Praise for Anna Nicholas's Mallorca travel series

'Terrific!' Lucia van der Post, contributor,   FT *How to Spend It*

'As intelligent as it is entertaining. From simple escapism to a much more complicated story about the difficulties of balancing life in two places...'   Leah Hyslop, *The Telegraph*

'Anna Nicholas is one of those lucky swine who has dared to live the dream and write about it.'   Harry Ritchie, *The Daily Mail*

'Witty, evocative and heart-warming. Another Mallorcan pearl from Anna Nicholas.'   Peter Kerr, author of *Snowball Oranges*

'A beautifully written and highly entertaining account of the upside of downshifting.'   Henry Sutton, *The Daily Mirror*

'A hugely entertaining and witty account of how to juggle life and work between two countries, keep fit and stay sane!'   Colonel John Blashford-Snell, CBE, British explorer & author

'An enjoyable read for anyone wanting to live their dream.'   Lynne Franks, OBE, broadcaster & author

'If you thought that glitz and glamour don't mix with rural country living you must read this book.'   *Bella* magazine

'This is Anna's comic and observational style at its very best.'   *St Christopher's Inns* magazine

'Endearing, funny and poignant. What more could one wish for?'   *Real Travel* magazine

Anna Nicholas is the most prolific British author writing about Mallorca today. Her successful series of six travel books explores the history, culture and delights of the golden isle. An inveterate traveller and experienced freelance journalist, she is on the Telegraph's travel team, and has contributed features to FT *How to Spend It,* the Times, and other leading British national newspapers. Anna regularly participates in humanitarian aid expeditions overseas and runs an international marathon annually for her favourite causes.

Haunted Magpie is her second novel in the new Mallorca crime series.

Twitter/Instagram @majorcanpearls

Also by Anna Nicholas

Mallorca crime series
The Devil's Horn

Mallorca travel series
A Lizard in my Luggage
Cat on a Hot Tiled Roof
Goats from a Small Island
Donkeys on my Doorstep
A Bull on the Beach
A Chorus of Cockerels

Memoir
Strictly Off the Record with Norris McWhirter

Burro Books,
403, Union Wharf,
23 Wenlock Road,
London N1 7SJ
www.burrobooks.co.uk

Published by Burro Books Ltd 2020

ISBN: 978-1-9996618-6-1
Ebook ISBN: 978-1-9996618-7-8

Printed and bound by CPI Group (UK) Ltd, Croydon, CR0 4YY

HAUNTED
MAGPIE

AN ISABEL FLORES MALLORCAN MYSTERY

ANNA NICHOLAS

burrobooks

LONDON

For Kay Halley
at Universal Bookshop

The most dedicated, enthusiastic and supportive
book shop owner in Mallorca.

Glossary

The following Mallorcan and Spanish words and expressions appear in the book. I hope these explanations prove helpful.

Adéu – goodbye (Mallorcan)

Ajuntament – town hall

Ánimo – cheer up

Autónomo – self-employed

Bocadillo – sandwich/roll

Bodega – wine cellar

Bona nit – good night (Mallorcan)

Botifarró – a local spicy pork sausage

Bu – boo

Ca rater – small Mallorcan dog breed

Café con leche – coffee with milk

Calambre – cramp

Campesino – farmer, countryman or peasant

Cariño – darling

Casita – little house

Comandante – commander

Coca – a popular rectangular-shaped local savoury pastry that is similar to pizza

Crema – cream (usually custard variety)

Cruz Roja- Red Cross

Diga – Tell me or speak!

El Cant de la Sibil.la – the song of the Sybil. Note the Mallorcan use of a full stop in Sibil.la

El meu amic – my friend

Ensaïmada – spiral-shaped Mallorcan pastry

Entrada – entrance

Escritura – title deed

Feliz cumpleaños – happy birthday!

Finca – country house

Gató – almond cake

Guardia Civil – the Civil Guard, Spanish military police force

Gloses – Mallorcan folk songs

Herbes – Signature Mallorcan herbal dijestif

Hombre – literally 'Man!' meaning, 'Oh, come on!'

Jefe superior – superintendent

Lotería – the lottery

Madre de díos – mother of God

Menu del día – lunchtime menu

Merienda – mid-morning snack

Moros y Cristianos fiesta – Moors & Christians festival

Moto – motorbike

No pasa nada – It's okay

Olivar – olive grove

Padre – father

Pastelería – cake shop

Plaça – village or town square

Porc amb col – pork with cabbage

Potaje – soup

Pues – well then

Ramallet – long-lasting local tomato

Reina – queen, term of endearment

Rondalles – Mallorcan folklore tales passed down through the generations

Sobrassada – famed Mallorcan paprika-flavoured, cured pork sausage

Sombreros – hats

Suerte – good luck

Torrente – river

Tostadas – toasted bread

Tumbet – a typical Mallorcan dish of cooked aubergine, potatoes and peppers

Uep – friendly Mallorcan greeting signifying surprise

Venga, amiga mía – come, my friend

Vino tinto – red wine

Vermutería –Vermouth bar

ONE

Paloma Crespí and a gaggle of companions clad in gaudy leggings, sweatshirts and trainers erupted noisily from the dance studio inside the converted barn, shrieking in dismay when they saw rain pelting from the inky sky. Waving and exchanging boisterous farewells, they careered off in all directions, heads bowed to the wind, jumping into awaiting cars, or grappling with stubborn umbrellas as they hurriedly headed away on foot. The instructor turned off the lights and locked the heavy wooden doors, leaving Paloma alone in the darkened doorway.

As the rain gave way to sulky drizzle, she listened impatiently to the monotonous purr from her phone. Why wasn't he picking up? Where the heck *was* he? Fast-flowing water gurgled and hiccupped along the gutters as she shivered in the chill night air and gave an exasperated sigh. Moments later, a man's voice, loud and plaintive, ricocheted around the quiet street. Paloma's face tightened as she listened to her boyfriend's volley of excuses. Nothing ever changed. Always the same old litany about the boss keeping him working late or a sudden urgent task that needed doing before end of play. This time he claimed to have texted but she'd switched off her phone during the class and there was no sign of a message when she'd turned it back on again. In the last month Pere had promised – and twice failed – to pick her up after her weekly salsa class, and she'd had enough.

After a biting exchange, Paloma cursed loudly and cut the call dead. Thrusting the phone into her pocket, she zipped up her jacket and pushed a few loose tendrils of dark hair under the hood. Carrer del Sol was now devoid of life, its inhabitants either absent or squirrelled away in their tightly-shuttered homes. Miserably she surveyed the jumble of terraced properties, garages and crumbling stone walls about her and shook her head in frustration. If she'd known Pere wasn't going to show up, she might have cadged a lift with someone from her class but it was too late now. They'd all gone. A few rogue stars glittered in the fathomless sky, as pearls of water began descending at a rapid rate. Slinging her rucksack over her shoulders, Paloma plodded along the glistening pavement, past the weepy streetlamps and potholes brimming with rainwater. She could have carried onto the main road for the long walk home, but instead cut though Carrer d'en Socies, passing the honey-stoned house museum of Rafel Ginard, the nineteenth-century Mallorcan folklorist and priest. As a child, she had loved the songs that her mother had sung from his famed book of verse and now as she stood outside the silent house, she began humming a favourite ditty. She'd visited the tiny terraced property often enough as entry was free. At the rear, there was a snug patio with an antiquated well and feeding trough where the family would have kept the few livestock and hens they could afford. Paloma particularly liked the cosy kitchen, where on a cold winter's evening Rafel and his family would apparently huddle about the stove and sing *gloses*, local country songs. She pulled her hood close as she contemplated the stark frontage of the lowly dwelling and thanked her lucky stars that her aunt and uncle's rural *finca* had oil central heating and a roaring fire in the hearth. Taking a right at the top of the lane, she turned into Carrer Major, and puffed up the hill, the silence and encroaching darkness making her jumpy and ill at ease.

A few minutes later, she reached Carrer del Vent, the long stretch of country road that curled out of the town towards Sineu. A few cars shimmied past, their teary headlights momentarily blinding her, but soon all was still. In the distance, an anaemic and mournful moon hung heavy in the sky, surrounded by clumps of grubby, bloated cloud. She progressed cautiously, casting fretful glances at the dense woodland around her, trying not to contemplate what might be lurking deep in the undergrowth. If her phone's battery hadn't been so low, she would have used its torch to guide her but she decided to preserve it for as long as possible.

Thirty minutes later she arrived in a wide valley flanked by small undulating hills and dotted with isolated farmhouses. Taking a right onto the main road, she strode purposefully ahead, lulled by the sound of the wind and her trainers noisily smacking the wet tarmac as she forged northwards. Occasionally her eyes roved the sooty fields and orchards on either side so characteristic of Es Pla, the agricultural heartland of Mallorca. Soon she passed a curving layby where motorists would often stop to stretch their legs, or in spring take pictures of the derelict barns that looked so picturesque set against a background of pastureland bursting with golden oxalis. She thought longingly about the warm, brightly-lit hallway that would greet her once she reached the *finca*. It would take only another fifteen minutes to arrive at the muddy track that led to her uncle and aunt's home close to the Torrent de Son Vent. She imagined that the river would be swollen after such torrential rainfalls the last few days but tonight was not the time to investigate.

Once at the house with its welcoming lanterns in the drive, she would pull off her soaking trainers and jacket in the porch and seek out her aunt Alba in the kitchen. Her uncle Paco would probably be settling the horses and other animals in the barn while her aunt prepared a warming broth or rice dish on the stove. Her mood lifted as she ploughed on, visualising a comforting supper accompanied by a bottle of lager.

Paloma had spent the morning making bouquets and selling seasonal blooms at La Rosaleda, the floristry shop in Sant Joan, and in the afternoon, had dropped off flower arrangements for an event at a local restaurant. November was proving to be a miserable month weather-wise but the sight of peonies, roses and margaritas had filled her head with thoughts of spring. With a few hours to spare before her salsa class, she had helped out at her friend's grocery store for a little extra cash and boy, did she need it. All in all, it hadn't been a bad day, despite Pere letting her down.

Rain began to fall more persistently just as Paloma turned onto her track. Veiled in slate clouds, the moon cast precious little light on the path ahead, and Paloma's trainers struggled to find purchase in the slick, glutinous mud. Wind, like a malevolent sprite, now whipped around the trees, shaking the branches so hard that leaves whirled about like charcoal confetti. Icy cold and soaked through, she felt a sense of elation when a flash of light pierced the gloom and a large vehicle lumbered towards her. It had to be Paco, no doubt anticipating that Pere had failed her again. She waved and, with a faint smile, stepped aside onto the grass verge, cupping a hand over her eyes as they strained to penetrate the dark interior.

The engine cut out and a door slammed. Silhouetted against the headlights' beam, a figure approached. Paloma called out her uncle's name but no response came. Instead, the silent figure continued towards her. When the face came into view, a sudden clarity mingled with abject terror sent her stumbling back along the track.

With heart pounding she turned and ran blindly through the rain and blackness, but the mud clung to her ankles and dragged her down, tilting her rucksack over her shoulders. Unbalanced, she pitched forwards and with a thump struck her forehead on sharp rocks and silt. She tried to breathe evenly and move her limbs, but they were shaking uncontrollably. Fear, red and deadly, embraced her with cool and ghostly fingers. She could smell and taste it. It infected every useless limb and made her clumsy and immobile like an astronaut in free fall. She had to get a grip. Reeling in shock and pain, she crawled onto her knees, but before she could rise, a gloved hand had clamped over her mouth and nose from behind.

Paloma hit out wildly, squirming and retching as a strong sweet substance filled her nostrils and throat. Now a thick and coarse cloth was covering her entire face, but in spite of her desperate struggles, the hand remained patiently in place, pressing forever downwards in a vice-like grip, holding her still. Paloma felt dizzy and disorientated but before losing consciousness her last thought was this: let me live. And then her body shuddered to a halt.

TWO

After a night of unremitting rain, Isabel Flores Montserrat was elated to feel the warmth of the sun on her face as she sat cross-legged in *Plaça* de Sant Martí, surrounded by boisterous children. Nearby, in a state of excitement, Furó sniffed around the sacks of clothes stacked up by the central fountain, emitting a low growl when she whistled for his attention. It was the local primary school's 'help a friend day' and all morning, villagers had popped by to drop off unwanted garments to add to the stockpile for the Cruz Roja.

As usual, Isabel had volunteered to help the two young teachers to control their wards at this annual jamboree. It was the children's role to sort out the clothes and pile them into bags, but their enthusiasm for the task often waned when the prospect of playing tag around the square or sneaking into the Bon Día grocery shop for a packet of crisps or sunflower seeds proved irresistible. Whenever this occurred, Isabel would devise group games and songs to keep them on track while the teachers engaged with locals and sifted carefully through the piles of donated items.

Having successfully lured Furó onto her lap, Isabel momentarily closed her eyes, allowing her busy thoughts a few minutes' refuge. Although November was a quiet time of year for Hogar Dulce Hogar, her holiday rentals company, with only a slow stream of hikers and cyclists making bookings, she and her assistant, Pep, were already preparing for the busy season ahead. Come Easter, their feet would barely touch the ground and there would be little time for such languorous village affairs. A small hand suddenly pulled at her sleeve.

'Wake up, Bel. Idò has brought the lemons.'

She fixed her gaze on the earnest little face before her and gave a heavy sigh. 'Okay, Sofia. You win.'

Her goddaughter offered a jubilant grin and tugged at Isabel's hand. 'Remember, me first. Will Furó play?'

Rising to her feet, Isabel twisted her unruly tresses up onto her head and used a biro from her jean pocket to keep them in place. She draped Furó around her neck so that he resembled a russet stole, and smiled. 'I'm not sure how accomplished ferrets are at juggling.'

Sofia reached up to stroke his bushy tail. 'But he's good at football.'

'And sleeping.' Idò approached, clutching two wicker baskets bulging with lemons. 'That's all that ferret ever does.'

Isabel tutted. 'You took your time!'

He placed his load at her feet. 'Well, some of us have been working all morning. First, I had to fix your mother's washing machine and then rush over to Can Caracol to replace the guttering otherwise you'd be chewing my ear off.'

She laughed. 'One of my best rental properties, lest you forget. I hope you did a proper job?'

'Give me a break, Bel!' he puffed. 'Now I'm off for a well-deserved beer at Jordi's.'

Isabel watched her uncle amble across the square towards Café Jordi before clapping her hands and commanding her juvenile troops. 'So, who wants to learn how to juggle lemons?'

Squeals of joy broke out around her as she began effortlessly spinning two plump golden fruits in the air. Next, she added a third and feigned horror when one smashed to the ground, releasing its aromatic zest into the air. In wonder, the crowd of youngsters looked on, jumping up and down with cries of 'Me next!'. Lining them up, and allowing Sofia first attempt, she spent an hour honing the children's juggling skills as lemons splattered around them to gales of raucous laughter. Villagers now stood about the fragrant *plaça* smiling and clapping while the teachers shook their heads good-naturedly.

Emerging from the town hall, Llorenç Bestard, Mayor of Sant Martí, made a beeline for her, his forehead creased like a grumpy bulldog. 'What a mess you've all made. Really, Bel, I wonder who's the bigger child!'

She leapt forward to kiss him on both cheeks, and, grinning, pressed two large lemons into his hands. 'Come on, have a go!'

He was about to demur but countless small voices pressed him to the challenge, so reluctantly he lobbed them both in the air, yelping when one landed heavily on his foot. Hysterical giggles filled the square as he turned to Francina, one of the teachers. 'I'm expecting all this cleared up by lunchtime,' he said with some indignation, and then with a wink added, 'and a big lemon pie on my desk when I return to the office.'

Grinning, she proffered a mock salute and handed round paper carrier bags to the children. 'Let's get cracking!'

Llorenç took Isabel aside. 'I'm afraid we have grave local matters to discuss.'

'We do?' She threw him a quizzical look.

'It's rather confidential. Have you a moment?'

Isabel indicated to Francina that she was taking her leave, and with Furó pattering along beside her, headed southwards across the *plaça* in the direction of Bar Castell. Llorenç gave a wry chuckle.

'Always loyal to Rafa.'

'True, but as Uncle Idò and his cronies are currently drinking at Café Jordi, I thought you might prefer a quieter place to talk.'

He tapped a finger to the side of his nose. 'Indeed. Good thinking, Bel.'

Isabel wondered what new calamity might have struck the village. Sant Martí was hardly a hotbed for crime with its six hundred fairly benign and well-behaved residents and yet the previous summer had tested both Llorenç and Isabel to the limit. There had been the grisly murder of an elderly villager, the discovery of a local drug cartel and the abduction of a young British girl in the northern resort of Puerto de Pollença to contend with. As a former policewoman, Isabel had been lured by Tolo Cabot, her old boss and close friend, into helping to solve the crimes. Since then life had proved mercifully uneventful.

The pair climbed the steep steps to Bar Castell, nodding to Rafael, who was stationed behind the antique mahogany counter, hunched over his vintage Bakelite telephone. Isabel headed for the sunny terrace overlooking the square and sank into a comfortable wicker chair. Fumbling in her large basket she pulled out a Chupa Chup lolly, which she hurriedly unwrapped and placed in her mouth. Llorenç pulled out a chair opposite her. 'Those things will make your teeth fall out.'

She waggled the gaudy red lollipop teasingly in his direction. 'So everyone keeps telling me, including my dentist, but you know how I like to live on the edge.'

Llorenç tittered, then leant forward confidentially. 'To business, Bel. Have you heard about the missing animals?'

Instinctively she patted Furó, who had jumped onto her lap. 'Are you talking about Alberto Bonet's dog?'

Rafael appeared and placed two *cortados* in front of them. 'Your usual.'

Isabel placed her lolly back in its wrapper and thanked him.

He turned to her. 'That plumber's always letting his boxer roam about.'

The mayor sighed irritably. 'We were having a private conversation, Rafa.'

'Suit yourself.' He shrugged and with an eye roll in Isabel's direction, pottered back to the bar.

Llorenç stirred his drink absentmindedly. 'It's not just Alberto's dog. Pau told me this morning that Llamp, his Alsatian, has vanished. We can't have our own police officer without his dog.'

'What happened?'

'Yesterday, he'd left Llamp in the back garden as usual but when he returned after his police shift, he'd gone.'

Isabel's brow furrowed. 'That's odd, but maybe he'd inadvertently left the back gate open.'

'He says not.'

Isabel ripped open a small packet of sugar and poured the contents into her coffee. 'Any others?'

The mayor shook his head. 'Not that I know about, but I don't like the smell of it. I've heard about foreign gangs stealing pedigree dogs to order. My Angélica is already fretting.'

Isabel resisted the urge to laugh. 'Well, I don't think she need worry about anyone stealing a *ca rater*. Just about every man and his dog has one on this island, no pun intended.'

Llorenç gave a sniff. 'That may well be but he's very special to her.'

'Of course,' she replied diplomatically. As Angélica was the mayor's only daughter and also the girlfriend of her assistant, Pep, Isabel had to tread carefully. 'I'll keep an ear to the ground.'

At the counter, Llorenç patted her arm. 'I feel reassured having our own detective in the village.'

'Former detective,' Isabel corrected.

He offered her a spirited hug, then turned and hastily scuttled down the stairs towards the *plaça*.

Rafael cast Isabel a knowing glance. 'Llorenç won't be able to keep the lid on this animal business. There are no secrets in this village.'

She turned at the stairs and smiled back at him. 'Oh really? I'm not so sure.'

*

Isabel strode across the *plaça* with Furó in her pannier, waving at the children who were following their teachers in crocodile formation towards the village school. A driver loaded the sacks of donated clothes into the back of his van, slammed the door and drove off towards Soller town. She'd enjoyed her carefree morning but now needed to post a birthday card to her brother, Eduardo, before getting down to some work back at the office. He and his wife and two young sons lived in Toledo and would soon be returning to Mallorca for a family Christmas, which filled Isabel and her mother with delight.

Cutting through the narrow alley by the church of Sant Antoní, she took a left, hoping to catch the postmistress before she closed for lunch. The door to the simple terraced house that served as the village postal hub stood wide open, much to Isabel's relief. As she approached the front gate, Señora Coll emerged in the doorway with her hands on her hips.

'I was just closing up, Bel. I've a terrible headache with all those kids making such a din in the square today. You'd think the teachers would keep them under control.'

'Well it was in a good cause, Señora Coll, and it only happens once a year.'

'Thank heavens for that. You should have heard the racket.'

Isabel feigned surprise. 'Really? I didn't hear a thing.'

Muttering to herself, the old lady turned tail and beckoned for her to follow. 'It's been a terrible week altogether. I'm amazed my heart hasn't given out.'

'I'm sorry to hear that,' replied Isabel, bracing herself for the volley of ailments that usually accompanied such an outburst. 'I thought those pills Doctor Ramis prescribed worked wonders?'

She nodded. 'Only thing keeping me alive, *reina*. Truth is, the terrible rains last weekend flooded my basement and then yesterday Carlos disappeared. I've not had a wink of sleep, worrying about him.'

Isabel squeezed her arm. 'I'm so sad to hear about your flooding. My mother's kitchen was a mess too. But might Carlos just have flown off somewhere? My cockerel, Salvador, comes and goes as he pleases.'

Señora Coll shook her head. 'He never leaves the garden, Bel. Someone's taken him.'

'But why?'

'There are some weird folk about. Anyway, let me get you a stamp for that letter.' She scrutinised the envelope and gave it a pinch. 'Writing to Eduardo? It feels like a card.'

Isabel stifled a grin. 'It's his birthday.'

'Such a lovely boy,' she replied glumly. 'Always so good with his hands.'

Isabel disguised a guffaw with a loud cough and scattered some coins on the polished wooden desk. 'Don't lose faith, Señora. Carlos might still come home to roost.'

She walked thoughtfully along Calle Pastor, her cobbled street with its denuded plane trees and caramel-hued stone terraced homes. If there really was an animal thief on the loose, what was the motivation and why steal a cockerel, too? That certainly ruled out the mayor's theory that it could be pedigree dogs stolen to order. She stopped in front of her home, Ca'n Moix, the house of the cat, and released Furó from her straw pannier. He scurried through the herb garden to the arched porch, and finding the front door ajar, crept inside. Isabel issued a long sigh. If her neighbours' beloved pets really were under threat, she'd make it her business to find the culprit. Whoever it was might well find they'd bitten off more than they could chew.

THREE

As Isabel entered her *entrada* with its graceful French windows overlooking the rear patio, she was greeted by the sound of laughter and clapping. She cocked her head to one side. The sound seemed to be coming from upstairs. Bemused, she tiptoed up the staircase and threw open the door to the office only to find Pep sitting back on his heels, throwing food pellets to her ferret.

'Whatever are you doing?' she asked.

He jumped to his feet. 'We're just playing catch. Come on, it's lunchtime.'

Furó was wagging his tail excitedly and now chased a small ball across the tiled floor, sending it flying under the old Chesterfield sofa.

'Goal!' cried Pep, clapping.

'Any chance of getting some work out of you today?'

Pep looked at her with big doe-eyes. 'Listen, I've been hard at it all morning. I've already made a booking for a cycling group and a couple on a hiking honeymoon.'

'What does that entail?'

'It sounds so boring. They're renting one of our apartments for a week next January and walking different routes in the Tramuntanas every day. Not my idea of a honeymoon.'

Isabel smiled broadly. 'Which is?'

'I'd go somewhere exotic, maybe South America, and do quad biking or sleeping rough in the jungle.' He flexed his ample muscles.

'I'm sure that would go down a treat with Angélica.'

He looked deflated. 'Of course, I'd forgotten she'd be tagging along.'

Isabel wafted into her own sunny office and opened the window. 'Yes, maybe tuck those thoughts away for a boy's own adventure.'

She looked down at the garden and the verdant orchard beyond, its trees brimming with golden lemons. A group of busy hens were clucking in the long grasses while her cockerel, Salvador, stalked about the gravel, pecking at bits of corn and seeds that she'd scattered earlier that morning. At this time of year, there were few flowers to brighten the land but rosemary bushes were in abundance, displaying delicate purple flowers, and thyme spilled luxuriantly from large terracotta pots. A few days earlier she had planted her broad beans and peas, ably assisted by Idò, but would need to wait patiently until the spring for the harvest.

Since leaving her former frenetic existence as a detective inspector with the National Police in Palma, Isabel had learnt to relish the slower pace of life in her mountain village. It was nearly three years since she'd decided to relinquish her police badge to run her elderly mother's holiday rentals agency and she had few regrets. With hard work and enthusiasm, she had turned a small enterprise into a flourishing business and had an international clientele. The tiny village of Sant Martí might have its limitations, but she enjoyed the novelty of belonging to a close community away from the hubbub, and besides, she had plenty of friends and contacts in the capital and beyond.

Pep stood in her doorway, smiling brightly. 'Florentina's just arrived. She's brought us lunch.'

Isabel tore her gaze from the garden. 'Does she think we're going to starve? I've already got her *tumbet*, and leftover pork with cabbage in the fridge from yesterday.'

He winked. 'Don't complain. Your mother's a great cook. If it makes her happy, let's just accept it gratefully.'

They exchanged complicit looks and descended the stairs to find Florentina and Isabel's neighbour, Doctor Ramis, standing by the front door.

Florentina rushed forward to give her a hug. 'I've left you both a *tortilla* and salad in the kitchen. I know how busy you are.'

'This is our slack time, Mama. You shouldn't go to so much bother, but thank you.' She gave Doctor Ramis a peck on the cheek. 'Are you not staying?'

He smiled genially. 'I'm taking your mother to see a splendid old film in Palma. It's the comedy, *Plácido*, one of my favourites of Luis García Berlanga, that genius of a director.'

'I don't think I've ever seen it,' replied Pep.

The doctor chuckled. 'It was released in 1961, well before you were born, so I'm hardly surprised, my boy. Come on, Florentina. We mustn't be late.'

At the porch, he turned back. 'By the way, did you know that Señora Coll's cockerel has gone missing? She's very distressed.'

'I've just heard.'

He shrugged. 'It's probably flown off somewhere. You'd have to be mad to steal such a cacophonous creature. Mind you, one of my other patients reported her pet going missing.'

Isabel bristled. 'Who might that be?'

'Old Magdalena Sala says her poodle has disappeared. It's a yappy little beast, so the neighbours are probably happy. Anyway, she doesn't keep it locked up, so it could have just gone astray.'

Isabel closed the door behind them. 'All very mysterious.'

'What is?' asked Pep.

'Llorenç told me that a few villagers have reported pets missing. Have you heard anything?'

'Angélica mentioned something but it's probably a load of nonsense. Animals are always roaming around this village unsupervised. Think of all the abandoned feral cats.'

'That's true. Ah, how I wish I could adopt them all!'

'Furó would leave home,' Pep scoffed.

Isabel pottered into the kitchen and took a seat at the table. 'Come and eat.'

She served Pep a big slice of omelette and heaped salad onto his plate.

'Not so much!'

'It's good for you,' she retorted.

'Like your Chupa Chups are…'

Isabel helped herself to a slice of crusty brown bread and poured them both a glass of home-made lemonade from an earthenware jug. 'We all have our small vices.'

He grinned at her. 'So, when are you seeing your beau?'

'Watch your cheek. Tolo and I are just good friends, as you know very well.'

'If you say so.'

She gave him a warning look. 'I'm seeing him for a drink in Soller later. He has a case that's worrying him.'

Pep stopped mid-bite. 'A murder?'

'I hope not.'

'Will you be working with him again?'

Isabel chewed thoughtfully on a chunk of tomato before answering. 'That all depends on the case and whether he wants my help.'

'There's not much action going on around here so why not? I can keep things ticking over in the office.'

Isabel tapped her chin. 'I'm not sure I still have an appetite for crime solving after last time.'

Pep laughed. 'Come on. It was exciting. You solved two cases and got a pat on the back from the Minister of the Interior in Madrid. What's not to like?'

She offered him a pert smile. 'If you consider the slaying of a pensioner – albeit a bad egg – the abduction of a child, two additional murders and a road death exciting, there has to be something wrong with you.'

Pep groaned. 'You know what I mean! At least it was a bit of an adrenalin ride.'

Before she could reply, her phone rang. '*Diga*!' she answered.

'I'd like to rent a haunted house in your valley. Can you help?'

Isabel broke into a smile. 'We have plenty, sir. Do you prefer ghosts or poltergeists or possibly both?'

Pep's eyes bulged. He had a loathing for the supernatural and a terror of ghosts. In fact, he was convinced that half the homes in the valley were possessed.

Tolo gave a guffaw. 'How's your day? I wondered if we might meet earlier? I have to leave for Madrid tonight for a training course. It starts with a finance crisis meeting early tomorrow.'

'Culling more staff?' she asked.

'Hopefully not mine. Gaspar and I are barely able to cope with our workload as it is.'

As chief inspector of the National Police on the island, Tolo Cabot spent much of his time juggling cold and live cases and having to decide which most merited funding. Fortunately he had an excellent deputy in Gaspar Fernández and a small and loyal team that watched his back.

He yawned. '5 p.m.?'

'See you at Bar Turismo.'

Isabel cut the call and looked across at Pep. 'Now, my friend, to work.'

*

As Isabel strolled along her front path happily studying the many lush shrubs and herbs, someone called out to her from the neighbouring garden. With so much foliage on both sides, it was impossible to peer over either of her neighbours' fences. For that reason, she kept a sturdy wooden box by the stone wall on the right, close to Doctor Ramis's terraced property.

For the last four years, the house on the left had lain abandoned following a dispute between three brothers who'd all inherited a share. The elderly parents had died and the squabbling siblings could not agree on whether to sell or refurbish the premises. As all of them lacked funds, the house was left to go to rack and ruin while discussions rumbled on. Finally, all had grudgingly come to an accord and decided to divide whatever monies came from the sale. As Florentina had wisely surmised, the house would have fetched a significantly higher sum had they sold immediately and ceased their petty scrapping. Isabel had been aware of various visitors to the property since, but was delighted to learn that a Brazilian family had recently purchased it.

Grabbing her wooden box, she crossed the lawn and placed it in front of a bush of wild creeping ivy, and carefully climbed aloft. She could now see the bronzed smiling face on the other side.

'Hola! I don't think we've met?'

The older woman beamed up at her. 'We've just moved in so I wanted to introduce myself. I am Juliana Santos. We are Brazilian.'

Isabel nodded. 'Welcome to Calle Pastor! I am Bel. You must come over for supper soon.'

'Thank you but it's our turn first. I'd like you to meet my husband, Lucas, and our sons, Bruno and Victor. We Brazilians like to party so we'll have you over for *feijoada* and *Caipirinhas* soon!'

'Perfect. Do let me know if you need anything in the meantime. My assistant, Pep, is a one-man Atlas and a dab hand at carrying furniture.'

Juliana rolled her head back and laughed. 'That's kind but you haven't seen my strapping boys yet!'

As Isabel headed down the street to where Pequeñito, her canary yellow Vintage Fiat 500, was parked, she smiled at the novelty of having new neighbours. It would be lovely to see the house redecorated and the gardens tamed, and on first impression, Juliana seemed warm and friendly.

Without a watch, she estimated that it was probably close to five o'clock, meaning that she would arrive at Bar Turismo at the back of five, offering Tolo ample time to order two cool bottles of Rosa Blanca, one of her favourite lagers.

*

As she had rightly predicted, Tolo was already sitting outside Bar Turismo in the waning sunlight, nursing a couple of glasses and bottles of lager, and smoking a slim cigar. He was unshaven with hair askew and had heavy shadows under his dark eyes. Isabel ruffled his unruly mop and pulled up a chair. Caught off his guard, he hurriedly dropped the cigar into an ashtray and leant forward to kiss her fervently on both cheeks.

'It's so wonderful to see you.'

Isabel laughed. 'Steady on. It's only been two days.'

Tolo grasped her hand. 'You're always a balm to the soul, and it's been a tough afternoon.'

Wearily, he rubbed his eyes and poured lager into their glasses. Isabel drew one towards her and took a grateful sip. Much as she adored her old friend, her feelings towards him were complicated. The previous summer, when he had persuaded her to take up her police badge again, they had become particularly close perhaps due to the intensity of the work. Despite becoming thoroughly absorbed in the baffling cases, she had been able to continue to run her rentals agency thanks to the assistance of Pep, her mother and Idò. Somehow though, their relationship had seemed much more straightforward when she had worked full-time at the Palma police precinct. During that period, they had been professional colleagues, and in their free time, close friends, but the dynamics had since changed. Tolo had freely admitted that he would like more from their relationship but she had resisted. In her mind, they had the perfect friendship and made excellent working partners. Why upset the applecart and ruin everything even if both did have latent feelings for one another? Besides, they had time on their side – or did they? Isabel would soon turn thirty-four and dreamed of having a family one day. On the other hand, she relished her freedom and single status. After many anguished late-night conversations on the matter, Tolo had reluctantly agreed to maintain the status quo for the time being.

Isabel now eyed him sympathetically, worried at his lean and hungry aspect. 'So, what's been happening?'

Tolo sat back in his chair and clinked her glass before taking a long draught from his own. 'It's been a heavy few days. Aside from a major drug bust, two violent domestic abuse cases, a night-time pyromaniac on the loose in Palma setting fire to vehicles, we now have a possible abduction.'

Isabel grimaced. 'Can't the Guardia Civil take off some of the heat? Where's our irreplaceable Capitán Gómez when you need him?'

The island's military force, which mainly controlled law and order in the rural zones, was headed locally by the imperious Álvaro Gómez. This green-uniformed force at times clashed with the National Police's boys in blue, who also had island-wide jurisdiction, though primarily in urban areas.

'Believe it or not, Gómez is off-island, walking the Camino de Santiago. He's a religious fellow, as you know. All that humanity shines through his reptilian eyes.'

Isabel grinned. 'What, he's actually taking a holiday?'

'His deputy, who's a civilised chap called Reynes, told me that Gómez's wife, Paula, has been nagging him for ages about taking a pilgrimage. They'll be away two weeks.'

She took a long sip of cool lager. 'And you're leaving us too? This will be music to the ears of the island's criminal fraternity.'

He gave her a long look. 'I'll be gone a week. Can't be helped. I'll miss you.'

Instinctively Isabel pulled a packet of sunflower seeds from her pocket and crunched one tensely between her teeth. 'I'm sure these training courses aren't so bad.'

He let the moment pass. 'Yes, at least I won't have to cook for myself. Meanwhile, I'd like your help with this potential abduction.'

'Tell me about it.'

Tolo uttered a sigh. 'I may be jumping the gun, but I don't like the feel of it. Two days ago, Paloma Crespí, a twenty-five-year-old florist, was walking home from an evening dance class in Sant Joan but never arrived at her uncle's *finca* just beyond the town. He reported her missing yesterday.'

'Why was she staying with her uncle?'

'Quick off the stops as ever. From what we can gather, her mother is dead and the father has a restraining order on him. She's been living with her mother's brother and his wife for the last year or so.'

Isabel nibbled on another seed. 'So, this happened Monday. If I recall, it was raining heavily that night. Did she not have a car or a lift organised?'

Tolo grunted. 'The Guardia boys spoke with her boyfriend yesterday. He was supposed to be picking her up but apparently left her a message claiming he'd lost track of time. He maintains that Paloma called him after the class and said she'd walk home.'

'Did they believe him?'

He shrugged. 'Gaspar's been liaising with them but they have no grounds for suspicion yet. One of our team also spoke at length with the uncle. Apparently, Paloma had a chequered history of running away, drug abuse and depression.' He eyed her intently. 'Of course, she might just have got a lift from a friend and is lying low, but why?'

Isabel puffed out her cheeks. 'Who knows, but if that's not the case, either the boyfriend is lying or she was indeed abducted on the way back home. Then again, the uncle could be leading you a dance and perhaps she did arrive at the house but something bad happened there.' She paused. 'It was a filthy night too, so she could have fallen or hurt herself along the route.'

'The Guardia has already checked the area and found nothing.'

'Presumably she's not answering her mobile?'

'It appears to be switched off. Gaspar's in touch with the provider about a trace.'

'Does she have a regular job?'

'She works part-time at a florist's called La Rosaleda in Sant Joan and also has freelance clients. The owner, Mar Planes, called her uncle when she didn't show up for work yesterday morning. That's when he decided to contact us.'

Isabel nodded slowly. 'I think you have grounds for concern, though as we both know, thousands go missing every year in Spain with the majority of cases resolved.'

'True, but what about the eight hundred or more that go unaccounted for? An elderly local named Luz Pujals disappeared without trace on the island three years ago. We never knew what happened to her and it's always disturbed me. We failed her.'

'Don't be hard on yourself. Unfortunately, we can't prevent some victims slipping through our fingers.'

Tolo glanced at his watch. 'You said business was fairly slack, so I'm really hoping you'll come on board with this case? Gaspar and the team have enough to deal with while I'm away and we could do with your lateral thinking again.'

'Is that supposed to be a compliment?' Isabel teased.

'Take your pick. Quirky, lateral, off the grid, instinctive, stubborn, and at times frustratingly impetuous and foolishly brave. All the things that made you an outstanding cop. So, it's a yes?'

She laughed. 'I suppose I could do with a little mental stimulation. It's a quiet time for rentals.'

'You're a star,' he replied. 'I'll get Gaspar to sort out the paperwork with you.'

She smiled. 'As it happens, I'm in Sineu tomorrow collecting a sack of feed for Furó from a local farm. I can pop by Sant Joan and Paloma's family on the way back and do some digging.'

'Perfect. Can I leave you to get up to speed with Gaspar?'

'Sure. I'll pop by the Palma precinct first thing.'

'And how are things in sleepy Sant Martí?'

Isabel wrinkled her nose. 'There's been a spate of pet disappearances and Llorenç is quite hot and bothered about it. It started with dogs but now the postmistress's cockerel has gone missing.'

He guffawed. 'You'd have to be deranged to steal a cockerel. Damn noisy buggers. You can't give them away.'

Isabel slapped his arm. 'I happen to love my cockerel, Salvador, but you make a good point. In fact, my neighbour, Doctor Ramis, said exactly the same. It's all very puzzling.'

Tolo yawned and finished his lager. 'There'll no doubt be a simple explanation. It's probably just a coincidence they've all gone missing at the same time.'

'I thought that too but now I'm not so sure.'

He nudged her. 'How about one more for the road?'

'My round,' she replied.

He protested but she stood up and headed to the counter. When she returned, she passed him a bottle and winked.

'Enjoy it, because when we solve this case, I'll be expecting more than a magnum of *cava*.'

FOUR

A restless grey sea spewed cool frothy water onto the sand at the far end of Can Repic beach, where Isabel sat nursing a mug of coffee. Her long, wet hair fell in straggles about her face, as she contemplated the metallic, marbleised sky from her eyrie, a jagged piece of limestone rock overlooking Soller bay. It was seven o'clock, an hour when she and Furó normally had the whole beach to themselves. Every morning, they pushed through the cold, briny waves, swimming and splashing about together before hurriedly returning to the beach. With chattering teeth and feet encrusted with damp, soft sand, Isabel then wrapped a huge towel about them both, and, once dry, they headed for her favourite rock. After throwing on a heavy woollen knit, she doled out some meaty snacks to Furó while she sipped on a mug of strong and sweet, warming coffee from a metal flask. As skittish seagulls circled above, Isabel welcomed the day quietly, allowing her cluttered thoughts to detangle while she breathed in the sharp and salty aroma of ozone and seaweed.

Although Isabel had a smartphone, she shied away from using it for anything other than calls while on the move. Mid-morning she'd cast a cursory glance at global headlines but would studiously avoid the plethora of social media sites and ephemeral news trends and online chatter. Frankly, she had better things to do with her time, as she constantly pointed out to Pep when she saw him poring over his Tuenti feed in the office. She was always disappointed at how her foreign rental clients would spend much of their precious holiday glued to phones around the pool, rather than exploring the coastline or hiking in the nearby Tramuntana mountains.

Now as she watched the glinting, ruby lights of a delivery truck reversing near Agapanto restaurant, her phone began to trill. In some trepidation, she put it to her ear, and smiled in relief when she heard the cheerful voice of Gaspar Fernández.

'This is early, even by your standards,' she teased.

'I know you're up with the birds so thought I'd disturb your early morning chill time,' he goaded. 'Tolo asked me to fill you in on this possible abduction. He said you'd be dropping by the precinct this morning on your way to Sant Joan?'

'That's my plan. How far have you got with the investigation?'

He groaned. 'We've been fire-fighting over here this week so this hasn't been our number one priority. There's no proof of anything sinister at this stage and by all accounts Paloma Crespí was known for disappearing.'

'But she's now been missing nearly three days and hasn't shown up either at home or at work. That's surely cause for concern?'

'Agreed, which is why I'm mightily pleased you're on the team again. What time can I expect you?'

'If there's a hot *cortado* and *ensaïmada* on offer, I'll be with you before nine.'

Gaspar laughed. 'As if you had to ask.'

*

Isabel parked on Carrer de Sol in Sant Joan and glanced at the file Gaspar had given her. First stop was Carlotta Pilar, the dance teacher at the salsa studio where Paloma was last seen. During her meeting in Palma that morning with Gaspar, it became clear that Paloma had a dysfunctional family and complicated history. Was that relevant or circumstantial, and how did the boyfriend fit into the equation? She looked across at Furó slumbering on the passenger seat and stroked the soft vanilla fur around his snout. After leaving Palma she had driven to the rural homestead near Sineu that sold her ferret's favourite food pellets. Furó had loved his time careering around the wild terrain, communing with the elderly farmer's own band of playful ferrets and being petted by him and his wife. He had returned to the car exhausted and hadn't stirred since.

Isabel left Furó sleeping and with a fleeting glance back at her beloved Pequeñito strode across the narrow street. She surveyed the old terraced property before her and surmised that it must have been a barn at some stage. The unassuming street had a forlorn air about it and was comprised mostly of modest terraced houses and ramshackle garages. After giving a tentative knock at the wooden door, she heard a key rattle in the lock and moments later an elderly woman with sagging, pale skin peered out.

'Can I help you?'

Isabel held up the newly issued police badge bestowed on her by Gaspar earlier that morning. The woman's gaze swept over it in perfunctory manner. 'You're here about Paloma.'

Isabel offered a reassuring smile. 'That's right. And who might you be?'

'Sara. I'm just the cleaner here but Carlotta Pilar will be back in a few minutes. She owns the studio.'

'Could I have a few words?'

The woman shrugged wearily and pulled back the door. 'I don't know much, I'm afraid.'

Isabel followed her into a large white open space with solid, shiny wooden flooring. The room was stark save for a huddle of giant blue exercise balls and exercise mats at one end. A mop leant lazily against a wall, the accompanying metal pail standing forlornly close by.

'This is where Paloma had her salsa class on Monday night?'

Sara nodded. 'She's one of the regulars and has been coming ever since Carlotta started the classes a year ago.'

'Are they friends?'

She averted her eyes. 'I think Carlotta knew her father. I'm not sure.'

'Is Paloma a familiar face in the town?'

'Of course. Sant Joan is a small place.'

'How would you describe her?'

She pushed out her bottom lip. 'She's very pretty and thin but a bit nervy. Everyone knows she had big problems with her old man.'

'Oh?'

The older woman spoke in hushed tones. 'He's called Jago Morey, a nasty piece of work.'

'But Paloma has a different surname.'

'She took her mother's maiden name of Crespí, and who could blame her? Jago used to beat Paloma and her mother and he was eventually sent to prison. Served him right too. A few years ago, he got out of the Palma penitentiary after completing his sentence and moved to Manacor. They say he's not allowed to have any contact with her.'

'When was the last time you saw her?'

'Just before the class on Monday. I always switch on the lights and heating before they arrive. She was chatting with a few of the other girls for a change.'

'She didn't normally?'

'Not really. Paloma likes to keep to herself. You should speak with Laura at the grocer's. She's her friend.'

'And what of her boyfriend, Pere Brotat?'

'He picks her up now and then after the class. They always seem to be rowing. I've never spoken with him.'

The front door banged. A middle-aged woman with an athletic figure walked into the studio and momentarily studied Isabel. 'Are you here about salsa classes?'

The cleaner scuttled into a side room as Isabel stepped forward. 'Actually, I'm with the National Police. I take it you are Carlotta Pilar?'

Flinging a leather jacket onto a nearby chair, the woman ruffled a hand through a clump of short, spikey red hair, her heavy bangles jangling with the effort. 'Poor Paloma. I'm glad you people are taking it seriously now.'

Isabel fixed her with an inscrutable smile. 'The National Police take every potential disappearance seriously. However, there are thousands of missing people reported every year in Spain so certain protocols have to be put in place.'

The woman threw her a withering glance. 'It can't be every day that someone completely vanishes.'

'You'd be surprised. There are more than twelve thousand active missing person cases in the country each year – and at least 130 here in the Baleares.'

Carlotta Pilar gave an insouciant shrug. 'Well, let's hope you find her.'

'Are you close to her?'

'Actually, I don't know Paloma very well. She's one of fifteen girls that attend my Monday class. It's hard to get much out of her. She's a little mouse.'

'Why would you say that was?'

'Just the way she is, I guess, but I believe she has a lot of issues and used to take drugs. The boyfriend looks scruffy and they always squabble whenever he deigns to turn up here after the class. You could say she was an accident waiting to happen.'

Isabel flinched. 'Let's hope not. Did you see Paloma leave the class on Monday night?'

'I locked the front door once the girls had left but saw Paloma hovering close by on her phone. Probably trying to get through to that oaf of a boyfriend. It was raining hard so I hot-footed it to a friend's house. I'd been invited to dinner.'

'Can I have her details?'

She raised an indignant eyebrow and grabbing a piece of paper and a biro, scrawled a name and telephone number down. 'Here.'

'Cati Marcer? We'll check that out. What time did the class end?'

'At around 8 p.m. I try to be punctual.'

'How did she seem on Monday night?'

Carlotta frowned. 'The same as she always is, quiet and shy but she cheered up being around the other girls. It's always a lively class.'

'Did you speak with her?'

'No. I arrived a little late so got the music on quickly. There was no time for chat.'

Isabel glanced around the room. 'This is a lovely place. Do you own it?'

Carlotta's tone was defiant. 'Yes, it's all mine and I've earned it.'

Isabel thanked her for her time but paused on the doorstep. 'I forgot to ask. How did Paloma hear about your classes?'

The woman stiffened. 'I can't quite recall. One of the other girls must have told her.'

'You don't know any family members?'

Carlotta offered her a bleak smile. 'No, I've never had that pleasure.'

Isabel returned to the car. She looked across at Furó. 'They were an odd pair, and neither seemed that upset about Paloma's disappearance. In fact, Carlotta Pilar had quite a notion of herself and was evidently hiding something.' She exhaled deeply. 'She knows a lot more than she's letting on. Any thoughts?"

Furó looked up at her for a moment, uttered a yawn, sneezed and went back to sleep. With a grin, Isabel revved the engine and after consulting her map set off along the route she imagined Paloma would have taken that night. On the way, she cut through Carrer d'en Socies as she had a soft spot for the little Pare Ginard Museum. It was closed but she still enjoyed viewing its quaint historic frontage. Carefully she navigated the little Fiat onto Carrer Major, and up the hill to Carrer del Vent. The road had multiple bends and was flanked on either side by pastureland and dense woodland. She imagined that walking alone along this winding, deserted road at night might feel quite creepy. All the same, dappled with sunlight and without the company of other vehicles, it was a joy to drive. Isabel regretted that she didn't visit Es Pla more often. It was the most fertile part of the island with its vineyards, olive groves and rich red soil that produced such an abundance of healthy crops and vegetables. She vowed that when the weather improved, she would drive Tolo over here one weekend for a picnic and to visit the many burgeoning local *bodegas*.

After a few miles, she reached a crossroads and carried on, the sweeping valley, flooded with soft light, opening out before her. Ahead of her, a row of forested hills like squat Buddhas rose up on the far side of the main road, their flanks dotted with lone farmhouses and Holm oaks. She took a right onto the empty highway, and a few kilometres further on noticed a layby surrounded by decrepit farm buildings and barns. Some five minutes later she turned onto a rough track of silt and gravel that was strewn with rocks and decaying branches. A phalanx of trees rose up on either side, as erect and silent as a firing squad, killing the sunlight as it struggled to break through. At first, Pequeñito protested loudly but Isabel coaxed him slowly forward, lowering the gear and carefully navigating each pothole and boulder along the way. Gradually, the track gave onto solid asphalt and a lone *finca* with outbuildings became visible through the trees. If she was right, this was the home of Paloma's aunt and uncle.

Isabel parked on the driveway and walked along a gravel path to the front porch. She called loudly through the open front door. Moments later came the sound of barking, and a man appeared with a young Labrador at his side. Isabel was glad to have left Furó in the car.

He regarded her with rheumy eyes and offered a tentative smile. 'Isabel Flores? Your colleague, Gaspar Fernández, telephoned to say you'd be popping by.'

'And you must be Paco?' Isabel reached forward and shook the thin, lined hand. 'That's some track you've got! Do you have many visitors?'

His face crinkled in bemusement. 'Once a month the oil delivery truck comes and that's about it. We're the sole users, though we don't go out much at our age. Just use my old pick-up truck for weekly errands and to fetch any post in town.'

'And were you and your wife here all day on Monday?'

Paco nodded. 'We haven't been out since Sunday.' He hesitated. 'Glad we didn't because the track was pretty water-logged and muddy.'

He led the way into a comfortable and traditional *entrada*, its floor covered in large, well-worn terracotta tiles. A stone staircase with mahogany bannisters looped up to the floors above while a grand fireplace took in the corner of the room. He ushered her through into a cosy parlour where a roaring fire burned in the grate.

'Let me fetch my wife, Alba. Can I get you a coffee?'

Isabel nodded gratefully and looked about the room. On the mantelpiece stood several framed photographs, one of a laughing young girl riding a bike and in another, a shy, fair-haired woman holding a baby. Isabel studied a cluster of certificates proudly hung on one of the walls. They had evidently been awarded at equestrian competitions. The door opened and Paco reappeared clutching a tray of cups, and – to Isabel's delight – a plate loaded with slices of cake. She hadn't eaten since her meeting with Gaspar, and had only consumed an *ensaïmada* pastry, albeit a large one.

Paco nodded towards the certificates. 'Those belong to Paloma. She's a natural horse rider. Taught her myself when she was a little girl. She won all the gymkhanas as a teenager.'

An amply-built woman with wiry grey hair bustled into the room and instinctively kissed Isabel on both cheeks. She appeared anxious and fretful.

'I am Alba, Paloma's aunt. Thank you for coming here. Please make yourself at home and do help yourself to coffee and almond cake. It's my own recipe.'

Isabel touched her arm. 'How kind of you. I haven't eaten much today and I love almond cake.'

The woman broke into a nervous smile and led Isabel to the sofa, sitting by her side.

'It's been such a worrying time for us. When Paloma didn't arrive home on Monday night, we were naturally concerned. She had been looking forward to having a quiet night in with us, and knew I'd be cooking. We tried calling her but the phone went to voicemail. Then we called Pere and Laura, her friend from the grocer's in Sant Joan. They knew nothing.'

Paco placed a coffee and sugar bowl in front of Isabel and passed her a plate with two thick slices of cake. She eyed it hungrily. It wasn't police protocol to accept such offerings as they could so easily be seen as bribes. All the same, Isabel had rarely adhered to protocols of any kind, so why start now? Besides, she wasn't strictly a member of the national police team any more so could eat as much cake as she liked.

'So, tell me, Alba, what time were you expecting Paloma home?'

'If she'd had a lift from Pere, she should have been home by 8.30 p.m. but on foot she wouldn't have reached here much before nine.'

Paco sat down heavily on a nearby armchair and cleared his throat. 'She's only been seeing that lad for about six months but he's not a reliable type. He's always letting the girl down.'

Isabel nodded. 'And why do you think that?'

He shrugged. 'I've only met him a few times when he dropped Paloma home but he was always playing loud music in the car and swearing. Paloma said he'd changed jobs a lot in the past but that's the building business for you. At least he seems to have hung on to the current one.'

'What did Pere tell you when you called him?'

'He claimed he'd forgotten to pick her up and that she'd decided to walk home instead,' he replied.

'Did he say if they'd rowed?'

'No, but they were always bickering. To be honest, she was about to break up with him.'

'Was there another man on the scene?'

Alba flinched. 'Not that she told us.'

Isabel took a bite of cake and watched as Alba held her cup protectively to her chest. She took a sip with quivering lips and absentmindedly tapped Isabel's knee. 'You know, Paloma had a terrible childhood. She was an only child and her father, Jago, was always drunk and abusing Estéla, her poor mother.'

Paco massaged his forehead. 'It was a living nightmare for us all. I was ten years older than Estéla and pleaded with Jago to see reason but he was aggressive and threatening. We tried to protect the two of them but it wasn't easy and Estéla would often beg us not to interfere. She was terrified of her husband.'

Alba continued. 'Jago would hang out with fancy women and come home late from local bars and terrorise them both, so finally social services intervened and he was given a prison term eight years ago.'

'How did social services find out?' Isabel asked.

'I was often in touch with them.' Paco shook his head and sighed. 'Within a few months of his incarceration, my sister was diagnosed with breast cancer and barely lasted the year. Paloma was only seventeen but losing Estéla was all too much for her. She skipped school, took up with a drug dealer and refused to meet with us.'

'She wasn't herself,' added Alba, 'but we couldn't do anything to help once she turned eighteen and was legally an adult.'

Paco took up the story. 'Out of the blue she made contact with us about two years ago saying she had turned her life around but had debts. She needed somewhere to live so we offered her a home. We've all got along well and she's been working hard as a florist.'

'Did she do any training for it?'

'We funded a floristry course for her in Palma soon after she moved in with us, and she began picking up a lot of work,' he replied.

'Would you say it is out of character for her to disappear like this?'

Alba eyed her intently. 'She used to go off quite a lot when she first came to stay here. Sometimes, we had no idea where she was and who she was with but in time she settled down.'

'Do you know if Paloma had made some enemies in the past?'

Paco studied his hands thoughtfully. 'We heard that she owed money for drugs and was trying to make things good but she was quite a secretive girl.'

Isabel finished the last of her cake. 'I believe that her father is working as a mechanic in Manacor now. Did he ever meet up with Paloma when he left prison?'

Paco regarded her fiercely. 'Not that we know. She was very frightened of him and besides, he still has a restraining order. He's not allowed any contact with her.'

'Mind you, what does that mean?' Alba huffed. 'The man's a violent thug. He wouldn't take any notice of the law.'

'Would you know why she took up salsa classes?'

Alba shrugged. 'She told us she knew the woman who ran them but I don't know how.'

Isabel drained her coffee cup. 'Where else did she work aside from La Rosaleda and with Laura at the shop in Sant Joan?'

Alba placed her cup on the small table at her side. 'In Palma and also Bunyola, but she didn't talk much about her work. When she was with us, she preferred to groom the horses and play with the dogs. She was a simple girl at heart.'

Paco ran a hand through his thinning grey hair. 'You should talk with Laura and Mar Planes, the owner of La Rosaleda. They might know something.'

Isabel stood up and straightened her jacket. 'Guardia Civil officers have already spoken with them but I'll be paying them both a visit tomorrow.' She hesitated. 'Was Paloma *autónomo*?'

There was an awkward silence.

Isabel smiled. 'Listen, I'm not a tax inspector. Lots of people around here still get paid in black money but if she is on the tax system, it would make life easier for us. We'd at least be able to find out who her clients were.'

Paco sighed. 'She'd only recently got a bank account and always seemed to be paid in cash so I don't think so.'

'Can I take a look at her bedroom?'

They led her upstairs to a cosy room with a low-beamed, wooden ceiling and views to the garden and forestland beyond. A few old-fashioned canvasses of pastoral scenes adorned the white walls but otherwise the room was sparse. While Paco and Alba stood in the doorway, Isabel donned latex gloves and inspected the wardrobe, desk and drawers. Everything was neat and in order, including the perfectly made-up double bed. There was a faint aroma of lavender on the pillows and on the bedside table, an inhaler. 'Does Paloma have asthma?'

Alba nodded. 'Yes, we hope she had a spare inhaler in her bag. She suffers severe attacks.'

Isabel sat at the desk, unplugged the laptop and flicked through a black diary. She noticed that in the margins of some of the entries Paloma had drawn small religious crosses underneath which she'd written the letters JC in capitals.

'Was Paloma religious?'

Alba touched the small gold cross around her neck. 'Not at all. She wouldn't darken the door of a church.'

'May I borrow these for a while?'

Paco nodded. 'Be our guest.'

'Would you know if Paloma carried her identity card with her?'

They eyed one another. Paco seemed doubtful. 'Maybe, but I think she'd often forget to take it with her.'

Isabel double-checked the desk, cupboards and bedside table drawers but drew a blank. The underside of the bed yielded nothing.

'Has anyone been into this room since Monday evening?'

Alba looked affronted. 'Only us and that was to check that she hadn't left her phone in the bedroom. We haven't touched anything.'

Isabel left the room and walked slowly down the stairs, deep in thought. 'Why didn't you report Paloma's disappearance on Monday night?'

Paco bit his lip. 'To be honest we thought she might have gone off the rails again or was trying to make Pere feel bad and had gone off sulking somewhere. We thought she'd turn up late after we'd gone to bed.'

Alba shook her head sadly. 'When she didn't turn up for work at La Rosaleda the next morning, we grew worried and Paco called the police.'

'One final thing, can I see your vehicle?' Isabel asked.

Paco nodded genially and ushered her out of the house. 'We only have one. It's over here.'

He led Isabel to a cherry-red truck parked in an open garage.

'That's an old beauty,' she said.

He smiled. 'She's a Ford Ranger. Bought her back in the late eighties and she's held up pretty well. A bit battered and bruised but still drives like a dream.'

Squatting down, Isabel took images of the tyre treads and examined the dried mud splattered on the chassis and bodywork. It was evident that it hadn't been driven for some days.

At the front door, Isabel pressed a hand reassuringly on Alba's shoulder. 'We will do everything we can to find your niece. No stone will be left unturned.'

The light was beginning to fade as Isabel set off back along the track. Furó had woken up and now began grunting and scratching at the passenger door. With a sigh, she parked as soon as she'd reached the uneven part of the track where the asphalt ceased.

'Okay my little friend, let's go for a quick wander.'

She released Furó from the car and watched as he scampered happily about the wild terrain, sniffing in the long grasses and under rotten logs and boulders. Isabel thought back to what Paco had said about the track being a muddy quagmire on the night Paloma walked home alone. Had she even reached this far? How would she have navigated the mud and water if she had? She walked slowly, using the bright light of her key torch to examine the impacted soil. There were plenty of deep tyre marks in the mud which presumably had been created by Paco's truck and yet, as she squatted in the grass, she noticed some that didn't match. One set of heavy-duty treads indicated that an unknown vehicle had attempted a three-point turn. She stood and looked up and down the track. Why would a car drive up here, stop before reaching Paco's farm and then turn around and head straight back to the road? Maybe someone had got lost but why drive onto an unmarked track if that was the case? She pulled out her phone and took several images just in case they might prove useful at some stage in the investigation. She shivered as the air grew noticeably cooler, and whistled for Furó. He hurtled towards her but quickly turned tail and began scurrying along the grass verge. Isabel clapped her hands. 'Come on! In the car now, you imp.'

Heading back to Pequeñito in the gathering gloom, she grinned when she heard a pattering of feet behind her and waited for Furó to catch her up. As he weaved excitedly about her legs, she noticed something gripped between his teeth and tried to coax him to drop it. Having no luck, she opened the boot and took a handful of food pellets from the sack she'd bought at the farm. As soon as she'd scattered them on the ground, he released his find, more interested in the feast before him. Instinctively Isabel pulled on her latex gloves and carefully scooped it up, brushing away loose flakes of mud. Bemused, she studied the smooth and rounded, honey-toned wooden heart sitting in the palm of her hand. It measured about four centimetres in length and breadth, and felt surprisingly solid for such a small keepsake. She placed it carefully in a plastic bag in her pannier and, removing her gloves, ushered Furó into the car. With headlights on, Pequeñito laboured along the forbidding track until the juddering vehicle was finally able to turn onto the highway. Isabel drove along the quiet, dark road deep in thought. Was the little heart just a random find or could it be connected in any way to Paloma? Inexplicably, she felt a sudden sense of dread and prayed that her uncanny instinct might this time prove her wrong.

FIVE

A hazy sun greeted Isabel as she approached the sand-hued town of Sant Joan. Low lying in the east of Es Pla, it shimmered on the horizon like a dollop of paradise, flanked by gentle hills, fruit orchards, vineyards, verdant pastures and lush fields. Windmills occasionally popped up on the arable land, a sight Isabel relished, along with mountains of hay bales, wooden shacks and ancient stone barns. As Pequeñito rumbled into the heart of the town, Isabel looked up at the stern limestone clock tower of the seventeenth-century St Joan Baptista church that seemed inordinately grand for such a modest place. Then again, other rural havens such as Selva and Muro also possessed gigantic churches that dwarfed every other edifice for miles.

In truth, there wasn't a lot to commend the centre of Sant Joan, aside from the old church and humble home of the island's folklore hero and priest, Pare Ginard, but it had an earthy character and compelling authenticity lacking in some of Mallorca's more polished enclaves. On the environs of the town, there was of course El Calderers, the rambling estate that had its roots in the thirteenth century. A certain Antoni Oliver, who worked for the privileged family at the turn of the century, purportedly educated local farmers in new agricultural techniques that he'd acquired on his travels overseas. He was consequently declared a son of Sant Joan and locals had forever tucked him into their hearts.

It was just past midday and the Thursday market was in full flow, yet, happily, Isabel discovered a parking place on a narrow street close to the church. Admittedly, Pequeñito's inside front wheel grazed a single yellow line but not enough to worry her. She was friendly with many of the island's traffic wardens and could usually wheedle her way out of potential parking disputes.

Isabel gave a yawn and stretched as she stepped out of the car. As usual she had started the day early and had driven to the Palma police precinct before nine o'clock in order to leave Paloma's laptop and the wooden heart with her good friend and former colleague, Nacho Blanco, head of the forensics team. The previous evening, Isabel had forwarded Gaspar the images of the tyre treads she'd discovered on the track leading to Paco and Alba's house, and hoped they might present a fresh lead.

Breezing through the market, she offered a cheery *'Hola'* to the various stallholders and treated herself to a *senala*, a traditional, hand-woven palm leaf basket from the town of Artà. Then she bought a string of fat garlic bulbs, a marrow, cauliflower and leeks. Some roughly hewn pottery bowls in bright colours caught her eye, so she negotiated a price for six and struggled back to the car with her wares, pausing to drink a *cortado* and to buy a freshly-baked brown loaf on the way. After dumping her load, she set off for Llard, the grocer's owned by Paloma's friend, Laura.

Close to the post office, and wedged between a garage and a hairdressing salon, the pretty store was festooned with rows of tiny white Christmas lights ahead of the festive season, and the windows were awash with fresh fruit, vegetables, and jars of homemade jams and pickles. Cured sausages of every size hung from hooks around the front door and from the ceiling and formed the centrepiece of a handsome product display on the pavement. As Isabel stepped inside, breathing in the delicious aromas of paprika and garlic, a friendly voice called out to her from a back room. Moments later, a young woman appeared, wiping her hands on an apron.

'I've just been making sausages in the kitchen. A messy business!'

Isabel laughed. 'I wondered how your shop came by its unusual name.'

'Llard was founded by my great grandfather, who was a butcher, and our speciality continues to be homemade sausages, so I suppose "fat" still fits the bill. He named it that for a bit of fun. When I took over the business from my father, I wanted to introduce general groceries but kept the name as it's well known and we still make the best *botifarró* sausage in the area.' She leant forward and offered her hand. 'By the way, my name is Laura.'

Isabel smiled. 'I'm Bel. Thank you for sharing such an interesting story. Sadly, much as I love sausages, I am here on police business. I believe you know Paloma Crespí?'

Laura's face darkened. 'She's my best friend and I have been sick with worry. There's no answer from her phone and the Guardia Civil officers called two days ago to say there'd been no trace of her since Monday night. Are you with the National Police?'

Isabel nodded. 'We are trying to create a clear picture of Paloma and her life. Have you known her long?'

'We were friends at school but lost touch when she moved from her family home in Sant Joan. Her father went to prison, she and her mother rented a flat in Manacor and Paloma got in with a bad crowd. Then two years ago, she came back here and moved in with her uncle and aunt and we resumed our friendship. She had changed for the better.'

'In what way?'

'Paloma had quit taking drugs and had decided to train as a florist. She has a wonderful way with flowers and makes the most stunning arrangements. All the same, she still has debts, so I offered her some hours here at the grocery for some extra cash.'

'Do you have any idea where she might be?'

Laura shook her head. 'This is very out of character. She only really hangs out with me or her boyfriend. Where would she go? I feel something bad has happened. My father and I retraced her route on foot on Tuesday afternoon but we found nothing.'

'You know her boyfriend?'

'I've met Pere a few times.' She lowered her eyes. 'He's not very reliable and to be honest she was about to ditch him for good.'

'Do you think he knew?'

'They were having a lot of rows and he could be quite aggressive and insulting. He probably knew she would split up with him soon.'

'She'd met someone new?'

'Not that I know of.' She hesitated. 'There is something else. Paloma mentioned that some young guy she'd met was a bit creepy around her. She thought he had a bit of a crush.'

'Did she mention his name or how they knew one another?'

'I'm afraid not. She tried to joke about it but she seemed quite scared.'

'Did she tell you the names or whereabouts of any other clients?'

Laura clicked her teeth. 'They were all rich people. One was in Palma and she had others in the countryside. She must have had a client in Manacor because she seemed to go there a fair bit.'

'Do you know how she got her work?'

She shrugged. 'It was all word of mouth. Most were one-off jobs for floral displays but she did have some regular weekly assignments too.'

'You've been very helpful, Laura. Please let me know if Paloma makes contact.' Isabel handed her a card.

She smiled sadly. 'Of course. Can I give you my special spicy *sobrassada* to take home? You've just missed the town's La Morcilla *fiesta* where my sausages sell out, especially the *botifarró*.'

'I'm not surprised. They look wonderful but let me buy a few instead as I'd like to bring a gift to my new neighbour and my mother. Also, I'll take some red wine.' She examined the shelves and proffered two bottles, Trispol, a biodynamic wine from the Mesquida Mora winery in Porerres, and El Galgo from the Oliver Moragues vineyard in Algaida. Laura laid out a selection of sausages on the counter, and after a robust discussion about the merits of each, Isabel made her choice. She added a bunch of parsley to the pile and some homemade pickles and flower honey.

With her pannier groaning, she set off to Carrer de Neu, just a short distance on foot from Llard. As soon as she walked into La Rosaleda and began sniffing the dark red roses by the door, a tall and elegant silver-haired woman approached. Isabel anticipated that she was the owner, Mar Planes, and noticed how her shoulders slumped when she presented her police badge.

'This is all so upsetting,' she sighed. 'Paloma has been working for me for less than a year but she's a lovely girl and very willing. In all the time I've run this business, I've never come across such a natural at handling blooms. Her knowledge and love of plants is extraordinary.'

'Has she ever missed work before?' asked Isabel.

'Never. One of the most reliable staff members I've ever had. She can be withdrawn and at times lacks confidence but lately she's really seemed much happier.'

'Did she talk about boyfriends?'

The woman shook her head. 'She never discussed personal matters with me.'

'What about her home life?'

Mar Planes gave a cynical cluck. 'That father should have been locked up for twenty years. Jago made all their lives hell. Thanks to Paco and Alba she now has a proper home life.'

Isabel nodded sympathetically. 'Does he ever pass this way?'

'Jago Morey is not allowed near her or he could be sent back to prison. I knew him in my teen days. He had good looks so was quite the ladies' man. Do you think he's involved in her disappearance?'

Isabel chose her words carefully. 'We are doing all we can to find Paloma. At this stage, it is too early to determine what happened that night.'

In contemplative state, Isabel drove to Manacor. Today, she didn't have Furó for company as he was staying with her mother, and she was quite relieved. If Paloma's father was as unpleasant as everyone had warned, she wouldn't want her beloved ferret to have to witness any angry scenes or be tempted to deliver the man a nasty nip.

*

As Isabel drove through the busy streets of Manacor, she thought about the oak dining table Florentina had purchased many years before from a local family that produced solid traditional furniture. It had stood the test of time and bore testimony to the craftsmanship of the town. It might not be the most picturesque of places with its industrial character but islanders flocked to its centre for their tables, chairs and wardrobes, and tourists for its sprawling Monday market and factories selling artificial pearls. The garage workshop belonging to Jago Morey was tucked away in a scruffy street to the west of the town, surrounded by tired apartment blocks and empty retail units. Parking Pequeñito in the forecourt, Isabel stood by the car, taking in her surroundings. There was no sign of human life but a pair of worn workman's boots jutted out from under an old jalopy inside the building. She strolled over to the entrance and issued a loud greeting. The boots stirred and a grumpy bearded face peered out.

'What do you want?'

Isabel bent down and presented her police badge. 'Mr Morey, I presume? I need to talk to you about your daughter.'

The portly man flinched and, with a lot of wheezing and cursing, wriggled out from under the car.

He wiped his big paws on the filthy overall he wore. 'You talking about Paloma?'

Isabel offered a beguiling smile. 'You have other daughters?'

He gave a hoarse cough and opened a packet of cigarettes, thrusting one between his lips. 'The Guardia were here Tuesday. I told them I haven't seen her for years. If I make any contact with Paloma, I'll be straight back in the slammer.'

'When did you last see her?'

Jago Morey offered a dismissive shrug. 'You should have done your homework. Eight years ago, when they put me in jail.'

Isabel nodded. 'So, in the three years since you've been out of prison, you've never had contact with your daughter?'

He took a long drag on his cigarette. 'That's what I said.'

'You do realise that Paloma has been missing since Monday evening and we are deeply concerned. Would you have any idea where she might be?'

He gave a snort of laughter. 'How the heck would I know? Thanks to her and her waste of a mother, I ended up in the nick. She wouldn't be welcome around here.'

Isabel felt her fists tighten, and made herself take a long breath. 'Do you know Carlotta Pilar?'

'Never heard of her.'

Isabel defiantly held his gaze. 'That's a shame. She speaks very highly of you.'

Jago Morey narrowed his eyes but said nothing.

'So where were you on Monday evening?'

'I told the Guardia. Home alone.'

'So, no witnesses? Did anyone call round?'

He cursed silently. 'I ate alone, had a few beers and went to bed around 10 p.m.'

Isabel smiled. 'How's work these days?'

'What's it to you?'

'Just wondered. Do you have any other business interests?'

'Like what?'

'You tell me. I'm sure you must have done some useful networking in the Palma penitentiary.'

Glaring at her, he hurled his cigarette butt on the ground and stubbed it out with his boot. 'You should keep your nose out of other people's affairs. It can get you into trouble.'

'One of the perks of the job.' Isabel offered him a bleak smile. 'Here's my card. If you hear anything, call me.'

She turned and was about to return to her car when he yelled after her. 'You're all the same, you cops! Always harassing innocent folks. Stay away and when you find the sloven, tell her not to come skulking around here.'

Isabel didn't look back but after revving the engine, she took great pleasure in reversing Pequeñito into a *moto* parked behind her. She enjoyed the sound of tinkling glass as the bike crashed heavily to the ground, causing the man to lumber towards her in rage. His eyes bulged. 'Hey! That's mine. Look what you've done!'

Isabel wound down the window and gave a mock gasp. 'Did I really do that? We women drivers are such a menace. Still, you're a mechanic so I'm sure it's easily fixed.'

With a wave, she roared out of the forecourt and patted the dashboard. 'Well done, Pequeñito. Team effort. We may not have made a friend, but we've meted out a little revenge on behalf of Paloma and her mother.'

*

It was late in the evening and a mischievous wind blew through the garden, upturning pots and sending debris flying about the orchard. A donkey bellowed in the distance and a choir of downcast dogs howled balefully at the moon. Having updated Tolo by phone as soon as she'd returned home, Isabel had devoured a bowl of lemon infused artichokes and *jamon serrano* left on the kitchen table by Florentina. She headed upstairs with a glass of red wine and a half-empty bottle of the Trispol she had purchased earlier that day in Sant Joan and curled up on her Chesterfield sofa with Furó by her side. Taking a sip of her wine, she lit a fragrant candle on the table before her, and began reading Paloma's diary.

Although it was nearly December, the entries for the previous eleven months, recorded in Paloma's neat and even handwriting, were thin and perfunctory at best. Isabel flipped through each page, carefully studying the limited content while jotting down thoughts in her own small notebook. As she had observed when at Paloma's home, on the first Monday of each month, a doodled cross had been inserted in the margin with the letters JC. The entry for these days simply read: pick up and deliver blooms. Various times and addresses had been written next to each one. Was Paloma talking about delivering flowers to private clients? Her aunt had said that she wasn't religious so what did the cross signify? Isabel jumped up and walked over to a white board she had set up the day before. Cracking open a handful of sunflower seeds heaped in a glass bowl, she surveyed the images and sticky notes before her. It was near midnight when she finally stopped her travails and flung the diary down on the sofa. She looked across at an expectant Furó before punching a number into her phone. Tolo answered on the third ring.

'You sound sleepy.'

'I was in bed,' he grumbled.

'Lucky you, living it up in a swanky Madrid hotel.'

He laughed. 'Trust me, the beds aren't that great. So, what news?'

'All is not as it seems, dear Watson. Contrary to what everyone has been telling me, I think Paloma was seeing her father regularly.'

'How come?'

'I discovered crosses in the margin of her diary with the initials JC which I initially thought signified Jesus Christ but they are evidently just a decoy. I'm now convinced they stand for Jago and Carlotta.'

'Carlotta, the dance teacher?'

'Yes, I think she and Jago are possibly lovers or associates and involved Paloma in something shifty. She mentions making monthly flower deliveries in her diary but I think she was delivering something else.'

'What then?'

'Drugs, most likely.'

Tolo responded sharply. 'You think her disappearance is drug related?'

'Not necessarily, but there is more to Paloma than meets the eye. Jago told me he hadn't seen her for years but he was definitely lying and Carlotta Pilar is a piece of work.'

'This case is getting complicated, Bel.'

'It certainly is. This morning when I visited Paloma's best friend, Laura, in Sant Joan, she mentioned that Paloma was going to Manacor regularly. Laura assumed it was a client but I think it was to see her father.'

'But why would she do that after everything that had happened to her and her mother?'

'I think he had some kind of hold on her. Laura also mentioned that Paloma had attracted some unwelcome attention from some dodgy guy but she couldn't tell me any more.'

What's your next step?'

'Yesterday Gaspar got local media to carry images of Paloma requesting information from the public, so hopefully tomorrow we might get some intel about Paloma's past and current clients. In the morning I shall be interviewing her boyfriend, Pere Brotat.'

'What about that wooden heart you found?'

'It's with forensics, along with Paloma's laptop and the tyre tread images I took. I sent a shot of the wooden heart to her uncle and aunt but both claimed never to have seen it before.'

'It could have nothing to do with Paloma.'

'I know.'

'Time is ticking and it's already been four days since she disappeared.' He paused. 'Let's hope she's still alive.'

As Isabel ended the call, Furó gave a whimper and scratched at her arm. Isabel kissed his head and, with a heavy heart, blew out the flickering candle before her and said a little prayer.

SIX

As Isabel clanged shut her garden gate and set off towards the *plaça* for her early morning breakfast at Bar Castell, she heard someone calling after her. Drawing to a halt, she spun round to find her new neighbour, Juliana, running towards her in what appeared to be bright orange pyjamas, her long mane of glossy black hair streaming about her shoulders. The woman stopped for breath, and began laughing.

'*Hombre*! You're a fast walker. I just wanted to thank you for the delicious sausage and wine you left on my doorstep last night.'

'A small welcome gift from the heart of Mallorca.'

'I'm so grateful. Also I want to invite you for lunch tomorrow. It would be a chance to meet the family. Please bring your mother.'

Isabel beamed. 'I'd love to come and I'm sure Florentina will too. We'll bring a dessert. Well, rather my mother will want to make one.'

'That would be wonderful. And what about Doctor Ramis and that handsome assistant of yours? I saw him leaving your house the other day.'

'I'm sure Doctor Ramis will be ecstatic. He adores a Sunday lunch and only the other day was telling me how he'd visited Brazil in his youth. I'll ask Pep, too, though he might want to bring his girlfriend, Angélica.'

'The more the merrier. We will prepare a big spread. I have invited the English couple who live on the other side of our house. They are called French, which is so funny, don't you think?'

Isabel grinned. 'Yes, I've always found it amusing, especially as they speak neither French nor Spanish. They are very friendly people though.'

Juliana waved her hand dismissively in the air. '*No hay problema!* At home we all speak English and of course Portuguese and Spanish too. We are one big cosmic family, are we not?' She kissed Isabel on both cheeks and wandered back to her house, sashaying her hips and singing as she walked. 'See you at two o'clock tomorrow, beautiful Bel!'

Isabel laughed to herself and carried on her way. Her new neighbour was certainly warm and gregarious. She wondered what Doctor Ramis and her mother would make of her. As she headed across the square towards Bar Castell, she clocked Llorenç Bestard standing in front of the sturdy wooden doors of the town hall, a frown painted on his forehead. Deep in conversation with Padre Agustí, he faltered when he spotted her and beckoned her over. She kissed both men's cheeks and squeezed the *padre*'s hand.

'You've been on my mind, Padre Agustí.'

'God is still waiting for you at the church, Bel. His patience knows no bounds.'

'That's just as well,' she replied as she shared a surreptitious grin with the mayor. When he saw the solemn expression on the *padre*'s face, Llorenç adopted an air of gravitas.

'Ah Bel, we have a real crisis on our hands. The animal thefts here are getting completely out of hand. An Alsatian, boxer and poodle have now disappeared. And of course we're also missing a cockerel and parrot.'

Isabel's eyes widened. 'Wait! You don't mean the grey parrot belonging to Dolores?'

'Sadly, I do. She was sobbing as she served drinks in Café Jordi yesterday. Bimbo is like her baby.'

Padre Agustí made a rapid sign of the cross and bowed his head. 'He's the only parrot I know that can speak Russian.'

Suddenly engulfed in sunlight, Isabel squinted at him in surprise. 'I knew he did card tricks but he's a linguist, too?'

The priest gasped. 'Card tricks? What a talented creature! God works in mysterious ways. Let us pray that the Lord finds our feathered friend.' He held up his hands in prayer before ambling off in the direction of the church.

Llorenç waggled a finger at her. 'How mischievous you are, Bel! Poor Padre Agustí will be telling everyone about the card-playing parrot.'

Isabel winked at him. 'Imagine life without humour! All the same, I do agree with you that we urgently need to find out who is behind all this. But where have all the animals gone? Have the municipal bins been checked?'

'Of course, but there's no trace of them. They've simply disappeared.'

Isabel tapped her cheek. 'Perhaps they were spirited away by magic like the children in the legend of the Pied Piper?'

Llorenç grinned. 'As Mayor of Sant Martí, I can assure you that I've seen no *Flautista de Hamelín* around here and we don't have a rat infestation yet.'

'Never say never, Llorenç,' she teased.

He eyed her earnestly. 'There's another delicate matter. Nicolas Garcia has lost his beloved cat and has summoned me to his estate tomorrow morning. I rather wondered if you might accompany me?'

Isabel eyed him thoughtfully. 'The Chilean sculptor? I have never been to Ses Fonts. I hear that he keeps to himself.'

'Indeed,' agreed the mayor. 'He is a charming yet private man and loved by all so this is unfortunate, to say the least. If the international media finds out that this maestro has had his pet stolen and that it's part of a spate of thefts, things could spiral out of control. We don't want reporters snooping around the village, blowing this all out of proportion.'

'When did he report the cat missing?'

'Yesterday. He was quite inconsolable. As you may know from press articles, he is wheelchair-bound and besotted with his pets, and also his loyal staff.'

'Yes, I have read a great deal about him. His bronzes are magnificent.'

The mayor cleared his throat. 'In truth I'm not an art man, but I appreciate that he is world renowned. So, would you come with me? It seems your reputation travels as Nicolas specifically asked that I bring you. He'd heard on the grapevine that you were a detective inspector.'

'That's history now,' she chided. 'I wonder who tittle-tattled to him. Still, if it helps you out, of course, though I must be back for lunch with my new Brazilian neighbours.'

Llorenç appeared affronted. 'What, you're seeing them socially? But they've only just moved into the village. You know nothing about them.'

'I'll take the risk,' she replied with a straight face. 'It's good to live dangerously, Llorenç.'

'So many foreigners moving here,' he muttered. 'Where will it end?'

'But we're one big cosmopolitan family, are we not?' With an enigmatic smile, she sauntered off towards Bar Castell. She was suddenly ravenously hungry and needed breakfast.

'Shall we say ten o'clock tomorrow?' he called after her.

Isabel gave a wave of accord, a smile playing on her lips. She'd always wanted to see the famed artist's sculpture park, and what better way to spend a Sunday morning?

*

A velvety blue sky spread like a cosy blanket over the valley, brushing the tips of the Tramuntana peaks and proving an idyllic playground for the island's feathered fraternity. Following a delicious breakfast of scrambled eggs and coffee at Bar Castell, Isabel sang at the top of her voice as she drove towards Sineu, only pausing to listen to the familiar toot-toot of Soller's century-old train as it rattled through dusty tunnels and along mountain tracks on its way to Palma. She relished the excuse to drive back to the interior of the island, and hoped, time permitting, to stop by the Sanctuary of Senyora de Curat that crouched aloft Randa, a graceful hill on the outskirts of Felanitx.

Isabel loved visiting the historic sanctuaries and hermitages of the area, not out of religious fervour, but just to enjoy their beauty and sense of peace. Another hallmark of Es Pla were the historic mills, a good number of which had fallen into disrepair, but a government scheme had seen many restored to their original splendour. Isabel cast an eye over a field where a handsome stone specimen with gigantic sails stood. She felt a surge of joy to see that it had been refurbished and was functioning as in days of yore. She fervently believed in protecting the heritage of her beloved island, and what could be better than starting with these precious relics? She recalled that the most ancient of Mallorca's mills was in happy retirement in the south-eastern town of Santanyi, and dated back to 1262. If memory served her right, it was built in the very same year that James I of Aragon bequeathed his kingdom to his second son, James, though the poor devil never lived long enough to accept the honour.

Just as she pulled up outside a squat block of flats on the fringes of Sineu, her phone rang. It was Josep Casanovas, the preening editor of *El Periódico*, one of the island's leading newspapers.

'This is indeed a pleasure, Josep.'

'Bel, it's been too long,' he simpered. 'But happily, I feel our lives are to be entwined once more.'

'How come?'

'I placed a story about the missing florist for our mutual chum, Gaspar Fernández. It seems that his boss is off gallivanting in Madrid yet again.'

'Tolo Cabot is on a training course. He doesn't have a choice,' she replied hastily.

He guffawed. 'A likely story. Anyway, his absence is no great loss as far as I'm concerned.'

Isabel felt her hackles rise but decided not to jump to the bait. The two men were old adversaries and though she found Casanovas trying, he had his uses.

'Besides,' he chirruped, 'to my delight, Fernández told me that you were now taking charge of the case.'

'I'm just lending a hand to the team again. We urgently need information about Paloma Crespí's contacts, particularly her private clients.'

'Perhaps we should meet to discuss all this, Bel? You can bring me up to speed on the case and we can work together to find this unfortunate girl.'

Isabel stifled a yawn. 'Good try, Josep, but you know I don't tout confidential information.'

His laughter rang down the line. 'Of course not, Bel, but we are close friends and can lean on one another.'

'So, I'm leaning on you now, Josep. Have you had any response to the article yet?'

'Obviously we issued a police helpline but the public aren't awfully bright and have been calling the newspaper directly. Naturally we've passed any leads onto Fernández. He'll no doubt bring you up to speed.'

'Were any clients of Paloma?'

'A butler called from Los Abetos, an estate near Bunyola, to report that Paloma used to arrange flowers at the manor each week.'

She shook her head. 'How the other half live, eh?'

'Actually,' he coughed, 'my local florist regularly arranges flowers at my *finca*. If you were there to brighten my home, I'd have no need.'

Isabel resisted a groan. At least she could always rely on the unctuous editor to keep her entertained. 'Did the butler say when Paloma last visited the estate?'

'Apparently she stopped working abruptly some weeks ago and gave no explanation.'

'Anything else of interest?' she asked.

He sighed impatiently. 'Some deranged woman rang about her old mother, droning on about how she'd gone missing three years ago and the police had failed to find her. Probably down to Tolo Cabot's incompetence. I don't have any time for the man, as you know.'

Isabel swallowed her irritation. 'You passed the details onto Gaspar?'

'Of course.'

'You've been most helpful, Josep.'

'So, when are we going to get together?' he gushed. 'You may have heard that I've been formerly nominated to become the next Mayor of Forn de Camp. Surely cause for celebration? I know a great seafood restaurant in Portixol.'

Isabel frowned, trying to dismiss the thought of how unbearably pompous Casanovas would become should he snatch the mayoral role. An image floated before her eyes of a gigantic pufferfish, its swollen belly full of pride at being one of the most potentially toxic vertebrates in the world. 'Have you ever tried blowfish?'

'Not recently.'

'It's also called pufferfish. It's a great delicacy in South East Asia but can be fatal if not prepared correctly.'

He gave a hyena laugh. 'Well, let's stick to the seabass when we meet! By the way, how is that charming ferret of yours?'

'As charming and irreplaceable as ever,' Isabel replied. As she terminated the call, she mused on the animal disappearances. Furó was safely ensconced in his basket in her office but how could she protect him against an invisible enemy? She would need to act fast to protect her village from further losses.

Deep in thought, she crossed the street and rang the doorbell of Pere Brotat's flat. He buzzed her into the building and stood anxiously at his front door on the ground floor. 'Do you want to come in?'

Isabel examined the lean-faced, greasy-haired specimen before her. 'Unless you want your neighbours to hear our conversation out here.'

Tetchily he led her into the flat and through to a small and chaotic kitchen cum living area. Every surface was strewn with empty pizza cartons, discarded cigarette packets, coffee cups and beer cans. Isabel's eyes roamed the room, noting an assortment of oily car parts sitting on a newspaper by the fireplace and an axe propped up against a wall.

'Nice pad you've got here,' she said. 'Does it come with a government health warning?'

He froze but relaxed when he saw the merriment in her eyes. 'I'm not great on housework. Can I get you anything? A beer or coffee?'

She grinned. 'Thanks, but that kitchen looks like a bacteria breeding station. So, to business. Tell me about you and Paloma.'

Sighing heavily, he stuck his hands in the pockets of his grimy jeans and slumped onto the messy sofa. 'I've been seeing Paloma for about six months.' He lowered his eyes. 'To be honest, I was on the point of splitting with her.'

'Oh?'

'Yeah. We weren't really getting on lately. She was becoming a bit of a drag.'

'In what way?'

He shrugged carelessly. 'You know, always complaining and expecting me to pick her up all the time. She said she couldn't afford her own car but often I saw her with bundles of cash.'

Isabel frowned. 'Did she say where it came from?'

He shook his head. 'All I know is that she'd go to Manacor each month and come back with a bulging wallet. I asked her if she was back to selling drugs and she punched me.'

She stared at the well-built youth before her and offered a sardonic smile. 'I'm glad you lived to tell the tale. Have you ever met her father?'

He frowned. 'No way. He's not allowed anywhere near Paloma since he left prison. She told me he used to beat her and her mum up. Sounds like a real thug.'

Isabel nodded. 'Okay, tell me about the night Paloma disappeared. What happened?'

'She asked me to pick her up from her salsa class in Sant Joan but I forgot. I'm working on a building site in Campos and the boss keeps me late sometimes.'

'How long have you been employed there?'

'About five months. It's a steady job and good money.'

'Do you take on other work?'

He hesitated. 'I'd like the extra money but I just don't have time.'

'I'll need your employer's details, and from your last job, too.'

'No problem,' he replied nonchalantly.

Isabel indicated for him to continue.

'Anyway, Paloma gave me hell on the phone and said she was going to walk to her uncle's house instead.'

Isabel nodded encouragingly.

'So, I just drove back here, had a beer and some pasta and played video games until about ten o'clock with my neighbour, Jorge.'

'What games?'

'FIFA. We both like football.'

'Can your neighbour confirm all that?'

'Sure. He lives next door. I told the Guardia Civil this before.'

'Carry on.'

'Paloma's aunt called me around nine o'clock. She thought Paloma might have come back here.'

'So what did you do?"

'I tried Paloma's phone but it just went to voicemail. The next morning, I called it again but it was dead.'

'Can you tell me about her work?'

Pere slouched in his seat and pulled a cigarette towards him. 'She helped at her friend Laura's shop and at La Rosaleda in Sant Joan but she had private clients in different places.'

He lit up and exhaled slowly. 'She used local buses and the train in Sineu to get around but she didn't tell me much about her clients except that they were all loaded.'

Isabel looked out of the dirty window at an unkempt patch of communal grass interrupted at intervals by bald patches of mud. Beyond were faded green pastures and bare, spiky almond trees lacking their characteristic verdant foliage and frothy blossom that early spring transformed into balls of pink candyfloss.

Pere peered up at Isabel from under his brown fringe. 'I was the only one who could have known that Paloma would be walking home alone on Monday night.'

'It certainly looks that way, which is why your alibi is crucial. It was raining heavily so do you think an opportunist, some random abductor, really just intercepted her en route?'

'What else?' he answered with a scowl.

'There are a myriad of possibilities. You for example, could have driven there, picked her up, stowed her somewhere and returned to your flat for a night's FIFA playing.'

'That's ridiculous,' he fumed. 'I'd never hurt Paloma. Anyway, where would I have put her and why?'

'Indeed, motivation is key. Why would you have done that? A crime of passion? Did she ditch you for someone else? Maybe you knew she was carrying a stash of money? Maybe you have a handy barn or cellar somewhere.'

'You're crazy. None of this is true.'

Isabel cocked her head and smiled. 'Relax. I know that, but I do need to see your car. Have you got the keys?'

Confused, Pere got to his feet and strode to the front door. 'You think I'm telling the truth?'

'Yes, because on Tuesday your concierge showed the Guardia video footage of you arriving home at 8.30 p.m. and there's no evidence that you left the building again. Your neighbour also confirmed your story.'

He looked at her aghast. 'So why all the questions?'

'I like to hear witness evidence for myself. Not second-hand.'

He ground the cigarette stub underfoot. 'There's no point in searching my van. She's not in the boot.'

'Let's make sure,' she replied dryly.

Isabel followed him out of the building and down into an underground garage. He led her to a decrepit white van and opened the front and back doors.

'There. Nothing.'

Isabel donned her police gloves and slipped into the driver's seat. She inspected the dashboard, glovebox and windshield and worked her way with her fingers around the seats and belts.

Irritated, Pere poked his head inside. 'What are you doing?'

Isabel ignored him as she methodically explored every crevice. After fifteen minutes she emerged, carrying a tiny device that she held up for him to see. 'Look what I found behind the rear-view mirror.'

'What is it?'

'A minute camcorder. Whoever planted this would have tabs on you the whole time and listened to any conversations you had by phone.'

For a second, Pere was too shocked to reply. 'It's like a spy movie.'

Isabel popped the apparatus into a plastic bag. 'There are more of these things around than you might think. We need to find out who placed it and why. Is your underground garage always open?'

Pere nodded. 'But maybe a security camera might show someone tampering with my van?' He pointed to a corner of the ceiling. 'There's one over there with a view to my car space.'

'We can but hope. I'll go and talk to your concierge.'

He seemed exasperated. 'You're the police. Can't you just trace the person that put it there and arrest them?'

''That would be nice and easy, wouldn't it? The pros that use these spy-cams usually have proxy servers to hide their identities. They're all encrypted so it's virtually impossible to find those responsible.'

'But how does it work?'

'A wireless signal is transmitted which means the video can be recorded and viewed elsewhere, even live.'

'That's so cool.'

'Not if it's your car being tapped,' she replied. 'Where were you when you spoke with Paloma on Monday night?'

'In the car. I'd just finished work for the day.'

Isabel took off her gloves and headed back to the building with Pere trailing behind her.

He caught her up. 'But this is serious, right? Whoever was listening on that device would have known from my phone call with Paloma that I wasn't picking her up, and abducted her on the way home.'

Isabel turned to him. 'Let's not jump to conclusions yet.'

She looked up at an ominous sky and felt a needle of rain on her skin. With an involuntary shiver, she hastily rang the doorbell of the concierge. Video footage of the garage might throw up some answers but she didn't hold out much hope. Who knew if the camera was even in operation? Whoever was behind Paloma's disappearance was no amateur, of that she was sure. Perhaps the device had been planted by an obsessed stalker, possibly the young man that Laura had mentioned, or was it the result of a business transaction gone sour? She wasn't ruling anything out at this stage. All she did know was that if by some miracle Paloma wasn't already dead, her life was in mortal danger.

SEVEN

It was half past seven on Sunday morning, a time when few regulars set foot in Bar Castell. All the same, at the first crow of the cockerel, Isabel and Furó had set off to Can Repic beach for their customary early swim while most villagers were happily still slumbering in their beds. Returning to the village with wet hair and a healthy glow, Isabel skipped up the stairs to her favourite bar and threw open the door with such ferocity that it banged noisily against the glass windows. Furó popped his head out of her pannier in some alarm.

'Steady on, Bel. You're like a raging bull!' Rafael growled from behind the counter. 'Even your ferret got a fright.'

She leant against the counter. 'Just an *ensaïmada* and coffee today, *el meu amic*. By the way, my police colleague, Gaspar, will be joining me any time.'

Rafael gave her a long look. 'Is he coming here about that missing florist I read about or our animals?'

'Hopefully we don't need to involve the police in our own little domestic matter,' she replied pointedly.

'But what's to be done, Bel? It's no longer a joke. You know Gabriel Reus?'

'Isn't he the manager of Blau Bank in Soller?'

'That's right. Well, his sister, Margarita, who's just moved to the village, says his black pug has vanished, just like all the rest.'

Isabel gave a long sigh. 'That is bad news. None of it makes any sense but I promise that Llorenç and I are working on it.'

She headed off towards her favourite table on the terrace overlooking the square. The sun was just rising and throwing off a duvet of soft cloud as a halo of dim light appeared in the sky. Furó clambered out of the pannier and curled up on Isabel's lap, his muzzle and whiskers still wet from his early morning baptism. Isabel felt a growing frustration about this new danger facing her village and instinctively held Furó close. It seemed that no animal was safe. She would urgently have to put her mind to the matter. Rafael soon appeared in the doorway accompanied by a beaming giant of a man. Isabel greeted him with a hug.

'Gaspar, it's so good to see you. Thanks for coming all the way here, especially early on a Sunday.'

'Any excuse to get out of Palma! Besides, I don't get to the Soller valley much these days.'

Isabel pulled a bag of lemons out of her pannier. 'A little gift from Sant Martí.'

He picked out a fruit and inhaled deeply. 'Perfect for my gin and tonics.'

She cast a critical gaze over him. 'Still sticking to the Kojak look, then?'

Gaspar clicked his teeth and ran a hand over his smooth, dark head. 'You liked my curls, didn't you? A little bit of my West African heritage shining through. '

'I like you just as you are, but yes, those curls were phenomenal.'

He rolled his head back and laughed. 'My girlfriend agrees but my new hard man look spooks the island thugs so I'm sticking with it.'

Rafael gave a discreet cough. 'Can I get you a coffee?'

Gaspar nodded. 'Thanks. *Café con leche* and *tostadas*.'

While Rafael pottered back to the counter, Isabel lent across the table confidentially. 'Don't keep me in suspense. Any intel on that wooden heart yet?'

Gaspar pulled a set of papers out of a rucksack.

'I'm afraid we got no prints from the little heart. All I can tell you is that it was crafted from laurel wood.'

Isabel frowned. 'That's interesting. Why laurel?'

He shrugged. 'I'm not a gardening man, so don't ask me.'

The shrill ring of the bar's telephone distracted them.

'It'll be Rafael's old mother at this time of morning,' explained Isabel. 'She lives in Es Pla and is always on the blower.'

'Mine too. Never get a moment's peace,' replied Gaspar, breaking into a big grin.

Isabel returned to the theme in hand. 'Laurel is an unusual wood to use for crafting, that's all.'

'Is that so?' Gaspar passed her a piece of paper. 'This is the analysis of those car treads you found on Paloma's home track. The tyres are the Continental brand and have a directional tyre tread, meaning they're particularly good in mud and snow.'

'And resistant to aquaplaning at high speeds, too.'

'Spot on. What it proves is that an unknown high-performance vehicle was on the track that night as the treads on the uncle's van don't match.'

'And what about Paloma's phone and laptop?'

He shrugged. 'The laptop is clean as a whistle. Her browser is full of knitting and floristry sites and her social media feed is virtually non-existent. However, her mobile's records prove that Pere Brotat was telling the truth about calling her on Monday night and leaving her a message during her salsa class. The phone now appears to be dead, probably destroyed. How did it go with Brotat yesterday?'

Isabel reached into her voluminous pannier and pulled out a small specimen bag, which she dangled it in front of him. 'Can you get this checked? It's a minute videocam I found in his van.'

Gaspar examined it closely. 'These little devices are ingenious and not too expensive. I wonder who hid it there.'

Rafael appeared and placed a coffee and toast smeared with fresh pureed tomato in front of Gaspar while Isabel received a plump, sugared *ensaïmada* with her steaming *cortado*.

'That looks very slimming,' winked Gaspar.

'Yes, calorie-free,' she grinned.

When Rafael had left, Isabel leant forward conspiratorially.

'Whoever it was would have heard Pere's conversation with Paloma as he called her from the car on Monday night, and known that she would be walking home alone.'

Gaspar gave a low whistle. 'What a web this is turning out to be. I'll see if we can get any intel on this device. Where was the van parked? Any chance of a surveillance camera in the vicinity?'

'There was one but the concierge told me it hadn't been working for months, so no luck there.' She took a sip of coffee. 'Any other interesting telephone numbers connected to Paloma's mobile phone?'

'We've called round all the others listed. Nothing much there, I'm afraid. Just numbers for the two women she worked with in Sant Joan and also her dance instructor.'

Isabel perked up. 'You mean Carlotta Pilar?'

Gaspar took a bite of toast and passed her the report.

She flicked through the pages and gave a sigh. 'What about her identity card? Do you think she was carrying it? If so, she could have left the island.'

He gave her a long look. 'Frankly, Bel, I don't know what to think. The whole case is baffling and Paloma herself, an enigma. Maybe she had a lover and planned on running away with him or disappeared abroad, but it doesn't hang together, does it?'

'No, not at all. Anything from the local press yet? Josep Casanovas called me yesterday. He said that he'd had some results.'

He passed her a file. 'All yours. We did some filtering of reader response from his paper and also *Ultima Hora, Diario de Mallorca* and *Majorca Daily Bulletin*. There are a few hot leads. Some we dismissed because they had only come into contact with Paloma very fleetingly.' He paused. 'A woman also got in touch about her mother, Luz Pujals, who went missing three years back. Tolo and I worked on that case.'

Isabel took a sip of her coffee and eyed him keenly. 'Yes, Josep alluded to her without giving me a name, but Tolo mentioned the case to me when we met.'

'Luz was a pensioner who'd gone out on a mountain hike early one Friday morning in Mortitx, close to her home, and never returned. It's a treacherous, wild piece of land and the poor woman probably fell down a sink hole or hit her head and died. We had trackers and dogs but her body was never found. We did recover a sweatshirt, though, and a few random items.'

'Was she accustomed to hiking?'

'The daughter said that every Friday she would walk around the nearby hills as regular as clockwork.'

'Curious then that she should come to grief in an area no doubt very familiar to her.' Isabel frowned. 'Can I see her case notes and evidence bag?'

'Of course. If you pop by the precinct tomorrow afternoon, I'll be in the office. The good news is that we heard from three of Paloma's private clients – a butler from an estate near Bunyola, an elderly man in Palma and a cook who rang from another estate near Soller.'

'Where?'

'The woman said she worked for a sculptor named Nicolas Garcia. He's apparently some big shot with an estate near Escorca. Paloma was employed on a freelance basis but failed to show up a few weeks ago. Ironically, he's a close friend of our commissioner.'

Isabel's mouth fell open. 'But that's where I'm going later this morning. Garcia has lost his cat.'

Gaspar gave a guffaw. 'Are you winding me up, Bel?'

She raised her hands in the air. 'This is a weird coincidence. It reminds me of that play, *The Importance of Being Earnest* by the Irish playwright, Oscar Wilde.'

'How?'

'There's a character called Lady Bracknell and she says this brilliant line, "To lose one parent may be regarded as a misfortune, to lose both looks like carelessness." It sort of suits Garcia, doesn't it?'

Gaspar stared at her uncomprehendingly. 'Sorry, Bel, you've lost me. I didn't do much foreign literature at school.'

'He's lost both his cat and his florist, rather careless, no?'

Gaspar nodded slowly. 'I think I get it.'

She stood up and smiled brightly. 'No matter, Gaspar. I'm not sure where any of this leads us but happily in the distance, I see a small glimmer of light.'

EIGHT

As Llorenç pootled along the winding mountain road that carved a gentle, scenic path through the mountains, he belted out traditional Mallorcan *gloses*, cheerily tapping the steering wheel to the rhythm of each song. Occasionally he'd cast a furtive glance at Isabel as she sat in the passenger seat, her eyes trained determinedly on the hills beyond. The road had been built by the American forces during the fifties at the same time as they embarked on constructing a radar tower on the peak of Puig Major, the island's highest mountain in the Tramuntana range. For that reason, locals christened it 'The American Road' and the name had stuck. It unfurled as far as the military base and, although forbidden to all but forces personnel, continued up to the summit of Puig Major. The mountain road climbed onwards past the military base and the placid turquoise reservoirs of Cúber and Gorg Blau, towards Lluc monastery, ending its journey at the picturesque northern town of Pollença.

Isabel looked up as they passed the two reservoirs, dazzled by the sun that danced across the glittering water. She turned to Llorenç.

'Isn't the estate near here?'

He stopped mid-song. 'It's just coming up. Hopefully, we'll be offered a coffee, or better still, a *vino tinto*, when we get there.'

'I'll be on the *caipirinhas* later so no wine for me.'

He grimaced. 'I wouldn't touch one of those lethal Brazilian drinks. You're safer with wine, Bel. Be careful. You never know what else they might put in it!'

Isabel grinned, resolving one day soon to persuade her mayor to dice with death and try a *caipirinha* for himself, preferably with her new neighbour. Seconds later, Llorenç indicated left at a small wooden sign and headed up a curving, bumpy track that twisted into the hills beyond. Isabel grabbed the handle above her door as the car jolted violently. Given that Llorenç's vintage Renault had seen better days, she pondered whether it would manage the journey home. Isabel had visions of the mayor and she hitching a lift on the lonely road or calling a disgruntled Pep to come to the rescue, which he would not appreciate on a Sunday. She was shaken from her reverie when an elegant estate with sweeping drive framed by woodland came into view. Luxuriant flora ran along the road's verges and phalanxes of towering cypresses and nude plane trees rose up on either side halting at a pair of formidable wrought iron gates. Llorenç leant out of his window and confidently pressed the buzzer.

'I am Llorenç Bestard, Mayor of...'

There was a crackle and a pleasant female voice rang out in greeting before he could utter another word. Immediately, the gate started to peel back like a ripe banana, leaving Llorenç scrabbling to get into first gear.

'This is rather grand,' said Isabel. 'It reminds me of a scene from a Grimm fairy tale or one of the *Rondalles*.'

Llorenç gave a sniff. 'These people have more money than we can ever imagine, Bel. This man must surely be a multi-millionaire. He has very famous clients all over the world.'

She leant out of her window to breathe in the sweet mountain air. 'I have no idea about Nicolas Garcia's worth. All that matters is that he's a decent human being.'

As if he'd been listening, the estate's owner appeared in a wheelchair by the porch, wearing a broad grin. He was middle-aged yet youthful and slim, with a good head of dark hair and chiselled features. Casually dressed yet immaculately groomed in a butterscotch cashmere sweater, tartan scarf and jeans, he cut a dashing figure. Deftly, he propelled himself along the stone path and smiled graciously as his two guests exited the car. The mayor lent forward to shake his hand.

'*Señor* Garcia! It is indeed an honour to see you again. I believe the last time we met was at a piano recital at Lluc monastery.'

He nodded. 'It was a charity concert, raising funds for the education of young disabled artists in the Baleares.'

'A noble cause,' simpered the mayor.

Nicolas Garcia smiled genially at him. 'A basic right, I'd say.'

With a flourish, Llorenç waved Isabel forward. 'I forget myself. Please may I introduce Isabel Flores Montserrat, our very own specialist police detective in the valley.' Colouring slightly at Isabel's stern expression he added, 'Well, former detective, actually, but she is still working alongside the National Police in an advisory capacity.' He tapped his nose and grinned knowingly at his host. Isabel took a sharp intake of breath and stepped forward to shake the man's hand.

'You have a stunning estate, Mr Garcia. The views over the Tramuntanas and to the reservoirs are spectacular.'

'Thank you. Let me show you around the grounds, but first let's have some coffee or a glass of wine or *cava*, as you prefer. And please call me Nicolas. We are all friends here.' He turned to Llorenç with a wave of the hand.

'Do leave your key in the ignition. Your car will be perfectly safe.'

Llorenç nodded a tad warily. 'Yes, of course.'

With Isabel in tow, he followed Nicolas as he nimbly manoeuvred the wheelchair up a specially-adapted ramp and into a vast, high-ceilinged entrance hall. Coloured light, delicately distilled through a lofty row of exquisite stained-glass windows, fell on a life-sized bronze of a woman with a mane of hair astride a horse. Above, a massive skylight cut into the roof allowed sunlight to spill like golden oil onto the sea of ancient grey flagstones. Isabel marvelled at the effect.

'A combination of history and modern-day architectural engineering,' Nicolas Garcia opined as Llorenç and Isabel stood in awe.

'And the beautiful bronze?' questioned Isabel.

'That was my wife, Francesca. The love of my life. It was my homage to her.' He pressed a small button on his armrest and looked away. 'Now for coffee.'

Moments later, a brisk figure, wiping her hands on an apron, arrived at his side. 'This is my wonderful cook, Lourdes. She has been with me for more than five years now.'

The young woman patted his shoulder affectionately before inviting them into a large but cosy kitchen. A fire crackled contentedly in the grate while a white Labrador stretched out in front of the hearth, its eyes closed and breath laboured.

'That is my British dog, Harry. He was given to me two years ago by an English artist friend. Sadly I can't take him for long walks but my valet, Andel, adores him. He's a dog fanatic. At least indoors, Harry is my constant companion.'

'He's a beauty,' replied Isabel. 'I have a pet ferret named Furó. He is my constant companion.'

Nicolas Garcia broke into a smile. 'What a pity you didn't bring him. I too used to keep ferrets before the accident.' He lowered his head for a second and then resumed his poise. 'So, what can we offer you?'

Isabel suggested a *cortado* while Llorenç was easily persuaded by the cook to have a glass of robust *rioja*.

'So, Nicolas, tell us about your missing cat,' said Llorenç as he enthusiastically accepted his glass of wine from Lourdes. He was delighted that it was accompanied by brown bread and *sobrassada*. 'I'm afraid we have a growing number of pet disappearances in Sant Martí.'

'Is that so?' he replied gravely. 'Misha is one of my oldest and most beloved cats. She is a white Maine Coon and I've had her fourteen years. Despite her age, she is a great huntress and very playful.' His eyes filled with tears.

'I see,' replied Llorenç, shooting a panicked look in Isabel's direction. 'I don't think I've ever heard of this species.'

'It's the largest domestic cat breed and it's native to Maine, hence the name.'

'And where is that?' asked Llorenç.

'The States,' Isabel replied hastily. 'Please continue.'

The man sniffed loudly. 'About a week ago, a car turned up here late one evening, while I was asleep. Fortunately, Andel was still awake and thought he heard Misha's cry. He left his room, as he lives on the premises, but the car had already sped away.'

'Does the cat roam at night?' she asked.

'She's a real prowler but always comes in around midnight through there.' He stopped and pointed towards a built-in flap in the kitchen door. 'Last Friday she never returned and we haven't seen her since.'

The mayor nodded sympathetically. 'We need to act fast. Your estate may be some way from Soller but my hunch is that this is related. What's your view, Bel?'

Taking a long sip of coffee, Isabel set her cup on the oak table and faced them both. 'The truth is that I have no idea who might be abducting our animals or why. It's highly unlikely, given the number missing, that they all just left of their own accord. As for Misha, she may well have met a natural death or strayed into the road. With luck she may return.' She paused. 'On the other hand, she may well have been stolen but whether her disappearance is related to those in our village, who can say?'

'An odd coincidence though,' mused Llorenç.

Isabel took a bite of one of the homemade biscuits that sat on a plate before her. She chewed thoughtfully and then eyed them all. 'I have a feeling that those involved are closer to home than we might think. The motive has eluded us so far but it will become apparent soon.'

The mayor coloured. 'I do hope you're not suggesting that a citizen of Sant Martí is behind this?'

'That's precisely what I'm suggesting,' she answered coolly. 'How else would the abductor or abductors have such detailed knowledge about the pets in our village? And if Mr Garcia's cat has been stolen, it follows that the perpetrator is a local or has visited the estate before.'

Before Llorenç had a chance to speak, Isabel rose and addressed the cook as she stood polishing glasses at the sink.

'Lourdes, I believe you have information about Paloma Crespí, who once worked here?'

The woman seemed startled and setting down a glass, ran a hand through her short fair hair. She looked tenderly across at Nicolas. 'I'm afraid that we have another upset. Our dear Paloma has gone missing. I read about her disappearance in the newspaper and rang the police to say that she had once worked here.'

Nicolas turned pale. 'Why didn't you tell me about this, Lourdes?'

'As you've been so distraught about Misha, I didn't want to add to your troubles.'

Isabel stood by the kitchen door and looked out at a perfectly ordered vegetable garden. A light drizzle shed tiny water droplets on a cabbage's rubbery leaves that like giant green petals protectively embraced its hidden heart. Rows of fledgling kale, spinach and Brussels sprouts trembled as water trickled along their stems and coursed its way down to the roots. Isabel's thoughts trailed to her own orchard, where an abundance of vegetables were ripe for the picking. She wondered whether she would have time to do that after her neighbour's lunch party.

She blinked and turned to Nicolas. 'When did you last see Paloma and how long did she work here?'

He struggled to compose himself. 'Paloma started with us a year ago and used to visit here twice a week to arrange flowers. She came highly recommended by a butler contact at Los Abetos estate near Bunyola, and so when she failed to turn up for work three weeks ago, I called him. He told me that she had become fed up with the long train and bus journey over here so decided to quit when she picked up other work locally. I was sad that she didn't confide in us as we might have found a solution.'

Lourdes nodded. 'We did try calling her on the phone number she'd given us but it just kept going to voicemail. I was so shocked to read that on Monday she'd disappeared.'

Nicolas sighed heavily. 'In reality she was more than just a flower arranger. Paloma used to accompany the gardener and me around the grounds and we'd discuss seasonal plants and flowers. I was devastated when she left us.'

'Was she happy working here?' asked Isabel pointedly.

'I paid her well and my staff always arranged transport for her to the bus stop in Soller. She seemed to love coming here but lately she had become troubled and anxious. I'm not sure why.'

Lourdes shook her head. 'She was shy and appeared to be quite lonely. Recently she confided in me that she had a difficult father.'

The mayor swung his gaze from Isabel to Nicolas.

'Does this have anything to do with Misha's disappearance?' he demanded.

Isabel offered a tight smile. 'I can't think how, Llorenç, but it is indeed a coincidence that both the cat and Paloma are missing.'

Nicolas placed his hands in his lap and turned to Isabel and Llorenç. 'May I make a suggestion? I am willing to offer a substantial reward for information pertaining to Misha and the other missing animals. Furthermore, I would like to fund a group of village volunteers to patrol Sant Martí, where all this seems to have started. My personal view is that Misha was taken to order.'

The mayor beamed. 'How generous of you! I think that's a great plan.'

Isabel clicked her teeth. 'It's a very thoughtful gesture but we don't want vigilantes in our village and offering rewards can bring out the worst in people.'

'But, Bel,' Llorenç protested, 'I see this as a way to reassure our villagers and keep our remaining animals safe. We may well smoke out the fiend yet!'

Isabel fiddled with a tendril of hair, a fleeting smile crossing her face. 'On second thoughts, I think we should try it.'

Nicolas appeared relieved. 'Excellent. And now I must give you a tour of the gardens and my sculpture park. Please excuse me a few minutes while I fetch the gardener.'

As the door closed, Lourdes turned to face them. 'You know this is all very traumatic for Nicolas. He is the best boss you could wish for and cares for us all as if we were his family. In reality, we are his only family now.'

'Very laudable,' replied Llorenç.

Isabel lowered her voice. 'Can I ask about Señor Garcia's wife? I read in the press that she'd died in an equestrian accident.'

Lourdes pulled out a chair at the kitchen table and sat down heavily. Isabel noticed how strong and wiry her arms seemed and imagined that she worked out a lot.

'Francesca was Italian by birth and a talented horsewoman. Tragically, seventeen years ago, when she was only twenty-eight, she was killed in a freak horse-riding accident in Argentina. She had been competing in an equestrian competition. Nicolas was spectating and saw his wife fall from her horse. He has never really come to terms with it.'

'What a sad story. And I understand from press reports that he was subsequently badly injured in a car accident,' Isabel replied.

Lourdes nodded. 'That happened just two years after Francesca died, when Nicolas was only thirty-two years old and already a prominent sculptor. It was a head-on collision with a drunk driver, and his spine was badly damaged. He lost the use of his legs.'

'It's a good thing that he can still produce his sculptures,' replied Llorenç. 'It must have proved a lifeline.'

'Very true. It is his passion and all of us here on the estate are one big family.'

'How many of you are there?' asked Llorenç.

She counted on her fingers. 'Apart from me and my husband Ismael, who is the estate's handyman, there's Andel Picó, Nicolas's valet, Elena, the maid, Linda, our launderess, and Raul, the gardener. We all live on the estate but we have other helpers who work on a freelance basis, just like Paloma did.'

'Do you have many staff changes?'

The cook laughed. 'You must be joking! No one ever leaves. This is such a happy place to work and the conditions so good. We've had scores of applicants to replace Paloma but Nicolas believes she's irreplaceable. '

'Has he been hoping that she'd return?'

She nodded. 'I imagine so. He's very sentimental about the staff.'

The door opened and Nicolas appeared with a genial elderly gnome at his side. Isabel was amused to see that he was donned from head to foot in green attire, even down to his rubber boots and protective leather gloves.

'Let me guess,' she teased. 'You're the gardener?'

The elderly man gave her a wink. 'That's right. I'm Raul. I've been gardening here since Nicolas bought the estate.'

Isabel smiled and addressed Nicolas. 'When did you decide to move here?'

'Thirteen years ago. I had endured three years of rehabilitation following my car accident in Chile, so decided to escape to paradise. My parents used to holiday here when I was a child, so I knew this area well.'

The mayor looked at his watch. 'As time is marching on I wonder whether we might take you up on that tour of the grounds before we leave.'

'Of course,' smiled their host. 'And you must have a quick peek at my foundry too, if time permits. It enables me to produce all my bronzes on the spot without having to leave the estate.'

'A good idea before the rain returns,' warned Raul.

At the porch, after their brief tour, Llorenç's eyes searched frantically for his Renault. Isabel smiled to herself. All their talk of disappearances was making him twitchy; maybe the mayor wished he hadn't left the keys in the ignition, after all.

Nicolas offered him a cheery wink. 'Andel has most likely taken your car to be cleaned in the garage. He's very zealous.'

They approached a handsomely restored barn that had been converted into a six-car garage. Llorenç puffed out his lower lip admiringly. 'This is a work of art. You know, I love cars.'

A young man, wiping his hands on a piece of crumped cloth, rushed forward to greet them all, introducing himself as Andel.

Isabel noticed the friendly and firm grip. 'What a great name. Where are you from?'

He smiled. 'Believe it or not, I'm Czech-Mallorcan. A good combination, eh?'

Isabel turned to Llorenç with a mischievous smile. 'Isn't it great that we have such a cosmopolitan community up here in the hills?'

'Indeed,' huffed Llorenç. He gasped when Andel led him over to his vehicle, which had been buffed to within an inch of its life.

'Is this your handiwork?'

Andel nodded modestly. 'I cleaned inside too. I hope it will save you a job when you get home.'

Llorenç patted him on the back. 'You're a *campion*! I owe you.'

'Not at all,' the young man demurred.

As they set off towards the Elysian plains before them, Isabel contemplated Nicolas Garcia's generous proposal to guard the village and to offer a reward for information. Somehow it had an ominous ring about it and yet an idea had formed in her mind. Despite earlier reservations, she now believed that creating a vigilante group might prove to be the very best way to catch the culprit.

*

Once showered, Isabel changed into a dress, a rarity for her, and left Furó dozing in his basket. Grabbing a woolly cardigan, she locked the house and strode along her neighbour's path with a bag of oranges and lemons, a dozen fresh eggs and bunch of sunflowers. On finding the door wide open, she allowed herself inside the *entrada* and looked about her. The structure of the room resembled Isabel's own but the wide hallway appeared sombre and dark, and possessed just one small, barred window overlooking an untamed back garden. It was devoid of fruit trees and touted a wild smattering of long grasses, weeds and sprays of fennel. A few haggard cypresses wilted by the back wall and a small pond was suffocated by pampas grass and bulrushes. As she was almost an hour late, Isabel wasn't surprised to hear music, laughter and chatter emanating from the back of the house, where she presumed the kitchen was located. She followed the sound and discovered Juliana presiding over a throng of guests seated informally around a large oak table. She whooped when she saw Isabel.

'Come in, stranger! We've been waiting for you. How was your morning?'

Isabel smiled and nodded at the familiar faces before her and noted her mother's exasperated expression. Pushing the gifts into Juliana's hands, she gave her a peck on each cheek.

'So sorry to be running late but Llorenç and I had a puncture on the American Road. Luckily I managed to fix the tyre with help from a passing cyclist.'

Laughter rippled around the table as Pep, his face creased with mirth, asked, 'Surely Llorenç can change a tyre?'

Catching sight of the mayor's buxom daughter at his side, she diplomatically replied, 'He was wearing his Sunday best so preferred not to ruin it with grease. Besides, I like changing tyres.'

'What a cop out!' Pep shrieked gleefully while his girlfriend, Angélica, gave him a sharp dig in the ribs.

Isabel hastily took a vacant seat next to Doctor Ramis and gratefully accepted a potent *Caipirinha* from her host. The members of Juliana's family sitting around the table, including an elderly uncle visiting from Palma, politely introduced themselves to Isabel. She looked in wonder at Juliana's twin teenage sons, Bruno and Victor, when they stood up to pass around wine. Both were more than six feet tall and towered over their swarthy father, Luca, whose weathered and lined face reminded Isabel of local fishermen who spent their days on the high seas and under the harsh rays of the sun. As Isabel tucked into a colourful plate of *tapas* and Brazilian specialities, Doctor Ramis, sitting by her side, gave her a nudge. 'Your mother brought along an orange, pomegranate and fennel salad, and an apple tart, which I cannot wait to try.'

Isabel laughed; Doctor Ramis loved food, possibly even more than she did.

'And how was your visit with the famed sculptor this morning?' he asked quietly.

'My mother told you, of course,' she said resignedly. 'Nothing is ever sacrosanct.'

'Florentina mentioned it fleetingly yesterday on our way to Pilates.'

Isabel nearly choked on an olive. 'Say that again?'

He offered her a cheeky wink. 'Ah, you didn't know? Your mother persuaded me to join the new Sant Martí silver sports club. You have to be over fifty, I'm afraid, so you can't join in.'

'Who's started it?'

'Our very own Juliana! She trained as a Pilates instructor in Brazil and held her first class here yesterday afternoon. As she builds up members she hopes to rent the recreation hall at the *ajuntament* once a week.'

Isabel supressed a smile. 'I'm sure Llorenç will be very supportive.'

They both laughed knowingly. Doctor Ramis tapped her hand. 'Tell me about Nicolas Garcia.'

'He's charming and the sculpture park is stunning. There are more than fifty bronzes in the grounds, some abstract, others full-scale models. The one of his wife astride a horse, situated in the *entrada*, was particularly poignant.'

Doctor Ramis shook his head. 'Yes, that was a terrible tragedy. It's incredible that Nicolas Garcia managed to keep going, especially after the car accident.'

'Do you know much about him?'

'Not really, but I'm a great admirer of his work.'

They were interrupted by Juliana, who, in high spirits, was gyrating around the kitchen to Brazilian music with a jug of *Caipirinha* in her hand, and urging her guests to help themselves to a selection of desserts.

Doctor Ramis eyed the many dishes being placed on the table before him and gave a mock swoon. 'Dear Juliana, I do believe I've just died and gone to heaven!'

She smiled across at him. 'But you can't do that just yet. I'm expecting to see your dance moves later.'

There was applause and whooping as the doctor blushed pink. Isabel smiled across at her animated mother and the assembled villagers. One thing was certain; the Sant Martí community and her new Brazilian neighbours certainly knew how to have a good time.

NINE

Back from her early morning swim with Furó at Can Repic beach, Isabel picked her way carefully through the trees of plump lemons and ripening oranges in her orchard. A gentle mist had covered the Tramuntanas like a veil of gossamer and the air was fresh and pungent. Unlike many of her neighbours and friends, she welcomed Monday mornings, when a delicious new week full of adventure and promise stretched out before her. Isabel always believed in having one or two small treats to look forward to every day and already she was contemplating the fresh warm eggs in her pockets that Mrs Buncle, her favourite red hen, had kindly left for her in the laying box. At the beginning of the week, Florentina always made iced *gató*, the local almond cake, and popped it in a tin in her larder. Surely, reason enough to want to face a new day?

The birdsong was so intense that Isabel closed her eyes momentarily, happy to have the garden choir all to herself while her busy hens and cockerel pecked at her feet. She had gathered an aromatic selection of wild flowers and herbs and was singing to herself as she inspected the rotund and dewy lemons on her trees. The sound of a cracking twig followed by coughing and muttering cut short her reverie. Close by, to her surprise, she discovered her uncle Idò on hands and knees clearing the weeds that had recently invaded her vegetable patch. By his side stood a hefty wicker trug teeming with leeks, cabbages, turnips, carrots and potatoes. He sat back on his heels and squinted up at her, mopping his brow with a soil-encrusted hand.

'What time do you call this? I've been toiling like a slave out here for hours!' he teased.

She tapped his head affectionately. 'Well, what a nice surprise. I've been meaning to do this for the last few weeks. Just been flat out with this investigation lately.'

Idò creakily rose to his feet, placing his hands on his lumbar region and emitting a low groan. 'Thought you might need a hand. Mind you, my back's been playing me up this winter. It's the humidity.'

'And possibly age?' she grinned.

'Nonsense! I've got the muscles of Atlas.' He flexed his right arm and winked. 'Anyway, I've planted the broad beans. It'll save you a job.'

She kissed his cheek. 'Well, for that noble deed, I think you deserve a coffee and croissant.'

'I'll say, and maybe you can tell me about this investigation. I knew you'd never be able to give up police work.' Idò picked up the trug and followed her back into the house, pausing at the back door to remove his muddy boots. Isabel went into the voluminous larder and placed the eggs in a terracotta dish while Idò huffed and puffed on the back porch.

He emitted a hearty yawn. 'And where's that young upstart? Probably still in his bed.'

'If you're referring to me, Idò, I'm here making coffee,' Pep replied from the kitchen. 'You'd better be nice or I'll give yours to Furó.'

Idò gave a rascally guffaw and, striding into the room, thumped Pep good-naturedly on the shoulder. 'At the office by eight-thirty. Now that shows dedication.'

'It certainly does when I'm nursing a hangover.'

At the sink, Isabel filled a vase with water for her flowers and laughed. 'I warned you not to stay late at Juliana's place. That's why I left after my third *caipirinha*!'

'Dancing on the tables, were you?' goaded Idò.

Pep passed him a steaming *café con leche*. 'Actually, we had a guitar jamming session at midnight but I left by two o'clock.'

'Ah, that's what woke me up,' cried Isabel.

'Did it?' asked Pep anxiously.

'Only teasing. I went out like a light and didn't hear a thing all night.' She rummaged in her pannier. Having retrieved a paper bag full of freshly made croissants bought earlier from Bon Día, she placed them on a plate and said, 'Come on, let's take our coffees upstairs. It's warmer in the office.'

As they made their way to the next floor, the front door opened.

'*Cooeeee*! It's only me,' called Florentina. 'I've just had an early walk with Juliana. Can I join you for coffee?'

'Just grab yourself one in the kitchen, Mama,' Isabel yelled from the top of the staircase. 'And don't forget to leave the *gató* in the larder!'

Moments later they sat around the communal office, enjoying their impromptu breakfast and discussing the disappearance of Paloma and the latest news of the animal thefts. Isabel dusted her lips after demolishing her croissant and stood up, a few crumbs falling onto the wooden floor.

Florentina reprimanded her. 'Look at that! You'll have mice up here.'

'Furó would like that,' winked Pep.

Isabel ignored the banter and approached her whiteboard. 'I was stopped by Teo Darder this morning. Apparently one of his three spaniels has gone missing.

Idò scowled. 'The constructor? He once double-crossed me at cards in Jordi's. Serves him right.'

'Oh really!' exclaimed Florentina. 'Where's your heart? The poor man loves his dogs. Besides, you've diddled him enough times at cards. This pet stealing has got to stop, Bel.'

Pep sat up in his chair. 'How many pets have supposedly gone missing?'

'Quite a few now,' Isabel sighed as she added Teo Darder's name to a list on the board. 'Six dogs, the cat belonging to Nicolas Garcia, the sculptor – Señora Coll's cockerel and Dolores's parrot.'

Idó scrutinised the list that Isabel had written in black marker pen. 'Old Magdalena Sala has lost her poodle too?'

'I'm afraid so,' said Isabel thoughtfully.

'All the same, she's a right old busybody and that dog never shuts up!' Idò replied. 'The thief's done us all a favour.'

'Really, Idò!' scolded Florentina.

Pep read the list out loud. 'So there's also Pau's Alsatian, Gabriel Reus's black pug, Alberto Bonet's boxer and the terrier belonging to Xavi Mir.'

Idó offered him a quizzical stare. 'Who's he?'

'The lawyer with the big *finca* on the road to Morells. He's got a black Vogue Range Rover.'

'Trust you to know the exact model,' laughed Idò.

Isabel tapped a pen against her lip. 'The key to the mystery is that there have been no remains found or sightings, despite Pau putting out an alert to his police and Guardia colleagues across the valley.'

'Angélica tells me that Llorenç is going to form a vigilante team to patrol the streets,' added Pep.

Isabel nodded. 'Indeed. It was Nicolas Garcia's suggestion and he's willing to assist with any costs as well as offering a reward for information.'

'That bloke must be made of money!' scoffed Idò.

'That's as may be, but it's very kind of him,' replied Florentina.

Isabel faced them all. 'The only possibility I see is that they have all been lured away by a modern-day Pied Piper to some kind of safe house.'

'Bel's finally lost the plot,' Pep goaded.

The others giggled.

'Hear me out,' she said, holding up a placatory hand. 'Why else would the animals have not been sighted since? They also appear to have gone willingly. No one heard a thing. Perhaps they were drugged or the perpetrator was familiar to them already. I believe someone has been targeting specific pets.'

'But it seems totally random,' insisted Idò. 'Who'd want to steal a cockerel or a moggy? We've hundreds roaming the valley.'

'True, it's a disparate group but there has to be a common denominator. What is the motivation behind it?' she replied.

'So, let me get this straight,' said Idò. 'You think some nutter is deliberately stealing certain villagers' pets, even though none of the owners are connected?'

'How do you know that, Idò? I think whoever took the animals is more interested in their owners,' Isabel said.

'In what way?' asked her mother. 'What on earth do a plumber, policeman and postmistress have in common?'

'I know!' replied Pep, straight-faced. 'They all begin with P.'

Florentina nudged him good-naturedly. 'Good one, Pep!'

Isabel nibbled a nail. 'Listen. We need to know about the victims' movements and activities over the last few months and if they share the same contacts. Pep, can you call round everyone who's missing a pet and arrange for me to pop by tonight?'

He nodded. 'Bookings are a bit thin at the moment so that'll keep me busy. Shall I slot them in from mid-afternoon?'

She shook her head. 'I'll be at the Palma precinct around that time discussing the Paloma case, so make it seven o'clock onwards.'

'The poor girl,' sighed Florentina. 'A week's gone by. Do you think you'll still find her?'

Isabel shook her head. 'It's not very hopeful, but we must pull out all the stops. Best case scenario is that she's being held somewhere against her will.' She paused. 'Pep, can you arrange about twenty minutes for me with each victim? I won't need to see Nicolas Garcia, whom I've already spoken with. Just text me the details.'

'That means you won't get home till late,' fretted Florentina. 'I'll leave you dinner in the kitchen.'

'There's no need,' Isabel replied, but seeing the obstinate expression on her mother's face, smiled and thanked her instead.

She drained her coffee cup. 'What time is it, Pep? 9.20 a.m.?'

He laughed. 'How do you do that? '

'What?'

'Know the time without a watch?'

She shrugged. 'I like to call it instinct. Now I need to head off to the bakery in Morells. I'm going to order a massive *ensaïmada* with *crema* for Marga's birthday party on Friday night. I can hardly believe she'll be thirty-four.'

'To think you were at kindergarten together and are still best friends,' smiled Florentina. 'It's lovely that her little Sofia is your goddaughter. One day Marga will hopefully be godmother to one of your children too.'

'Not that old chestnut again,' complained Isabel. 'She may have to wait some time.'

Pep smothered a grin and gave her the thumbs up. 'Keep your freedom, Bel. Look at Angélica and me. I'm already a slave and we're not even engaged yet.'

Isabel laughed and strode into her office. Grabbing the keys to Pequeñito, she thrust a handful of Chupa Chup lollies and a bag of sunflower seeds into her pannier and returned to the communal office.

She turned to Pep. 'Can you make sure those cyclists have left Can Marc in Fornalutx in a good state? The cleaning team did an interim tidy round last week and told me the group was very rowdy and messy.'

He grinned. 'That's the Brits for you. They like their beer, but it's all under control. The lads are leaving late morning and I'm popping by to check they've left the property in order.'

'What about the couple at Can Oliver in Biniaraix?'

Pep groaned. 'They complained about the number of crowing cockerels early morning. I politely told them to consider an urban dwelling next time.'

Isabel shook her head. 'Remember the woman who asked us to remove all the geckos from the garden?'

Pep laughed. 'She was a real nut.'

'I remember her,' huffed Idò. 'You wonder why such fussy folk don't just stay at home!'

Isabel grinned. 'I'm off! Pep, please make sure Furó is locked in my office before you leave. I don't want our prowler to have designs on him.'

Her mother and Idò gave her a hug, but Pep interrupted their goodbyes. 'When will you be back after doing the interviews tonight?'

Isabel paused at the door and winked. 'Don't hold your breath. I've a feeling it's going to be a long and eventful evening.'

*

As Isabel made her way to the bakery in Morells, she found the tranquil *plaça* devoid of life. Although a fretful breeze teased the crisp, brown leaves in the gutters, a radiant sun glimmered through a scrum of clouds, dusting the plane trees along the square with golden light. The bell tinkled as Isabel stepped into the shop and immediately Juana Ripoll came scuttling out from behind a curtain, wiping her hands on her apron.

'Ah, dear Bel! What a lovely surprise. What brings you here?'

Isabel stepped forward to kiss her on both cheeks and proceeded to place her order.

'This is an *ensaïmada* with *crema* for thirty guests?' quizzed Juana. 'Marga will love that. She has to be my number one client, aside from your mother, of course.'

Isabel smiled. 'Your reputation precedes you. And how is Aina?'

Juana cocked her head and took on a confidential tone. 'I'm relieved to say that after getting rid of that no-good boyfriend, Felip, she's been studying hard at her archaeology course.'

Juana's daughter, Aina, had been a gifted student at the local university until she'd got caught up in her boyfriend's attempt at a murky drug deal the previous summer. When his plan backfired she was lucky not to have been implicated and had gone on instead to win a bursary to study at Barcelona University.

'I'd love to see her when she's back home,' replied Isabel.

'Well, you're in luck. She's here for three days, doing an archaeological field study in Deia . Her professor isn't collecting her until lunchtime today so you'll find her down by the *torrente*, reading.'

'In that case, I shall go and surprise her,' she said.

Isabel set off towards the river and smiled to see Aina stretched out on a bench, her head propped up on a rucksack, immersed in a book. She crept up from behind and shouted, '¡*Bu*!'

The girl gave a start but grinned widely when she saw Isabel and scrabbled to her feet.

'Are you trying to scare me to death!' she said, offering Isabel a hug.

'What's this earnest-looking tome you're reading?' Isabel whisked up the book and read the title out loud before flipping to the chapter that Aina had been reading. '*The Oxford Handbook of the Archaeology of Death and Burial*. Well, that sounds cheery.'

'I've just got to the bit about cremations in culture and cosmology. It's thrilling stuff.'

So, what have you learnt so far?'

Aina gave a snort of laughter. 'A lot, actually! It's all about the European Bronze Age and Iron Age death rituals. For example, the deceased would be cremated and with the metals they heated in the same furnace, they created shields and swords. They believed that death was therefore transformed into new life.'

'A bit sinister,' joked Isabel.

'By modern-day standards it was, I suppose. I've got to give a presentation about it all when I return to Barcelona. I'm getting nervous.'

'Nonsense! It'll be a huge success. And how is life now?'

The girl beamed. 'I'm loving my course and life in Barcelona. I've also got a new boyfriend. He's doing a PhD in palaeontology, so we have a lot in common.'

'Boffins together. Well, I'm so happy to hear all is well but now, sadly, I must head off to Es Pla.'

'What for?'

'I'm helping with another police case, which you've no doubt read about. It's the young florist who's gone missing.'

'It's so shocking, and she's only a few years older than me. I hope you'll find her.'

Isabel kissed Aina goodbye and headed back to Pequeñito along the edge of the river. As she reached the car, her mobile buzzed. It was Gaspar.

'Bel, I thought you'd like to know that Carlotta Pilar's alibi didn't check out. We got hold of Cati Marcer this morning. She's been away in Madrid for two weeks and has only just returned. Obviously she couldn't have met Carlotta Pilar last Monday night. You said you'd be seeing her today?'

'You bet! So where was she, I wonder? Perhaps with Paloma's charming father.'

Gaspar clicked his teeth. 'She'd better have a good answer. Anyway, see you later at the precinct. You'll bring her in?'

'Naturally,' she replied. 'Save you sending an officer.'

'By the way,' he said, 'I've located the archive containing the Luz Pujals file. The storage facility promises to have it delivered with the evidence box by the time you get here. The curator will need to be present while you examine it. They have strict protocols about inventory control. '

'Of course,' she breezed.

Isabel ended the call and, sinking into the driving seat, tapped the wheel. 'Come on, Pequeñito, let's pay a visit to Señora Pilar. She's certainly going to have some explaining to do.'

*

By the time Isabel had reached Sant Joan it was past noon and her stomach was rumbling. Should she visit Carlotta Pilar on an empty stomach or seek sustenance first? Her mind was quickly made up when she walked past a café where she spied *empanadas* in the window. Five minutes later she was sitting on the sunny front terrace with a delicious *cortado* and the crown-shaped little savoury pastry. Normally a hallmark of Easter baking, this hearty local delicacy filled with peas and lamb was, as her mother always insisted, good to eat at any time of the year.

Duly satiated, Isabel headed for the studio on Carrer de Sol. She had called Carlotta Pilar in advance to check that she would be on the premises and had received a cool response. With a look of undisguised disdain, the salsa teacher reluctantly opened the door and ushered her inside. She marched into the empty room and turned to face Isabel. 'I'm not sure why you need to see me again. I've told you everything I know.'

'Can we sit down, perhaps. This will take a little time,' she replied.

Carlotta Pilar moodily indicated a sofa in an ante room and sat defensively at one end while offering Isabel the other. She fixed the woman with an icy stare.

'I'm afraid that Cati Marcer, your alibi for the night of Paloma's disappearance, didn't check out, and we have reason to believe that instead you were in the company of Jago Morey. Naturally this has very serious implications.'

The woman put a hand to her throat. 'Cati ratted on me? A great friend she is!'

'Actually, she only got back from Madrid last night and had been away for two weeks so even if she'd been willing to lie for you, it wouldn't have stacked up.'

The woman uttered a frustrated growl. 'I left her a voice message on the house telephone asking her to be my alibi but she obviously never got around to listening to it.'

'It was silly of you to think we wouldn't have checked her own whereabouts the last week or so. Anyway, tell me about your relationship with Jago Morey and the drug running. Naturally his testimony has shone the spotlight on you.'

Carlotta Pilar looked aghast. 'Was he interviewed this morning? He told you about the drugs?'

''I'm not at liberty to discuss the matter, but should you lie again, you may well be implicated in the likely abduction of Paloma.'

'So he's sold me out too? Well, let me tell you about him, the two-faced pig.'

Isabel nodded encouragingly. 'Please do. We have plenty of time.'

The woman gave a long sigh. ' Last Monday night Jago picked me up at the local bus stop after the class and drove me to his flat in Manacor.'

'You don't drive?'

'No. I've never got around to learning.'

'So what were you doing over there?'

'Jago and I do some business together. I don't earn much as a dance teacher so the money comes in handy.'

'I did wonder how you afforded this place. Drug pushing is a lucrative business.'

'I work hard. A little illegal drug selling on the side helps me make ends meet. Jago gets the stuff and I help distribute it locally.'

'What do you sell?'

She shrugged. 'Marijuana, MDMA, GHB, ketamine and meth – nothing heavy.'

'A matter of opinion. Where does he source it?'

'No idea. He knows a lot of cons from inside.'

'How long have you been lovers?'

The woman balked. 'He told you that too?'

Isabel didn't speak.

The woman resumed. 'Okay, we were once, not anymore. I called it off six months ago when I caught the imbecile with someone else.'

'Tell me how Jago found a way to contact Paloma.'

She groaned. 'You know about that?'

Isabel nodded. She knew that strictly speaking she shouldn't be spinning Carlotta Pilar so many fibs, but if it got fast results she was willing to take any fallout later.

'About a year ago, he did some sniffing around and approached Paloma on her way home from work. He'd heard she had debts and promised her a way out. She's always been frightened of him so she did as he asked.'

'Which was?'

'She supplied local kids with his drugs in Manacor and Sineu.'

'How?'

'Through some of her old school connections. Not that prissy cow, Laura, though. She was always trying to reform Paloma. Little did she know what was going on.'

Isabel ploughed on. 'In fact, Jago introduced you to Paloma and that's why she attended your salsa classes.'

'True. It was a good way for us to liaise without raising suspicion. But lately, Paloma stopped playing ball. She faced up to Jago and told him she wanted out. That was a month ago.'

'How did Jago take it?'

'He was livid but he couldn't change her mind. She said she was going straight and would build her own floristry business. The girl is so naïve.'

Isabel laughed. 'You were the naïve one, foolishly putting your trust in a convicted criminal.'

'I needed the money,' she replied sullenly.

'And you all met on a designated date once a month in Manacor to pick up the next assignment and to get paid?'

Carlotta Pilar cursed. 'Jago told you all this?'

'Regardless of what Jago might have told us, Paloma itemised all your assignations in her diary.'

'You've got to be kidding?'

'I'm not in a joking mood,' replied Isabel. 'Last Monday night, did you and Jago tail Paloma and force her into your car? Are you both holding her against her will?'

The woman stood up. 'Are you mad? Neither of us has touched Paloma. Jago's still angry with her but he wouldn't harm her. He assumed she'd done a runner.'

Isabel rose to her feet. 'I need you to accompany me to the Palma precinct to give a statement.'

'What, now?' Carlotta Pilar screeched.

'Indeed. You are the very last person to have seen Paloma alive and therefore are a prime suspect. Furthermore, you and Jago have a motivation for abducting Paloma. She let you both down and may owe you money. Perhaps you wanted to punish or frighten her? Or was it to keep her quiet because she simply knew too much about your operation?'

The woman stared at Isabel in disbelief. 'No! You've got it completely wrong. I don't know what's happened to her, I swear to God.'

Isabel retraced her steps to the front door with Carlotta trailing behind.

'I need to be back here for my class tonight.'

Isabel shook her head. 'I'm afraid, Señora Pilar, that will not be possible. You won't be back here for some time.'

'I need to call my lawyer,' she barked.

'There'll be plenty of time for that at the precinct.' Isabel opened the door and offered a tight smile. 'After you.'

TEN

Isabel sat in an armchair in Tolo's office munching on a packet of sunflower seeds and looked up when Gaspar walked in. He gave her a grin as he closed the door and propped himself up against his boss's desk.

'Well that was an easy interview. You did a good job getting Pilar to spill the beans but I'm not entirely sure it was ethical.'

'Oh?'

'Well, for one thing she seemed to think Jago Morey had already shopped her in an interview when he's not even been officially questioned yet.'

The telephone rang; they both started. After a curt exchange with the caller, Gaspar hung up.

'What do you know? Our boys have just dropped off Jago Morey here for questioning. Surprisingly, before they picked him up, he invited them to search his premises and the flat upstairs, but so far they've found nothing.'

'That figures. He'd hardly leave a drug trail in his own backyard.'

'And another thing. He's lodged a complaint about you. He says you deliberately vandalised his *moto*.'

'Just an unfortunate little accident when I reversed the car,' she replied, holding Gaspar's gaze.

'Really? Well perhaps you can try to be a little more careful in future,' he smirked. 'And that goes for fibbing to suspects too.'

'Just saving time,' she winked.

He looked at his watch. 'Are you happy for me to conduct the interview with Morey?'

'Be my guest. I'd rather study the file and evidence bag of Luz Pujals when it arrives.'

'What are you hoping to find?' he asked.

'I'm honestly not sure, but I have a feeling there's a connection with Paloma's abduction.'

Gaspar frowned. 'I don't see it. An elderly widow gets lost on a hike three years ago and now a florist vanishes. What's the common ground?'

'We can't assume she got lost. She may well have been abducted.'

'But what was the motivation? She was just a retired woman. At the time, her daughter claimed she led a happy, peaceful existence and was well liked locally.'

'I don't know,' sighed Isabel. 'Sometimes I just get a mental itch. There's much more to this case than meets the eye.'

Gaspar rapped the desk. 'Too right. By the way, we've checked out both Paloma's other clients in Bunyola and Palma. They seemed to know precious little about her and both had alibis the night she disappeared. The old chap in Palma is ninety and uses a Zimmer frame. At least you got better intel from the guys on the Ses Fonts estate.'

'Hardly. All I learnt was that she was good with plants and had seemed preoccupied before she left. Any news on the bug found in Pere Brotat's car?'

'Predictably, forensics couldn't glean much from it aside from it being a highly sophisticated device. We're evidently dealing with an intelligent player.'

'In that case, it's unlikely that either Carlotta Pilar or Jago Morey placed it there,' she said dryly.

'You've got a point.'

Isabel stood up and paced the room. 'Have you asked the officers to check all the vehicles in Morey's garage too? Carlotta Pilar hasn't got a driving licence and that checks out, but we need to find the vehicle that was on Paloma's track last Monday night.'

'We'll know more later. Meanwhile, where do you think Paloma is, providing she's still alive? Do you think Morey and Pilar could be holding her somewhere? Did they think she'd blow their operation, if she walked away?'

Isabel shook her head. 'I don't think they have anything to do with her disappearance. They're petty drug dealers and just a side show. Paloma wouldn't have posed a risk. She'd have implicated herself if she'd opened her mouth.' She paused. 'It's obvious that whoever was on the track that night planted the Vidcam in Pere's car and heard his conversation with Paloma. The perpetrator then lay in wait and abducted Paloma before she could reach her uncle's house.'

'So who is it? A jilted lover, random stalker or maybe one of her dodgy druggie clients?'

'Her friend, Laura, mentioned that Paloma had complained about a creepy guy. I think he could be our lead. I told Tolo about him.'

'And how do we find him?'

'Through good policing and deduction,' she replied with a hint of a smile.

The door opened and Corc, Tolo Cabot's highly-strung assistant, burst in.

'Sorry to disturb you both, but the evidence custodian has arrived with the file on Luz Pujals. Shall I let her in?'

Isabel smiled. 'Yes, of course. I've been waiting for her. Corc, could you kindly offer her a coffee and fetch me a *cortado* too?'

He nodded. 'Ah, how nice it is to have a task! I miss the boss when he's not here. It makes me very stressed.'

'It makes me stressed when he is here,' joked Gaspar. 'He's just swanning about in Madrid having fun while we're slaving away.'

'Not at all,' replied Corc. 'Tolo Cabot is undertaking critical police training.'

Isabel patted his quivering arm. 'It's okay, Corc. Ignore Gaspar, he was just teasing.'

In some confusion, Corc scuttled out of the office and was soon engulfed in a long, dark corridor.

Gaspar shook his head. 'That guy's the limit. No wonder Tolo's close to strangling him half the time. Mind you, he's devoted to the boss. You've got to credit him for that!'

As he slung on his jacket and headed off to interview Jago Morey, Isabel welcomed the prim evidence custodian who entered the office with a large box, sealed plastic bag and file. She set them down on Tolo's desk.

'I'll just sit on the sofa quietly and let you work through them,' she said. 'Take your time.'

Isabel nodded. 'Thank you. Hopefully, our coffees will be here soon and if we're lucky, Corc might even bring us a biscuit, too.'

*

Isabel rubbed her eyes. Two hours had quickly swept by, in which time she had scrutinised the cold case file of Luz Pujals and made copious notes. She now moved on to the tamper-proof bag and box of her possessions. The evidence custodian glanced across at her.

'The bag contains a few items found at Mortitx and the box some smaller bits and bobs discovered near the scene.'

Isabel held up the clear bag and wrote down the visible contents that included a blue sweatshirt, collapsible walking stick and guide to island wildlife. She wondered why these possessions would have been left sitting by a rock if the woman had been walking. If she'd fallen down a sink hole or tripped and knocked her head in undergrowth, surely they'd have been with her? If she'd removed them from her rucksack, she'd hardly have strayed far – and in that case, why was her body never recovered close to the scene? After all, in the file it was stressed that there had been an exhaustive search. Carefully she lifted the cover of the evidence box and froze in her tracks. There were smaller bags inside containing a woolly hat and compass, but only one bag beckoned to her. It contained a little wooden heart, an exact replica of the one she had found on Paloma's track.

*

It was late in the evening by the time Isabel had finished conducting her interviews with the villagers in Sant Martí. Despite valiant efforts to concentrate on the task in hand, she had found her mind constantly wandering back to the discovery of the heart in the evidence box of Luz Pujals. Her worst fears appeared to be confirmed. She was convinced that both Luz and Paloma had fallen victim to the same abductor – or possibly a copyist – who had left the same puzzling calling card. And yet three years had elapsed since the disappearance of Luz, so why had the perpetrator struck again now? Where was the motive and what possibly linked the two women, if anything did at all? Isabel had seen the look of horror on Gaspar's face before she left the precinct and she was already dreading updating Tolo. She had left an urgent message and would speak with him on her return to the house. She felt some relief to know that he was due to return to the island the following day and would be popping by for supper. No doubt the Ministry of Interior would be in uproar at the latest developments. The last thing the national or Balearic regional government needed was unwelcome publicity about the golden isle, which so relied on tourism.

Although she didn't want to articulate her worst fears, Isabel acknowledged that a potential serial killer might be on the loose, one who could have already committed a historic crime and who might strike again. She wandered through the dark and empty *plaça*, her thoughts now returning to the animal thefts that had left her community nervous and wary. All of those she had interviewed believed that their beloved pets had been snatched and drugged by a stranger, but Isabel wasn't so sure. How, she pondered, had the animal thief known the exact whereabouts of the animals and when to make off with them? Whoever it was would have needed detailed information about the owners' timetables and habits.

Hungry and shivering in the chilly wind, Isabel fastened up her jacket and headed towards the cut-through by the church. She had just turned right into Calle Pastor when a blood-curdling scream stopped her in her tracks. She turned around and some way off, saw Señora Coll standing under a dim streetlight with a look of abject misery on her face. Isabel ran towards her, her breath laboured as her pannier swung heavily back and forth from her shoulder, nearly tipping her off balance. She had no idea what had taken place but her immediate thought was to comfort the elderly matron. But as Isabel leant forward to clasp her in a hug, the woman struggled free and pointed with a shaky finger at a small bundle close to her feet. Isabel looked down, her eyes adjusting to the gloom, and gasped in dismay when she saw the bloodied corpse of the postmistress's beloved cockerel, Carlos.

ELEVEN

A group of regulars had gathered in Café Jordi, some crammed around the bar while others squeezed into seats at wooden tables. Most were dishevelled in old overalls or scruffy working attire, as befitted local tradesmen. In customary fashion, Jordi held court at the counter, handing out coffees and cognacs and draught beers while yelling at the top of his voice at a television screen showing a replay of a football match held the previous evening.

'Cretins! What were they doing? That's the last time I'm visiting Sevilla!'

Chico, the young assistant of Bernat, the mechanic, shook his head sadly. 'I can't watch that match again. Turn it off. Broke my heart last night. Mallorca should have won. Sevilla got lucky.'

Jordi banged a fist on the counter. 'Of course we should have won! It was that referee. The whole thing was a shambles.'

A general clamour ensued as ripe expletives were exchanged between the various customers and hands were waved in the air. When Jordi passed around fat *bocadillos* of *chorizo*, *jamon serrano* and *sobrassada* sausage, all smeared generously with olive oil, garlic and a paste made from *ramallet* tomatoes, the men fell on them with gusto. It was only nine o'clock in the morning, but for most of those present, this was *merienda* hour, when a hearty snack and drink were enjoyed following a few hours of early morning labour. Watching this spectacle from the doorway, Isabel and Llorenç exchanged grins. The mayor chuckled.

'Honestly, Bel, if some poor tourist pitched up here for a drink, they'd think there was a fight going on inside and quickly turn tail.'

She nodded. 'We Spaniards know how to make a din, that's for certain.'

'Mallorcans!' Llorenç corrected.

She folded her arms and eyeballed him. 'Well, remember that I'm half mainlander, so don't play that card with me. I'm proud to be a hybrid.'

He demurred. 'Of course, your father Juan was a very good man and an outstanding police superintendent, even if he was from Castilla-La Mancha!'

He threw open the door before Isabel could take him further to task. The room fell momentarily silent as everyone gawped at the newcomers. Isabel nodded and smiled at the men, all citizens of Sant Martí whom she knew well. Jordi clapped his hands together. 'We can begin the meeting now. Bel, want a *cortado* and *ensaïmada*? The usual, Llorenç?'

Isabel gave him the thumbs up while the mayor waved an impatient hand in Jordi's direction. He puffed out his chest like a proud robin and faced them all.

'As you will all be aware, a pestilence has come to Sant Martí in the form of an animal thief.'

A loud murmur swept like a wave across the room as Llorenç solemnly observed them all.

'Today we share the grief of our very own Señora Coll, whose beloved cockerel, Carlos, had his life cruelly cut short last night. Some heartless individual has chosen to play a vicious game of cat and mouse here in our village, but we will not be cowed.'

There were a few initial sniggers and wry expressions visible but as Señora Coll was a village treasure, all felt a degree of indignation on her behalf and bowed their heads.

During the lull, Isabel gratefully accepted her coffee and pastry from Jordi and took a seat next to Pau. Llorenç displayed the ghost of a frown when voices became too boisterous again but Jordi roared for attention and the room fell still. The mayor continued. 'Today we will create our own taskforce to tackle the problem head on. Very generously, the famed sculptor, Nicolas Garcia, whose own cat has gone missing, has offered to meet any costs and will fund a reward to the tune of one thousand euros for information leading to the arrest of the felon.'

There was a frisson of surprise across the room.

'Now, my idea is to have villagers patrolling the streets during the hours of *siesta* when things are quiet and from early evening until eleven at night. I would like eight volunteers to form four shifts.'

A few men raised their hands in the air, but Llorenç subdued them.

'I will set up at one of the tables and if you would like to come forward, please do so. For those working a shift, I will offer lunch or dinner at Jordi's each day. Now, are there any questions?'

Many hands shot up in the air.

'Are all the animals going to be killed like Carlos?' Alfonso, the village artist, asked tremulously. 'It's just that I couldn't survive without Bianca, my Persian. She's my world.'

There were a few guffaws but Llorenç appeared stern. 'A good question. Let us hope not, but the signs aren't good. Perhaps the cockerel is the first teasing step. The culprit must be a sadist to hurt an old lady's pet. Poor Señora Coll is very distressed but fortunately Doctor Ramis has prescribed her some excellent calming medication.'

Isabel touched his arm. 'Can I say something?'

The mayor nodded enthusiastically. 'Now let us hear from Bel, our very own resident sleuth!'

There were smiles of approval as all eyes were trained on her. Isabel offered a taut smile. 'Evidently, this is a serious situation and the death of Carlos is very upsetting. All the same, we must err on the side of caution. It is possible that the cockerel was killed by another party. We cannot be sure that there is only one abductor.'

Llorenç's mouth dropped open in shock. 'Are you suggesting that we have multiple abductors, Bel?'

She breathed deeply. 'All I'm saying is that we need to keep an open mind. Carlos was not the first pet to have gone missing. Why was he killed and was there possibly another motive?'

'But he wasn't the only bird. What about Dolores's parrot?' asked a workman.

Ruben, the carpenter, raised his hand. 'Maybe Bimbo swore at the abductor in Russian and he decided to turn him into a feather duster!'

Isabel stared anxiously around for Dolores, but relaxed when she remembered that the waitress only worked night shifts. In the midst of the heckling and laughter, Llorenç eyed his watch and cut short the meeting. 'I have important business back at the town hall so please form an orderly queue over here and let's set up our first vigil tonight.'

As Alfonso, Pau, Ruben and an assortment of men lined up at the mayor's table, Isabel slipped quietly out of the café. She had a busy day ahead and was still feeling uneasy about the fate of Carlos. There was something unsettling about the brutality of his killing that didn't stack up with the theory forming in her mind about the abductions. Was she on track or was there something she had somehow overlooked?

*

Furó rushed to greet Isabel as she stepped into the office, wagging his tail and making excitable grunts and wheezes. She picked him up and wove him around her shoulders while Pep observed her from his desk. He replaced the telephone with a resounding thump and issued a groan. 'That was hard work! A German woman was trying to make a booking for July with possibly the worst English I've ever heard.'

'Really, and how's your German?'

He shrugged. 'Admittedly not good but at least I speak reasonable English.'

'More importantly, did you confirm the booking?'

He shot her a frustrated look. 'Yes, of course. Two weeks booked at Ca'n Fiol.'

'Excellent. I shall allow you to leave the office tonight. Now, did Tolo call?'

He picked up a small notepad and grinned. 'He's flying into Palma early evening and plans on coming here around eight o'clock tonight. He said he hoped you'd be cooking *paella*.'

'What impertinence!' she said with a smile and pottered into her office, flinging her pannier on the desk. Pep followed after her.

'So are the vigilantes all signed up?' he snickered.

'Just about, but I'm not entirely happy about it. Still, it may bring about an unexpected result.'

'How did you get on with the interviews last night?'

She sat down at her desk and scrolled through her emails. 'It was a useful exercise but I need to cross-reference the information. In fact, you can help with that. I don't want you sitting idle during this quiet period.'

His face lit up. 'Excellent! I like playing sleuth.'

Isabel took out her notepad and beckoned him over. 'I have taken detailed notes of the victims' contacts and movements during the last few months. I need you to make lists of any common ground. For example, Alberto Bonet recently had new windows fitted and so did Pau. Did they use the same workmen? Teo Darder and Dolores both use the same hairdresser so...'

'You're kidding! Teo goes to that Atelier place in Fornalutx? It's a bit grand for the likes of a builder, isn't it?'

'That's not your concern. Besides, it rather elevates him in my opinion. Now, off you go and find what parallels can be drawn. Please follow my notes carefully and include every last detail under the headings I have highlighted.'

'Ever thought of being a headmistress?'

She winked at him. 'Teaching pupils to juggle lemons might not take them far in life.'

Pep glanced at her notes and tapped his lips with a pen. 'You still believe that the thief knows all the victims, then?'

'Most assuredly, yes. My gut tells me that this might be some kind of vendetta or punishment.'

'But gut isn't enough in police work, is it? You taught me that,' he baited.

Isabel nodded. 'In police work, hard evidence is always key, but never underestimate instinct. It doesn't matter whether a suspect is a king or a judge, if something feels awry, even in lieu of hard facts, you must follow your gut, regardless of the consequences.'

'Is that what you learnt when you trained as a detective?'

'Good heavens, no.' Isabel paused. 'Now, before I forget, can you also start work on a map of Sant Martí for our rental guests? It must be attractive and informal, something we can produce as a postcard to put inside the complementary basket of goodies we leave guests on arrival.'

He nodded. 'An illustrative map?'

'Yes, you're very good at drawing. Just a black and white line drawing highlighting the most useful businesses and of course our offices.'

He was about to reply but Isabel has begun tapping at her computer keys, a sure sign that in her own mind, she had concluded the conversation.

As Pep sloped off to his desk and began studying her neatly written notes, Isabel looked up and eyed him thoughtfully. She felt it important to entrust him with investigative tasks, knowing how excited he was that she was continuing her role with the National Police. Although the animal thefts didn't appear to enthrall him as much as the case of the missing florist, she was delighted to find him so keen to be involved in her police work. At any rate, it surely had to beat taking rental bookings or tiling for that matter, his previous apprentice post. Her thoughts were interrupted by the shrill cry of the telephone from the main office.

'Hogar Dulce Hogar, home sweet home,' Pep trilled. Isabel noticed that his face set when he heard the voice at the other end of the line. It was Emilio Navarro, a private investigator from Barcelona, who had been helping Isabel to unravel the whereabouts of Hugo Flores Romero, her father's missing brother. Three years had elapsed since a female witness claimed to have seen the controversial journalist being frogmarched from his Barcelona office into a black limousine bearing a small Colombian flag. He had not been heard of since and the sole witness had subsequently died in suspicious circumstances. Pep sighed and transferred the call to his boss.

Isabel took it in some trepidation, wondering what the investigator might have discovered on his recent trip to Colombia in search of clues. She swivelled round in her chair so that she faced the garden, depriving Pep of the opportunity to gauge her reaction.

Anticipating that the call might bring bad news, Pep jogged downstairs and started to brew coffee and froth milk. He peered into the large tuck tin that always sat in the adjoining larder and examined the contents. To his delight, he discovered a freshly-baked orange cake, drizzled with lemon icing, that Florentina, like a benevolent genie, had left. Cutting two large wedges, he placed them on a small tray with Isabel's *cortado* and his own *cappuccino* and carried it carefully upstairs. He was surprised to discover Isabel staring blankly across her desk, her hands clasped firmly under her chin. She offered a wan smile when he tapped on her door and placed the treat in front of her. 'Dear Pep, you certainly want me to get fat. A piece of cake in addition to my *ensaïmada* this morning?'

'Who can refuse your mother's homemade orange cake?'

'Who indeed?' she replied, popping a delicious morsel into her mouth.

'Is everything alright?' he asked, hovering by her office door.

She shrugged. 'There's no real news, but at least Navarro has found solid evidence that Hugo was smuggled into Medellín some months ago. We still know nothing of the perpetrators or the motive for his abduction.'

'Is Navarro going to keep on the trail over there?'

'I've connected him with Julian Mosquero, my old police chum in Bogotá, so hopefully they can collaborate and compare notes.

He'll stay another week and continue the investigation back in Barcelona.'

'And what is your instinct?' asked Pep, his voice quiet.

'My instinct, Pep, is that my uncle is still alive, perhaps kept in captivity, and that one day we shall bring him home.'

*

Isabel finished a call with Gaspar and spying her ferret's whiskery face under her desk, handed him a soft ball. He gripped it with his teeth and scampered off to his basket. Pensively, Isabel picked a green-papered Chupa Chup from the big bowl of colourful lollipops on her desk, and slowly removed the wrapper before popping the treat into her mouth. She strolled over to her open window and took several deep breaths of cool, fresh air. Below in the garden she could see her favourite hen, Mrs Buncle, nursing a new clutch of six chicks. Much as she loved seeing new life, she knew that few of the golden fur balls would live to seize the day because of the various predators on her land. Recently, in the early hours, she had seen both a genet and pine marten prowling about the terrain, seemingly impervious to Furó's habitual scuttling about in the orchard. Mercifully, Mallorca had no foxes, but her chickens still had too much unwanted attention, especially from rats, eagles, hawks and peacocks. She opened the window when she caught sight of Idò entering the patio with a basket and secateurs.

'Back again for more punishment?'

He looked up at her. 'Florentina needs more lemons. She's making lemonade so I'm only too happy to oblige.'

'Save some for me,' Isabel replied.

'If you're good,' he grinned. 'By the way, I've signed up to patrol the streets.'

'Laudable, but is that a good idea? I don't like the thought of you surprising some would-be attacker.'

Idò pulled a face. 'I could see off any thieving blighter single-handedly. Besides, Llorenç has ordered us to work in twos like responsible toddlers. We'll be told to hold hands next!'

Muttering under his breath, he trudged off, blowing his nose loudly and scattering the skittish hens.

Isabel turned when Pep burst into her office, a look of unbridled panic on his face. 'Guess who's downstairs? You'll never believe it! Capitán Gómez!'

Genuinely stunned at the news, Isabel stood stock still for a moment. 'What, here in the house?'

'Yes,' he hissed. 'I told him you were on the phone to buy some time but he is insistent that he speak with you.'

'He's supposed to be walking the Camino de Santiago,' she interjected.

'He's got a terrible cold so maybe he came home early. I was too scared to ask.'

Isabel gave a sigh. 'Is it Friday the thirteenth?'

'No, it's Tuesday the twenty-third.'

Isabel patted his shoulder and smiled. 'I know, Pep. Okay, offer him a coffee and send him up. This day can only get better.'

As her assistant dashed from the office, Isabel nuzzled Furó and placed him in his basket. 'Whatever happens, you must neither bite the good Capitán nor expect him to play ball. That is something he rarely does.'

Isabel heard urgent steps in the adjoining room and suddenly the looming form of Álvaro Gómez filled the doorway, his immaculate sage ensemble giving him the appearance of a dapper grasshopper. He was mopping his nose with a neatly folded, white handkerchief while his rheumy eyes fixed on Isabel with the zeal of a magnet. Isabel stepped forward to shake his hand but he stepped back, colliding with the doorframe.

'I am lamentably contaminated. However, I may sit at some distance if that is acceptable to you.'

Isabel nodded and watched as he gingerly lowered himself into the chair across from her desk and wiped his fevered brow.

'It's always a pleasure to see you, Capitán. I mistakenly thought you were enjoying the Camino de Santiago with your wife, Paula.'

He placed his phone and a pair of pristine, black leather gloves on the desk, and issued an impatient cough. 'As I had predicted, it was a mistake to have been persuaded to participate in such frivolity. After six interminable days plodding along bland paths in the rain with Paula in loquacious flow at my side, I had to endure the additional inane chatter of passing hikers, the majority neither spiritual nor cerebral.'

'So how far did you get?'

Irritably he flipped a hand in the air. 'Leon to Ponferrada, at which point I came down with a fever and a fearsome cold and insisted on returning to the island.'

'So maybe Hippocrates was wrong about walking being a man's best medicine? Did Paula plough on?'

'Of course not. She's my wife.'

Isabel waited for further explanation but none came. Pep stuck his head around the door. 'Here is your coffee, Capitán. I've poured you a fresh orange juice too. It will help your cold.'

He placed a tray between them and with a surreptitious wink at Isabel, left the room. Capitán Gómez gulped the juice and then reached for his coffee.

'It seems, Isabel, that once again Tolo Cabot has lured you away from your day job to assist him with this unfortunate florist case. One wonders why he doesn't offer you his own position as head of homicide while he's at it. I should point out that the Guardia has jurisdiction in this matter and yet, like a reckless bull, Cabot muscled in to take control from the outset.'

'In reality, both forces have been cooperating but your deputy made it clear to Tolo that he was short-staffed while you were absent, and would welcome the assistance of the national force.'

'Reynes is a good man but as jumpy and pliable as a rubber band. I am convinced Cabot pressured him to relinquish authority in my absence. This is why the state prosecutor handed Cabot the lead in the case. And where is he? In Madrid!'

Isabel cracked open a sunflower seed and smiled. 'Happily he returns later today.'

'No matter, I am now back and intend to be fully apprised of developments. We all have a part to play.'

'Of course,' soothed Isabel. 'It will be a delight to cooperate with you again. Has Gaspar Fernández brought you up to speed?'

He sneezed into his handkerchief. 'He sent me a progress report last night. It is evident that Paloma Crespí is a wayward and degenerate young woman who allowed her life to be corrupted by drugs. I would not be surprised if her father and his moll, the dance teacher, were involved, or one of their unpleasant associates.'

'I think not. They may be a loathsome pair but I have just spoken with Gaspar, who says both had an alibi last Monday night. Two independent neighbours of Jago Morey saw them arrive by car at 8.30 p.m. and the vehicle remained in front of Morey's garage all night long.'

'The girl may well have left the country. After all, she most likely had her identity card with her as it wasn't found in her home. Perhaps it was all pre-planned and she was on the run from some of her nefarious drug contacts.'

Isabel frowned. 'In that case, why would she have arranged for her boyfriend, Pere, to pick her up that night? Why was his car bugged and what is the significance of the tiny wooden heart found on the uncle's track? I discovered the very same object in the cold case evidence bag of pensioner Luz Pujals, who three years ago also disappeared.'

Capitán Gómez eyed her glumly. 'Isabel, I cannot explain all these things as I am new to the case, but I am sure we will find logical explanations. I would advise not becoming fixated with the wooden trinket. There are no doubt countless sentimental baubles of this kind on the market and sold in souvenir shops. Women love them.'

'Do they?' asked Isabel, crunching hard on a seed. 'Has Paula invested in one?'

'I would hope not,' he replied sourly.

'Listen, Capitán. Whether you like it or not, we are possibly dealing with a serial offender, a potential killer who for whatever reason has decided to resurface.'

He chuckled. 'There are no serial murderers in Mallorca! This is your frenzied over-active imagination at work as ever. You'll tell me next that "instinct" led you to this conclusion.'

Isabel glared. 'Good policing, Capitán. The wooden hearts were both unique hand-carved pieces and fashioned from laurel. It is an unusual wood and unlikely to be used for souvenir tat. For an identical keepsake to be discovered close to where two unconnected women seemingly vanished into thin air is remarkable. The truth is that this is no coincidence. '

'If you are right, which I strongly dispute, what is its meaning?'

'I think it is the abductor's calling card.'

'And your theory is based purely on two cases?'

Isabel exhaled deeply. 'I have asked Gaspar and his team to identify all the cold cases of missing people in the last few decades. We need to find connections and to re-examine the evidence.'

'A pointless task, in my opinion.' With a violent cough, Capitán Gómez stood up and shook his head solemnly. 'You are spreading the net too wide and making sweeping assumptions. This will cost both our forces time and money.'

'It will be money well spent.'

'For your own sake, Isabel, I do hope so, because your reputation is likely to be in shreds when this is all over.'

Isabel opened her door with a flourish and waved him through. 'It's a risk I'm willing to take. Besides, I've nothing to lose. I'm just a hick rentals agent. In the meantime, I do hope you make a swift recovery.'

As the Guardia Civil captain walked stiffly out of her office, Isabel picked up Furó's soft ball and flung it against the wall.

*

Isabel and Tolo sat together at the kitchen table enjoying the dregs of a bottle of potent local red wine. He fixed his eyes on her. 'It's good to be back, though the Paloma case is becoming more troubling by the hour. I'm sorry I got you involved.'

Isabel gave a snort. 'Fibber!'

He touched her hand. 'If, as you believe, we have a serial killer on the loose, we need to keep a handle on the media. If that strutting cockerel, Casanovas, gets wind of this, we're all doomed.'

'Josep isn't so bad. He's already helped us track down two of Paloma's previous clients. We just have to keep stoking the fire, feeding him titbits to keep him on side.'

'I'll leave that to you, since he fawns all over you.'

Isabel shifted in her chair. 'Forget Casanovas.'

He nodded. 'You're right, we need to focus. My team will pick over cold cases while hopefully you can try to track down the mysterious "creepy guy" Paloma mentioned to her friend, Laura, and find out who had access to Pere's car to place that Vidcam.'

'Easier said than done. So far, we have no DNA and no motive, but there will be one. What interests me most is what links Paloma Crespí with Luz Pujals and why our abductor has resurfaced again now. The heart surely signifies love?'

'They're both women. Could be sexual.'

'A fair point, but the profiles vary greatly. We have a twenty-five-year-old woman and a seventy-four-year-old pensioner, both living in different zones of the island.'

'Still, a deranged sex attacker will pounce wherever there's an opportunity.'

'True, but these attacks appear to have been pre-meditated and carefully executed. No witnesses or tangible evidence aside from the hearts. I'm convinced our abductor knew his victims.'

'You used past tense. You don't think we still have a chance of finding Paloma alive?'

'It's likely that she was despatched either on the day of the abduction or shortly afterwards – Luz Pujals too.'

'But where are the bodies?'

'Where indeed?' Isabel wandered over to the dresser. 'Fancy a little *digestif*?'

He smiled. '*Herbes*, thanks.'

She placed the bright green liqueur on the table and poured them both a generous dollop. She added a lump of ice to each glass and clinked hers against his.

'You know, the last two cases we handled were complex, but we finally cracked them.'

He sighed. 'Mostly thanks to you.'

'It was down to team effort. Although, this time I hope our good Capitán will not become a nuisance.'

'I've involved his force in monitoring the movements of Jago Morey, Carlotta Pilar and Pere Brotat. They've also been doing intensive door-to-door checks and searching disused outbuildings in the Sant Joan and Sineu area, but they're widening the search. That'll keep them busy.'

'Good. Meanwhile, tomorrow I shall interview the daughter of Luz Pujals and the builder who employs Pere Brotat. I've got to take care of some local village business too. As I mentioned to you, we have our own spate of disappearances.'

Tolo was taken aback. 'You're not suggesting they're connected?'

She shrugged. 'Not at all, but as you know, various pets have gone missing here in Sant Martí. The sculptor, Nicolas Garcia, has galvanised Llorenç into organising a group of male villagers to patrol Sant Martí every day.'

'I don't like that. It smacks of vigilantism.'

Isabel savoured a mouthful of *herbes*. 'I agree, but at the same time I think it might flush out the culprit.'

'Why is Garcia getting involved anyway? His estate isn't that close.'

'He's lost a rare breed cat and is convinced it's been taken by the same perpetrator. He's even offered a reward of one thousand euros.'

'A well-meant gesture, but not a good move. You know how these things pan out. Neighbours will denounce one another and there'll be all sorts of trumped up sightings and stories in order to claim the bounty.'

'Actually Nicolas rang me today and asked if I would pop over to the estate to discuss the thefts, without Llorenç in tow. He wants my advice on how to handle the matter with delicacy.'

Tolo rubbed a hand over his forehead. 'I met him some years ago. He funded an impressive facility for young disabled artists and musicians, which he still supports.'

'So I believe.' She drummed her fingers on the tablecloth. 'My life has suddenly become crowded with missing animals and people. I heard from Emilio Navarro today about my Uncle Hugo.'

Tolo's mouth fell open in surprise. 'Why did you leave this until last? What has he discovered in Colombia?'

'He now believes that Hugo was smuggled out of Spain a few years ago and held captive in Medellín and also Bogotá.'

'Has this got anything to do with that monster, Ortega?'

A recent case in which Tolo had sought Isabel's help had involved Enzo Ortega, a former elderly resident of Sant Martí, a murderer and stooge of the Colombian drug baron, Pablo Escobar. He had been killed by his housekeeper who, unbeknown to him, proved to be a relative of one of his victims.

'Maybe. Emilio is following the trail for another few days and promises to give me a full report on his return. He is currently in Medellín and cooperating with Julian Mosquera, my old police chum.'

'Please keep me in the picture. If Navarro's intel is compelling enough, we should visit Colombia together and try to locate Hugo.'

As Tolo rose to his feet, she gave him a bear hug. 'You are the best friend anyone could wish for.'

He eyed her ruefully. 'In truth as you know, I'd rather be.....' His words were lost in the violent blare of his phone. 'Gaspar? *Diga*!' he growled.

Isabel watched as his face tensed and he began delivering short, urgent questions to his deputy. He finished the call and with a heavy sigh heaved on his coat and headed for the front door with Isabel hot on his heels. 'I need to go. There's been another disappearance. I'll call you from the office when I have more information.'

'Is it a woman?' asked Isabel anxiously.

He turned to her with a bleak expression. 'It's a man, a German, and one who has only just stepped back on the island.'

TWELVE

As Isabel drove through the impressive gates of Ses Fonts, her heart leapt with joy when a gaggle of baby lambs gambolled across her path, causing Pequeñito to break sharply. She parked up close to the house, remembering to leave her keys in the car, and walked into the sunny lobby. Nicolas Garcia greeted her cordially and led her through to an elegant drawing room. The French doors gave directly onto the rear garden, with views to the sculpture park and orchards beyond. Isabel wondered how an artist might feel presented with such a vision of beauty and perfection. Once seated on one of the cream linen sofas, she quickly scanned the room, impressed by the antique kilim rugs, fine contemporary art and many bookshelves lining the walls.

Nicolas caught her eye. 'Do you enjoy reading?'

Isabel nodded. 'Too much. If I had my chance, I'd read all day.'

'I'm just the same. When not in my studio and foundry, I like nothing more than to sit by the fire with an excellent book and good glass of red wine, with Chopin playing in the background.'

'I love Chopin too, but let us not forget home-grown composers such as Albéniz, Granados and the likes of classical guitarist Tárrega.'

'Indeed. *Suite Espanyola* and *Iberia* by Albéniz are masterpieces, and Granados needs no introduction.'

'A favourite of mine is *Mallorca* by Albéniz.'

He laughed. 'I'm afraid you're a hopeless romantic and evidently very patriotic.'

Lourdes appeared silently at the door and gave Isabel a warm smile. 'Can I get you a coffee or tea?'

'A *cortado* would be perfect, thank you.'

When the woman had left the room and discreetly closed the polished mahogany doors behind her, Isabel turned to her host.

'We should talk about the animal thefts. I know you are concerned.'

'Yes, I am deeply disturbed by them. In truth, when you visited with Llorenç, I felt that you were unhappy about my offer to finance a reward and a watch group. That is why I invited you here. I need you to understand that I just wanted to help as best I could. I am physically useless so at least I can offer funds.'

Isabel digested his words carefully. 'Can I be blunt? Your estate is in the municipality of Escorca, some distance from Sant Martí, so your cat is highly unlikely to have been taken by our offender.'

He ran a hand through his perfectly groomed hair. 'Maybe I was grasping at straws. I become attached to all my animals, so when I heard about the thefts in Sant Martí, I convinced myself that it might be the same perpetrator.'

'Your valet thought he saw a car the night she disappeared. Could it just have been a lost driver?'

'Unlikely, given how hidden away we are.'

'And how would the car have entered your land? You have voice-entry gates?'

He sighed. 'After our shepherd brings the animals through to the barns early evening, we are often a bit lax on security as the gates are mainly there to protect our livestock. We don't have video cameras either.'

'I'm sorry to have to ask, but do you know of anyone who might hold a grudge against you or the estate?'

Nicolas looked away as if to avoid her gaze. 'I'd hope not. We look after our staff and tradesmen very well.'

Isabel smiled. 'Whether or not your cat is part of our problem in Sant Martí, it was generous of you to offer to finance both a watch and reward. All the same, money can bring out the very worst in humankind. I strongly dislike locals taking the law into their own hands, too.'

'Maybe emotion got the better of me. Is there a better alternative?'

'To be vigilant, sit tight and wait for the thief to make a mistake – or a demand.'

He eyed her keenly. 'What kind of demand?'

Isabel shrugged. 'The perpetrator may want money, or perhaps revenge.' She paused. 'Or both.'

'Do you have evidence to suggest this?'

'No, but logic tells us that if the animals are still alive – and there's no proof to the contrary yet – they may have been stolen for another purpose.'

'But Lourdes told me that the postmistress's cockerel was found dead.'

'True, but perhaps that was an unconnected killing.'

'You've lost me,' he replied with a deep sigh.

Lourdes returned with their drinks and handed a coffee to Isabel. She placed a handsome Japanese teapot and a dainty china cup and saucer in front of Nicolas.

She leant forward. 'Will that be all?'

He thanked her and began pouring his tea. 'It's green. Are you a fan?' he asked Isabel.

'I like English teas like Darjeeling and Assam but I'm more of a coffee girl.'

He nodded slowly. 'So, returning to the matter in hand, where do we go from here?'

'We wait. Let's leave the home patrol in place for now. They are all local men and are enjoying their moment of glory. I will monitor the situation.'

He nodded. 'I'd be grateful if you'd keep me informed of any developments. Meanwhile, tell me about your work as a detective. Llorenç is obviously very proud to have you in the village.'

She took a sip of coffee and laughed. 'I am no longer a detective. I reached detective inspector rank while serving with the National Police in Madrid and Barcelona, and retained the position when I came back to Mallorca.'

'For one so young that sounds like some feat?'

Isabel brushed off the compliment. 'I was fortunate enough to have handled some high-profile cases but that's all in the past now. I'm very happy running my rentals agency which my mother founded some years ago.'

'Yet Llorenç mentioned that you are still an advisor to the police here.'

'I occasionally cooperate with the head of homicide when he needs a little lateral thought.'

Nicolas gave a hearty laugh. 'You are a truly remarkable woman, Isabel. I feel privileged to have met you. Sant Martí is safer in your hands.'

Isabel hastily finished her coffee and stood up. 'I'm afraid I need to set off soon as I have a long day ahead of me. I have one small favour to ask, though.'

'Of course. How can I help?'

'It sounds a little foolish, but I have never seen an artist's studio. You'll remember that when I came with Llorenç we only had time to visit the sculpture park. Would you be kind enough to give me a quick peek?'

'It would be a delight! Come, let us do a tour together and I will give you a brief explanation of how I conceptualise my bronzes through to completion.'

Isabel beamed. 'Fantastic. Thank you!'

As they left the property together, chatting easily in the sunshine, Lourdes stood observing them from the front door, a small scowl blighting her pretty face.

*

Isabel relished her peaceful drive back along the winding country road with its sweeping views of the Tramuntana mountains and dense woodland of wild olives and holm oaks. The recent rainfall had brought the landscape into sharp relief with the bushy trees daubed a rich, silvery sage against a backdrop of shimmering, powder-blue skies. She had enjoyed her visit to Ses Fonts and her tour of Nicolas's studio though she hadn't had time to visit the foundry. The whole artistic process seemed somewhat arduous and painstaking, and yet Isabel appreciated the dedication and creativity that accompanied the craft. She wondered whether one day she would ever be able to afford a sculpture by the Chilean maestro and smiled at the thought of winning the lotería and nonchalantly rolling up to the estate to stake her claim. Nicolas's valet, Andel, had even washed and buffed Pequeñito during her visit so the bright yellow vehicle now gleamed under the sun.

Singing happily along to the Gypsy Kings with her window rolled down, Isabel contemplated her meeting with the daughter of Luz

Pujals. She was hopeful that it might disclose another small piece in the ever-expanding jigsaw. As the peak of Puig Major came into view, she glanced across at the glinting Gorg Blau reservoir on her left and frowned. She could see a distraught-looking couple gesticulating at one another by a lone black car. Something must be amiss. Isabel veered off into the small parking area. Jumping out of Pequeñito, she grabbed her pannier and strode towards them. Judging by the couple's fair hair and the hire car sticker on the boot of the vehicle, they were tourists, so she addressed them in English.

'Have you a problem?' she called out.

The young woman appeared relieved to hear her own mother tongue. 'I'm afraid we do. We left the car and went hiking early this morning around Cuber but returned to find the driver's window smashed and all our belongings gone.'

Isabel clicked her teeth. 'What have you had stolen?'

The woman's bearded partner stepped forward in an agitated state. 'Everything of importance. Our passports, money and flight tickets – and our jackets.'

Isabel examined the stray shards of glass still clinging to the car's window frame. 'This is an old trick. Thieves use a rock to break inside and try their luck, especially out of season on a weekday when this area is devoid of life.'

'At least we still have our phones,' the man muttered.

'You know it's always a good idea to keep valuables with you at all times or leave them in a safe at your hotel. Where are you staying?'

The woman's eyes filled with tears. 'At the Soller Plaza. I'm not sure what we'll do without money.'

Isabel patted her arm. 'Follow me to Soller and I'll lead you to the local police office to file a report. It's close to your hotel.

You'll need to cancel your bank cards. Do you have travel insurance?'

'We didn't bother,' the man replied.

Isabel sighed. 'You'd be best to contact the British Consulate in Palma. The hotel owners are charming and will help you. Come on, follow me.'

Before they returned to their vehicle, she pointed to the reservoir. 'Did you know that an ancient Moorish settlement called Almallutx was recently discovered underneath the water here?'

The man looked across at the placid, moss green water. 'We had no idea. Is it intact?'

Isabel shook her head. 'Sadly not. Still, local archaeologists discovered the remains of a mosque and cemetery, and a lot of pottery but with erosion, the site's not in the best shape. It was believed to be the last Islamic stronghold after the Christian invasion under James I of Aragón in the thirteenth century.'

'What happened to it?' asked the woman.

'There was evidence of fire, so perhaps they were flushed out by the troops of James I. Many Muslims hiding in the Tramuntanas were enslaved at the time.'

The man stared at her. 'Are you a mountain guide?'

'Not at all, but I love the history of my island.'

Dispiritedly, the couple got into their car and drove behind Isabel back to Soller. She parked on the street next to the town hall and indicated to them to do likewise. As she was manoeuvring into a space, a local police officer ambled over.

'Hey Bel, Pequeñito is looking very spruce today, but that doesn't qualify you to park here,' he said with a grin.

She leant her head out of the window and indicated the couple in the car behind her. 'Can you look after these tourists? They need to file a report.'

'What happened to them?'

'The usual, I'm afraid. They left their hire car by Gorg Blau and—'

'Theft, then?' he interrupted.

'Exactly. They have no passports or money now.'

The man whistled. 'Okay. Will you join us?'

'Sorry, I can't. I have to interview someone. Pau from our village may have told you that I'm assisting the Palma squad again.'

He cocked his head to one side. 'Yes, he did. You've also got your own funny business going on in Sant Martí.'

She winked. 'We certainly do. Nothing like a challenge, eh?'

With a rev of the engine, she waved and roared off up the road. Although she had no watch, she guessed it was only about eleven thirty, surely time for a quick pit stop and a coffee and a *bocadillo*?

*

Isabel had been forced to park up unexpectedly on a grass verge on the outskirts of the peaceful village of Costitx, which lay hidden like a rare jewel among soft, velvety pastures and verdant orchards in the very heart of the island. She had been on the point of entering the driveway to an attractive stone *finca* when Tolo had called to give her an update on the latest citizen to go missing. With phone to ear, she listened carefully and after finishing the call, gave a hefty sigh. It appeared that Gunter Weber, a forty-six-year-old freelance arborist and talented yachtsman, had left the island two years previously for a sabbatical. He had rented out his apartment through an agency in the town of Artà to fulfil an ambition of sailing around the world in his 46ft Fisher motorsailer. Isabel had secretly admonished herself for feeling a twinge of envy when Tolo had mentioned the vessel. It had always been her dream to restore and sail one of these powerful and reliable fibreglass beauties that hailed from the UK, but life had somehow got in the way.

Sadly for Gunter Weber, what should have been a triumphant return to his erstwhile home in Mallorca following a successful two-year sailing trip had not ended so well. After a month of partying and catching up with old friends, he had suddenly disappeared without trace. Patricia Colom, his rentals agent, confirmed to Tolo that she had visited him at his apartment two days previously. She had needed him to sign some documents and was shocked to find the kitchen and living area littered with bottles. He had reportedly told her that he was enjoying life for a while before settling back into work again. The agent had subsequently arranged for him to have a full-time cleaner, especially as he had recently acquired a young Jack Russell pup that was creating havoc around the apartment.

On the day of his disappearance, he was due to have lunch with a friend in Palma and meet a potential client at 6 p.m. before attending a private dinner party in the small, north-easterly town of Capdepera. He had failed to keep any of his appointments. It was only when his cleaner had arrived the following morning to find his bed made and the Jack Russell chained up and crying pitifully from the bathroom that she had alerted the agent. The police had been called and were puzzled to find that most of the German's personal effects were in evidence, including his wallet, identity card, passport and car keys. His vehicle remained untouched in its garage. All the same, there was no sign of a computer or phone in the apartment.

Isabel tapped impatiently on the wheel of the car while her mind whirred. Today was Wednesday, ten days since Paloma had vanished; the new week had barely begun and Gunter Weber had now also disappeared. In her call with Tolo she had offered, once forensics had finished their sweep of the premises, to visit the man's apartment the following evening in case any clues might have been missed. She would also visit Patricia Colom, Weber's agent. Fortunately, she knew the woman well as they often recommended one another's agencies to potential clients when their own property lists were full. Tantalisingly, Tolo had not been able to confirm whether forensics had discovered a wooden heart among the man's personal belongings. She would have to wait patiently until the forensics team had finished its task.

Revving the engine, she set off up the driveway and parked in front of the *finca*, admiring the plentiful ivy that had smothered most of the façade. Before she had reached the arched doorway, a red setter came tearing out of the house to greet her. She stroked his muzzle while a cheery woman looked on from the porch.

'He's a fine guard dog, as you can see,' she laughed. "I'm Angela, and I take it you must be Señora Flores Montserrat?'

'Yes, I'm Bel.'

The woman smiled and welcomed her through the hallway and into the kitchen. 'Would you like a glass of my homemade lemonade?'

'That would be perfect. What a wonderful situation you have here.'

Angela placed a jug of her brew and two glasses on the robust wooden dining table and offered Isabel a seat. She pulled out a chair opposite her and poured their drinks. Isabel watched as the ice cubes plopped noisily into the dark blue glasses.

The woman fiddled unconsciously with her watchstrap. 'I must admit, Bel, I was surprised to hear from you. It's been three years since my mother disappeared and the police never got to the bottom of it at all. We never knew what became of her and so there's never been any closure for the family.'

Isabel offered a sympathetic nod. 'I can understand how frustrating and heart-breaking it must have been for you. By all accounts, Luz was very independent and happy with her life.'

'Oh yes,' she replied. 'After my father died, she lived in their remote cottage in Pollença on her own and never asked for any help. My husband and I would visit with the kids most weekends but she was quite content with her own company and that of her two cats.' She paused. 'We still have them.'

'You were an only child?'

Angela nodded. 'My parents married late in life. They were both walking guides and met in the Tramuntanas. Quite romantic, really.'

Isabel smiled. 'And so when did Luz give up her work? I was told she was a cook?'

'Fifteen years ago my father suffered a cerebral embolism and died quite suddenly. My mother was already sixty-two by then and lost the heart for guiding. A friend of hers named Tia, ran an agency for freelance chefs and roped her in. As my mother was always a great home cook, she took to it like a duck to water. It helped her get over my father's death and gave her a new lease of life.'

'And how long did she and Tia work together?'

'Until my mother turned seventy and decided to retire.'

'Is her friend still around?'

'Sadly she also passed away a few years ago.'

Isabel took a long draught of lemonade. 'I suppose you wouldn't know anything about Luz's clients?'

'Not really, although my mother kept an old album of images from those days. She was very proud to have cooked for some important and well-known people on the island.'

'How fascinating. Do you have the album here?'

'I'm afraid not but it's still in the bookcase in my mother's cottage. We left the property as it was and still go there for long weekends. We don't want to sell it yet as it holds too many memories for me.'

'Would you be happy for me to visit the house and take a look at the album?'

'By all means. We leave a key under the front mat as there's nothing of value in the property. The album is blue. You won't miss it.'

Isabel decided to take her leave and, thanking Angela, set off towards Campos to have a chat with the builder who employed Pere Brotat. She wanted to know if Paloma's boyfriend worked solely for his construction company or took on other work, as she firmly suspected.

*

Isabel arrived back in Sant Martí just before the hands of the old church clock struck nine. She was ravenously hungry and as she felt too tired to rustle up something at home, popped into Bar Castel, hoping that Rafael might still have some leftovers from his *menu del día*. He sloped back from the kitchen, damp tea towel flung over his shoulder in the fashion of a Roman emperor and nodded.

'You're in luck, Bel. We've still got a plate of *potaje* and a portion of *porc amb col*. Let me get you the soup first.'

Isabel sat at the counter and savoured a glass of red wine while she waited. She cast an eye over the well-thumbed copy of *El*

Periódico and gave a low growl when she saw the face of Gunter Weber on the front page with the single word 'Missing'. Trust Josep Casanovas to be quick off the mark. She wondered which of his many contacts he'd bribed or threatened for the information. Next to her glass, Isabel's phone winked, and for the first time she noticed a WhatsApp message from the obsequious editor that he'd evidently left earlier that day. It simply asked her to ring. She toyed with the idea of calling him back but decided it could wait. Food should always come first.

For the next hour she enjoyed chatting with locals while she tucked into a bowl of vegetable soup followed by pork and cabbage. Placing ten euros on the counter, she jumped off the bar stool and bumped straight into Idò.

'*Uep*!' he yelled cheerily, uttering that favourite of island greetings that signified surprise. 'I'm having a quick break from my night shift.'

'Drinking on the job, are we?' she teased.

'One beer won't hurt. We've been patrolling the streets for a few hours and haven't seen a damned thing.'

'Hardly surprising when the culprit is probably aware of your shifts.'

'You really think it's someone from the village?' enquired Rafael lugubriously. 'I tend to agree. How else could someone know about all our pets and how to steal them so easily?'

Idò gave a whinny of disapproval. 'Not a chance! This is definitely the work of outsiders. Anyway, one piece of good news. Dolores's parrot has returned. She found him on her balcony this afternoon trying to get into his cage. She thinks she might have left the catch loose the day he went missing.'

'Fancy that!' smiled Isabel. 'I'm happy for her. It also narrows the field.'

'I don't see how,' replied Idò. 'Anyway, Bel, could you do me a small favour before you go home?'

'Depends how risky it is,' she said with a grin.

'I forgot to feed Perro before I left for my shift. Poor little blighter will be starving. The garden door's open as usual.'

Isabel scrunched his arm. 'As you've been so active in my orchard of late, I'll return the favour.'

She ran down the steep steps of the bar and zipped up her jacket against the cold. There was a hint of rain in the air and the breeze was cool and damp. In descending mist, she walked quickly along the labyrinth of cut-throughs and winding alleys which were the hallmark of her beloved village. The odd cough alerted her to a passer-by in the gloom and both exchanged a hurried *bona nit* before going on their way. Reaching for the torch in her pannier, Isabel headed out of the village towards the *torrente*, contemplating the sharp ascent uphill along a stony track to her uncle's *finca*. Stopping midway, she suddenly heard the sound of yapping and growling and the unmistakeable cry of Perro. Without a moment's thought, and in spite of a full stomach, she ran as fast as she could uphill towards the house. As she hurtled into the driveway, a large white van, its headlights glaring in the ghostly mist and blackness, roared towards her, causing her to leap into the nearest flowerbed. As she grappled to her feet, an image flashed before her eyes of Perro's terrified face staring directly at her from the rear window of the racing van.

THIRTEEN

As Idò walked into Isabel's offices, he found his sister and Pep in a glum state. Even Furó wore a mournful expression as he sat curled up on the sofa next to Florentina, making faint whimpering sounds. Idò could hear the familiar animated cadence of Isabel's voice from the other office and felt relief that she was still at home.

'She's on the phone to Tolo Cabot,' said Pep unnecessarily, and with a sudden sense of urgency sprang from his seat and offered to make Idò a coffee. He was agitated and not quite sure what to say. After all, Idò was a crusty old soldier and not one for emotion, and yet the theft of Perro had affected him badly: his face was drawn and pale and he had lost his customary bite and sparkle. While Pep set off down the stairs, Florentina smiled across at her brother.

'I know things look bad but Perro is a feisty little dog. I'm sure he'll keep his tail up until he's home safely.'

Idò eyed her plaintively. 'But he may never come back. Whoever took him is just playing with us. It's so cruel. He's an old dog and I worry about his ticker.'

Florentina rose and patted his hand reassuringly. 'All will be well.'

Isabel had finished her call and now came over to greet Idò with a hug.

'*Ánimo*, Uncle! We will find Perro but more importantly we will catch this creep. I have been working with the local Guardia and police teams this morning to identify white van owners in the village. There are thirty in total.'

'Who'd have thought it?' muttered Florentina.

Idò frowned and sat down heavily in a chair. 'Thirty? Does that mean you'll have to interview all the owners?'

'Hopefully it will be a simple matter of deduction. Pep and I have been cross-referencing the contacts and activities of everyone who has lost a pet. Each has some common ground and so we'll focus on that.'

Pep returned with a coffee and huge slice of Florentina's homemade plum tart, which he placed in front of Idò. He noticed that the very sight of it elicited a glimmer of a smile from the elderly man.

'What exactly do you mean?' asked Idò, taking a large bite of his prize.

Isabel stood in front of her whiteboard. 'Pep has done an excellent job in identifying any commonalities between these villagers. For example, all of them have set routines each day and, apart from Pau, place their keys under doormats and plant pots when they leave the house. A dream ticket for a thief.'

'Another thing,' added Pep, 'is that five of them were having DIY jobs done, such as painting and home improvements, and used various local tradesmen.'

'I'm not doing any repairs,' growled Idò. 'I do everything myself.'

'Maybe not,' replied Pep. 'But you do leave a key under the mat and have a predictable routine.'

'Not to me, it isn't,' he sniffed.

Florentina interrupted. 'Actually, Idò,' you recently had to fetch the plumber when you had a blocked drain. He's got a white van.'

'Old Alberto? He'd hardly steal Perro. We went to school together! Besides, his own dog is missing.'

'We're not saying that it's Alberto, but he might unknowingly be connected to someone who did steal Perro. Maybe someone else has access to his van,' replied Pep, blushing at the approval in his boss's eye.

Isabel resumed. 'We have a long list of names and will need to do some investigating, but I am certain that the culprit is in amongst them or certainly a close associate. Remember, we are looking for a male.'

'Why's that?' asked Florentina.

'No woman would have driven at me in that dangerously macho manner,' she replied with a wink.

Furó yawned and leapt up onto Idò's lap, making him smile. He ran a hand over the silky-smooth chestnut hair on his back and muzzle. 'I never thought a ferret could be such a good friend, but he's as companionable as my Perro. No wonder they get on.' He turned to his niece. 'How is your police investigation going?'

She exhaled deeply. 'We're making slow progress, but there is a chink of light. Yesterday, I spoke with the constructor who employs Paloma's boyfriend and he said that Pere often did work "on the black" for another client after his day job finished. The boy had fibbed about that, so I will need him to give me the details of that other client. It could be the person who placed the camcorder in his car.'

'Why would Pere Brotat lie?' asked Pep.

'He wouldn't want the National Police to know that he was working cash in hand in case we contacted the tax office.'

He laughed. 'Can't blame him!'

'I have also just spoken with Josep Casanovas and we will be meeting tomorrow to see how his newspaper might assist with the investigation.'

'That man is still sweet on you, Bel. I'm sure he'd do anything for you!' clucked her mother. 'To think he could be the next Mayor of Forn de Camp.'

'Heaven help us,' Isabel retorted.

Her mother, duly chastised, rose to her feet. 'I must away. The good doctor and I are off to a Tai Chi class.'

'What the heck is that?' quizzed Idò.

'Don't ask!' cried Pep. 'Yesterday, Doctor Ramis showed me his new Lycra cycling shorts. The world is truly going mad.'

'Less cheek, young man!' Florentina scuffed Pep's head as she bustled out of the room. 'We oldies have got to keep fit and I for one think Miguel looks very handsome in them. He has good knees for a man of his age.'

Florentina descended the staircase and sallied forth along the garden path, blissfully unaware of the raucous laughter emanating from the upstairs office of Ca'n Moix.

*

Isabel enjoyed her car journey to Pollença along the quiet, twisting mountain road. It gave her an opportunity to rein in the various theories and frenzied thoughts galloping like wild steeds through her brain. A bizarre hypothesis so dark and unfathomable as to give her goose pimples had formed in her mind. She convinced herself that her highly fertile imagination had overstepped the mark this time. With an involuntary shiver, she rolled down the window, allowing cool air to engulf the vehicle. She inhaled deeply and smiled when the sharp peak of Penyal des Migdia peered from behind a bend in the road. She loved to climb in the Tramuntanas and had scaled many of the island's highest peaks, though she preferred canyoning most of all as it afforded a true adrenaline ride and required accomplished technical skills. Thanks to her brother, Eduardo, an outdoor sports fanatic, she had honed the craft in her early twenties, though she would never be able to match his ability. All the same, she enjoyed occasional weekend excursions with her canyoning friends, and especially the delicious picnics of homemade fare they all shared along the way.

Sometime later, Isabel passed the turning for Lluc Monastery, knowing that she wasn't far from Mortitx, her next destination. She would take the track as far as Ses Basses, a wild and remote plateau close to the north coast where the grizzled cliffs plunged down to a sea the colour of bluebells. As she sang softly to herself, her phone rang. Putting Tolo on the loud speaker, she listened as he gave her an update on the forensic team's findings at the flat of Gunter Weber.

'I'm afraid no wooden heart has been discovered there, but Nacho Blanco wanted you to know that they have found fresh remnants of blood spatter. It's a small amount but enough to justify a full investigation. Nacho's hypothesis is that Weber was surprised and knocked out before being bodily removed from his apartment. The place had been cleaned up as there is evidence of the use of domestic bleach on floors and surfaces.'

'It sounds as if our abductor wasn't very prepared this time, or something went awry. Why did he or she not use an oxygen-based bleach? That would have taken care of those blood stains.'

Tolo grunted. 'Perhaps he or she should have consulted you first. By the way, the commissioner has officially upgraded our abductor to serial killer status, so that is how we will refer to our felon from now onwards.'

Isabel sighed. 'Better to call a spade a spade, I suppose.'

'Are you on your way to the cottage of Luz Pujals?' he asked.

'I'll be there in another few hours or so. I need to take a quick look around Ses Basses, where she was last seen hiking.'

'It's very isolated, so be careful. I'm still fretting about the animal thief in Sant Martí. You could have been killed last night.'

'Whoever it was just panicked. I don't think he intended to harm me.'

'Cold comfort, Bel. Either way, I'm glad we've opened an official enquiry into the matter in conjunction with the Guardia. With Gómez taking the lead, my team should be free to concentrate on the Paloma investigation with you.'

'A good compromise, and his team has already offered to help with cross-checking names of white van drivers in Sant Martí. Before I forget, could you please thank Nacho for couriering the Fluorescein over to me this morning.'

'You think you're going to need it?' Tolo asked in surprise.

'I hope not, but I'd like to quell one theory in my mind when I get to Luz Pujals' house.'

Isabel ended the call and took a left at a sign for the Mortitx vineyards. There wasn't a car in sight, and having parked by a grass verge, she sighed with pleasure to see nothing but rocky paths and abundant nature in all directions. Quickly she changed her plimsolls for heavy duty hiking boots and pulled on a warm, hooded jacket. The sky had turned sullen and there was a spit of rain in the air. Before exiting the car, Isabel placed her customary cardboard sign on the dashboard. In Mallorquí it read: *Dear would-be thief, there is nothing of value in this elderly car so please leave him in peace. Be conscious that one thoughtless action can destroy a life. There are always alternatives.* With her rucksack strapped over her shoulders, she patted Pequeñito and set off with a walking pole towards the lonely cliff face.

*

An incandescent wind stormed around the lonely plateau as Isabel stumbled over limestone boulders. With some difficulty, she made her way to a sheltered area surrounded by dense box shrubs to consult her map. Having identified the place where Luz Pujals was supposed to have left her belongings, Isabel studied the coordinates and, battling the violent gusts of wind, strode close to the cliff edge and looked across at the black and brooding sea. As she fought to keep her map upright inside its protective cover, a pewter sky began shedding heavy raindrops which found their way inside her jacket and trickled down her face.

There wasn't a soul in sight across the barren and shrubby plain, and yet an uneasy and prickly sensation coursed through her. Irrationally, she had the feeling that her every movement was being monitored by an invisible force, but all she could see in the tumbling rain were lone, spindly holm oaks, pistacia trees, steep cliffs and countless gleaming white boulders. Pulling her jacket close, she turned and set off along the stony track that Luz Pujals would have taken back to Mortitx. Despite the uneven terrain and occasional, well-defined sinkhole close to the route, there was precious little to concern an experienced hiker. Unless the elderly woman had been forcibly dragged to the cliffs and hurled into the sea below, it would have been nigh impossible for her to lose her way in daylight.

In contemplative state, Isabel walked back along the rocky path leading to Pequeñito, hurled off her wet jacket and drove onto the main road to Pollença. Twenty minutes later, she turned left along a rough track and after half a kilometre followed a wooden arrow to the single-tiered white cottage of Luz Pujals. Isabel parked the car and walked through the pretty, overgrown front garden. The front door key was, as Angela had promised, under a dusty old mat in the porch. Inside, Isabel switched on the dull overhead light and placed her rucksack and damp jacket on a wooden table in the hallway. The shutters in the property were closed tightly and a stale aroma hung in the air. Stepping into the gloomy open-plan living room, Isabel made her way carefully over to the windows and wrestled with the rusty fasteners. She gave a little gasp when a crash of thunder sounded overhead and a thud, possibly a branch, knocked impatiently at one of the windows. Pulling hard, she released one of the catches, breaking it in pieces at the same time. Cursing under her breath, she pushed open the shutters and allowed fresh air to rush in. How was it that she was always breaking things? Pep had given her the sobriquet King Kong, but she would argue that things just weren't made properly anymore.

With the sudden flash of daylight she was able to take in her surroundings. A modest kitchen lay to her right and a bedroom and bathroom to her left. The main room evidently served as both a dining and living area and was simply decorated with white walls and traditional terracotta floor tiles. The low-beamed ceiling was festooned with translucent spiders' webs that hung from the gnarled wood like long strands of saliva. A fireplace huddled in the corner near to a built-in white plaster bookcase while a table crammed with framed family photographs rubbed shoulders with a sofa. Two walls were adorned with a collection of ancient wooden walking sticks and old seafaring stills. Despite the layer of dust that smothered the dining table and most surfaces, the place was neat and homely.

Isabel retrieved her voluminous rucksack and took out her latex gloves and the testing kit biked over to her home that morning by Nacho Blanco. The spray of Fluorescein and hydrogen peroxide offered one of the most reliable ways to detect historic blood stains, and she intended to test its efficacy around the premises. Turning on her powerful flashlight, she set off first to the bookcase to locate the blue album of images that Angela had mentioned. She started on the top level, and worked her way diligently along each row. It was only when she reached the third shelf that she discovered a large gap between two volumes and a smudge in the dust where a tome had been winkled from its snug resting place. She examined the remaining shelves in vain, rattled that someone had evidently beaten her to the prize. Perhaps, more unnerving, was the realisation that someone other than her police colleagues and Angela knew that she would be visiting the place.

Apprehensively, Isabel crept about her, opening the larder door in the kitchen and checking the contents of a deep broom cupboard. Before she entered the en-suite bedroom, she removed the collapsible walking pole from her rucksack and gripped it tightly in her right hand. Pushing back the partially-open door, she sprang inside, only to find the room deserted but for a bed and built-in wooden wardrobe. She checked the pokey bathroom, and, satisfied that she was quite alone, closed the shutters and windows in the living room using string and duct tape to secure the broken catch, then turned off the hallway light.

In the darkness, she sprayed the surfaces, walls and wooden floor of the kitchen with the concoction Nacho had given her and used a high intensity white light to explore them. During her time on the force, it had been standard procedure to use the chemical Luminol, which emitted a bright blue glow when blood stains were detected. It reacted with the iron in haemoglobin but when criminals used oxygen-bleach at crime scenes, it could prove destructive and completely clean away evidence. Ordinary chlorine-based detergents weren't a problem for investigators as they couldn't eradicate the haemoglobin in blood which was visible using chemicals such as Luminol. In the past, Isabel had often attended meticulously clean crime scenes where an inexperienced killer had used ordinary bleach detergents, not realising that chemicals such as Luminol would clearly reveal blood stains undetected by the naked eye. Although Isabel had never tried Fluorescein before, Nacho had assured her that it was extremely effective in conjunction with a high intensity white light in a darkened room.

On her hands and knees, she worked her way slowly around the living room and progressed to the hallway. It was only then, after thirty minutes, that she issued a loud *madre mia!* Along a wall and on the tiled flooring, close to the front door, the bright light clearly revealed dense blood staining. She removed her gloves to take images with her phone, and then, sitting back on her heels, called Nacho.

'I've found historic blood stains at the house, thanks to you. As I had suspected, Luz Pujals never disappeared on a hike. She was abducted after a struggle in her own home.'

Nacho listened attentively. 'Good work, Bel, and I'm glad the kit was so effective. I'll get my team down there to go over the whole house. Of course, it was never done at the time as the focus had always been on Ses Basses.'

Isabel nodded. 'The abductor must have taken some of Luz Pujals' hiking gear from the cottage and left it there to throw the police off the scent.'

'In fairness, at the time, no one would have imagined that she had been abducted from her own home.'

'I'll cordon the place off outside and let the daughter know not to visit,' Isabel replied.

'Okay, will you be hanging about there for a while?'

'No, the evidence I sought has already been taken. Someone knew I was on my way and got here before I did.'

'I don't like the sound of that. Where does that leave us?'

'Searching for answers,' she replied.

As she gathered her belongings together, and pulled on her jacket, she heard the muffled sound of a *moto* beyond the garden gate. Isabel instinctively ran from the front door and out onto the track, just in time to see a motorbike riding away from the cottage at significant speed.

FOURTEEN

The hilltop idyll of Artà lay in the north-east of the island and of all the rural inland towns enjoyed the most tourism with its welcoming restaurants and cafés, gift shops and galleries. It had a large, shady *plaça*, a mecca for family gatherings during the summer months that also offered a welcome refuge from the sizzling heat for elderly locals by night. The townspeople had built a handsome railway station in 1921 with a line that ran to Palma via the town of Manacor, but it had been disbanded in the late nineties. All the same, the rather grand three-storey edifice still proved an attraction and, it was rumoured, might function again in the future. The cherry on the cake was the church of Sant Salvador with its medieval fortress walls that occupied prime position at the top of the hill.

On the outskirts of the town were the well-maintained remains of the Talayotic village of Ses Païsses, the best-preserved prehistoric settlement on the island. It was here that Isabel decided to have a brief pit stop before popping by the rentals agency of her friend Patricia Colom. Isabel found herself alone at the Bronze Age site; having parked close by, she perched on a rock and munched her *bocadillo* of *jamon serrano*, Manchego cheese and tomato in blissful peace. As she listened to the birdsong, she looked across at the area where in 1959 several hearths had been ex*cava*ted. Archaeologists had discovered human bone fragments among the ashes, as well as the remains of vessels and coins. She thought back to her conversation with Aina in Morells about how in prehistoric culture the deceased were often cremated with other metals such as copper to create artefacts that symbolised new life. Maybe the concept was not as peculiar as Isabel had originally thought. After all, there was something rather noble about recycling human remains and fashioning them into something new and metallic that would stand the test of time. It was one way to gain immortality.

With a yawn, she brushed some crumbs from her lips and made her way back to Pequeñito. Barely had she started the ignition than her phone bleated and Tolo's voice filled the void.

'Bel, sorry not to have returned your call. It's been crazy at the precinct. I'm still stunned that you found blood at the cottage. A full forensics team is working over there now. We evidently failed Luz Pujals three years ago.'

Isabel sighed. 'Don't beat yourself up. The evidence was at Ses Basses and you had no reason to believe she'd been abducted from the cottage.'

He groaned. 'Unfortunately your instincts have been proven right. Some cold killer has re-surfaced and for whatever reason has begun picking off new victims.'

'Don't forget that we have no evidence of murder yet, but it's certainly looking that way.'

'The media will lap this up. All we can do is try to keep them off our backs for now. Our press office will be evasive at this stage but it won't be long before the likes of Casanovas will be on our trail. As you can imagine, Gómez is as excitable as a bee on caffeine.'

'Actually I've arranged to meet Josep tomorrow evening. His newspaper might be able to help us track down our killer. Someone must have seen suspicious activity in the vicinity of Gunter Weber's apartment on the night he vanished. Even the sighting of a car would help at this stage.'

'Don't trust Casanovas. He's not reliable and would sell his granny down the river.'

Isabel emitted a sigh. 'I think I can handle him.'

'And what's your plan now?'

'I'm going to catch up with Patricia Colom in Artà and then I'll do an inspection of Weber's flat. She said she could give me a spare key.'

'It's already six-thirty. Why not visit the flat tomorrow morning instead and get a good night's rest? It's a long drive home to Sant Martí.'

Isabel tuttted impatiently. 'I'm a big girl. I can look after myself. I'll report in tomorrow morning.'

She finished the call and popped a bright red Chupa Chup in her mouth before roaring off along the quiet country road to Artà.

*

Having exchanged hugs, Isabel and Patricia caught up on local news. The rentals agent was in her late thirties and was already married with young children. She wore a weary expression as the topic of Gunter Weber reared its head.

'Bel, in all honesty I found Gunter quite a difficult man. He was very amusing and had a wonderful *joie de vivre* but he was as fidgety and irresponsible as a child.'

'In what way?' Isabel asked.

She shrugged. 'He had some great clients on the island and had built up a lucrative business but then just upped sticks to go off sailing.'

'That could be viewed as rather brave,' Isabel baited.

'We all have dreams but sometimes it's just not practical.'

Isabel pondered whether Patricia's scepticism was born from envy. As the main bread-earner it couldn't be easy juggling her job and raising three children while her bone-idle husband worked on and off at various local building sites when the fancy took him.

Patricia took a sip of her tea. 'Besides, Gunter returned to Mallorca and within only a few weeks had rashly bought a Jack Russell pup. Then he left it alone all day while he hung out with friends. The flat was a tip and I had to hire a cleaner for him.'

'It was this cleaner who discovered Weber missing and the dog chained in the bathroom?'

'Correct. She found his bed unmade from the day before and the dog had been chained to the bath taps.'

'Did it have food and water?'

She frowned. 'Is that important?'

'You never know.'

The woman grabbed her phone and made a call. After a brief, animated conversation, she replied. 'My cleaner says the dog had fresh water, food pellets and a dog basket in the bath.'

'That's odd, don't you think?' mused Isabel.

The woman offered a puzzled expression. 'The whole situation is.'

'Do you know where Weber had been working before he set off on his yacht?'

'He had many horticultural clients, most of them very wealthy. I think the majority were foreigners. If you want to know more, his best friend is Archie Brookes, an Englishman, who lives beyond the town in a secluded *finca*. Here is his address and phone number.'

Isabel took the fluorescent pink sticky note and nodded. 'Any lead would be helpful at this stage. Where is the puppy?'

'Archie took him. He already has an elderly dachshund.' Patricia looked at her watch. 'I'm sorry, Bel, but I have to pick up the kids from my mother. Just call if you need anything else.'

Isabel offered her a peck on both cheeks and, placing the key to Gunter Weber's flat in her pocket, walked out into the street. She had parked Pequeñito up on the kerb directly outside the office and saw, to her chagrin, that a traffic warden was buzzing around the bonnet. What was it Tolo had said about Gómez? As excitable as a bee on caffeine. She laughed and sauntering over to the young, uniformed man, flicked her police badge at him.

'I'm so sorry for leaving the car here but I'm on urgent business. I didn't have time to park. And you are?'

Taken aback, he replied, 'Serge.'

'An excellent name. Now, don't let me delay you any longer. I'm sure you have important work elsewhere.'

She smiled cheerily and waved as she drove off. He stood watching her, his pad and pen poised in the air. It was as if he'd been frozen in time.

*

Isabel found Gunter Weber's apartment block on a secluded cul-de-sac on the environs of the town. She was tired and longing for her bed but decided that a quick inspection would leave her time for other pressing matters the following day. It was already 8 p.m. and a long drive home beckoned but she was keen to make contact with Archie Brookes before heading back to Sant Martí.

She called his mobile phone, wondering whether she might have time to visit the man briefly en route home. Archie Brookes was polite but sombre.

'I take my old dachshund for an hour's walk around 8.30 p.m. in nearby woodland so can you come after then? I've also got Gunter's Jack Russell pup to care for now.'

'Will you keep him?'

'If possible, but a few weeks ago I broke my right arm skiing so am a little handicapped at present. Should probably give it up at my age.'

'Ouch. Well, I promise not to keep you long. I just need a little private information.'

In somewhat guarded manner, he asked, 'What particularly do you want to know about Gunter? Is this to do with his sexuality?'

Isabel was somewhat taken aback. 'Is that relevant?'

'He was gay, as am I.'

'It would only matter if it related in some way to his disappearance.'

He sighed. 'Gunter was always getting into difficult relationships. The last one was with a yachtie he met during his round-the-world trip. It ended in tears before he returned here. The guy sounded creepy to me, so I wasn't unhappy about it.'

'Creepy, in what way?'

'He just seemed a bit obsessive. A young man with a lot of insecurities from what Gunter told me. He was always turning up on his boat unexpectedly when he docked in different ports and was constantly accusing him of infidelity.'

'Was that unfair?' she asked.

'Not really,' he drawled. 'But Gunter was a sweetheart. He loved everything and everyone. In his book, life was for living but sometimes he broke promises and hearts.'

'Do you think this man could have wanted to harm Gunter?'

'I've no idea, but I'd check him out if I were you. His name was Jet, some kind of nickname, that's all I know.'

Isabel rubbed her eyes and stifled a yawn. 'I do need to know about Gunter's clients when he lived on the island. Would you be able to help? There was no evidence of a computer at his apartment.'

'That's weird. He lived on his laptop. But yes, I have a real estate business and I referred many clients to him at the time, so I should have all their names still logged on my computer. He had one or two favourites; some real oddballs I can tell you about.'

Isabel smiled. 'Great. I'll be over around nine-thirty.'

*

Gunter Weber's apartment had been pulled apart by the forensics team and there were markers on floors and walls in the various rooms. With great care, Isabel donned her gloves and shoe covers and padded about the place with her torch. She didn't turn on the main lights so as not to unnerve neighbours who would undoubtedly have been disturbed by the recent police activity. The bathroom where the dog had been discovered was cordoned off, so with great care, she stepped over the police tape and shone her torch about. She inspected the small cabinet where three toothbrushes, still in their wrappers, were neatly piled, but there was precious little else. Forensics would have taken away anything of significance.

She wandered into the living room and spent some time examining the bookshelves, which mostly exhibited tomes on gardening and tree species. The smoky grey walls were covered with historic black and white stills of yachts and happy-looking crew members on the high seas. She recognised a younger Gunter than the one in the police images she had been given, looking tanned, relaxed and carefree with pale blue eyes, a set of perfectly even white teeth and floppy blond hair. He wore casual but chic clothes in every image and evidently worked out. From recent images she'd seen of him, he was still strikingly handsome.

Isabel walked into the kitchen and pulled open drawers and cupboards. There was precious little cooking paraphernalia, which indicated that Gunter was a man who dined out a good deal. In the right-hand drawer of a large black desk in the study, she found some recent letters from his mother, written in a frail German hand. Isabel read through them and with a stab of pity wondered how she would be feeling about her son's disappearance. A shoebox sitting on the floor contained a mountain of invoices and business cards. She sifted through them, taking images of any that might prove useful. On a coffee table of artefacts, she found a large framed image of a sporty-looking youth sitting on the deck of a yacht. He wore a cautious smile and eyed the lens suspiciously. She picked up the frame and smelt it. It had a whiff of newness about it. Could this man be the mysterious Jet? With a shrug, she put it in a plastic bag in her rucksack with the intention of showing it to Archie Brookes. Perhaps he would be able to identify the man.

In the stillness, she froze when her ears detected the whine of a departing motorbike. Her eyes had adjusted to the darkness and with the beam from her torch, she bounded over to the window in time to see the bike's red taillight melting into the inky night. Nothing stirred outside.

It was then that it struck her how quiet the apartment block seemed. Perhaps in November there was low occupancy if the property was mostly rented by expats and tourists. She would check with Patricia the next day. Something about the sound of the bike had disturbed her. She was no mechanic but the *moto* had emitted a distinctive rattle that was all too familiar. Recently, Pep's Yamaha Sniper had made the very same noise, and he had told her that it was the fault of the chain drive. The bike that she had seen leaving the house of Luz Pujals had made exactly the same jarring sound. Someone was definitely tailing her, but how could they know her every move?

With a sinking feeling, Isabel turned on the main light and threw open the bedroom door, the only room she was yet to explore. In the centre of the bed, seemingly mocking her, lay a perfectly poised little wooden heart.

*

With Isabel at the wheel, Pequeñito tore through the quiet streets on the perimeter of Artà and onto the main road for Alcudia just as gentle rain began to fall. Through the blurred windscreen, she saw the bright forecourt of a garage in the distance and made a left turn shortly before it. Barely two kilometres later, amidst fields and dense shrubs, she spotted a clearly visible wooden sign for *Finca* La Vinya. She took a sharp right along a curving, muddy track and arrived at a smart, recently renovated farmhouse surrounded by pretty gardens and forestland.

Jumping out of the car in her hooded jacket, she approached the porch and immediately triggered several bright external lights. She blinked and, casting her gaze around, saw nothing but an elderly Range Rover and antiquated trailer parked up by the side of the house. A Scops owl called out, its methodical sonar beep as clear as a bell in the encroaching silence, and somewhere nearby came the persistent hiss of running water. Isabel vaguely wondered whether Archie Brookes lived close to a stream or had inadvertently left a hose running at full tilt. She'd done the same thing herself often enough in her garden.

She rapped on the arched wooden door, frightened by her own rapid heartbeat, and paced about the porch. Why was Archie not answering and where were the dogs? Wouldn't a Jack Russell pup bark at the sound of a visitor? Instinct was kicking in; without another moment's hesitation she rattled the handle. As if by magic, the front door yawned open, displaying the lifeless silhouette of a hallway in an equally still and empty house.

In frustration, Isabel turned back along the garden path and considered her options. Close to the gate, she noticed a well-worn track that led into dense woods. This was the most likely route Archie Brookes would have taken for his walk with the dogs. Crouching down, she examined the impacted soil by the light of her torch and determined the boggy paw marks of two small canines, though the human prints were unclear. There appeared to be several impressions of heavy boots over-layered by a distinctly different set of shoes, possibly trainers, but the rain had all but destroyed them. With a sense of foreboding, she stole along the path, keeping her torch low and her eyes trained on the rustling leaves and untamed undergrowth all about her.

After ten minutes of brisk walking in the encroaching dusk, she stopped still. She had lost all sense of direction but somewhere in the umbra beyond she could hear the muffled, anguished cry of an animal. Despite the moaning of the wind and drumming rain, she picked her way carefully through the trees, determinedly heading towards the sound, using her torchlight as a guide. Twigs cracked underfoot and branches creaked overhead like the beams of an old galley, but Isabel doggedly ploughed on. She had worn robust hiking boots but as she veered off the path into cloggy and unforgiving mud strewn with clumps of wet leaves, they became slippery and cumbersome and she nearly fell. Although her jacket offered some protection, heavy rain danced in the light beam like fine gold needles, pricking her cheeks and neck.

Exhausted and ravenously hungry, Isabel began to doubt her her decision to leave the relative security of the *finca*, but as she entered a patch of scrubland, she felt vindicated as the sound of whimpering grew stronger. To her relief, her eyes suddenly alighted upon two shadowy creatures cowering on the forest floor. Cautiously she crept forward, making soothing noises, while swinging the light beam about her, unsure who else might also be out there. The sodden faces of an elderly dachshund and young Jack Russell loomed at her, their eyes blinking in the sudden light. The collars of both had been attached to a rope secured to a tree and close by lay empty pouches of dog food. As Isabel bent down to release them, they howled and cavorted giddily about her, licking her face and hands. She patted them both tenderly and, grabbing the rope, looked about her. Where was Archie?

It didn't take her long to find out as both animals steered her roughly and excitedly towards a bank of trees where the slumped form of their master lay. Isabel bent down and examined the icy-cold, inert figure. He was facing downwards in the mud and rain with his left arm crumpled by his side while his plastered right arm appeared stiff under his chest. By the light, Isabel discovered a gaping wound on the back of his skull. It had evidently bled profusely but the rain had washed away much of the gore, leaving a tell-tale pink residue in the tiny rivulets of water running along the forest floor. The thick grey hair now appeared clean and slick, and the wet skin on his hands, sallow and waxy. She felt his pulse, knowing that it was a lost cause but the erstwhile disciplines of police protocols persuaded her to follow procedure. There were no signs of life, but feeling inside the man's jacket, she felt residual warmth. Even without Nacho's good counsel, it was obvious that she had narrowly missed the killer of Archie Brookes. Isabel sank to her knees, the dogs huddling by her side, and rang Tolo.

He picked up on the third ring. 'Has something happened?' he said.

'How did you guess?'

He gave a heavy sigh. 'I had a bad feeling. Where are you?'

Forty minutes later, as Isabel huddled near Archie's body with both dogs asleep on her lap, she became aware of voices and heavy footsteps. Torchlight ripped ribbons of darkness from the sky as police officers left the path at the sound of her whistle and flashing of her torch. Isabel was shivering with cold and grateful for the warmth of the two dogs. She was already worrying about what would become of them. Could she possibly find a home for either in Sant Martí? Ghostly uniformed figures now appeared before her and to her delight, Tolo was among them. He helped her to her feet and wrapped her in a hug.

'Let's get you home and into a hot shower.' He looked down at the inanimate form and shook his head sorrowfully. 'I take it this is the unfortunate friend of Gunter Weber?'

'I'm afraid it is. Our killer has been one step ahead of me all day but one thing's for certain, he has become reckless.'

'You think that's good news?' he jested.

'Yes, I do because we are now in a duel to the finish and I intend to win.'

FIFTEEN

A vibrant blue sky greeted Isabel as she strolled across the *plaça* of Sant Martí to Bon Día. Jesus, the owner, was in a cheerful mood, munching on a sticky bun as he served locals at the counter, occasionally wiping his hands on a stripy cotton apron. Isabel whisked up a freshly baked baguette, a packet of flour and some cans of tomatoes and waited in the modest queue. In front of her, Gori, the next-door neighbour of Señora Coll, was clasping a large box of chocolates to his chest and a bottle of *rosé cava*.

Isabel winked. 'Pushing the boat out, aren't we, Gori? An anniversary?'

His cheeks flushed pink and he whispered confidentially in her ear. 'It's for Señora Coll. She's been very upset.'

'That's very kind,' she replied, 'but she doesn't drink alcohol, so maybe don't bother with the bottle?'

He bowed his head for a second and then smiled, nodding. 'Don't worry, the *cava* is for me and the wife.'

It was his turn at the counter and in a fluster he pushed the items into a straw basket, and with an '*Adeu!*' rushed off.

'He's a funny one,' laughed Jesus. 'He hardly ever buys anything here except the odd croissant or packet of fags on his way to the construction site, but today he's really going the whole hog.'

'Maybe he's won the *lotería*,' a wag commented behind Isabel.

She giggled. 'Well, if that's the case, I hope it's drinks all round!'

Leaving the jollity of her companions behind, she set off towards Bar Castell, bracing herself for her encounter with Josep Casanovas. She was keen to gain his support with the Paloma case and needed his newspaper's cooperation. She found him sitting on the terrace overlooking the square, a smile etched on his full pink lips. His hair was perfectly coiffed and highlighted so that it glinted like gold thread under the sun's rays. He rose quickly as Isabel entered.

'What a glorious start to my day. Blue skies, sunshine and Bel!'

Isabel gritted her teeth but managed a tight smile as she bent forward to kiss him on both cheeks.

'It's really good of you to find time to meet, Josep.'

He waved a hand languorously in the air. 'Oh don't mention it. I never need an excuse to see you. Besides, I'm keen to have your take on the death of that Englishman last night.'

She gave him a cool stare. 'The death of Archie Brookes is not for discussion while under investigation.'

He winked conspiratorially. 'Come on, spill the beans! Is it connected to the Paloma case or is it something else? A local said he was gay and that a jealous lover murdered him.'

'What colourful imaginations people have on this island.' She stared at him. 'I'm sure all will be revealed in the fullness of time.'

Rafael appeared at the table, fixing the dapper editor with suspicious eyes, his order pad lying slack in his hand. Isabel managed to nip a grin in the bud when she saw his gaze fall on the would-be mayor's luxuriant locks.

'The usual Friday special for me, Rafa, and what about you, Josep?'

'Can you rustle up poached eggs and sautéed spinach or possibly sliced avocado on rye bread?'

'No', replied Rafael. 'Would you like a coffee?'

Slightly deflated, Josep turned to Isabel. 'What are you having?'

She shrugged. 'A *cortado, tostadas* with tomato and scrambled eggs.'

'I'll have the same but normally I try to avoid gluten.'

Rafael exhaled slowly and offered Isabel a wry grin before plodding off to the kitchen.

'How do you keep your figure with such an appetite, Bel?' Josep asked.

'I was brought up to be grateful for whatever was on the table and nothing's changed. I do a lot of exercise, otherwise I'd be the size of a hippo. And now, Josep, to business.'

He sat up straight and, clasping his hands together on the table, leant forward. 'I'm all yours.'

'This is of course in strictest confidence, but we are moving on significantly in the Paloma case.'

'Really? That's not what I heard on the grapevine. Cabot is as usual dragging his heels and—'

'Is that what our friend Gómez has fed you? I'm hardly surprised when he's been demoted on the case.'

He flinched. 'Oh, that comes as a surprise. To be honest, he did sound downbeat.'

'*Plus ça change*,' she muttered. 'What I need from you is help in tracing business colleagues or friends of a woman named Luz Pujals. She was a seventy-four-year-old pensioner who disappeared three years ago in Mortitx.'

He raised a hand. 'Wait. Remember I told you that her daughter called the newspaper when we flagged up Paloma's disappearance? I thought she was some nut, going on about her missing mother.'

'Yes, I do.'

'The case rings a bell. Didn't the poor woman get lost on a hike and was never found?'

Isabel smiled encouragingly. 'What an excellent memory you have. Well, I am keen to know more about her life and contacts. So far, we've hit a dead end.'

Josep's lip curled triumphantly. 'If you're re-opening this cold case, it must in some way relate to the Paloma disappearance. I knew it! We do have a serial killer on the loose.'

Rafael pottered over to their table with a full tray. He set each item in front of them, and left wordlessly.

Isabel sighed. 'We have nothing to back such a theory, but I'll admit that there are similarities in the two cases. If you promise not to run with that notion until I have hard evidence, I'll give you first dibs on the story.'

He took a sip of coffee. 'Why would I do that?'

'Because if you don't, we'll discredit you, ensure that you'll never get a headline again and manifest a campaign against you becoming Mayor of Forn de Camp.'

He sounded hurt and aghast. 'Bel, you wouldn't?'

Isabel stuck a fork in her scrambled eggs and beamed at him. 'Relax, Josep. We're old friends. I know you'd never stab me in the back, and in the same way, I'll always offer you what I can. Just don't push your luck.'

He threw her a mournful glance. 'Anything else you want to share with me?'

'Actually, yes. I'd like to know if any of your readers in the Artà area noticed anything untoward on the night of Gunter Weber's disappearance.'

'Such as?' he asked.

'A driver acting suspiciously or something unusual in the zone where Weber lived.'

He took a cautious bite of the bread and, pulling out a notepad, offered her a wide smile. 'Come on then, let's set to work.'

*

As Isabel approached her garden gate, she noticed Gori Bauza's downbeat wife leaving the house of Doctor Ramis. The woman stopped to greet Isabel and pointed to her throat. 'I've just been to the surgery. I think I'm coming down with a cough.'

'Sorry to hear that,' she soothed. 'I hope the *cava* will help that Gori bought in Bon Día this morning.'

The woman gaped. 'My Gori? He's as mean as a monk! He usually buys our *vino* by the barrel.'

'Maybe he's had a change of heart. He was thoughtfully buying Señora Coll some chocolates as well.'

'Are we talking about the same man? Has Gori suddenly found God? He can't stick that old busybody, and her cockerel did nothing for his insomnia either. He used to get up in the early hours and wander the streets before work, just to be free of it.'

Isabel shook her head. 'Maybe I was mistaken.'

'You most surely were!' she huffed.

Isabel watched her flounce off and smiled to herself. 'Well, well. What a tangled web we weave.'

As she entered the office she found Pep hunched over his desk, nursing a coffee, a morose look in his eye. Furó lay curled up cosily on the sofa, making faint snuffling sounds in his sleep.

'Whatever's the matter with you?' she asked.

'Oh, it's just Angélica. She's making endless hints about getting engaged. This morning I dropped her off in Soller for work at the *pasteleria* and she was ogling diamond rings in the window of that Estela shop. They cost a fortune.'

'Do you want to get engaged?'

'Are you mad? I'd rather walk barefoot across burning lava.'

'Steady on. In that case, just take her out for dinner, explain that she's the girl for you but that you'd rather responsibly first build resources for your joint future.'

'What kind of resources?'

'Money, of course. Llorenç would be impressed with that.'

He nodded slowly. 'Maybe it's worth a go. By the way, did you hear about the death of a British guy in Artà last night? It was on the radio this morning. You were in the town poking around Gunter Weber's flat, weren't you?'

Isabel sat on the arm of the sofa and flicked through some post. 'It's a long story.'

'Don't tell me he and Gunter were connected!'

Isabel looked up at him and smiled. 'I'm glad to see you're joining the dots, but before I take you through last night's excitement, tell me how the local Guardia are getting on in their search for the white van belonging to our animal thief.'

His eyes shone. 'Good news. An officer called earlier. They've narrowed the list down to five white vans in the village. They're interviewing all the owners.'

'Excellent. And I think I've solved one small part of the mystery. It's a tricky one to deal with though.'

He stared hard at her. 'What do you mean?'

'As I suspected, we have two unconnected animal abductors and one has just shot himself in the foot. It will take some delicacy in handling the matter.' She gave a sigh. 'I know who killed Carlos, the cockerel.'

Pep stood up in some bewilderment. 'Let me make us some coffees. I think I'm going to need caffeine to process whatever you're going to tell me.'

Isabel watched as he ran down the staircase, and answered her phone on the first ring. It was Tolo.

'How are you feeling after last night's exertions?'

She smiled. 'Thanks for cooking supper and the lift home. I slept like a baby.'

'It was the wine, and of course my excellent pasta,' he replied.

'I couldn't agree more. So, any news?'

'You'll be pleased. We've discovered the true name and whereabouts of the mysterious yachtie in that photograph you discovered at Gunter Weber's flat. He is the man named Jet that Archie Brookes mentioned to you. We circulated his image last night among the local maritime community and this morning a yacht master in Puerto Portals called. He described him as an itinerant deckhand.'

'Have you got him in for interview yet?'

'Hold your horses, Bel. He is currently on his way back from a working trip to Cartagena and the yacht will be docking in Palma tonight. We've already radioed through to his captain and Gaspar will pick him up on arrival.'

She smiled. 'Great work. One more piece of our jigsaw. Any news from forensics yet about the vehicles over at Jago Morey's place?'

'Nacho says they're all clean. I think we can eliminate Morey and his fancy bit, Carlotta, from the enquiry as you suggested.'

'That's helpful. Meanwhile, I'm going to speak with Paloma's boyfriend about his other freelance work. We need to know who might have placed that bug in the car and why. I've also just been with your favourite editor.'

'Not the ghastly Casanovas?' he boomed.

'Despite what you might feel about the man, he has his uses and he does edit the most popular newspaper on the island. He'll be running a piece for us tomorrow requesting information about Luz Pujals, and also about any suspicious activity in the Artà neighbourhood on the night Gunter was abducted.'

Tolo issued a sniff. 'All the same, keep an eye on him. The man's not to be trusted.'

As she finished the call, Pep bustled in with two coffees and set them on the table by the sofa. Grabbing a pad and pen from his desk, he sat close to the sleeping Furó, his face animated. 'I'm all ears.'

Isabel sunk into an armchair and blew on her coffee. 'I'm impressed, Pep. You have the makings of a proper sleuth.'

*

An hour later, Isabel sat in front of her computer, nibbling sunflower seeds. Whenever she spoke with Capitán Gómez, she felt the need to crack shells with her teeth; today was no different. She waited for him to clear his throat. A sneeze exploded in her ear; she pulled the phone away. There came the sound of a nose being blown and finally, after heavy coughing, the voice of the cold-ridden captain resumed. 'I apologise, Isabel. My flu has taken a turn for the worse but there's no time for rest. What were you just saying?'

'I was congratulating your team on identifying potential suspects with white vans in the valley. With any luck we'll soon find the culprit.'

'It is indeed progress, but we will hopefully know more following interviews with them. All five vans fit the description you gave and were in the San Martí area on the days when animals went missing. The only anomalies are Nicolas Garcia's missing cat, which took place out of the village, and the postmistress's cockerel.'

'Yes, all the missing pets are dogs apart from these two.' Isabel took a deep breath. 'Actually, I think Garcia's cat is not relevant to the case and Señora Coll's cockerel was killed by someone else entirely.'

'What on earth do you mean?'

'Rather than discuss the matter by phone, Capitán, why don't we meet with Llorenç Bestard at the town hall?'

'A highly irregular arrangement. Still, if it solves one part of this tedious mystery, so be it. Tomorrow at eleven.' Isabel heard the click of the phone and the line went dead.

She crunched on a seed and then rang Llorenç. The diminutive mayor would not be happy that the Guardia captain was calling the shots, but curiosity would no doubt get the better of him. To her relief, he was full of bonhomie.

'Ah, Bel, I have just had a marvellous lunch at Can Busquets,' he trilled. 'How can I help?'

*

It was six o'clock and Pep was in high spirits. Surrounded by colourful balloons and bunting in Bar Castell, he carefully descended a ladder, having taped a shiny 'Feliz cumpleaños, Marga!' sign on the wall facing the entrance. Rafael stood with hands on hips, surveying the room, now cleared of its tables and chairs. Instead, trestles had been set up with plates, cutlery, glasses and ice buckets in preparation for Marga's birthday celebrations. Pep adored his eldest sister. She was nine years his senior and had always spoilt him as a child. He also had a twin sister and a brother, five years older than him, but the two remained as thick as thieves and now lived in Palma with their respective families. He enjoyed seeing them at family gatherings, but Marga and he had formed their own special alliance years before and had remained close.

It had been Isabel's idea to throw a surprise birthday party for her closest girl friend at Bar Castell, much to Pep's delight. They had tricked Marga into believing that they would bring food dishes to her home for an intimate supper with her husband, Luis and daughter, Sofia. In reality, Isabel had invited Marga's extended family and good friends and neighbours to Bar Castell, and she and Rafael had devised a buffet menu to suit local tastes. As Marga was a regular, Rafael had offered Isabel wine at cost price and permitted himself only a small margin of profit on food. Isabel had driven to Morells to collect the giant *ensaïmada* from Juana's bakery before picking up her mother and Furó on the way home. Luis had agreed to lure his wife to the bar for a glass of *cava* at 7 p.m. supposedly before heading home for supper.

Fifteen minutes before Marga and her husband were due to arrive, a lively gaggle of friends and family was already milling about Bar Castell with glasses in hand. Everyone gasped in expectation then laughed when the front door swung open and a puffed Idò entered.

'Trust you to be late!' scolded Pep. 'Quickly, come into the main room and hide. It's supposed to be a surprise.'

'Alright, alright,' he grunted. 'It's only her thirty-fourth birthday, so I'm damned if I know what all the fuss is about.'

Isabel gave him a playful punch on the arm. 'Why can't we throw a party whatever the age? Besides, Marga has had a tough year, so I wanted her to have a special birthday.'

Idò patted her cheek. 'That's true enough. I stand corrected.'

Isabel thought back to the various unhappy incidents that had thwarted her friend's past year. Her beloved grandmother had suffered a sudden heart attack, a client had caused a serious fire in her hair salon by throwing a burning cigarette butt into a bin in the bathroom, and in September, Marga had slipped in rain and broken an ankle. Things could only get better.

As the hands of the church clock struck seven, there was a hush in the bar. It seemed that everyone held their breath as the sound of footsteps and cheery voices grew nearer. Pep nudged Isabel, a look of excitement on his face when the front door creaked open and Luis and Marga were greeted by an uncharacteristically exuberant Rafael at the counter. Isabel smiled when she heard her friend asking why the door to the main room was closed. With a calm voice, Rafael told her that he was redecorating and invited her to check his progress. The door slowly opened and the room erupted into laughter, as a surprised and clearly confused Marga gaped at them all in wonderment. Her husband squeezed her arm and proffered a kiss, while friends and family rushed to hug and greet her. A local musical trio began playing jazz and *cava* stoppers popped.

Isabel waited for her turn and, passing Marga a flute of bubbly, embraced her.

'Was this all your idea?' she yelled above the din.

'Pep and I plotted together,' Isabel laughed. 'It's nearly December. This is a precursor to a fantastic Christmas for you and an even better New Year.'

Marga nodded and took a sip of her drink. 'I'll drink to that! I have an amazing brother and you truly are the best friend a girl could have.'

Isabel bit her lip and, suddenly overcome with emotion, blinked hard. 'Come on, you must mingle with your guests while I sort out food with Rafael and my mother in the kitchen. I hope they're keeping an eye on Furó or there won't be any meatballs left. '

As she headed for the door, a little hand clasped her own and with delight she saw her goddaughter, Sofia, at her side.

'Come on,' Isabel whispered. 'Let's get cooking.'

Before disappearing into the kitchen, Isabel turned to see Pep receiving a bear hug from his ecstatic sister. In that moment, she'd truly never felt happier.

*

Isabel's phone was bleating before she'd even reached her front door. In the darkness, she sighed with relief to see that it was only Tolo calling her.

'This is late. I'm only just back from Marga's party.'

'I figured you might be. How did it go?'

'A riot. She was over the moon. Is everything okay?'

'Aside from the fact that I'm missing you as ever.'

Isabel gave a breezy chuckle. 'We did see one another last night, or have you forgotten already?'

'No, but I wish I could see more of you.'

'We just need time. There's so much happening in our lives.'

Tolo was quiet for a few seconds. 'True, but sometimes we have to prioritise. Anyway, that's a discussion for another day. I have some important news.'

In some relief, Isabel propped herself up against the wall in the porch. 'Come on, don't keep me in suspense.'

He stifled a yawn. 'A few things. Gaspar picked up Jet fresh off the boat in Palma. He has cooperated fully so far and in Gaspar's view is not involved at all in the disappearance of Weber. He was on the island at the time but has a solid alibi for the likely time of his abduction.'

Isabel nodded. 'I thought as much but we had to be sure.'

'Any luck with Paloma's boyfriend?'

'Pere Brotat? I had a good phone conversation with him earlier today. He has at last admitted to doing freelance work for a builder in Bunyola and picking up Paloma from Los Abetos estate there. He also collected her once from Ses Fonts.'

'How does that help us, exactly?'

'It tells us that he had direct contact, even fleetingly, with both estates where Paloma worked. Could someone on either estate have planted the bug in his car? I know that Gaspar interviewed the butler from Los Abetos and he had an alibi for the night of Paloma's disappearance, but maybe we need to look at all the staff from both residences. Remember, Paloma had been bothered by a young man.'

'But these were former clients. Why focus on her past?'

'The past is fused with the present. We have the hearts as proof of that. Everything is connected, trust me.'

'And how does this help us with the disappearance of Weber and death of Brookes? How were they connected to Paloma Crespi or Luz Pujals?'

'I don't know yet, but Gunter most certainly was. We need to dig deeper into their pasts. As for poor Archie, he was just in the wrong place at the wrong time. The abductor silenced him because he had a record of Gunter's past clients on his computer and I was on my way to retrieve them. I feel partly responsible.'

'Nonsense. You were just doing your job. Don't veer down that path.' Tolo continued in a softer tone. 'I trust your instincts on this, Bel, but tread carefully with the likes of Garcia. He's a respected sculptor and if he feels his household is under scrutiny, he may put up barriers. Los Abetos is also owned by a big-fish Madrid lawyer, so act cautiously over there, too.'

'Don't worry, I'll be discretion itself,' she replied. 'By the way, Pere mentioned that when he was at Ses Fonts, he briefly met Lourdes, Nicolas's cook. He said that she was keen to emphasise that the household was like one big family. It reminded me of a similar conversation I had with her. She's an odd one.'

'In what way?'

'She's very protective and cloying with Garcia. The relationship is a little too close for my liking. When we met, she mentioned several times how like "family" the staff were. It made me uncomfortable.'

'Staff on these estates often are close. It's a modern-day feudal system with benefits.' Tolo yawed heavily. 'Sorry, Bel, I've had a long day. The pressure is on from Madrid, so please just crack on.'

Isabel jangled the door key in her hand. 'One last thing. How is the team progressing with the other cold cases?'

'Fortunately, nothing else significant has shown up so far. There's just a handful that have anomalies. We've held them back for you.'

Isabel frowned. 'I'll be at the precinct tomorrow, so will look over them then. I need to see Nacho's forensics report on Gunter's apartment and Archie's crime scene.'

'He should have something to show you by tomorrow. I'll be back from a meeting late afternoon. We can catch up with Gaspar then.'

Isabel suddenly frowned. She remembered that she'd been meaning to check Pequeñito for possible listening devices. How else had the motorcyclist been able to track her movements? Or was she just being paranoid? Either way, under the cloak of darkness was always best for such a task. Clutching the phone, she turned and headed wearily back along her path.

Tolo's voice brought her back to the present. 'Bel, are you still there? I was just asking whether after tomorrow's meeting we might get a bite in Palma together?'

Isabel hesitated, but the thought of breaking bread and sharing wine with the man she trusted more than anyone else in the whole world proved too irresistible. 'Perfect,' she replied.

SIXTEEN

Isabel parked up close to her house and smiled as Furó jumped out of Pequeñito, shaking the last remaining drops of water from his fur. Her own hair was still dripping wet but she gathered it up in her hands and squeezed it over the kerb, as she might a sopping shirt in a sink. With a satisfied smile she pulled a biro from her pocket and used it to twist her hair into a tight topknot. With basket over her shoulder, Isabel opened the gate to Ca'n Moix, allowing Furó to pad ahead of her through the sunlit *entrada* and up the steps to the office. She could hear laughter and was puzzled that anyone should be in her home on a Saturday morning. In the height of the tourist season, Pep habitually worked several hours over the weekend, but she had encouraged him not to bother during the peaceful winter period when bookings were low.

A pair of smiling faces greeted her as she opened the door. Pep and her neighbour, Juliana, were sitting together on the sofa peering at her phone while the Gypsy Kings crooned enthusiastically in the background.

Juliana rose and gave her a peck on both cheeks. 'I just popped by to say hello before taking my seniors' Pilates class, and Pep and

I got talking about holidays. I'm just showing him some images from Brazil and South America.'

Isabel looked over Pep's shoulder. 'Can I see them too?'

'Of course,' Juliana cried. 'I was just showing him the beaches of Río de Janeiro, my home city, and some of the local *favelas*. The rest are family trips to Argentina and Chile.'

Pep stood up and patted Isabel on the shoulder. 'You sit down and I'll get you a coffee. I've seen them all.'

When he'd left, Juliana said to Isabel. 'He's such a sweet boy, isn't he? So polite. You've trained him well.'

She laughed. 'I think it's his sister, Marga, who's trained him, or possibly his girlfriend, Angélica. All the same, I like to take a little credit.'

Isabel browsed through the sunny images, and was particularly drawn to the shots of *favelas*. She had heard a lot about the infamous shantytowns around Río where there was great poverty and crime.

'Do these people get financial help?' she asked.

Juliana shrugged. 'The people of the *favelas* are very proud and most don't want sympathy or handouts. They work hard and eke out a living, though drug crime and robberies can make life difficult for the communities.'

Isabel nodded slowly, her eyes attracted by a stunning image of some tall wooden statues. 'What are these?'

Juana frowned. 'Ah, yes, those are *chemamüll*, made by the Mapuche people. I think we saw them in Argentina or Chile. It was some years ago.'

'They're enormous,' Isabel replied.

'Some are over four metres in height and are all made by hand.'

Isabel flicked to another image. 'And what are those? Two poodles wearing tutus and *sombreros*?'

Juliana threw her head back and laughed. 'I took that shot during the animal parade on Copacabana beach! Aren't they cute?'

'You Brazilians certainly know how to live!' Isabel handed the phone back to her. 'So who is attending your class this morning?'

'Your mother and Doctor Ramis and my nice English neighbour, Mrs French. I've also signed up Señora Coll and some other local elderly ladies.'

'So is Doctor Ramis the only male attending?'

'Yes, and he's loving it!' She looked at her watch. 'Gosh, I must be on my way. The class starts at 9 a.m.'

Pep stepped aside at the top of the staircase as Juliana waved and hurtled past. He placed the coffee in front of Isabel and exhaled deeply.

'That woman is a ball of energy. She must be at least fifty but she's like a teenager.'

Isabel picked up the cup and offered him a grateful smile. 'If you don't dwell on age, it's amazing what you can achieve. Fifty is hardly old, Pep! Anyway, why are you in the office today?'

Pep sat on his desk. 'It beats going to Soller market with Angélica and her mother. I'm also trying to get my head around this animal kidnapping. It's bothering me.'

'Admirable, Pep.'

'Those five white vans the Guardia identified all belong to locals we know. None of them would steal dogs.'

'Really? You think they're all law-abiding citizens?'

He gaped at her. 'All of them own their own dogs, for one thing.'

'A perfect alibi, Pep.'

'You think?'

'Indeed. I'm sure that the thief is a pet owner. That is how he knows how to handle animals. The problem with the list of white van owners is that all of them lease or lend their vans to others, so it widens the net.'

Pep offered a deflated sigh. 'That's what I thought. So we're no closer to catching the guy.'

'Yes, we are. All the dogs have been stolen for a purpose and I believe it is blackmail. To our knowledge, none have been hurt yet, and let's hope it remains that way.'

'Blackmail?' he remonstrated. 'But none of the owners have received any demands, have they?'

'Not that we know about, but I'm sure they will soon. Each and every one of them must have a connection with the thief. Let us keep digging that seam first before worrying too much about the various van drivers.'

Isabel whisked up Furó under her arm and carried him to his basket. She returned to the communal office with an open packet of sunflower seeds and knocked back the last dregs of her coffee. 'Talking of poor Carlos, the cockerel, I now have a meeting with Llorenç and Gómez to discuss that very subject.'

Pep pulled a face.

She nodded. 'Exactly. So, wish me luck.'

*

Isabel strode across the *plaça*, offering a friendly wave to Padre Agustí on the way. He stood with hands crossed benevolently in front of him, talking to an elderly parishioner outside Bon Día. Fearful that he might question her about her next attendance at the parish church, she lowered her head and stepped determinedly towards the large wooden doors of the town hall. As she reached the top floor office of Llorenç Bestard, her phone rang.

'Hello Josep. Any news?'

'Nothing on the Gunter Weber front, I'm afraid. No one has reported witnessing anything peculiar in Artà that night. However, a woman named Ana Blanes rang in connection with Luz Pujals. She handled work assignments for her.'

Isabel caught the eye of Sandra, Llorenç's secretary, who pointed urgently to the mayor's closed door. Isabel gave her a thumb's up sign.

'That is fantastic, Josep, but I will have to call you back. I have a meeting with the mayor.'

He laughed. 'Llorenç Bestard? Ah, do send the dear old boy my best. Soon we will be attending functions together, shoulder to shoulder, as island mayors.'

Isabel sighed impatiently and, offering hurried platitudes, finished the call.

'Hurry,' hissed Llorenç's secretary. 'Capitán Gómez has already arrived. He's in a grumpy mood.'

With a groan, Isabel knocked on the door and entered the room.

The Guardia captain was sitting across the desk from Llorenç and blowing heartily into a large white handkerchief. He observed Isabel with red-rimmed eyes and rose to his feet with a sniff.

Isabel waved him back into his chair and smiled at Llorenç. 'Please, gentlemen, don't get up for me. I'm sure you both have busy agendas, so let's get down to business.'

Llorenç nodded and beckoned to his secretary who had appeared at the door. 'Coffees all around and some tasty rolls would be nice.'

Capitán Gómez shook his head sombrely. 'Just a black coffee for me. I have no appetite with this cold.'

Isabel winked at Sandra. 'I'm starving as always.'

The woman chortled and bustled out while Llorenç fixed his beady eyes on Isabel.

'Come on, tell us what's going on. Who killed poor Señora Coll's cockerel?'

Isabel shifted in her chair. 'I believe the culprit is Gori Bauza, her next-door neighbour.'

'Bauza? But he was the first to raise the alarm!' he exclaimed.

'I'm sure he was,' replied Isabel with irony. 'It didn't strike me as odd at the time, but when I put two and two together, it all made sense. For one thing, all the abducted animals were dogs, so the cockerel was an anomaly. Furthermore, if one wanted to get rid of a neighbour's annoying pet, our animal thief would offer a perfect alibi.'

'So what did Bauza have against the postmistress and her cockerel, and where is your evidence, Isabel?' asked Capitán Gómez.

'I bumped into him at Bon Día buying chocolates, supposedly for Señora Coll. He was also purchasing a bottle of *cava* so I advised him not to bother as she doesn't drink alcohol.'

The mayor nodded. 'That's true enough.'

'But Gori Bauza told me the *cava* was for him and his wife. This was refuted later when I ran into her. She insisted that he disliked Señora Coll and that the cockerel had stopped him from sleeping.'

Capitán Gómez leant forward in his chair and placed a hand on his forehead. 'This village tittle tattle is giving me a headache. Do we have hard evidence such as a weapon with Bauza's DNA?'

Llorenç burst out laughing, his eyes lighting up when Sandra arrived bearing a huge tray of assorted *bocadillos* and coffees.

'If we got the forensic team up here every time a cockerel was found dead, they'd soon have to open their own Sant Martí unit.'

'That's true, but this was a nasty, premeditated killing by Gori Bauza who used the dog thefts to mask his own crime. It's abhorrent that he should kill Señora Coll's beloved Carlos and get away with it,' replied Isabel.

'All supposition,' said Capitán Gómez, helping himself to a coffee. 'Without evidence you have no case. Just because this Bauza chap pretended to buy chocolates for the postmistress doesn't make him the killer.'

'Nor an adulterer,' replied Isabel.

Both men stared at her.

'Well he was obviously buying the chocolates and *cava* for a lover if neither his wife nor the postmistress were the recipients. Who else?'

'Again, supposition,' replied the captain, massaging his temples. 'Maybe he was going to gorge them all himself!'

The mayor threw out his hands dramatically. 'Returning to Carlos, how can we get evidence, Capitán, if the cockerel is now dead and buried?'

'You can't,' he replied flatly. 'I concede that your suspicions are probably correct, Isabel, but without hard proof, I'm afraid you have no case.'

The mayor took a huge bite of his roll. 'Then we'll have to find it. All the same, at least we only have to worry about one thief now, though there's still the mystery surrounding Nicolas Garcia's cat.'

Capitán Gómez cursed silently. 'To think someone of my rank has to deal with such frivolities. As far as I'm concerned, the owners of these unfortunate lost animals should just invest in replacements and save my force wasted time and effort. We have a lot of other work currently.'

Isabel chewed thoughtfully on her Manchego cheese and salad roll. 'Perhaps you're right, Capitán.'

He eyed her suspiciously. 'Still, I would like to find the maniac who nearly ran you over in that white van, Isabel. We cannot tolerate such behaviour.'

Taking one last sip of his coffee, he stood up and faced them both. 'My force will continue to question the owners of the white vans, and in the meantime, I would forget the whole cockerel affair. None of us should lose sleep over a wretched bird.'

Isabel wished him better and as soon as he'd left, helped herself to another roll.

'That man is obnoxious!' grumbled Llorenç.

'He's even more unbearable with a cold. Let's leave him to get tough with those van owners while we sort out Bauza.'

'But what can we do without evidence?' he asked miserably. 'I thought you agreed with Gómez to let sleeping dogs lie?'

'Of course not,' she winked. 'Besides, you and I might know we don't have proof, but does Gori Bauza? I think it's time to call his bluff.'

Llorenç banged a triumphant hand on his desk. 'Excellent. So what's the plan?'

*

On the country road from Sant Martí to Fornalutx, a three-hundred-year-old *finca* was being lovingly restored by one of the valley's most powerful contractors. A large team of construction workers, most paid cash-in-hand, were toiling over large rocks and boulders. In the busy throng, Isabel recognised the weary form of Gori Bauza as he transported a pile of debris in a wheelbarrow to the site's dump. Placing her thumb and forefinger between her lips, she emitted a sharp whistle and saw the man look up and squint in her direction. She watched his shoulders rise as he tipped the barrow up on its front wheel and scattered the rubble. Casting it aside, he set off in her direction with a wolf-like lope, looking over his shoulder to check he wasn't being monitored by his companions. The sun was high in the sky and the man's plump face was basted in sweat. Isabel smiled cheerily as he approached.

'Sorry for interrupting your work, Gori, but I do need a quick word.'

'About what?' He nervously ran a hand through his thick chestnut locks.

Isabel led him over to a low stone wall and invited him to sit. 'I'm afraid, Gori, the cat's out of the bag.'

'What are you talking about?'

Isabel shook her head sorrowfully. 'I'm afraid the remains of poor Señora Coll's cockerel were exhumed by the police some days ago and Llorenç received a report from the forensic team this morning.'

Gori Bauza's mouth fell open. 'The Guardia dug up the cockerel?'

'I'm afraid that with this animal thief still on the loose, the captain in charge felt no stone should be left unturned. Naturally Llorenç was shocked to see the name of the culprit that was revealed from a direct DNA match. I think you know what I'm going to say.'

The man sat perfectly still as the full weight of her words hit home. Isabel set unblinking eyes on his face until he could bear the silence no more. He put his head in his hands.

'It was driving me mad. Night and day, the damned creature crowed and gave me no rest. That woman is a menace. She's always snooping on me.'

'I find it curious that you were only recently disturbed by Carlos, the cockerel, bearing in mind that he lived next door to you for four years. Could it have more to do with the problems in your marriage and a guilty conscience? Is that why you didn't like Señora Coll's snooping?'

Gori Bauza cursed. 'What don't you know? Who told you about Elisa? '

Isabel maintained an air of calm. 'I'm afraid I cannot divulge my sources, but you haven't helped yourself buying chocolates and *cava* from Bon Día for your secret trysts. You might as well have announced your affair to the whole queue.'

'Elisa's been upset recently because I won't leave my wife. We've been seeing each other for almost a year and she's growing restless. I thought if I bought her some gifts, I could calm her down and put things right.'

'And has it?' she asked crisply.

'No. After you talked to my wife, she asked me what was going on. I told her the truth. Now Elisa doesn't want to see me anymore and the wife's not talking to me.'

'How sad. Well, you could always drown your sorrows with the *cava*, I suppose. Does your wife know that you killed Carlos?'

'Of course not. She gets on alright with the old busybody next door.'

'In that case, if you don't want your problems to get a whole lot worse, I'd advise you to agree to Llorenç's conditions unless you want a jail term.'

'What conditions?'

'You will buy Señora Coll a new Carlos. For now, let's call him Carlos II, but he will not be just any cockerel, he will be a king among birds and the envy of the village. I have located a breeder of the rare Ayam Ketawa Indonesian variety on the island. It is known as the laughing chicken.'

'Why's that?'

'Because it has a loud and manic laugh. It is very rare and was revered for generations by the Buginese royal family in Indonesia. It represents heroism, courage and a high social status, attributes you appear to lack. Naturally it doesn't come cheap. It will cost you four hundred euros.'

'You've got be joking! I haven't got that kind of money, and no way am I buying the old boot another damned cockerel. It would drive me mad.'

'Yes, this one possibly will. It's also known as the asylum bird for good reason. You will buy it, and in doing so, will buy our silence. Otherwise, you will be handed over to the Guardia Civil for punishment.'

'That's nearly a quarter of my monthly wages,' he grumbled.

'Maybe next time you'll think hard before killing your neighbour's pet. In fact, you're lucky. The only reason Llorenç isn't turning you over to the authorities is to ensure that poor Señora Coll never finds out that her next-door neighbour acted so callously.'

Isabel stood up. 'You will come to the town hall tonight at 7 p.m. sharp to agree to the purchase of the bird and to sign an official document in Llorenç's presence. We will shortly arrange a surprise presentation in the village square at which you will hand over the Ayam Ketawa to Señora Coll. I'd save those chocolates too. She'll enjoy them.'

'I'll be the laughing stock of the village.'

'Far from it. I think you'll be applauded for such a generous gesture and Señora Coll will hopefully have a new spring in her step.' She paused. 'You never know, it might prove the first time in your life that you'll actually have something to crow about!'

SEVENTEEN

As office bookings were slow and Pep had shown so much interest in her police work of late, Isabel decided to invite him along on her visit to Los Abetos. It was already 1.30 p.m. and she still had a lot to squeeze into the rest of her day. When Pequeñito pulled up at a set of large and showy wrought-iron gates, Pep emitted a low whistle.

'Who'd have thought these places existed here. This pile has to be worth at least three million.'

Isabel laughed. 'Trust me, Pep, this will be worth about ten times as much. I did a little research online. The house has twelve bedrooms, two pools, a subterranean spa and gym, staff quarters and five guest houses. It also has a tennis court, cocktail bar, stables and helipad.'

'Maybe I should have been a hot shot lawyer,' sighed Pep.

'Why? So that you could make piles of money back in the city and visit your palatial estate only once a year? And probably be miserable, stressed out, unloved and surrounded by sycophants and finally, after never really appreciating life, die alone of a heart attack.'

Pep rolled his eyes. 'I knew I shouldn't have said anything.'

A voice crackled through the intercom. 'Señora Flores, do drive up to the front of the house and I'll meet you there.'

Isabel nudged Pep. 'That must be Vincente Diaz, the butler. At least we're not being sent to the back door.'

'What does he do if the owner is away all the time?'

'I imagine he potters about, keeping an eye on other staff and making sure the house is shipshape for when his master returns.'

'Not a bad job. I could do that.'

'I think you'd be bored stiff, Pep. Besides, you'd have to wait hand on foot on the owner whenever he pitched up.'

'If I was paid enough, I could do it.'

Isabel laughed. 'Angélica might have a view on the matter.'

'No doubt,' he replied cheerlessly.

A tall and elegantly attired man stood on the gravel drive watching as Isabel approached the courtyard. With a welcoming wave, he came towards Pequeñito and with a flamboyant flourish, opened Isabel's door and shook her hand as she exited the vehicle.

'It is a delight to welcome you here, Señorita Flores.' Then, eyeing Pep, he rushed to the passenger door and ushered him out.

'I'm fine, thanks,' said Pep, appearing rather abashed.

The butler returned to Isabel. 'Just leave the keys in the ignition. Your car will be parked in the garage and given a nice buff.'

'Is that normal practice around here?' she asked.

'Indeed. It is a sign of hospitality, especially as our tracks are so muddy and dusty. Surely it's the very least one can do for a guest?'

Isabel cocked her head to one side and examined the affable man before her. He had smooth, honey-coloured skin and deep-set, dark eyes that resembled woodland berries. 'Señor Diaz, I believe?'

He smiled genially and nodded.

'So how long have you worked here?'

He waved an arm expansively in the air. 'I met my boss in Neuquén, where I was born. It is a city in the east of Argentina. At the time, I was a twenty-year-old waiter in a hotel, and when he told me he was looking for a butler, I begged him for the job. He agreed to give me training and I moved over here. That was eighteen years ago.'

'And does he visit here often?' asked Isabel.

He exhaled deeply. 'Sadly not. My boss is a very busy lawyer and is always travelling. He has homes in London and New York, so is rarely here.'

'It must be a stressful job,' she replied.

'He is always under pressure, and when he divorced last year, he had a lot of problems.'

Isabel offered Pep a surreptitious wink. 'Well, I always say money doesn't buy happiness.'

'So true.' He said soberly while Pep gave her a nudge.

The butler broke into a smile. 'Anyway, I am forgetting my manners. Do come through to the drawing room for a coffee. I'll do my best to help you in any way regarding poor Paloma.'

Isabel and Pep followed him to a bright and graceful parlour with views to a pristine lawn and rose garden. The luxurious sofas and chairs appeared to be liveried in sage velvet and the oak floor was strewn with exquisite wool and silk rugs in a palette of greys and greens. Mushroom-coloured walls were dotted with abstract paintings and perfectly poised citrus trees stood to attention in large decorative terracotta pots on either side of a stone hearth. Isabel fretted about how they might be affected whenever a fire was lit and wondered whether staff relocated them. When Vincente left the room to organise their coffees, Pep faced Isabel with hands on hips.

'I've never seen a place like this. It's so grand.'

'It certainly is,' she replied, studying the ancient leather-bound tomes in one of the vast bookcases. 'He seems a friendly chap. Maybe Amerindian? He has a beautiful face.'

'Don't tell Tolo that or he'll be jealous.'

Isabel frowned. 'He wouldn't mind at all. We're just good friends.'

'So you keep saying,' Pep smirked.

The door opened and Vincente returned bearing a silver tray loaded with coffees, mineral water and tiny iced cakes. Pep was captivated by the apparition, his eyes trained on the tray until it was set down in front of him.

The butler smiled. 'Our chef creates wonderful sweets. These are made with honey and macadamia nuts and the others are dark chocolate fondants with agave syrup. Do help yourselves.'

Isabel almost burst out laughing as Pep stuffed a whole fondant into his mouth, the dark icing giving him a shiny moustache. The butler rushed forward and placed a white linen serviette on his lap, then handed Isabel her coffee.

'I wonder if you might give me a list of all your employees?'

Vincente turned to her. 'Of course, but it is a short list. Just the chef, valet, gardener and me. We also have a small team of local women who come here most days to clean and deal with the laundry.'

'And returning to Paloma's disappearance, can you tell me about your dealings with her?'

He shrugged and the corners of his mouth twitched. 'It is such a tragedy that she has still not been found. She was a lovely girl, always so willing and conscientious. As I told your colleague, Gaspar, she worked here as a freelance florist for nearly eighteen months, visiting the estate every week. We were all very sad when she left without explanation. That was a fortnight before she disappeared.'

'Why do you think that was?'

'I have no idea. She seemed to love her job.'

'But she also quit the Ses Fonts estate shortly before that.'

He nodded. 'I knew about that. She had told me that the journey was getting too onerous and she'd found more work locally in Sant Joan. She promised to continue with us but a week later, she was gone.'

'Did she get on with the other staff?'

'Yes, indeed. She was well liked by all. Marc, my chef, was devoted to her, always picking her up from Bunyola station and making her nice snacks for lunch. She was very much part of the team.'

Isabel nibbled on her honey cake. 'Your chef has been here a while too?'

'He arrived two years ago. He is a young man who studied catering in Switzerland and Italy. He is quite a perfectionist and comes from a respected family in Palma. He may only be twenty-seven years old, but he has an impressive work history in Europe and speaks several languages.'

Pep stopped mid-bite, trying to read Isabel's face. 'These are delicious!'

Vincente smiled. 'I'll get Marc to give you a box to take home. You must meet him.' He pushed a staff call button discreetly mounted on a wall, and minutes later, Marc, a tall and well-built figure dressed in an unsullied white apron, appeared. He gave a slight bow as he was introduced. Isabel found herself transfixed by his smooth, shiny skull and muscly torso. He seemed as strong as an ox.

'Our kind guests were admiring your cakes, Marc. Can we send them home with a selection?'

'Of course, sir.' He stood by the door with hands clasped in front of him, casting a nervous eye over Isabel. She offered him an encouraging smile.

'Señor Diaz was just telling me that you and Paloma Crespí were close friends.'

His face went blank. 'Not really. We got on well but she was quite distant. It's a pity that she left.'

'It's even more of a pity that she's gone missing,' she replied.

'Yes, of course. I hope she's found safe and well.'

'Where were you on the night of her disappearance?'

He shrugged. 'Here in the house all night. I rarely go out in the winter. It's a long way to the village from here.'

'Did Paloma ever tell you anything about her life or friends?'

He shook his head. 'We only really talked about our jobs and music.'

'What music did she like?' asked Pep, wiping his fingers on his napkin.

Marc stared across at him. 'She liked jazz and singers like Joni Mitchell. She had a ring on her third finger with a J on it for Joni.'

Pep grinned. 'That's a bit obsessive.'

'Why? If you like someone enough, you'll always want to keep a part of them with you.'

'Even a complete stranger?' balked Pep.

'Yes, I think so,' he replied with a faint smile. He turned to Vincente. 'Will that be all, sir?'

The butler looked across at Isabel and nodding, watched as Marc left the room.

'Does he always call you sir?' asked Pep.

'Only when guests are here. We have certain protocols in place.'

Pep smiled. 'Your chef looks fit. Does he work out?'

Vincente chuckled. 'We have a subterranean gym and he spends most of his spare time there. He could lift a horse.'

Isabel looked up from her notebook, pen hovering in the air. 'Our team in Palma will need to take statements from all your staff members about their whereabouts on the night of Paloma's disappearance. They are not implicated in any way. We are just trying to eliminate all possibilities. '

'No problem. As Marc said, we were all here at the house. A few nights each week we dine informally together at around 6 p.m. and that Monday was one of those occasions. We must have cleared up in the kitchen around 7 p.m.'

'What happened after dinner? Asked Isabel.

'I took a scheduled call with my boss, who was ringing from London. We spoke for about an hour. You can check the phone records. The others all returned to their quarters. Marc and Julian, our valet, live in the main house like me, and the gardener has a small cottage in the grounds. He is elderly and lives there with his wife.'

'Did either your valet or chef leave the house that night?'

'I did explain to your colleague, Gaspar Fernández, that I heard the shower being used in Marc's suite and the television was on in Julian's room. He is in Valencia currently visiting his sick father, but when he returns, I will arrange for him to contact you.'

'Did you see either man again that evening?' she asked.

'Indeed. Julian and I played rummy at about nine o'clock and had a few glasses of wine. Then we chatted and played music.'

'And did Marc join you?' asked Pep.

'No, but he likes to get an early night as he is up at dawn, busy in the kitchen.'

'Who assumes the valet's responsibilities when he's away?' Isabel asked.

'That depends, but Marc and I share most of his duties, such as overseeing the laundry, car maintenance and the like.'

'Can I see the cars you keep here on the estate? I'm afraid our time is short but it would be marvellous to have a quick look.'

The butler rose slowly and placing his napkin on his plate, buttoned up his dark jacket. 'Our home is your home. We have no secrets.'

As they headed towards the hallway, Isabel turned to him. 'Do you remember a young man picking Paloma up in a car one day? His name was Pere.'

He nodded. 'Yes, quite a shy boy. He came in for a drink while he waited for Paloma and was thrilled to see that his car was cleaned while he was at the house.'

'Who cleaned it?' she asked.

'I think it was Marc as our valet has been away off and on in Valencia during his father's sickness. I will check for you now.'

While he was gone, Isabel called Gaspar and arranged for statements to be taken from members of the household and also those at Ses Fonts. Every person Paloma was in recent contact with had to be eliminated. Vincente returned.

'As I thought, it was Marc. If he wasn't a chef, he'd be a mechanic! He adores cars and fast bikes. We all muck in here, especially if someone's absent. Let me take you to the car port.'

Isabel smiled politely and followed him to a large outbuilding with sliding doors that was able to hold multiple vehicles. She took images and studied the various number plates while Pep walked around in wonderment like a child in a toy shop.

In the front courtyard, after their visit, Isabel stood with arms outstretched, smiling in front of Pequeñito. 'My car is gleaming!'

'That will be Marc.'

'It's very kind of him but I worry that Pequeñito will grow to expect this kind of treatment. At Ses Fonts, my car was also cleaned.'

'Nicolas Garcia has an excellent valet in Andel and a very special cook named Lourdes. She is devoted to him.'

'Ah yes, we have met. Aside from recommending Paloma to Nicolas, did you assist him with finding other staff?'

'On occasion, we've recommended freelancers. I'm not sure how he came across his core team. Lourdes and her husband Ismael are from Soller, and Andel and Raul, the gardener, have both been there donkeys' years and hail from the nearby village of Escorca. Those of us on large estates try to help one another with staffing matters when needed.'

'How cordial,' Isabel replied.

As they drove away, she gnawed agitatedly on her lower lip. 'There's something strange about all these people. It's the phrase "like family" they all use that gives me the shivers.'

Pep ran a hand through his wavy, dark locks. 'That chef is a right weirdo. Imagine being stuck up there all winter with him? Mind you, his cakes are pretty good. Angélica will love these.' He tapped the pink-ribboned carton sitting on his knee.

As they turned onto the main road into Bunyola, Isabel looked across at him. 'You noticed that there were two powerful motorbikes in the garage, and, more importantly, an Alfa Romeo?'

'A Giulia Ti, to be exact. There was an article about it in one of my car mags recently. To be honest, I was more interested in the Porsche and the Nissan GT-R. They also had two Range Rovers.'

She slid him a grin. 'But dear Pep, only the Alfa Romeo had Continental branded tyres.'

*

Isabel was shouting at her speaker phone in the car but Josep Casanovas's voice kept petering out. Finally, Pep rang him manually and held the phone to Isabel's ear as they passed through the Soller tunnel.

'Bel, I was just saying that this woman, Ana Blanes, who called our newspaper, used to run an employment agency for wealthy estate owners here in the Baleares. She remembers Luz Pujals well.'

'Brilliant. What is she doing now?'

'I've no idea. I'll leave that to you to find out. Remember you owe me.'

'Sure. Drinks on me next time.'

'I'll hold you to that.'

Isabel indicated to Pep that she'd finished the call.

'Is he still following you around like a lapdog?' he asked.

'Lapdogs have their uses, Pep.'

He sat back in his seat. 'After you've dropped me off, are you going straight to the precinct?'

She nodded. 'I'll try to pay a visit to Ana Blanes first if she's free. I've also got to return to Ses Fonts.'

'Why?'

'Because I need to talk to Nicolas Garcia about his missing cat and find out more about the staff there.'

'You think they're all suspects too?'

'Everyone who came into contact with Paloma or Pere is currently a suspect. We need to erase as many people as we can from our enquiries.'

'But say it's just a random psychopath?' he quizzed.

'It isn't. Whoever abducted Paloma also abducted Luz Pujals and Gunter Weber, and who knows, there may be others out there we're completely unaware of. According to Tolo, he has a few cold cases he wants me to see.'

'So there's some maniac on the loose who abducted people before and has now started again?'

'I don't think he or she ever really stopped. There was a lull and that must have been for a very good reason. Don't for a moment believe that these abductions aren't connected. We are dealing with a cunning serial killer who is back on the trail and must be stopped. Once we unravel the stitching, the garment will all come apart very quickly.'

'What have they got in common?'

'I don't know, but if we can ascertain that they all had connections in some way with these two estates it would be a big help.'

Pep was silent for a while. 'Do you think any of them are still alive?'

Isabel pulled a face. 'What, like in the Hollywood movies, being held in an underground cellar waiting for the *caval*ry to arrive? Sadly not. I think they were all disposed of soon after they were taken. I can't explain why, but I feel they did something that made certain parties angry and disappointed. The wooden heart is the key. Why leave it?'

'Because whoever took them is a complete lunatic?'

'Think, Pep. What does a heart signify?'

'Romance? Love?'

'Exactly. Whoever did this wants us to believe that the abduction was as a result of love. Maybe this is about betrayal.'

Pep wrinkled his nose. 'So Paloma and Gunter are both dead?'

'I can't say for certain, but it's highly likely. They were punished.'

'Could there be more than one killer?'

'Anything is possible. We must rule out nothing at this stage.'

As Isabel parked abruptly outside her front door, she saw a flash of blue uniform and Pau approached the car. She slammed her door and eyed him expectantly.

'Can I have a private word, Bel?'

Pep, offered a friendly and discreet nod, and set off along the garden path to the house while Isabel waited by the front gate. She looked up and down her quiet street to ensure that there were no eavesdroppers.

Pau spoke in a low tone. 'As the local officer for Sant Martí, Llorenç took me into his confidence about Gori Bauza killing Señora Coll's cockerel. I'm angry that he did such a vile thing, but I do understand why this should be kept under wraps. We don't want a community at war.'

'Quite. If it makes you feel better, when the Ayam Ketawa arrives, he'll wish he was never born.'

He grinned and then his face fell. 'There is something else. Teo Darder and I are on patrol tonight. It's been quiet and aside from your scrape with that speeding van, there haven't been any more animal thefts. All the same, we've no idea what has happened to our pets or if we'll ever find the culprit. I can't bear to think that my Llamp may have been killed.'

Isabel gave a sigh. 'The Guardia has narrowed its search of potential white vans but there are probably twenty people who have access to those vehicles. One of them is certainly our man.'

'I know that, but what if we get too close and the culprit panics and kills all of the dogs?'

'That would be the worst-case scenario but I think there is more to this. These animals were stolen for a purpose. Out of interest, is there anyone here in Sant Martí who might hold a grudge against you?'

He laughed. 'I'm the local copper. Probably most people.'

'You told me that you made some home improvements recently and so did the other victims.'

'Come on, Bel, I don't think having new windows installed is of great interest. Ruben, the carpenter, fixed them.'

'Does he rent his van and is it white?'

'Of course. Loads of workmen around here rent vans and they're always white. Anyway, I've got to go. Let's keep in touch.'

Isabel was about to enter the house when she heard a '*Uepppp!*' from the other side of her garden wall. Staring down at her aloft a rickety wooden ladder was Doctor Ramis.

'How long have you been there?' she asked suspiciously.

'Only this second, Bel. I just heard Pau saying his farewells as I came down the path. So how is life?'

'As complicated as ever.'

'That's what makes it so compelling, my dear girl. Take my afternoon. I thought I'd do some deadheading of these roses, and then escort your mother to see a fine film, followed by a good sherry in a Palma *vermutería*.'

'Another movie?'

'Why not? We have our own exclusive film club *à deux*. This afternoon we are off to see *Muerte de un ciclista*.'

'Death of a cyclist, that sounds cheery. I won't be recommending it to any of my cycling clients.'

'It's quite a masterpiece by Juan Antonio Bardem. It was a huge success at the Cannes festival in 1955.'

'What a charmed life you lead, Doctor Ramis,' she said with a wink.

'And so would you, if you'd only disengage yourself from the criminal world.'

Laughing, Isabel entered the house and discovered Pep upstairs standing in front of the whiteboard.

'I'm trawling through all the notes you took. I think it's worth studying the timeline of those who've had pets stolen. It might rule out some of those van drivers. Can you remember anything else about the vehicle?'

'As I told Capitán Gómez, it came straight at me with its headlights on full beam. It was a large van with panels, maybe a Renault, but I couldn't say for certain.'

'That's the kind of van every workman has.'

Isabel nodded. 'Regardless, it's a great idea to go over those notes. Police work is mostly about meticulous checking. The devil is always in the detail.' She puffed out her cheeks. 'And we mustn't forget that a good percentage of white van owners and those borrowing vehicles from them will fib about their whereabouts at the time of the animal disappearances as most will have been working on the black.'

Pep sighed. 'I hadn't thought of that. A local Guardia officer told me yesterday that they've got some very urgent matters to deal with in Soller, so our pet problem is an extra hassle. I don't think they're taking it too seriously.'

'That doesn't surprise me. Our friend Capitán Gómez certainly isn't.'

Pep opened a drawer. 'Before you head off for Palma, I wanted to show you the map of San Martí you asked me to draw.'

Isabel studied it closely. 'I love it. It's so pictorial and fun. Well done. I like that you've got Marga's hair salon in there, and also our offices.'

He grinned. 'I also put in the town hall and all the bars, of course.'

'Our renters will really appreciate it. When you've drawn the final version, can you get a hundred copies printed on good quality paper?'

Having left him absorbed at his task, Isabel telephoned Ana Blanes, the former employment agent in Palma. She was polite and helpful but unable to meet until the following day as she was staying with her elderly mother out of town. Isabel looked out of her window and called to Mrs Buncle. The rotund and tawny figure looked up at her and clucked copiously before disappearing into the undergrowth. Isabel thought about the Ayam Ketawa that would be presented to Señora Coll. She had seen an online video of the unusual cockerel and found the manic laugh rather cheering. If she saved up to buy one, would her cockerel approve? As if he'd read her thoughts, Salvador strutted in front of the window below and hollered loudly.

'So you don't like the idea?' she asked him. 'Fair enough. You'll remain my king.'

Kissing Furó gently on the head while he slept in his basket, she grabbed her car keys and a Chupa Chup lolly. Pep looked up.

'When will you be back?'

'Late, so please lock up and make sure Furó has his afternoon feed.'

'Yes, madam.' Pep gave a mock salute. 'As if I'd forget.'

'What are your plans for tonight?'

He offered her a sheepish glance. 'I'm taking Angélica for dinner at Can Busquets to talk about putting off the engagement.'

Isabel's eyes popped. 'Maybe have a large glass of wine before you go. *Suerte*!'

At the gate, she studied the towering, denuded plane trees that lined her peaceful street, and felt their sorrow. How they must yearn for their springtime bushy cloak of leaves that gave them such a svelte appearance. Once in the car, Isabel turned on the ignition and Pequeñito roared into life. Delighting in the dense woodland on either side of her, Isabel coursed along the mountain road in the direction of Palma, singing cheerfully at the top of her voice.

EIGHTEEN

Isabel sat on a white plastic chair in Nacho's office. It was a slow Saturday afternoon and there was an air of exhaustion at the precinct. Most of the officers unlucky enough still to be on a shift were already dreaming of how they would spend Sunday away from their desks. Nacho was no different. It had been a long week and he was happy that by 7 p.m., he would be able to return home to spend time with his wife and baby. Luckily he lived in central Palma, a swift cycle ride from the office, so didn't have the headache of parking and traffic jams that many of his colleagues had.

As he returned to his pokey office – more a glorified walk-in cupboard – balancing two hot coffees, he smiled to see Isabel playing with his Rubik's cube. Placing the cups on his desk, he watched as she calmly twisted the multi-coloured object around until each face displayed one solid block of colour. He clapped, and then pulling a hair tie from his drawer, gathered his dark mane into a loose ponytail and took a sip of coffee. A small gold stud glinted in his right ear.

He smiled at her. 'When did you learn to do that?'

'My father used to have a Rubik's Cube on his desk at home and he'd time my brother and me as we raced to finish it. His was an original from the seventies.'

'You know its inventor was a Hungarian professor?'

Isabel blew on her coffee. 'Ernö Rubik, I remember. My father hailed him as a genius. Rubik credited his engineer father for being his inspiration.'

'You come from a competitive family.'

'If only it was that simple,' she laughed.

Nacho sat down opposite her and drummed his fingers on the desk. 'Why is it, Bel, that every case you get involved in turns out to be horribly complex and frustrating?'

She shrugged. 'I guess Tolo just likes giving me all the fun stuff to work on.'

He smiled. 'Well, I've a few things of interest for you. I can tell you with some confidence that judging by the blood spatter found in Gunter Weber's apartment that there was a significant struggle between two people. I'd wager that Weber was badly hurt before he was removed unconscious from the apartment. I'd be amazed if the neighbours didn't hear a rumpus.'

Isabel issued a sigh. 'There were no neighbours. I called Weber's rentals agent, yesterday and she told me that the other flats in the block were all rented by holiday owners. None are on the island at present.'

'So our abductor had a bit of luck then. After he knocked out the victim, he attempted to clean the kitchen area, where the struggle took place.'

'You're sure the assailant was male?'

He shrugged. 'Fairly certain, but it could have been a very fit woman, I suppose. Whatever, it looked like a rushed job, so I would assume that things hadn't gone according to plan.'

'What do you mean?'

'It seems that the attacker had hoped to subdue the victim without a fight using chloroform as we detected traces of it in a saliva sample at the crime scene, but it appears that Weber chose not to go quietly. This is mostly supposition, but it hangs together.'

Isabel eyed him thoughtfully. 'And what about the wooden heart that I found?'

He sighed. 'I'm afraid it was completely clean and only Weber's DNA was evident at the apartment. It's extraordinary that the abductor risked returning to place that heart on Weber's bed. Whoever it is evidently enjoys taunting you.'

He opened a file in front of him and swivelled the contents towards Isabel.

'As for poor Archie Brookes, he was attacked from behind with a heavy metal object. It would appear to be a monkey wrench judging by the force of the blow and the damage inflicted.'

'And what about the house and grounds? Anything of interest there?'

He shook his head. 'Your abductor had unplugged a laptop and there was no mobile phone to be found. There had evidently been a frantic search of his office. Files were strewn all over the floor.' He paused. 'We did find faint motorbike tracks and footprints close to the house but they had deteriorated badly in the rain.'

'Would you say it was a pre-meditated or spontaneous killing?'

As if reading her mind, he patted her hand. 'You know the answer to that but don't blame yourself. Your swift actions galvanised him into an unplanned murder but the killer would have tracked Brookes down once he realised that he might hold background information about Weber's past clients.'

Isabel leant her elbows on the desk and cupped her chin in her hands. 'I keep wondering about the dogs. Whoever did this went out of his way to treat them humanely, giving them food and water while he pummelled their owner to death. Such a dichotomy.'

'As you know, psychopaths often like dogs as they can be controlled and mostly show obedience.'

'Good point,' Isabel replied. 'That's if we are dealing with a psychopath.'

'You're doubtful?'

'I think we have a serial killer on our hands but not necessarily a psychopathic one.'

'That's a comfort,' he said dryly.

She frowned. 'The abductor leaves a hand-carved laurel-wood heart at the scene of each crime and removes the victim, but what does he do with the bodies and how are they disposed of? All those taken have different profiles and ages and yet are connected in some way. It seems that violence is only used when victims put up resistance. There were no signs of a struggle in Paloma's case and yet Luz Pujals had seemingly fought back.'

'Whoever takes away the bodies has got to be fit and strong, another reason for it being a male,' he replied.

Isabel frowned. 'You don't think two people might be involved?'

Nacho finished his coffee and scrunching the plastic cup, threw it in a wastepaper bin. 'My guess at this stage is that the crimes are carried out by one man, perhaps the guy you have seen on the motorbike. If there were two aggressors, the victims would have been subdued more easily.'

'One last thing,' Isabel asked. 'What did you make of the images of the Continental tyre treads I sent you?'

'It's a popular tyre brand but that particular model is a very close match to the vehicle treads discovered at the scene of where Paloma was abducted.'

'Good enough for a forensic search of the vehicle?'

'Definitely. I gave Gaspar the report this morning, so he should be organising a warrant.'

Isabel rose and set off upstairs to the homicide department. Corc was flitting around the communal office like a hyperactive bluebottle.

'Ah, Bel!' he cried. 'It's been a terrible day. The commissioner came by and shouted at Tolo and the team. He said Paloma's abductor and the killer of that Englishman must be found.'

She patted his shoulder. 'It doesn't take a genius to surmise that, does it?'

'Can I get you a coffee?'

She smiled and shook her head. 'Water would be great.'

As he scuttled off to the kitchen, she knocked on Tolo's door. He was sitting at his desk opposite Gaspar. Both wore morose expressions.

'Has someone just died?' she asked.

He waved her inside. 'We had a battering from the commissioner earlier.'

'So Corc told me.'

Gaspar slapped his forehead. '*Hombre*! That guy has the discretion of a popular bar owner.'

'Rafael at Bar Castell would take you to task,' quipped Isabel. 'He is the keeper of many secrets.'

He held up his hands. 'Fair play. Have you seen Nacho? He sent me a report on those tyres you photographed over at Los Abetos.'

She nodded.

Tolo tapped the desk. 'We've organised a warrant. We'll send our forensic team up there later to check out the Alfa Romeo in particular. You think our killer could be one of the staff?'

Isabel shrugged. 'There are a number of suspects in my mind but I definitely want to know more about the butler and the chef. I'm going to do a little delving into their backgrounds.' She looked at them both. 'I discovered that when Pere Brotat popped by there to pick up Paloma, Marc, the chef, had cleaned his car. Perhaps he could have placed a bug there.'

'A perfect opportunity,' Gaspar replied. 'I hope you haven't had your car cleaned at either estate.'

'If that were the case, it would explain how the killer knew where you were heading when you visited Luz Pujals' cottage and also Gunter's apartment in Artà,' Tolo considered.

'Yes, I'd already thought of that. Today, it was cleaned by Marc at Los Abetos estate but it's been valeted before at Ses Fonts prior to both those happenings. But last night I did a preliminary search of Pequeñito and couldn't find anything.'

'Remember these devices can be tiny,' said Gaspar.

'The only place I haven't checked is behind the dashboard and engine. I'll see if Bernat, my mechanic, can take a look.'

'I'd be happier if you did,' remarked Tolo. 'You told me Marc was friendly with Paloma so he's definitely a person of interest.'

Isabel nodded. 'He's also good with cars and a gym fanatic.'

Tolo frowned. 'And what about other potential suspects at Ses Fonts?'

'I'm planning on visiting the estate tomorrow and informally interviewing key staff so hopefully I'll have a better picture.'

'So what do we know so far about our killer?' asked Gaspar.

Isabel turned to him. 'He's got access to a powerful vehicle with Continental tyres and a motorbike, so obviously good with cars and also gadgets, hence the placing of the Vidcam. He's most likely handling the abductions – and killings – alone, is determined, resourceful and ruthless. He also has good body strength and a soft spot for dogs...'

Tolo smirked. 'Is that important?'

'Yes, I think so. After killing Archie Brookes in cold blood, he was very particular about making sure both the dogs in his care had food and water. He also ensured that the Jack Russell puppy was comfortable in the locked bathroom at Weber's flat. Even though under obvious pressure, he still found time to care for both animals.'

Gaspar ran a hand through his hair. 'Beats me. He's obviously a very mixed-up individual.'

'In a nutshell, our killer had a strict and disciplined childhood, probably mother issues, and constantly sought approval from his father,' replied Isabel. 'He's a control freak; intelligent and cunning yet insecure and obsessive. Shall I go on?'

Tolo raised an eyebrow. 'And all that from your crystal ball. You're a wonder.'

She grinned. 'You'll high-five me when I'm proven right.'

The door flew open and Corc stumbled in, a tray of water glasses in his clutches. He crashed it down on the table in the centre of the room and in furtive manner, left without a word.

'Gaspar, remind me what you were saying about mixed-up individuals,' growled Tolo.

Isabel passed round the glasses and took a gulp from her own. 'By the way, I called the builder on the site in Bunyola where Pere Brotat was moonlighting. He had a firm alibi for the night of Paloma's abduction. He told me that Pere worked there a few nights every month for cash in hand.'

'So many people on this island operate on the black,' muttered Tolo.

'If the government charged less tax, they wouldn't have to,' Isabel winked.

'Okay, so what's our next move?' he asked.

'Thanks to Josep Casanovas, tomorrow I'm meeting with Ana Blanes, the employment agent who found work placements for Luz Pujals in her day.'

'I'm glad he's proved of some small use,' Tolo replied.

Isabel finished her water. 'Gaspar, I think you have some cold case files for me?'

He stood up and passed her a pile of manila folders. 'I've made you dupes of all of them. There are some anomalies in each one. All these people went missing but in every case the conclusion was misadventure. There's an old shoeshine guy there who a decade ago disappeared in Colònia de Sant Pere.'

'What about him?' asked Tolo.

'In the notes, his son swore blind that he was an experienced swimmer and that it was his ritual to bathe every morning in the same bay. He was an eighty-year-old but had won swimming championships even in his seventies.'

Isabel stared at Gaspar intently. 'Did he do any other kind of work?'

'He was an odd-job man according to his son. He worked all over the island.'

Isabel tapped her glass. 'Is there an evidence bag?'

He shook his head. 'It was assumed he'd drowned. Body never recovered. End of story.' Gaspar looked at his watch. 'Sorry, guys, I've got to leave. It's my parents' wedding anniversary, so a night of Creole cuisine!'

'Lucky you,' she replied. 'Your mother's cooking is legendary.'

When he'd left, Tolo smiled across at her. 'It's seven o'clock, time for a cool beer and a good dinner.'

Isabel packed the files into her pannier. 'You're right, it's been a long day, but first let me call my mother. I need her to check up on Furó. With all these abductions going on, not even a savvy ferret is safe.'

*

By the time Isabel arrived back in Sant Martí, it was late and the *plaça* was deserted. A golden thread of light glimmered behind the locked shutters of Jordi's bar, no doubt for the card players and heavy imbibers who preferred to stagger home in the early hours. She drove along Calle Pastor and growled when she couldn't find a parking place. In a moment of inspiration, she double-backed, reminding herself that Bernat had a muddy yard at the end of her street. He wouldn't mind her leaving Pequeñito there overnight. As she parked in a vacant slot on the bumpy *tranche* of land, she looked up at the dark sky and marvelled at the plethora of glinting stars.

Patting her beloved Fiat on the bonnet, she wandered along the street, but instead of going home, disappeared down a cobbled alley in search of Pau and Teo who she remembered were both on animal watch that night. There wasn't a soul about, though muffled music and children's giggles could be heard from a few of the terraced stone houses that she passed. There was a nip of ice in the air as she strode along, bobbing her head up and down alleys and narrow lanes, in the hope of meeting the two men. She was just rounding the corner on Calle Amar when she heard hurried footsteps and the sound of a dog baying. Following the sound, she ran at speed along the road, and onto a narrow track lined with old garages, parked vans and *motos*. The dog's cries grew louder as she searched in the gloom for presence of life. An intermittent light flickered in the near distance, and so she headed quickly in that direction. Moments later she thumped into a bulky human form and yelped in surprise. The face that loomed in the darkness belonged to Teo. He stepped back, his eyes wide in panic.

'Bel! You nearly scared the living daylights out of me. What the heck are you doing here? I heard footsteps and a dog in distress so rushed down here but there's no one about and the dog's gone quiet.'

Isabel bent over double to catch her breath and then watched as Teo shone his torch around with a shaky gloved hand.

'Where's Pau?' she asked.

'He wasn't feeling too good so I told him to call it a night. He went home about an hour ago.'

'Just now, did you see anyone?'

He nodded. 'I thought I saw a shadowy male figure running past the garages but my torch isn't up to much.'

'Where did he go?'

He pointed vaguely in the distance. 'Somewhere over there.'

Isabel hushed him. 'Just a moment. Let's listen.'

At the sound of whimpering, she pulled a powerful torch from her pocket and ran stealthily alongside the parked vehicles to the far end of the track. Behind a gate, Isabel spied the outline of the agitated hound, and shone her torch towards it. As soon as the dog saw her, it began barking and wagging its tail. In relief, she bent down to stroke it through the wrought iron bars, seeing that it was the old mongrel mutt belonging to Bernat. She laughed. In her disorientated state in the blackness, she hadn't realised that she was at the back entrance to her mechanic's house.

Her mirth suddenly changed to confusion when she saw a thick coiled rope lying outside the gate and a tin foil tray containing the remnants of raw meat. She pulled on her gloves and called to Teo as she carefully examined both items. He picked his way towards her in the patchy light, his face pinched and anxious.

'Look what I've just found.'

He bent to examine the tray. 'Well, I never. I'll bring it to Llorenç tomorrow.'

She shook her head. 'Don't worry. Better that I hand it over to the Guardia as soon as possible to have it analysed. We may be lucky and find some DNA.'

He wore a doubtful expression. 'I don't think our thief would be so careless as to leave a trace.'

'Don't be so sure. Just the tiniest fibre can be the source of DNA.'

She bagged up her finds and suddenly turned to him. 'Actually, would you mind taking them to the *ajuntament* in the morning? I can ask Capitán Gómez to have them picked up by a Guardia officer, if that suits? As it's a Sunday, the town hall will be closed to the public but Josep, the caretaker, starts work at 8 a.m.'

He nodded and carefully transferred the wrapped items to his rucksack. 'Of course, I'll drop them off as soon as he opens up.'

They walked in silence to the village square.

'Where's your car parked?' she asked.

'I came on foot. It's not far to my house.'

With a wave, he set off towards the *torrente*, pulling his jacket tightly about him.

NINETEEN

Isabel sat on the terrace of Bar Castell with her feet up on the railings. It was Sunday and she was rewarding herself with a hearty breakfast after her early swim with Furó. A half-filled coffee cup sat in front of her and an empty plate. She had managed to demolish scrambled eggs and fried tomatoes with two slices of brown bread slathered with virgin olive oil and sea salt. She looked up as Rafael pottered into view.

'Feeling restored?' he asked.

'You bet. How about a fresh cup of coffee?'

He began clearing away the dishes. 'Your wish is my command.'

At the next table, a couple of hikers were scrutinising a map and trying to decide what to eat. The woman smiled across at Isabel.

'Do you speak English?

She nodded.

'I'd be grateful if you could suggest something on the menu that locals eat. Is the orange juice sweet?'

Isabel smiled. 'I'd recommend the scrambled eggs and tomatoes followed by *ensaïmada* pastries. At this time of the year, the oranges aren't ripe unless you want imported ones – not a good idea. The best on the island for juice are from here and are known as Canoneta. It is said that King Louis XIV of France would consider no other orange at his court.'

The woman gasped. 'Gosh, is that true?'

'Who knows,' she winked, 'but it makes a nice story. Where are you hiking?'

'We plan on climbing Puig L'Ofre, so we're going to park the car by the Cuber Reservoir,' replied the woman's husband.

'A wonderful hike, but please don't leave valuables in your car,' said Isabel.

He tutted. 'There are chancers everywhere, aren't there?'

'Yes,' she replied. 'Even in paradise.'

Rafael returned with her coffee and turned to the hikers with notepad poised. Tentatively they gave their order in English and looked slightly concerned when he simply nodded and walked off.

'It's okay,' said Isabel. 'He understands English perfectly, just prefers not to speak it.'

They laughed. 'Well, our Spanish is non-existent,' the man replied.

The wife remonstrated. 'We can order wine and at least we've learnt how to say please, thank you and help.'

Isabel gave the thumbs up. 'What more do you need?'

As she took a sip from her cup, Pau walked in and took a seat opposite her. He wore an anxious expression and appeared pale and haggard. In hushed tones Isabel asked if he was alright.

'Not really,' he answered.

'I bumped into Teo last night and he said you were feeling ill.'

'That's not strictly true,' he said. 'Something terrible happened on Friday but I didn't tell anyone, not even my girlfriend.'

Isabel frowned. 'Can you tell me?'

He bowed his head and looked close to tears. She noticed that his hands were shaking.

'Have you had anything to eat today?'

'No. I haven't slept the last few nights and I can't face food.'

'Let's get you some breakfast.'

He shook his head. 'Just a coffee would be fine.'

Unhappy about his agitated state, she jumped up and headed for the bar. She was determined to organise something nourishing for him. In the kitchen, she took Rafael aside and asked him to rustle up some eggs, toast and coffee.

When she returned to her seat, Isabel noticed that Pau was lost in his own world. Unblinkingly, he stared morosely across the square, and gnawed at the inside of his lip. Isabel took his hand and smiled encouragingly.

'I think I know what has happened.'

He shot her a panicked glance. 'That's not possible.'

'Is it about Llamp?'

He nodded.

'Have you received a ransom note seeking money for his safe return?'

Pau's face filled with surprise mixed with relief. 'Yes!' he blurted. 'I received a note in cut out letters demanding five hundred euros or I'd never see Llamp again.'

'What have you done with this note?'

He looked furtively around the room and, seeing that the hikers were deep in conversation, slowly took out an envelope. He passed it to Isabel.

'How did you know?' he asked.

Isabel shrugged. 'This whole animal theft business had to be about blackmail or revenge. Not all of the dogs were pedigree pooches and several were old, so they'd hardly have been snatched to order by a gang.'

Drawing out the piece of cheap white paper, she examined the hotchpotch of letters stuck on with glue. With a frown, she massaged her chin, recognising the typeface as that used by *Ultima Hora*, one of the local daily newspapers. Her eyes scanned the message.

This Saturday at precisely 10.30 p.m leave five hundred euros in ten bills of fifty inside the metal bucket of the disused well by the torrente bridge. If you contact the police I will kill your dog. Be warned I will be watching you.

'Appalling punctuation.' Isabel took a slug of her coffee and handed the note back to him. 'Not very imaginative, is it?'

He gawped at her. 'That well is difficult to reach, though. It's covered in briars.'

'I'm talking about the ransom. Our thief doesn't think big.' Isabel frowned. 'You're a police officer. Tell me you didn't do as instructed?'

He gave a nervous cough. 'I'm afraid I did, but I wasn't thinking straight.'

'Has Llamp been returned?'

'Not yet. That's why I can't sleep. It's horrible not knowing whether this madman will keep to his side of the bargain.'

'What side? He never gave you one,' she replied.

Rafael appeared with a tray and placed the dishes in front of Pau. He frowned at him. 'Eat or I'll have to shoot you.'

As he plodded away, Isabel winked at the hapless police officer. 'Don't worry, I haven't told Rafael anything, but he's intuitive.'

Without registering his actions, Pau began pouring olive oil onto his toast and took a hefty bite.

'So last night you pretended to Teo that you felt ill so that you could leave the money in the well.'

He nodded miserably. 'I don't have a lot of spare cash. That was money my girlfriend and I saved towards renting a bigger flat. She'll go mad when she finds out.'

'And did you see anyone when you left the money?'

'The woods were as silent as a stone and pitch black. I just left the money and drove away.' He paused and looked up at her. 'I can't believe that the culprit struck again last night. At least you and Teo stopped him from stealing Bernat's dog.'

'A case of being in the right place at the right time.'

He set imploring eyes on her. 'Do you think Llamp will be returned?'

'It wouldn't be easy without someone noticing, but I'm hopeful we'll find Llamp and the others soon.'

As he tucked into his breakfast, Isabel weighed up options. 'Two things interest me. Why five hundred euros and why you?'

Helplessly he waved his fork in the air. 'Search me.'

'You're a police officer. Come on, focus. Who would do this to you?'

'An angry citizen. Maybe I fined someone or referred their case to the Guardia and this is a payback.'

'Now you're thinking. Also, if you received a ransom note, what about the others? Surely if they haven't already received one, they will soon?'

'That's true.' He wiped his mouth with a paper napkin. 'I can draw up a list of likely candidates. I'd have to go back over my notes to see whom I've arrested or fined in the past.'

'Good. Do it as a matter of urgency and let's keep this matter to ourselves for now. I need to think about how we entrap our Pied Piper. We don't want him extracting money from anyone else, unless he already has, of course. Equally, we don't want any of the animals hurt.'

'I shouldn't have left the money. He may still kill Llamp.'

'Let's just concentrate on finding him. *Ánimo!*'

Isabel stood up and giving Pau a comforting hug, waved goodbye to the English couple. At the bar, she held out a twenty-euro note to Rafael. He waved it away.

'On the house today. Pau is a good lad and keeps an eye on this place. I don't know what's going on, but I have a good idea. So, Bel, I'm counting on you to catch the fiend. Do whatever it takes, won't you?'

Isabel patted his arm and with a quick nod, ran down the staircase to the *plaça*. She felt a spark of anger. Heaven help the culprit because if he hurt any of the dogs in his care, she would make it her mission to torment him for the rest of his days.

*

Isabel got to Bernat's yard and found him with his head under her bonnet. He threw her a cheeky grin.

'I like the way you operate, Bel.'

'Really?'

He stretched his back and wiped his hands on a greasy old cloth. 'You park Pequeñito here all night as if you owned the place and wake me at seven o'clock this morning to ask me to check her over for GPS trackers and Vidcams. If it had been anyone else, I'd have thought it was a wind-up.'

'I like to keep you on your toes. Anyway, there was plenty of space here for my tiny car.'

He laughed and pointed to a row of vans. 'See these vehicles? All of them were parked here by locals last night and not one of them has been collected yet. They think this is a free car park. Damned nerve, eh?'

'You're all heart, that's your problem. But to be fair, it's difficult to find anywhere to park in Sant Martí some nights.'

'True enough,' he agreed and shook his head. 'Well, as to your little problem, I have news. I unscrewed just about everything and then, Eureka!'

'You found something?'

He nodded. 'Come here. I've left it intact as you requested but there's the tiniest device hidden behind your dashboard.'

'Well, I never. I thought there must have been. You're a genius, Bernat!'

She leapt forward and planted two big kisses on his cheeks.

'Steady on. This isn't exactly good news, is it?'

'For me it is.' She stretched forward to view the tiny gadget. 'That is so small.'

'These trackers get more sophisticated by the day. Some are even connected via phone tower triangulation. Looks like this one can monitor you in real-time when you're on the move.'

Isabel clicked her teeth. 'It must have an audio link to a mobile phone too.'

Bernat shrugged. 'Probably. Are you sure you want me to keep it in place?'

'Yes, indeed. Now I can have some fun.'

He frowned. 'I'm not sure what you're getting yourself mixed up in, but be careful, my girl.'

As he replaced the dashboard and screwed the glove compartment back on, she turned to him. 'I have to tell you that late last night, our animal thief tried to steal your dog. Luckily Teo was patrolling and surprised him and I arrived soon after.'

His face registered complete surprise before he muttered an expletive under his breath. 'Who is this son of a gun, Bel? We have to catch him.'

She exhaled deeply. 'I promise that we are closing in. Can I ask you if you've had any recent run-ins with locals or neighbours?'

He laughed. 'I've had the odd falling out with clients who've disputed their bills but it's usually resolved amicably.'

She nodded. 'Could you do me a favour and consider any time where matters haven't ended quite so well? Please call me with any names.'

He lowered his head. 'I'll have a think.'

Isabel returned to the office and after telephoning both Tolo and Llorenç, she studied her emails and did some online research, her face a picture of concentration. Even when Pep slipped into the room bearing freshly baked apricot cake and a coffee, she hardly stirred. Some time later, she drummed her fingers on the desk, and grabbing the phone, dialled Julian Mosquera. As Colombia was seven hours behind Spain, she knew he'd pull her leg for calling him so early. All the same, she urgently needed him to point her in the right direction on a matter that was troubling her. It was a long shot but in Isabel's experience, it was always the most unlikely hunches that came good.

*

Pep strolled into the communal office just as Isabel was heading out. He stopped in his tracks with arms outspread.

'That's nice. I walk in the office and you leave before I've had a minute to say good morning or update you on news.'

Isabel sighed. 'I'm sorry, Pep, but I had a perplexing dream last night and had to carry out a little research. It got me thinking.'

'About what?'

'The mindset of our animal thief and Paloma's abductor. One is a vengeful Pied Piper and the other is delusional and killing out of love.'

'A strange way of showing it.'

'True. Key is that we stop them both before more animals and people go missing. So what's your update?'

'It's about those white vans. There could only have been three van drivers in Sant Martí around the time of each of the animal disappearances. More importantly, I've got the names of the registered owners of the vehicles too. One is a pretty good match for the van that nearly knocked you down. '

Isabel scanned the list and with a faint smile pushed the paper into her bag. 'Excellent work, Pep. You passed your intel onto the Guardia?'

He laughed. 'They thanked me but said it would have to wait as they've got a drugs bust and a sheep-killing dog to deal with today.'

As Isabel stood in the doorway, she tilted her head towards him. 'How did your dinner with Angélica go last night?'

'She was sulky at first, but when I said I'd rather save money towards buying us a house, she cheered up. I said we could think about getting engaged in the next year or so.'

Isabel laughed. 'You've bought yourself some time, so make the most of it.' She paused. 'Why are you in the office today? Doesn't Angélica's family prepare a slap-up lunch on a Sunday?'

'Too right. Sometimes, I just need some time on my own. I told them you needed me here.'

She winked. 'Perfect. As you are now my deputy sleuth, I'd like you to perform a little investigation. Can you call all of our pet owners and find out if any of them had fallen out with someone over the last year? It could be a supplier, neighbour, client or family member. Anyone at all.'

'You mean someone who might have wanted to take revenge on them by stealing their pets?'

'Exactly. I've already talked with Pau and Bernat. '

'Bernat, the mechanic? No one's stolen his dog.'

'Someone made an attempt last night. Teo and I thwarted the theft.'

His eyes widened. 'Okay, so I'll call Alberto Bonet, Magdalena Sala and Xavi Mir. I'll chase up Idò as well. He was supposed to have thought about anyone he might have annoyed. Where will he start?'

'Poor old Idò!' she laughed. 'Don't forget Gabriel Reus, the bank manager, either.'

'And Teo?'

'Don't worry, I'll be speaking with him.' She sighed. 'It's a delicate matter but I also need to know if any of them have received a ransom demand and whether they have acted on it. If they have, be sure to tell them to keep the matter to themselves.'

'That would be terrible,' he said quietly.

At the door, she lifted her chin in the direction of her office. 'And please keep an eye on Furó. Lock both the front and back door when you leave.'

He stared fretfully after her. Things must be serious if his boss was advocating locking doors. This menace surely must be found.

TWENTY

As Isabel parked in front of the grand porch of the Ses Fonts estate, she stopped momentarily to breathe the intoxicating air. The sun spread its rays like a golden net across fields and orchards so that the grass, trees and flowers glinted like jewels. Stretching her arms in the air, Isabel turned to see Lourdes observing her from the steps. She wore a serious expression and a furrow had formed on her brow. Isabel gave an exaggerated wave and strolled towards her, noticing how the woman immediately switched on a welcoming smile. Isabel had just reached the porch when her phone rang and, apologising to Lourdes, she pulled it from her pocket. Capitán Gómez was in ill humour.

'Isabel, it appears that someone has walked off with the evidence you and Teo Darder discovered at the potential crime scene last night.'

Isabel kept an even tone. 'How exactly?'

'I wondered the same thing. Teo deposited the two bagged items in the entrance hall of the *ajuntament* early this morning but that incompetent old caretaker, Josep, apparently failed to pick them up immediately and someone removed them. Presumably the animal thief. If your mayor had bothered to install video security cameras, we'd have caught our culprit.'

'We don't need security cameras in Sant Martí,' she replied.

'Really? Well, your little idyll is proving to be a den of vice these days so maybe you all need to move with the times.'

Isabel resisted a sarcastic riposte. 'I'll speak with Josep.'

'A bit late for that. Our thief has what he wants. Anyway, I must press on. We have rather more urgent matters to deal with at the Guardia today.'

Isabel threw the phone into her bag and ran up the steps of the porch. Lourdes stood patiently by the front door, ready to greet her.

'Nicolas is in his studio in the gardens. He would like you to join him there.'

Isabel followed her through several large, sun-dappled salons until they reached a pair of open French doors. Lourdes beckoned Isabel through and onto terracotta stepping stones that wove a meandering path through a plush green lawn. Beyond lay the glass-fronted studio, and next door, the foundry. As Lourdes tapped on the window, Nicolas waved from a large, white designer desk strewn with drawings.

'Come in, come in!'

With a deferential air, Lourdes showed Isabel to a seat and after offering to fetch them both coffees, discreetly left.

'You've arrived at a significant moment, Isabel,' Nicolas beamed.

'Why's that?' she smiled.

He manoeuvred his wheelchair over to a door in the studio. 'Follow me. I have just finished a maquette in the foundry. I want you to be the first to see it.'

Isabel followed the sculptor as he wheeled himself down a winding, zig-zag slope to a brightly-lit basement with white walls.

Adeptly, he steered himself along several corridors until they reached a double door that led into the foundry block.

'I always keep the foundry door secure these days.'

'Why's that?' Isabel asked. 'You can't have many thieves up here in the hills.'

He shook his head. 'You'd be surprised, but alas, my studio was recently broken into, so I take no chances. A few paintings and miniatures were taken and some euros from my desk drawer. Thankfully nothing was stolen from the foundry. I have many valuable materials and sculptures down here.'

Isabel frowned. 'Did you report the break-in to the Guardia?'

He shrugged. 'What was the point? I imagine the thief would have been far away by the time they got here.'

'All the same, fingerprints could have been taken and a report filed. How much cash did you lose?'

'Only about five hundred euros.' He waved a hand in the air. 'I'm really not bothered. It's more edifying to concentrate on the positive things of life such as my art, animals and garden, and of course, the health and welfare of my household and their families.'

Isabel looked around the large foundry room. On one side, traditional Mallorcan plaster shelving was filled with metal castings and maquettes crafted in clay and wax. A large grinder of some kind stood in a corner next to a pile of tools, and silicone and plaster moulds. There was an enclosed area on the left of the room which appeared to be home to unfinished life-size abstract works and small bronze sculptures. It was surrounded on all sides by metal grilles, and the strong wrought-iron door was secured with a massive padlock.

Nicolas turned to her. 'Those are commissioned works awaiting approval. They are worth a great deal of money so need to be protected.'

'How often do you work down here? It must get very hot,' she asked.

He laughed. 'Spot on. That is why I have a sophisticated cooling system and a state-of-the-art modern steel furnace. It was specially designed for me in Germany.' He paused. 'My latest maquette is here.'

Isabel followed his gaze to a statue formed from clay.

'Do feel free to touch it. It's the start of the process. Do you see what it is?'

'A cat?'

He smiled. 'It's my homage to Misha, my missing Maine Coon.'

Isabel sighed. 'That's why I called you yesterday and asked if I could pop by this morning. I'm afraid I have no positive news.'

He held up a hand. 'I didn't expect there to be because my Misha will never return. Whoever took her will not bring her back. Why would they? She was the most beautiful creature on the planet.'

Isabel was momentarily lost for words and somewhat grateful when Lourdes arrived with a tray of coffee and cakes.

'I thought I'd find you here, Nicolas. You were so excited about showing Isabel your lovely Misha.'

She placed the tray on a table and came over to admire the maquette. 'Isn't she exquisite? Imagine what she will be like when cast in bronze.'

Isabel nodded diplomatically. 'Is it a long process?'

Nicolas pulled a coffee towards him. 'You bet. I use the traditional, lost wax-casting method. First of all, you create the master pattern and make a plaster or silicone mould from it.'

'After that,' interjected Lourdes, 'You need to fill the mould with wax to create what is called a "wax positive". This is left to cool before being removed.'

The sculptor beamed. 'Impressive, Lourdes. You have paid attention.'

'Then you create a ceramic shell from the wax positive?' asked Isabel.

'Yes, indeed, but first you need to attach a network of rods and a pouring cup to it. It's complicated. After that, you melt the wax out of the ceramic shell using a burner and pour the molten bronze into it via the pouring cup.'

'Presumably you have to melt the bronze?'

He laughed. 'Of course. It comes in ingots that need to heat to at least twelve hundred degrees centigrade. That's why I have the furnace over there. It's fired by gas and needs to be treated with care. Andel and local workers help me to pour the hot bronze into the mould via a series of pulleys as I haven't the strength to do it. Then we let it cool overnight. The next day we chip away the ceramic cast and solder off the pouring cup and rods, and *voila*, you have your bronze.'

'This is all new to me,' smiled Isabel. 'And bronze is mostly copper?'

'Yes, about eighty-five per cent is copper, and the rest, zinc and other metals. It melts quickly once at a very high temperature. Usually about 150lbs of bronze can melt in forty-five minutes.'

'Gosh, that's fast,' she replied. Taking a sip of her coffee, she looked about her. 'Is it safe to have a furnace down here?'

Nicolas wheeled himself over to the large object that occupied half of one side of the room. 'This is one of the safest machines you can buy. It has a cooler and secure metal lid that opens and shuts via a pulley system, and we adhere to strict safety protocols. I don't want Andel or any of my helpers at risk during the firing process. When I am doing large sculptures, I have to cast the pieces individually and need at least three strong men to assist me.

I get help from a builder and two of his workers from the nearby village of Escorca.'

'Well,' Isabel replied. 'I've learnt a lot today. I had no idea the whole operation was so complex.'

Lourdes stood by the door with her arms crossed, silently studying her. She turned to Nicolas. 'Do you need anything further from me?'

He looked up at Isabel. 'When you rang, you said that you wanted to have separate chats with my full-time staff members?'

She drained her cup. 'That's correct. Would you be able to organise that for me?'

He smiled. 'It's all arranged. Lourdes will set you up in the drawing room and you can speak with each of them one by one.'

Isabel addressed her. 'Perhaps we can start with you first and then your husband, Ismael? I'll catch you up. I just need a quick word with Nicolas.'

The woman gave a curt nod and set off back to the house. Nicolas eyed Isabel quizzically.

'Was there something else?'

She nodded. 'I'd love your professional opinion about something.'

Pulling a small plastic bag from her pannier, she shook out the wooden heart within and handed it to the sculptor. He held it up in his fingers and swivelled it around. 'This is beautifully crafted by hand. See how smooth it is?'

'It is made of laurel. Do you know much about carving?'

He shook his head. 'Not my area of expertise, but you know laurel is important in some tribal communities. For example in Argentina the famed Mapuche people carve from this wood.'

'Yes, I was reading about the chemamüll statues made from laurel. They are known as wooden people and were placed at the grave of the deceased in pre-Colombian times.'

'You are very well informed, Isabel. Have you ever seen one of the gigantic statues? They can often stand seven feet tall.'

'My neighbour showed me a photo of one. She is from Brazil.'

Nicolas gave a coy smile. 'Did someone make this for you? Someone who is close to you?'

She smiled. 'Not at all. I found it in woodland and wondered who might have created it.'

'Whoever it was had a talent for carving. It would have taken a lot of patience and skill to make this. I would treasure it if I were you.'

He caught her gaze, and leaning forward, pressed it back into her hand. For a moment his hand lingered over hers until she released it in some haste and returned the object to its home.

*

Isabel rubbed her eyes. She had interviewed the key members of Nicolas's household and had found them polite yet unforthcoming. Mallorcan Ismael, at six feet tall and with a gruff manner, maintained that he'd only met Paloma twice and that on the night of her disappearance he and Lourdes had been watching television in their quarters and had gone to bed at ten o'clock. Both had recently turned thirty-two and in their respective interviews impressed on Isabel that they enjoyed a privileged existence on the estate and regarded it as home. Andel, the twenty-eight-year-old valet, told Isabel that Paloma was friendly and professional. He recalled meeting Pere briefly when Lourdes had introduced them in the kitchen. On the fateful night that she went missing, he had dined early and at 8.30 p.m. watched the vintage comedy film *Some Like It Hot* with Nicolas before helping him to his bedroom two hours later.

He explained that as he was half Spanish and Czechoslovakian he enjoyed watching old films with Nicolas: they helped him improve his English.

Raul, the elderly gardener, had little to impart, though he remembered Paloma well and described her as a pretty and friendly young woman. Both Elena, the maid, and Linda, the launderess, maintained that they'd never met Paloma and had been at home with their respective husbands and families the night of Paloma's disappearance. The least enthusiastic of the staff was Lourdes. Somewhat guardedly, she reiterated that she had liked Paloma and backed her husband's version of events. She told Isabel that she had met Pere on one occasion and made him a coffee. Isabel noted that she failed to recall the television show she and Ismael had been watching on the night Paloma vanished. By contrast, Ismael had named the Spanish television soap and channel with great alacrity when questioned by her.

Before heading back to the kitchen, Isabel walked through the still and peaceful sculpture park that lay beyond the extensive, meticulously groomed lawn. The scent of rosemary and thyme lifted her spirits, prompting her to pluck some leaves from a shaggy lavender bush and breathe in the sweet aroma. Dotted around the garden, some bronzes exhibited engraved signs on their plinths, offering a title and date of creation, while others, mostly abstract, life-size figures stood modestly under trees and by fountains and bowers with no mention of their subject matter. As she ambled around studying each and every masterpiece – geese caught in flight, leaping hares and playful cats and dogs – she took a call from Tolo and updated him on her interviews and the events of the morning in Sant Martí. She spoke softly so as not to let her voice carry to the house, which had its doors and windows open to the fresh air.

As she finished the call, she touched the smooth coppery-toned statue by the gate; it depicted a woman releasing a flock of tiny birds into the air. It was a piece of such immense beauty that she marvelled at it for some minutes until the hoarse and ominous cry of a magpie caught her attention. Isabel looked up at a nearby pine tree and there, with its dark and cold beady eyes fixed on her, stood the slim, masked raider crowing with all its might. With its black, glossy beak, head and tail and white bib, Isabel thought it rather resembled a macabre butler. She felt a modicum of pity for the much-maligned bird, and yet there was something distinctly sinister about it. Although a symbol of good luck in Asia, the magpie was often accused of stealing shiny objects, hence the title of Rossini's opera, *La Gazza Ladra*. She held its gaze until, with a loud caw and menacing expression, it flapped its wings and flew directly towards her, almost brushing her face before soaring high into the sky. The sound of crunching gravel startled her and she turned to see Andel strolling towards her. His face was pinched with concern.

'Are you okay? It looked as if that magpie was gunning for you.'

Isabel put a hand to her face. 'That's never happened to me before. It came so close that I felt the rush of cold air between its wings.'

They both stared up into the sky until Andel broke the silence and pointed to the statue before them.

'Talking of birds, isn't this beautiful? It is the goddess Artemis releasing sparrows to the heavens. I worked with Nicolas on it over many months.'

'I imagine he is very reliant on you in the foundry,' she replied.

'Since his accident, he has had to learn to trust others particularly with handling heavy production work. I came here straight from school and he trained me in valet work and also bronze production.'

They walked back to the house together.

'Do you enjoy being a valet and a sculptor's right-hand man?' she asked.

He laughed. 'I love being a valet but also helping in the foundry. Isn't variety the spice of life? Ses Fonts is home for me. Everyone here is devoted to their work, and, of course, to Nicolas.'

'Were you brought up here?

'In Escorca village. My mother was Mallorqui and my father Czech. We led a lovely rural life.'

'Is your family still living there now?'

He shook his head. 'When I was eighteen, my parents died in a terrible car accident one rainy night on the road back from Pollença. The car slid down the mountainside and they were both killed on impact. I don't have other relatives here.'

Isabel offered a sympathetic smile. 'I imagine that Nicolas was a lifeline for you at that age?'

'Yes, indeed. He took me under his wing. I owe him everything.'

Having made her farewells, Isabel stepped onto the drive and was unsurprised to see Pequeñito gleaming as if new. Evidently, the valet had given her a good polish. Her smile vanished when she noticed the ignition key missing. She strode over to the garage and walked among the parked vehicles, surreptitiously taking the odd image on her phone, but there was no sign of life. Returning to the house, she summoned Lourdes, who emerged from the kitchen in a starched white apron.

Somewhat tetchily the cook picked up her phone and rang Andel. Soon after the valet appeared.

'Is anything wrong?'

'Would you know where the key is for Señora Flores's car?'

The young man looked mystified. 'I left it in the ignition, as we always do.'

Scowling, Lourdes wiped her hands on her apron and stopped when a jingling was heard from her pocket. Andel and Isabel exchanged looks. Somewhat tentatively, she reached inside and pulled out Isabel's key. She flushed pink and quickly handed it over to her.

'I've no idea how that got in there.'

Andel cast her a long look. 'Maybe I left it on the kitchen table after all, and you picked it up without thinking.'

Isabel dangled the key from her finger. 'No *pasa nada!* It's easily done.'

With a wave, she headed off to the car and drove along the curving mountain track and back onto the main road leading to Soller. She glanced at the ignition key and gave a sigh. There was something amiss at Ses Fonts, and she had a feeling she knew why.

TWENTY-ONE

As Isabel approached La Rambla in Palma, she was dismayed to see long queues of cars snaking along both sides of the avenue. The car thrummed gently as it stood patiently at a set of red traffic lights close to the elegant Misericòrdia and its shady garden while streams of pedestrians strolled all around.

Isabel loved this landmark building that had served for many years as a charitable foundation for the impecunious. During its lifetime, it housed one thousand impoverished inmates of all ages, and conditions had been harsh. The original religious institution had been founded in 1677 on a tranche of land next to the historic cemetery of Camp Roig. In the nineteenth century, the property had been transformed into an exhibition space and included a library and historic archive. The pretty garden was still home to the capital's largest tree, a double-pronged Australian banyan, planted in 1830, whose long, creeping roots stretched from the soil like gnarled fingers. Its elephant hide-coloured trunk leapt up into the sky, sprouting broad, rubbery evergreen leaves that strained to kiss the clouds.

Isabel snapped out of her reverie and, leaning out of the window, whistled to a passer-by.

'Sorry to bother you, but what's going on here?'

The elderly man threw out his arms dramatically. 'Someone told me it's a demonstration about using plastic bags and straws. Can you believe such nonsense, *reina*?'

Isabel thanked him and, smiling to herself, indicated right. As a fervent believer in maintaining clean beaches across the island, she applauded any group that flew the flag for nature and keeping the environment free of rubbish. Few tourists realised that the Loggerhead and Silly turtle species that frequented Balearic waters often mistook plastic bags floating in the sea for jelly fish and after ingesting them died a slow death. It hurt Isabel to think that at least one million sea creatures across the globe died in this manner every year.

When the lights changed, an impatient male driver behind her began tooting his horn. Blowing a kiss provocatively in his direction, she left the chaos and turned into the wide stone patio in front of the ancient Convent de Santa Magdalena. Surely the nuns wouldn't mind her leaving Pequeñito there for a short while? She looked up at its forbidding creamy-grey frontage and contemplated Catalina Tomàs i Gallard, Mallorca's beloved saint, who hailed from the mountain town of Valldemossa, not far from Sant Martí. Born in 1531, she had entered the convent at just twenty-one years of age and devoted her life to it. Aside from its famed erstwhile inhabitant, the convent also garnered popularity for its Christmas home bakes that it sold in the lead up to the festive season. As if her prayers were answered, an elderly woman wearing a habit and grey pinafore came hobbling towards her.

'Are you lost, *reina*?'

Isabel shook her head and held out her police pass. 'To be honest, I'm on urgent business and with the demonstration, there's nowhere to park. Can I leave my car here?'

The woman waved her out of Pequeñito and smiled. 'We will take care of it, but if you could be back within a few hours, that would keep the local wardens happy. '

Thanking the kindly nun, Isabel patted her trusty vehicle and strode off towards a drab sixties-style apartment block on La Rambla. Ana Blanes lived on the fourth floor and there was no lift in the dark and dingy entrance hall. Taking the stairs two at a time, she walked along the landing until she found the apartment. The woman welcomed her with a coy smile and set off to make coffee while Isabel lingered in the kitchen doorway.

'How long have you lived here?' she asked.

'Twenty years. For some time I had an office in Carrer Jaime III, so it was just a quick walk to work every day. I've often thought about buying a rural house but I've probably left it too late. The prices are very high now.'

'You can still get a bargain in Es Pla and other rural villages if you hunt around. It all depends on how authentic a *campesino* life you want to lead.'

The woman ushered her through into the neat and perfunctory living room that looked out onto the broad avenue and central pedestrianised area where florists plied their trade. She handed Isabel a coffee and stirred sugar into her own.

'In truth I like living here. Every morning I watch the florists setting up their stalls and it's lovely to see such an abundance of fresh flowers on display. I'm not sure as a retired woman on my own I'd enjoy country life.'

Isabel smiled. 'Yes, the grass often seems greener, so if you're happy here, it's maybe better to stay put.' She sipped her hot coffee. 'I'd be grateful for your thoughts about Luz Pujals.'

Ana Blanes nodded. 'My agency offered freelance and full-time contracts to staff accustomed to working on private estates across the island. These people needed to have impeccable references and to offer at least two or three different languages. Occasionally, apprentices were sought, but usually clients were seeking experienced help. Luz Pujals had an excellent CV and was never without freelance work.'

'When did she first approach you for contracts?'

'She worked with a friend named Tia who ran a catering agency. She and I often collaborated and it was she who connected us. Luz worked for Russian magnates, Spanish rock stars and European and Middle Eastern royalty, and they all loved her. She was a first-rate, no nonsense Mallorcan cook and also did guided nature walks for clients and their guests. She was always in demand, despite her years.'

Isabel fixed her with bright eyes. 'Did you ever send her to Los Abetos estate near Bunyola or one named Ses Fonts in Escorca?'

'Definitely to Los Abetos. A respected Argentinian butler ran the estate and requested Luz for events and freelance catering during the summer.'

'And Ses Fonts?'

'I will have to look at my notes. I still have all the files for my past clients even though it's been five years since I retired. One moment.'

Ana Blanes rose slowly and made her way over to a desk and began tapping at her computer keys. There was something careworn and sad about her; Isabel suspected she lived a solitary life. It was obvious to her that the woman had been devoted to her work, but what of her personal circumstances? Had life passed her by as she pursued her career? The printer whirred into life and a few minutes later, Ana wandered over and placed some sheets of typed paper in Isabel's hands.

'You'll see all of her placements here. They go back many years. I cannot see Ses Fonts mentioned here and I don't remember taking on such a client.'

Isabel studied the print out, running her finger along each line as Ana took her seat. 'Of course, Luz may have worked at Ses Fonts on an assignment for Tia, or perhaps she was recommended by one of the other island estates.' She paused. 'I remember visiting Luz once she'd retired and she showed me an album containing images from every place where she'd ever worked. She had faithfully captioned and dated each picture. She was very proud of her achievements. Maybe her daughter will have kept it?'

Isabel looked across at her. 'Sadly, the album has gone astray. Is there anything else you can recall about Luz?'

The woman shrugged. 'She was a very loyal person, but when she was in great demand, some clients were unhappy that she couldn't attend to them. I remember a Saudi princess offered triple the fee to employ her for an event, but Luz wouldn't budge.'

'She was evidently a strong and principled woman who was devoted to her work,' replied Isabel.

'Indeed, but when she decided to retire, she stopped work immediately and never gave her regular clients another thought. She was very black and white.'

'I rather admire that,' said Isabel. 'The ability to start a new life without regrets or living in the past.'

'Yes,' she replied sadly. 'Some are able to do that.'

Isabel drained her cup and stood up. 'You have been very helpful.'

At the door, Ana Blanes offered her a wistful smile. 'Whatever befell poor Luz, at least she had some happy years in her retirement, hiking and enjoying time with her family. I envy her that.'

Isabel touched her arm. 'It's never too late to make a new start. Do you have a pet?'

The woman shook her head. 'I'd love a dog, maybe a puppy, but say something happened to me? It would be left all alone in the world.'

'It pays to celebrate the now. Who knows what lies in the future for any of us? What breed?'

She shrugged. 'I'm not fussy but a small dog would be best.'

'I might be able to help. Would you consider two?'

The woman gasped. 'Oh I'm not sure about that. Why two?'

'I know of a lovely old dachshund and a Jack Russell pup in desperate need of a loving home. Sadly, their owner died suddenly.'

The woman bit her lip and then with a smile, nodded. 'Maybe it's fate that you came here. Can I meet them first?'

Isabel smiled broadly. 'Of course. They are currently being held at a local animal refuge. I'll pass your details to the manager.'

'Thank you so much.'

As Isabel hurried back through the rumbustious young demonstrators waving slogans and placards, she wondered whether Ana Blanes had any family and friends, or just spent her days living vicariously through the lives of others on the busy Rambla, dreaming of what might have been. Isabel pondered whether she should have bounced the woman into considering the two dogs now made homeless, following Archie Brookes death. On the other hand, she had a feeling that they might transform Ana Blanes' life. Who knew, perhaps with two dogs as companions, the woman might one day buy that country house after all.

Before Isabel drove back to Soller, she dashed across to the imposing church door and rang the bell. When a very elderly nun appeared, Isabel offered a winning smile.

'Sister, I'm sorry to inconvenience you but is there any chance of buying some of your homemade Christmas sweets and cakes?'

The woman hesitated. 'We do keep certain hours, you know. This is the day of rest. Can you return on Monday?'

Isabel shook her head. 'I'm heading back to Soller now. Don't worry. I'll come another time.'

The nun hesitated. 'Ah, the Soller valley! The blessed place where our own dear Catalina Tomàs was born. For that reason alone, I'll serve you. What is it you'd like?'

'That's so good of you,' Isabel replied. '*Pues*, how about four packets of your cinnamon, coconut and almond biscuits, and a banana cake? Oh and maybe some aniseed doughnuts and nougat?'

The woman grinned. 'Are you planning a party?'

Isabel shrugged. 'No, I'm just greedy but I will be sharing them with my family and friends in Sant Martí.'

'Sant Martí? Surely you must know my nephew, Llorenç? He is the mayor.'

'Llorenç is a very good friend. I had no idea he had an aunt here.'

The woman clapped her hands. 'I will gather your home bakes and a few extra for you all as our gift. What a wonderful chance meeting this has been.'

She returned with two bulging paper bags and would only accept payment for the items that Isabel had ordered.

'Please give an almond cake to Llorenç from me and enjoy the other gifts with your friends and family. Visit us again soon.'

Isabel leant forward and kissed her on both cheeks before carefully stowing her booty in Pequeñito. She would certainly share the goodies with members of her community, though she might draw the line at offering Capitán Gómez a slice of the action.

En route home, Isabel put a call through to Tolo. He had agreed with her reasoning about keeping the listening device intact in the car. The last thing they wanted was to alert whoever had placed it there to its discovery. It could also prove useful in setting traps. Tolo sounded cheery.

'Ah Bel, you've just caught me having a beer with the team. It's been a long day so we thought we'd have one for the road.'

'It's alright for some. I'm in the car heading home to Sant Martí. It's been a productive day.'

'Anything interesting to report?' he replied in a slightly wooden manner.

'I'll fill you in when I see you but I visited Nicolas Garcia and interviewed all the staff.'

'Any concerns?'

'The cook is a little tense but I'm satisfied that they all had alibis for the night of Paloma's disappearance. I showed Nicolas the wooden heart, hoping that as a sculptor, he might be able to shed some light on it. He confirmed some information I discovered online that laurel is famously used by the Mapuche people of Argentina.'

'That's interesting. Isn't the butler at Los Abetos from that part of the world?'

'Yes, he is. I thought I might find out a little more about him and the rest of the staff members. Remember that Laura mentioned Paloma being scared of a creepy young guy? Maybe it's one of the team over there?'

'Yes, indeed. And how did you get on with the cold case files Gaspar gave you?'

Isabel pulled up at a roundabout, and waited for a large truck to pass. 'I'm glad you mentioned them. The evidence bag for one of the victims has thrown up something really important. Any chance of your swinging by in the morning to take a look at it?'

Isabel could just picture Tolo narrowing his eyes; evidence bags were only viewable under strict conditions at police headquarters. She hoped that he understood this conversation was also for the benefit of an unknown listener.

'I've a full day but I could send a police courier early morning to collect it?'

Isabel was grateful to Tolo for playing the game. 'Excellent. Later tonight, I'll leave it on the table in my *entrada* ready for collection.'

Loud chatter and laughter came from the speaker. 'Are you having a knees-up without me?' she laughed.

'Just the boys in the bar getting excited about the Barca match coming up next on television.'

Isabel smiled to herself. 'Let's speak in the morning.'

It was early evening by the time Isabel reached C'an Moix. She headed up to her office and discovered Furó in his basket, snuffling as he twitched and whined in his sleep. She kissed his head and sat down heavily at her desk, longing for a glass of red wine and a plate of good food. No doubt Florentina would have left some delicious savoury goodies for her in the fridge, but first she needed to check for an email she was expecting from Julian Mosquera.

As she waited for her emails to download, she noticed that Pep had left a neat report marked 'Sant Martí Animal Victims – potential enemies' at the top of her in-tray. She pulled it in front of her and read the contents with a satisfied nod. Her assistant was becoming quite an asset in her life and had all the makings of an excellent trainee detective. His work was thorough and methodical and he presented his findings intelligently. Who would have thought it? Pep was just an apprentice tiler when she'd lured him to come and work for her, but since then he had impressed her with his diligence and hunger for self-improvement and knowledge. Her eyes flicked to the screen and she bent forward to read the message that she had been anticipating. She thumped the desk triumphantly. It seemed that her gut had not betrayed her.

She wandered downstairs to the kitchen and opened a bottle of Ribas, a delicious and smooth local red wine. Sniffing the cork, she poured herself a large glass and left it on the table while she investigated the fridge. To her delight, Florentina had left a dish of baby broad beans, artichokes and diced *jamon serrano* in virgin olive oil, fresh goat's cheese with grapes and chicory leaves and a huge portion of aubergine bake. Without hesitation, Isabel switched on the oven and placed the earthenware dish inside while she helped herself to the cold dishes, accompanied by fresh bread. She rolled the wine around in her mouth and gulped it back enthusiastically; this reliable brand never failed her. She'd only recently discovered that it also held the accolade of being one of the oldest *bodegas* in Spain, having been established in 1711.

While her main dish was warming in the oven, she slipped upstairs with glass in hand and put on a CD by Joni Mitchell. She felt a stab of sorrow to think that Paloma would never hear her favourite artist's voice again. Standing in front of her whiteboard, she scanned the side devoted to the Sant Martí animal thefts. Picking up a red marker, she ringed a name and exhaled deeply.

'I know who you are and where you are, but how do I find the animals without you knowing?'

The sound of pattering feet caused her to turn; with a smile she bent down and picked up a sleepy Furó. 'What do you think, junior detective? Where would he be keeping the animals? I need to focus.'

Furó wriggled out of her arms, and landing softly on the wooden floor, darted under Pep's desk. Deep in thought, Isabel watched him squirm underneath until only his nose and whiskers were visible. She clapped her hands together. 'Of course, Furó. I take your point. He must have some secret hiding place where he's keeping them. Perhaps a remote barn or outbuilding away from his work premises? I need to look at any properties that he and his family might own or have inherited.'

She picked up the office phone and called Llorenç.

He sounded gruff. 'What a time I've had with that oaf, Gómez! He nearly wiped the floor with me over that missing evidence left by Teo at the town hall this morning.'

'It wasn't your fault.'

'Nor should poor old Josep get the blame. He left the bag in the foyer ready for collection by one of Gómez's officers and went about his work. When he returned downstairs minutes later, the package had gone, so he assumed it had been picked up.'

'These things happen,' she breezed.

'The front door was closed. It's a mystery how someone could have entered without being seen or heard.'

'That's very true. As it happens, I'm not bothered about the evidence going missing. In fact, it's rather helpful.'

'Whatever do you mean?'

'I'll explain soon but for now I do need an urgent favour.'

'What's new?' he chuckled.

'With luck it will lead us to our Pied Piper and hopefully to all of our stolen pets.'

'In that case, of course I'll help.'

'Good. Can you grab a pen and paper to take down what I need? Meanwhile, I have an almond cake for you from your aunt at the Convent de Santa Magdalena.'

Llorenç gasped. 'How on earth do you know my aunt?'

Isabel laughed. 'It's a long story.'

*

At eleven o'clock, Isabel closed the cold case files that Gaspar had given her. They included five missing person enquiries, two of which held close parallels with those currently under investigation. There was the disappearance eight years previously of Lucy Vila, a young woman from Bunyola who had served as a maid in various wealthy households on the island. She had simply vanished one afternoon on a country walk and had never been seen again. Her photograph showed a delicate, shy looking girl of about twenty-five years old; there was something strangely familiar about her face which disturbed Isabel. She knew of the other case from Gaspar. It concerned eighty-year-old Manolo Suarez, who, a decade earlier, had seemingly drowned off the coast of Colònia de Sant Pere. He had been itinerant during his working life, serving first as a shoe-shiner in *Plaça* Mayor in Palma before taking odd jobs island-wide. If Suarez and Vila had also been victims of the serial killer, that meant that over a period of ten years, there had been six known victims, including Archie Brookes.

Concerned, Isabel acknowledged that recently something had radically changed in the mind of the killer. Two abductions had occurred in quick succession, including the callous murder of Archie Brookes. What was the reason? Hubris, misplaced confidence and a desire to mock and frustrate her and her national police colleagues at every turn? She felt that it marked the beginning of an elaborate and dangerous game, but one that would inevitably lead to careless mistakes. That comforted her.

Isabel drummed her fingers on the desk, then, springing up energetically, crossed the room to the dark communal office that fronted the street. She crept over to the shuttered windows and peered through the slats like a spy, awaiting unwanted company. The street was devoid of life, save for a nimble-footed hound that clung to the shadows like a sleuth as it headed furtively in the direction of the *plaça*. With a pet-napper on the loose, she hoped it would make it home safely. Isabel scrutinised all the parked vehicles and bikes on the road, and then, grabbing Pep's chair and a golf club, sat close to the window and waited.

The rest of the house was in blackness and, although tired, she had no intention of falling asleep. As she kept vigil at the window, a bright message pinged on her phone. It was from Tolo, begging her to be careful. Of what? An invisible enemy. She had laid a trap like an industrious spider luring a fly to land in its web, but would her tracker take the bait?

Some hours later, Isabel felt her eyes closing, despite having consumed several *espressos*. She shook her head and attempted to sit upright but soon her body slumped forward in the chair as she drifted into sleep. Not long after, there came the familiar nagging sound of a motorbike before its engine cut out and a figure in black dismounted. Had Isabel been awake, she might have recognised the discordant rattle caused by a faulty chain drive but she had already tiptoed into a dream world, light years away from Calle Pastor. The sound of quiet, decisive footsteps accompanied by the distant shriek of a cat jarred in the silent street just as a handful of crisp and excitable leaves, driven by the breeze, took shelter in a gutter. Isabel's gate emitted a sharp squeal as a gloved hand pulled it open and a figure stole silently up the path. The flash of a bright blade winked in the moonlight before it was thrust into a leather sheaf on the visitor's belt. With head bowed, the hands worked quickly and efficiently at the front door lock, using a fine pick. Isabel moaned in her sleep as Furó suddenly emerged from his basket and, with a warning growl followed by a loud hiss, pattered over to the window.

TWENTY-TWO

Disoriented, Isabel awoke with a jolt in the darkness as Furó cried out and clawed at her legs. Wincing, she picked him up and held him close, her ears suddenly aware of a noise coming from the front door below. She rose quietly and, grabbing the golf club at her side, slowly groped her way down the staircase with Furó hot on her heels. When she reached the bottom step she stopped and, with heart thumping, watched as the front door slowly opened and a figure slipped inside. Isabel gripped the club and was about to pounce when Furó uttered a low and menacing growl and scuttled ahead of her into the dark *entrada*. There was a scuffle followed by an anguished cry of pain and then the front door slammed.

Isabel grappled with the light switch, and seeing that Furó had taken refuge under a chair, rushed onto her front path and out of the gate. Looking frantically right and left, she became aware of someone astride a motorbike some way further along the street. The engine roared into life just as Isabel ran at speed along the centre of Calle Pastor towards it. The sound of rattling caught her attention as the bike sped away, its rider speeding recklessly to the end of the cobbled street before screeching around a tight corner. Isabel pulled out her phone and called Tolo. He answered on the third ring.

'Did someone come?'

She breathed heavily. 'I nearly caught the intruder in the *entrada* but Furó attacked before I could intervene. There was a yelp, so Furó must have bitten whoever it was, in which case we might find DNA at the scene.'

'You shouldn't have taken the risk.'

'At least now we know that someone is definitely listening to my conversations in the car and getting jittery about potential evidence. With any luck, our killer will start making serious mistakes.'

Tolo exhaled deeply. 'I should have sent an undercover officer to keep watch.'

Isabel remonstrated. 'But we didn't know anyone would show up. Besides, we need a lot more evidence and I think I know where to find it.'

'It's late, so let's get some rest. Can I send over Nacho first thing?'

'Sure. I'll take Furó for a quick run and we'll be back by 8 a.m.'

'When can we meet?'

Isabel was momentarily lost in thought. 'How about lunch? I have some urgent business with Llorenç tomorrow morning.'

'Does that concern the animal thefts?'

'Spot on. I've identified my Pied Piper, but now I need conclusive proof.'

Tolo gave a snort of laughter. 'Our friend Gómez would be proud of you. He's all about hard evidence, as you know.'

'Trust me,' she replied. 'I'm going to drown him in it, but first I need Llorenç to confirm my suspicions, then it's all stations go.'

'Good, but make sure you have full back-up from Gómez and his team if you're springing any kind of arrest.'

'There's only ever one kind of arrest in my book,' Isabel replied impatiently. 'You might recall, Tolo, that I've made quite a few in my time. I can take care of myself.'

'I'm counting on it.'

Isabel finished the call and walked slowly back to the house, stopping in some alarm when she noticed a ghostly yet cumbersome figure lurking by her gate. Drawing nearer, she saw that it was Doctor Ramis clad in a billowing white nightshirt and cap, accompanied by bright red espadrilles. She stifled a giggle, marvelling at the eccentricity of her elderly neighbour. The apparition brought back memories of a verse she was made to recite as a child by her strict father, a *jefe superior* for the national police in Castilla-La Mancha. It was a Scottish poem from the nineteenth century that he thought might improve her grasp of the English language but it only served to confuse her. She found herself uttering aloud 'Wee Willie Winkie rins though the toon upstairs an' doon stairs in his nicht-gown.'

'What's that you're saying, Bel?' called her neighbour.

Isabel pulled herself up sharp. 'Hello, Doctor Ramis, you're up early.'

'Well, I'm not accustomed to break-ins in the middle of the night. I take it you had an unwelcome caller?'

She cocked her head at him. 'You were awake?'

He issued a yawn. 'I went downstairs for a glass of water and thought I heard light footsteps outside, but looking between the slats of the shutter, I couldn't see anything. Then when I returned from the kitchen, I was aware of someone yelling in pain.'

Isabel shrugged dismissively. 'That was just Furó offering my visitor a welcome bite.'

Doctor Ramis offered a bleak smile. 'As good a reason as any for making a hasty exit.'

'Did you get a clear view of him?'

He shivered in the chill night air. 'I only fleetingly saw a figure dressed in black and wearing a hood.'

Isabel nodded. 'Don't worry. It was just on the off chance. Now, hurry back to your bed. I don't want you getting cold.'

'All I care about is that you're okay. I do wish you'd give up all this police work. Your mother is always frantic with worry.'

At his gate, he turned to her. 'Just one small thing. Are you sure it was a male? I thought whoever it was had a slim, athletic build. You never know, it might well have been a woman.'

*

Isabel stood in her *entrada* and called for Furó but he remained silent under a chair. Frowning, she bent down to inspect him and gasped to see blood staining his fur. Was it his or the intruder's? With a lot of coaxing and soothing words, she managed to pull him into her arms while he issued a series of warning growls. In the kitchen cupboard she unearthed her ferret medical box and gently cleaned the fur on his head with peroxide. She discovered a deep cut on the crown that was bleeding profusely. Carefully, she dabbed it with styptic gel and lightly covered it with a dressing.

'We will need to visit the vet in Soller as soon as he opens. No early run for you in the morning.'

Furó whimpered and burrowed under her arm. 'Come on, my little hero. It won't be that bad and you like Tomeu.'

Isabel carried him upstairs to her bedroom and swaddled him in soft blankets in his basket. Fretfully she lay down on her bed and attempted to get a few hours' rest but sleep evaded her.

She was thinking about her intruder. The hypothesis that had gradually been forming in her head about Paloma's abductor had not included a female suspect. What if she was wrong? If Doctor Ramis was correct, where did that leave her? She sprang out of bed and tiptoed downstairs to the office, where she stood in deep contemplation in front of her whiteboard. Taking a black marker from a pot on Pep's desk, she drew dotted lines to connect various names listed in different large bubbles. Then, scuffing her head with her hand, she groaned and scribbled the word Continental tyres and underlined it. She wandered into her office and send an email marked URGENT to Gaspar, and felt some relief when it whooshed off into the ether.

Grabbing a woolly jumper off the back of her swivel chair, she pottered down to the kitchen and opened the back door. The garden was cool and still, but the bird fraternity was already busy. Salvador stood in the midst of the orchard bawling at the top of his voice while a chatty group of hens formed an adoring halo around him. In some frustration, Isabel stomped up to them.

'You wonder why he's got an ego! Pathetic behaviour, girls. Get a grip and stop fawning over him. Just act nonchalantly and get on with your own business.'

Mrs Buncle's tawny head bobbed up and she gave an embarrassed cluck. Isabel waggled a finger. 'Yes, you of all people should know better.'

Having rebuked her feathery female clan, she smiled to see the first crop of oranges hanging like fiery pendants from a tree. The juice would be a little tart but she didn't mind. Staring up into the sky, she watched an eagle, caught on the breeze, glide by while a cushion of soft rosy cloud rested on the tips of the Tramuntanas. She observed the grizzly grey mountains for a few minutes, then, stretching her arms in the air with an orange in each hand, began juggling. After a while, she tired of her exertions, yawned, and turned to one of her plump hens.

'Look, Cleopatra, a pink sky, so I'll need my umbrella today.'

The hen tilted her head thoughtfully before continuing her frenzied scratching in the long grasses. Heading back to the kitchen, Isabel made herself a freshly-squeezed orange juice and prepared a strong *cortado*. When the coffee had brewed, she raided her cake tin in the pantry and found, to her delight, that Florentina had, like a genie, conjured up a homemade almond cake topped with citrus icing. Cutting herself a huge slice, Isabel placed her spoils on a tray and wandered out to the patio, where she enjoyed her early breakfast to the sounds of the awakening valley. She studied the rosemary bush that had gradually invaded the patio and resolved to ask Idò to give it a trim. On all sides, she had planted borders of rosemary, thyme and lavender and it was this heady mix of tantalising aromas that lured her to the garden during hot and sticky summer nights. With feet up on the table, she would sit entranced, reading a crime novel by candlelight, while savouring a glass of fine Mallorcan wine and crunching on oven-roasted salted almonds and briny olives.

Having finished her breakfast, she tiptoed up to her bedroom to check on Furó. He slept soundly, though occasionally his limbs trembled and he emitted a low whimper. Although the dressing was bloodstained, the wound hadn't worsened, and to the touch her beloved ferret did not appear to have an abnormally high temperature. All the same, a small volcano of rage was burning inside her, threatening to explode when she would finally come face to face with her nemesis. Whoever did this to Furó would pay a heavy price. As she descended the stairs to her office, the doorbell rang. She knew that such an early caller could only be

Nacho. Unshaven and smiling, he stood on the doorstep like a supplicant with a paper bag in his hands.

'The best croissants from Panadería Fiol,' he announced.

She smiled. 'I love that place but I must be a pedant and argue the point. In Soller we also have some excellent bakeries, and Forn de Barri in La Huerta does the best almond croissants in the world.'

'In that case, you're buying breakfast next time.' He waved vaguely towards Isabel's path. 'I've done a sweep of the front garden and dusted down the gate, porch and front door. What about inside?'

Isabel scrunched up her nose. 'Sorry, but the *entrada* is fairly contaminated. You'll find my prints pretty much everywhere. I think the intruder was bitten by Furó near the table, but there are no obvious bloodstains.'

'Good for Furó. I'll check.'

'Sadly my little hero was struck with some kind of weapon in the scuffle and sustained a deep head wound. There was a lot of blood, so I'll take him to the vet when he opens.'

'In that case, the culprit made a fatal error of judgement.'

'You think?'

'Much as I love you, Bel, you're not someone I'd like to cross when you're angry.'

'Really?' She winked.

In the *entrada* Nacho got down on his haunches in his white overalls and studied the tiled floor with a sharp light while Isabel brewed coffee. She looked longingly at the fat butter croissants, wondering whether she could justify scoffing one when she'd just hoovered up so much almond cake already. A voice in her head propelled her into action. *Listen, Bel, you only live once, and who gives a damn if you've eaten more calories in one hour than the average Sumo wrestler does in a day? You swim and run, so you deserve it. Be happy. The serial killer could finish you off, and who'll be worrying about your excess calories at the funeral?*

'That's so true,' she said aloud.

Nacho offered her a curious expression as he entered the kitchen. 'What is?'

She stared at him. 'That life's for living.'

'Hell, yes!' he laughed. 'I'm afraid your *entrada* is as clean as a whistle, though I've taken some images and tiny fibre and hair samples. Did you notice anything else about our man? Height, stature, gait?'

Isabel exhaled deeply. 'Slightly built, agile, and strong. A cool customer. I've been assuming our killer is male but my neighbour, Doctor Ramis, woke in the night and suggested that it might have been a woman. It's discombobulated me.'

'Is that a medical term?'

Isabel swiped at him with a newspaper. 'Don't joke. If the good doctor is right, my theory is shot to pieces and I've no idea who the killer is.'

Nacho gratefully took the coffee Isabel handed to him. 'You think you know who it is?'

'Now I'm not so sure. I have no proof and I'm trusting my gut, but if I'm right, this is the most troubling and gruesome case I will ever have dealt with.'

Nacho observed her with serious eyes and made the sign of the cross. 'You're frightening me.'

She bit her lip. 'I'm frightening myself. Aside from disturbing nightmares, my head is constantly swamped now with unsettling images. I'm not sure I can handle what comes next.'

Nacho placed his coffee on the table. 'We don't have the easiest of jobs but every time I tremble or think I can't take any more,

I remember that our victims are voiceless and seeking justice. We cannot afford to make mistakes or weaken. We must steel ourselves and see things through to the bitter end. Always.'

As he relinquished his hold, Isabel nodded. 'That's so true.'

'True again?' he grinned.

Isabel placed a croissant in front of him and breathed deeply. 'The trouble is that since I've returned to police work, I've started getting these odd feelings again.'

'What do you mean?'

'It sounds crazy but a tremor comes over me when something seems awry on a case. I can't explain it but it's raw and animalistic, as if I am on the scent of putrid meat. It gets stronger, more pungent until my head is reeling.'

'Do you feel that now?'

Isabel took a long draught of coffee. 'It's infecting my dreams, and stifling sleep. I see a face and it grows more grotesque by the day. It's just like Dorian Gray.'

'Whose face? Who is Dorian Gray?' Nacho sounded concerned.

Isabel shook her head and laughed. 'Sorry, ignore me. *The Picture of Dorian Gray* was a famous story by Oscar Wilde, one of my favourite writers. You'd have to read it to understand.'

Nacho took a thoughtful bite of his croissant. 'Are you okay to continue with this case?'

'Of course, but sometimes our work can be overwhelming, as you said. Trust me, I will see this through to the end for the sakes of Paloma, Luz, Gunter and Archie, and others we may not even know about whose lives were cruelly cut short through no fault of their own.'

Nacho smiled. 'Good. That's more like the Bel I know. How about another coffee before I go?'

*

Isabel arrived back at Ca'n Moix with a bleary-eyed Furó in her arms. At the veterinary surgery, he had needed three stitches and an antibiotic injection for the gash on his head, but otherwise Tomeu felt he had suffered few ill effects from his nocturnal encounter. Pep jumped to his feet when Isabel entered the office and rushed forward to inspect Furó. She had called him from the surgery to explain the events of the night.

'Did Tomeu patch him up?' he asked. 'I will kill whoever did this to him.'

'You and me both,' she quipped. She placed Furó in his basket. 'A few stitches but he'll be fine, thankfully.'

'Can I get you a coffee?'

Isabel yawned. 'Thanks, but I've had more than enough this morning.'

'By the way, Pau rang and left some names of people he might have angered. It's quite a long list, but then he is a cop.'

She walked into her office and cast a cursory glance at her emails while she grabbed a packet of sunflower seeds from her desk drawer. A message from a contact at INTERPOL had her whooping loudly.

'Everything okay in there?' yelled Pep.

She breezed out of her room and, sitting on the sofa with her seeds, studied him.

'I've had some potentially good news. Meanwhile, I want to congratulate you on your interviews with the victims of the animal thief. The notes you left yesterday were excellent.'

Pep flushed pink. 'I felt like a real investigator talking with Alberto and all the others, though I didn't discover a common enemy for them all.'

'That doesn't matter. When I called Teo, he claimed to have no foes, whereas Bernat said that he might have many because people often blamed their mechanic for the failings of their cars.'

'But it's obvious from the targeted thefts that they all share one adversary?' Pep persisted.

'Of course, but it's so subjective. How many of us have silent enemies unbeknownst to us, waiting to pounce? We may have no idea that someone out there is holding a grudge, or worse, a vendetta. It could be built on old animosities or simply envy – the most insidious of all.'

Shifting uncomfortably in his chair, Pep regarded her with troubled eyes. 'I hope I haven't any enemies.'

Isabel giggled. 'Only admirers, Pep.'

His shoulders relaxed and he grinned. 'Talking of enemies, Idò wasn't much help. He seemed to think that at least ten people disliked him and might have nicked Perro.'

Isabel laughed. 'You know my uncle. The suspicious type.'

'And the bank manager and lawyer said loads of people resented them.'

Isabel gave a derisive snort. 'I can believe that.'

'All of them had been having house improvements, though using different local tradesmen, so not much to go on there.'

Isabel fixed him with a faint smile. 'Are you sure?'

'What's amusing?'

She shook her head. 'Nothing. So, of all those you spoke with, only two reported receiving ransom notes?'

He nodded. 'Two days ago, Magdalena Sala was sent one demanding five hundred euros. As instructed, she left the money behind a municipal bin on the outskirts of the village the same evening. Meanwhile, Xavi Mir received a demand for one thousand euros to be left tonight at the old washstand in Biniaraix village.

273

He told me that he was in two minds about going to the Guardia, so I told him you'd advise. Both notes were made using letters cut out from a newspaper.'

'*Ultima Hora*, to be correct.'

'How do you know that?'

'I recognised the font.' Isabel tapped her chin. 'I'm concerned that the abductor hasn't mentioned returning the pets, if that's his intention.'

'What do you mean? Of course he will.'

Isabel eyed him doubtfully. 'Often these blackmailers are as cold as ice and simply kill their victims – whether animals or humans – once they have the ransom money. It offers less risk. All the same, our abductor is good at handling dogs and gaining their trust, so we can assume he likes them.'

Pep turned to her, seemingly weighing up whether he should test a theory. 'I've been wondering about that. What if the animal thief is the serial killer too? They're both abductors and like dogs. Gunter Weber's Jack Russell pup hadn't been harmed and at the crime scene of Archie Brookes, you said that the two dogs had been left food and water. What kind of a killer does that?'

'A very confused one but you're barking up the wrong tree, dear Pep.'

'Why?' he replied, a tad sulkily.

'Because our animal abductor is trying to make a quick buck and punish locals who've angered him at some stage, but our serial killer is something else. Far more dark, deranged, deluded – and cunning.'

'It would have been handy if it was the same person,' he muttered.

'Yes, but nigh impossible.' Isabel offered him a steady gaze. 'I am planning a sting operation, Pep. The fact is that I know who the abductor is but need to catch him red-handed.'

'You already know?' he exclaimed.

'I do, but Llorenç and I will need to map out a plan with our dear Capitán Gómez to ensure we have hard proof. You said in your notes that Mir's money drop is supposed to happen tonight?'

Pep nodded. 'At eleven o'clock.'

'We have no time to lose. I will call him now and then pop by to see Llorenç. Tonight we must act.'

Pep's eyes were bright with excitement. 'You'll involve me too?'

'Naturally. You have proven an invaluable part of the operation so far.'

He beamed and punched the air. 'So, will you tell me who the culprit is now?'

TWENTY-THREE

Isabel was strolling across the *plaça* in the direction of the *ajuntament* when she was stopped in her tracks by Padre Agustí. He had a long black scarf wrapped around his neck and was clutching a hymn book.

'Dear Bel, I am saddened to hear that the animal thief is still in our midst. May God flood his heart with love so that he may see the error of his ways.'

Isabel offered a lukewarm smile. 'I think it's a bit late for that, *padre*, but rest assured, he will be brought to justice soon.'

He hung his head sorrowfully. 'I will pray for his soul. And meanwhile, Bel, any thoughts about the Christmas Eve service? You promised to give a reading.'

'Christmas? But it's weeks away.'

'Two to be exact, Bel.'

Isabel gave a gasp. 'Heavens. I have been so preoccupied with work of late. Of course, I'll do a reading.'

'Something uplifting and encouraging would be perfect for these troubled times.'

'Yes, of course,' she muttered. 'I'll put my thinking cap on.'

With a wave, she skipped up the steps to the town hall and turned the heavy round brass handle. To her dismay, it came away in her hand and clattered loudly to the ground.

A few heads bobbed up at tables outside Café Jordi while Alfonso, the village artist, out walking his dog, came over to inspect the damage. He clasped a hand to his mouth and tittered.

'To think that has probably stood the test of time for centuries only to be destroyed in seconds by a slip of a girl like you.'

'I'm sure it was coming loose, Alfonso. Josep will have it fixed in a jiffy.'

He giggled. 'I hope so for your sake, or Llorenç will never let you hear the end of it, *cariño*!'

As he wandered off, Isabel picked up the offending item and dusted it down. A small dent winked in the sunlight, one she hoped was a scar from a previous misadventure. Pushing the door open, she discovered the elderly caretaker plodding down the stairs.

'Ah, Josep! Just the man. By chance, the front door handle fell off, but I'm sure it's easily mended.'

He joggled the heavy golden ball in his hands. 'Fell off? I doubt that very much, Bel. That doorknob hasn't budged in at least a century.'

'And you can vouch for that personally, Josep?' Isabel folded her arms. 'What, are you trying to compete with Methuselah?'

'I don't know the gentleman in question, but I have on good authority from Llorenç that the handles in this building have never been removed in modern day history.'

With a shrug, Isabel turned to him. 'Well, I guess there's a first time for everything.'

'That's as may be, but I'm not taking the can for this, young lady. I see a dent in it that wasn't there before. After that Guardia captain made a song and dance about Teo Darder's missing package and accused me of being negligent, I'm keeping my head down. I'll have to report this to Llorenç.'

Isabel passed a hand through her hair. 'Don't fret, Josep. I'm having a meeting with him now so I'll confess to my crime. Hopefully I won't be sent to the tower.'

The old man shook his head and watched disapprovingly as she sprinted up the staircase. In the absence of his secretary, Isabel knocked on Llorenç's door and strode inside. The mayor was in the middle of a phone call, but he waved her to the polished mahogany chair in front of his desk and grimaced conspiratorially. Serenely, Isabel placed her hands in her lap and looked around the office, smiling at a newly installed image on the wall of the local police dog, an Alsatian named Arnie. This intrepid canine patrolled local school playgrounds and pupil hangouts to check for drugs, and was beloved by all the children. On the rare occasion when he sniffed out a few rogue spliffs hidden in a school locker, he was rewarded with a hefty steak on his return to police base.

Llorenç finished his call and cupped his head in his hands. 'That was our mutual friend, or should that be fiend?'

'Let me guess, Gómez?'

He gave a growl and nodded. 'As you suggested, I tried to arrange a meeting for this morning but he maintains that he is far too busy and can't see us later either.'

'Presumably you explained that we are on the brink of catching our Pied Piper?'

'I told him, Bel, but he wants proof. He is not prepared to go on a hunch, nor will he waste his so-called valuable resources on a sting operation.'

Isabel offered a defiant stare. 'That's an inconvenience, but we are quite capable of handling this ourselves.'

The mayor sat up in his chair, a slightly apprehensive look on his face. 'Handling what exactly?'

'We need to flush out our animal thief tonight. It's too risky leaving matters another day while precious lives are at stake. I've spoken with Xavi, and he is happy to make a dud drop at the *rendez-vous* cited in the ransom note he received. He will bulk up a pile of notes with some real bills on top and leave them taped in a plastic bag at the Biniaraix washstands at 11 p.m.'

'But what happens if our thief turns up and sees that they're fake?'

'He won't risk checking them there in case he's seen. Key is that I'll install Pep close by to take images of him collecting the package. We'll then move on to the second part of the plan depending on how you fared at the land registry office?'

Llorenç sighed and pulled a sheaf of papers towards him. He gave her a long look. 'You know how much I trust your judgement, Bel, but this makes me nervous. From what you are suggesting, a respected member of our community is responsible for this unpleasant wave of animal kidnappings.'

'Correct.'

He passed her a piece of typed paper and awaited her reaction. Isabel read the official document intently and triumphantly slapped it on the desk. 'This is just what I had suspected. I knew he must have another property tucked away in the hills.'

Llorenç sighed. 'The property is ten miles from here among olive groves high above Biniaraix village. Pretty remote.'

'And as you can see, it's surrounded by five acres of land, so a perfect place for hiding dogs.'

'The deeds are actually in his wife's name, but I'd hazard she knows nothing about any of this,' he replied miserably.

A weight of silence fell between them.

'You really think it is him, Bel? How can we be one hundred per cent sure?'

Isabel looked him straight in the eye. 'Our Pied Piper is Teo Darder, and whether you like it or not, I am telling you the truth.'

Llorenç ran a shaky hand through his cropped grey hair. 'But he installed the pool in my garden and constructed our garage. His daughter was in the same class as Angélica. We've been to barbecues at his home and I've played golf with him. He's one of the largest constructors in the valley.'

'And your point is?' she replied coolly.

'It just doesn't make any sense. Why would such a nice chap do such a terrible thing?'

'For all the wrong reasons,' she replied. 'I checked his bank records and the company is on its uppers. He has over-expanded and now can't meet interest payments.'

'I did hear rumours that he recently re-mortgaged his home and was behind on rent for his business premises. '

'All true. Blackmailing locals would not have got him out of his troubles but might have proved a quick fix. It was also a childish attempt to punish those he felt had slighted him in some way.'

Wearily, he pulled off his reading glasses and rubbed his eyes. 'So, what next?'

Isabel leant forward in her chair. 'As I explained by phone, you need to call Darder to tell him that council tax is being reduced on certain remote properties in the valley and that by luck one of his wife's qualifies.'

'The one above Biniaraix village?'

'Exactly. You must tell him that a council assessor will pop by the property at 9 a.m. tomorrow morning for a viewing in order to confirm the new charge and to review his *escritura*.'

Llorenç bit his lip. 'What if he's suspicious?'

'Just be your charming and persuasive self and I'm sure he'll bite. Who wouldn't want a reduction in rates? It would look odd if he refused to let an assessor visit when it's to his advantage.'

'So what do you think he'll do?'

'He'll try and stall you but don't let him off the hook. Tell him that the visit must take place tomorrow morning. Once he knows there's no way out, he will collect the ransom money left by Xavi at the washstands. Then he will either move the dogs in the night to a new location or finish them off, bury them on his land and cut his losses.'

'Surely he wouldn't do such a heinous thing, Bel?'

'We won't give him the chance.' Isabel clicked her teeth and stood up. 'Please make the call, Llorenç. I'll be in touch later to confirm arrangements.'

At the door, she hesitated. 'Just one other small matter. I'm afraid the door handle fell off as I was entering the building today. There's the tiniest hint of a dent on it.'

He grinned and shook his head. 'You don't change. Where is it?'

'In the safe hands of Josep. He isn't having the best of weeks.'

'I'm sure it's easily sorted. You and I have bigger fish to fry.'

Isabel thanked him. Skipping down the staircase, she was relieved when Jesus from Bon Día pushed open the front door of the town hall and ushered her through with a smile. As she crossed the *plaça*, she cast a look back only to see Josep kneeling like a devout monk in front of the solid arched doors, a pained expression on his face and the brass door knob cradled protectively in his hands.

*

Isabel returned to Ca'n Moix to find her house brimming with noise and people. Florentina and Doctor Ramis were performing stretching exercises in the *entrada* while two of her cleaning team and Idò were fussing over piles of towels and sheets on the kitchen table. With an exasperated sigh, she stood in the hallway and surveyed the scene in some bewilderment.

'Ah! There you are, Bel,' said her mother. 'Miguel and I are just back from Juliana's exercise class and doing a few stretches before we head off for lunch and a film in Palma.'

Isabel spread out her hands. 'Sorry, did I miss something? Has my *entrada* suddenly become a dance studio?'

'Don't be silly! It's good to keep flexible. We just happened to see the cleaning team and Idò arriving here as we headed home and thought we'd pop by to say hello.'

'Sure. It's not as if I need peace and quiet to think in my own house.'

Doctor Ramis offered her a genial hug. 'Still stressed after the night's events? I'm hardly surprised.'

'What events?' Florentina exclaimed. 'You didn't say anything, Miguel!'

He pulled a face. 'I apologise. It completely slipped my mind this morning. I was so fired up about our class.'

Isabel gritted her teeth. 'Nothing very exciting happened, Mama. Just a random burglar who didn't get very far.'

In a faint voice and making the sign of the cross, Florentina repeated, 'Burglar?'

'Well, he or she got their comeuppance. Furó sank his teeth into the felon and sustained a bit of a head injury himself, poor boy,' Isabel replied.

'What did Tomeu have to say?' asked the doctor.

'It's a flesh wound. He'll soon be as right as rain. The interesting thing will be to see if any DNA was left behind.'

Doctor Ramis nodded. 'Have the police already been here?'

'Nacho came early this morning,' she replied.

As Florentina sat down in a chair, her face ashen, Isabel waved at the others in the kitchen through the open door. Idò sauntered over to her.

'Morning, Bel. We can't remember which of the two houses you need cleaned first – Son Julia or Casa Ana?'

'It doesn't matter. We don't have new arrivals at either for a few days.'

He smiled. 'That's what I like to hear. I think we'll do Casa Ana this afternoon and I can get the pool engineer round at the same time. The filter is playing up.'

'If it's the motor, it'll be expensive to fix,' she replied gloomily.

Idò shrugged. 'Hopefully it's just a malfunction with the timer.'

'There are always problems with these old *fincas*. A never-ending job,' lamented Florentina.

Idò leant against the wall, a downbeat expression on his face. 'Any news on the animal thief, Bel? I miss my little fellow. Daft old bugger that I am.'

The chatter stopped, and Bel was aware that all eyes were on her.

'By tomorrow I hope to have good news, but it is vital that you keep this to yourselves.'

Idò laughed. 'I'm not sure what we need to keep to ourselves. You haven't told us anything.'

'I'm sorry. You're just going to have to trust me. By the way, where's Pep?'

'In the garden,' Florentina replied. 'He's smoking again. That's what working with you does to people!'

'Thanks for the vote of confidence, Mama.' She nudged Idò. 'Anyone making coffee?'

Her uncle slipped back into the kitchen and began grinding beans while the two cleaning ladies bustled out, having sorted their linen into a neat pile in a large wicker basket. They waved cheerily as they exited the house, leaving Florentina and Doctor Ramis to chat loudly together about the vintage film they would be viewing in Palma.

Isabel sloped over to her uncle and patted his shoulder. 'I'll get Perro back, I promise.'

He gave a wan smile. 'Don't make promises you can't keep, Bel, but I know you'll do your best.'

As they stood deep in thought, Pep sauntered in from the patio, reeking of tobacco.

'Smoking again, I hear,' Isabel remarked.

He spoke under his breath. 'It's the only way I can cope in this madhouse.'

'He's got a point,' Idò quipped. 'It's hardly a normal rentals office.'

'Normal is so overrated,' she replied. 'Anyway, Pep, we have important work to do before I go for lunch with Tolo.'

Florentina cut short her conversation with the doctor and stood with hands on hips in the doorway. 'So what's going on with you and Tolo?'

Isabel frowned. 'That's my business.'

Pep squirmed past and began ascending the staircase. 'I'll duck out of this conversation, thanks.'

Florentina flapped her arms. 'Just asking. He's such a lovely man and so devoted to you.'

'We are exceptionally good friends and that's really all you need to know. Now I must press on.'

Florentina was about to reply when she felt Doctor Ramis gently but firmly guide her towards the front door.

'We too must be off. I'm taking your mother to see *El Verdugo*, a wonderful satire released in 1963.'

Isabel stood at the bottom of the staircase. 'The Executioner? That sounds like a real rib tickler.'

'Oh, but it's a delicious black comedy and a black and white masterpiece, dear Bel. It was directed by Luis Garcia Berlanga and is considered a classic.'

'The plot is set in Mallorca too,' chipped in Florentina. 'It's about an execution that goes wrong.'

'Side-splitting stuff,' Isabel quipped.

'One day you should join us on one of our film excursions,' the doctor replied.

'I'll think about it. For now, I'm rather more preoccupied with real life executions.'

And with that, she walked slowly upstairs. Pep threw her a sympathetic glance when she entered the office.

'Don't mind Florentina. All mothers are like that. They just want to marry us off as fast as they can.'

'Then I shall be a big disappointment.'

Sitting at her desk, Isabel quickly dialled the main line for Ses Fonts and was surprised to find herself speaking with the sculptor himself.

'I'm afraid we're all over the place today. I'm heartbroken to report that our wonderful Lourdes has handed in her notice quite unexpectedly.'

Isabel frowned. 'I'm very sorry to hear that. She seemed devoted to you and the estate. Did she offer an explanation?'

Nicolas sounded distraught. 'Merely that it was impossible for her to continue due to personal reasons. Worst of all, she has left us abruptly with no time to find a replacement. We are hiring an agency chef until we can recruit a suitable candidate.'

'What about her husband? Doesn't Ismael know where she's gone?'

'Seemingly not,' he answered stiffly.

Isabel felt uncertain how to proceed. 'Perhaps this is a bad time to ask whether I could pop by tomorrow. It would be good to tell you about our findings so far in the Paloma case and to update you on the animal thefts.'

'It would cheer me up to see you. When did you have in mind?'

Isabel bit her lip. 'It would be better early evening.'

'In that case, do join me for supper around 8 p.m. I crave company on these dark winter evenings.'

'Thank you. I look forward to it.'

Isabel pressed the phone against her chin, a concerned expression on her face. Why had Lourdes taken off so suddenly? With a sinking feeling, she thought she knew.

*

Tolo and Isabel tucked into the seafood *paella* sitting between them at Can Busquets while Fabian, the proprietor, placed a basket of chunky brown bread on the table. He yawned and pulled up a chair.

'I just wanted to mention that I've a few cases of the house wine for sale, if you're interested. We're using a new vineyard from next week.'

'But I like it. Why change?' Isabel replied.

He shrugged. 'It's a small local *bodega* and they can't keep up with production, and I need consistency. I'm going to be working with an eco-producer in Felanitx.'

Tolo nodded. 'It's good to have a change. All the same, I love this red, so keep me back a case.'

'I'll have one too,' said Isabel.

Fabian stood up and winked. 'A special price for special clients.'

Tolo smiled across at Isabel. 'No wonder you love living here. It's like one big family.'

She laughed. 'Yes, it is to some extent, but don't forget we have someone in our midst who has been stealing pets.'

'But you have your culprit.'

'I do, but Gómez isn't keen to help with my planned operation tonight. He still claims that we only have circumstantial evidence.'

'The man's a fool. He doesn't seem to have had his horizons broadened doing the Camino de Santiago.'

Isabel toyed with a forkful of rice. 'But he only went for a few days. He complained about Paula talking too much along the way.'

'He'd have stuck to it longer if he'd gone with Maria instead.'

She tutted. 'Isn't it outmoded to have a mistress these days?'

'I agree,' he replied. 'But there are plenty of men who still have them.'

'Thank heavens you're different.'

Tolo placed his hand over hers. 'There's only one woman for me, that's if she'd agree.'

'She does agree, but she's too preoccupied with life at the moment and just wants to maintain a special friendship for now.'

He withdrew his hand with a heavy sigh. 'I know, I know. Okay, so tell me about your sting operation tonight, and then we can discuss your hypothesis on our serial killer.'

She nodded. 'You're going to be unnerved. As serial killer cases go, this one is as bizarre as it gets.'

Tolo studied her face. 'Nothing about human nature and the depths of its depravity surprises me anymore. All I care about is that we make an arrest imminently and put a stop to more abductions. The commissioner is running out of patience.'

'He'll have his prize, I promise. If you trust my reasoning, we're now urgently going to need a search warrant and be ready to make an arrest tomorrow night.'

'Have we enough to go on? You know that the commissioner and judge will need to be convinced.'

'I believe so, but more importantly another life could be in danger, so we have to act fast.'

'Whose life?'

'First things first,' she pulled out a file and thumped it on the table. 'You and Gaspar need to absorb this, but let me talk you through it now, step by step.'

She was about to continue when her phone bleeped. It was a message from Llorenç. It simply read: 'Our Pied Piper took the bait. On standby for tonight.'

Her eyes filled with zeal. 'Good news, Tolo. By this time tomorrow, I hope our animal thief will be firmly behind bars.'

TWENTY-FOUR

A grubby moon swung low in a muddy sky as Pep crouched against an old stone wall some distance from the ancient washstands in Biniaraix village. A few locals were giggling and chatting as they walked home along the narrow, cobbled street in the direction of Fornalutx. Enviously, he imagined they'd just enjoyed a few drinks at the bar in the tiny *plaça*. He scanned his watch and yawned. It was well past eleven-thirty. Where was Teo Darder?

Silence fell and a chill wind sent soft leaves fluttering like butterflies along the stony track of El Barranc. He zipped up his leather jacket and puffed out his cheeks while idly scrolling through messages on his phone. Pep gave a groan when he saw one from Angélica asking when he'd be home. He had told her that he was on important business with her father and could not divulge the nature of their assignation yet. She had been affronted not to have been entrusted with the information, but was somewhat mollified by his promise of a slap-up dinner at swanky Kingfisher restaurant in Soller port the following weekend.

Pep gave an involuntary shiver when he heard crackling sounds in the long dark grasses. He wondered whether rats were scurrying about, or was it perchance a genet or pine marten? The rhythmic single-note bleep of a Scops owl rang out in the stillness, followed by the raucous barking of frogs. Most of the valley's amphibians disappeared from the valley in the colder months but he'd noticed how during the past few winters they seemed to be hanging around all year. Why was that? Angélica blamed it on climate change but he believed they just couldn't be bothered to hop off anywhere else. And why should they? Living in an old water cistern in the heart of the Tramuntanas with plenty of tasty insects to gobble was probably as good as it got.

A loud cough caught his attention, followed by heavy footsteps. Peering out from his shadowy spot, he saw an elderly man with a wild beard, grizzled locks and crooked staff marching along the track with the determination of Job. What had he been doing in the mountains at this time of night, and how had he found his way to the village in the darkness? As he squatted quietly in thought, Pep saw the man hesitate on the track and sniff the air. For a while he didn't stir, but with a cock of the head, he suddenly swung around with a vivacity that belied his years and prodded his staff in Pep's direction.

'What are you doing down there, boy? Come out.'

Pep thought his heart might explode. In some panic he rose unsteadily and whispered hoarsely to him, 'I'm on a reconnaissance mission for the police, so I'd be grateful if you didn't blow my cover.'

'Is that so? Well if it's true you're not very good at it. I could see you some way off. Come here.'

Pep felt edgy and cross. Why did the old fool have to come along, and what if Darder pitched up now? All would be lost and Bel would be furious with him. Not wishing to incur the man's wrath, he decided to humour him.

'If I were you, I'd hide there,' the pensioner advised. 'Just inside that slight curve in the wall, behind the blue car.'

'That might not suit my purpose. I need to see anyone who comes to the washstands.'

'Try it,' he commanded.

Irritated, Pep headed towards the blue car and to his surprise found a dark crevasse, large enough to accommodate him, in the wall behind it.

'Actually that's a very good hidey hole,' he conceded. 'Thanks.'

The man smiled. 'I used to crouch in there as a nipper when I was in trouble with my father. It's never been bricked up. Be careful, lad.'

Striding forth in his baggy shorts and leather hiking boots, he carried on nonchalantly up the road and disappeared into the dusk.

Pep regulated his breathing. This sleuth work wasn't all it was cracked up to be. He was cold and achy and had spent more than an hour waiting for Darder to arrive – that's if he did. He was embarrassed that a wily and eccentric elderly local had discovered him in his hiding place, even though he thought he had been well out of sight. To counteract boredom and to keep Isabel informed, he quickly texted her. She replied that she was already stationed with Llorenç in woodland just beyond the rural property belonging to Darder's wife. The gate was padlocked but she was going to scale it and lie in wait. He texted back, asking her to be careful but then chuckled to himself. As if Bel would listen to him. She was a law unto herself and as stubborn as an ox. Still, he wouldn't change her for the world. Having put his phone in silent mode, he suddenly became aware of the sound of an engine and a white van, its lights low, slowly rumbled along the road in his direction.

Pep could feel his heart beating fast as he strained to see where the driver was heading. As the van passed the washstands, it halted close to where a few other vehicles were parked and the engine was silenced. By this time, Pep had squirmed out of his hidey-hole and crept on all fours around the side of the blue car. The door of the van creak open and Teo Darder stepped out. He was wearing jeans and trainers and looked furtively about as he walked slowly towards the washstands. Pep angled his phone and began taking shots. He hoped that in night mode and by the light of the streetlight and moon his images would be clear enough to provide the vital proof needed by his boss. He watched as the builder fished the small package out from below the washstand, examined it closely and walked back to the van. Even in the dull light, he could see a scowl forming on the man's face. Why was that? Had he already guessed that the package contained mostly scraps of paper or was he just in a foul mood? Pep kept taking images until he was convinced he had enough. Waiting until the van had left, he quickly checked his phone and in some relief rang Isabel.

'I got some clear shots of him collecting the package, and several more of his number plate and the van.'

Isabel sounded breathless. 'Fantastic, Pep. Well done. I've just climbed over the gate and have left Llorenç back in the car. I need to prepare for Darder's arrival.'

'What are you going to do?'

'I'll scout out the building and see if I can gain access. We need to establish that the animals are there. After that, I'll surprise him and hopefully you and Llorenç can back me up once the gate's open and you can drive through.'

Pep bit his lip. 'I don't like you being in there on your own. He might do something desperate. Can't you wait till we arrive before approaching him?'

Isabel sighed. 'Okay, but he might lock the gate after him. If worst comes to worst, you'll need to smash the padlock or scale the gate. It's high, so be careful.'

'What if you don't find the animals?'

Isabel was silent for a few seconds. 'If Darder comes to the property now, there must be a good reason for it. I'm convinced they're here. I must go. He could turn up in the next twenty minutes.'

Pep felt a swell of anxiety in his stomach as he ended the call. What if Darder didn't drive up the mountain to the remote property, or worse, came with a weapon? And what if the dogs weren't even kept there at all? Quickly, he got to his feet, jumped on his *moto* and set off. He had a small toolkit on board if needed and he could always use a spanner for self-defence. Should he call Capitán Gómez and beg him to provide back up? He hesitated. That would serve little purpose given that the arrogant Guardia chief still didn't believe Isabel had a solid case against Darder.

It was gone midnight, and as Pep curled up the dark and unforgiving mountain road, a soft ochre mist swirled eerily about the trees. Specks of rain began to stain the visor of his helmet and gradually increased, making the road wet and hazardous. The conditions didn't bother Pep as he'd been coming up to the olive groves since he was a boy. His grandparents owned an old *casita* and *olivar* high in the hills and his visits had always been a highlight of his childhood. Every Sunday, like clockwork, Marga, he and their siblings would accompany their parents up the steep, winding road to pick olives and enjoy an *al fresco paella*. While his grandmother and mother swirled the rice around in the voluminous pan of bubbling stock on an open fire, he and Marga would climb the olive trees like nimble monkeys and gather the fruit for his grandfather. They would first spread green cotton nets under the trees and delight in seeing the precious bounty grow before their eyes. Sometimes, Pep would risk chewing on a fruit and spit it out in disgust as the bitter taste suffused his mouth, but it didn't stop him trying again in the hope that one day it might improve. Meanwhile, his father would sit alone with his thoughts on a rocky summit under a blue and white marshmallow sky, cool beer in hand, oblivious to the frenzied and noisy activity around him.

Pep imagined he could drive this road in his sleep. He instinctively knew every bend and pothole and the worst of the hairpins. As he climbed higher, he became aware of the taillights of a van in the distance and cut back on his speed. It surely had to be Darder's? Who else would be navigating such treacherous bends and a road as slick and black as molasses, at this hour of the night?

Soon, the van pulled up sharply, and after a short while, rumbled along a track off to the left. Pep listened to the sound from his open window and hung back. Cutting the engine, he fretfully texted Isabel to warn her that she might have company and received a single word response: Great. Pep almost laughed. The woman was unhinged. What aspect of this perilous operation could be considered *great*?

When he was certain the van was well out of sight, he carried on along the road and turned onto the same narrow track. To his dismay, he was greeted by a vast metal gate that was closed and secured with a robust padlock. He dismounted his bike, and after examining it, returned to fetch his toolkit. Isabel might have enjoyed the challenge of scaling it but he'd prefer to take the easy route.

*

As rain tumbled down, Isabel was grateful that she'd chosen to wear her trail running shoes. Even in wet mud and on loose stones they rarely failed her. Having walked a good distance from the main gate she now stood outside the large and sombre *casita* wearing an anxious expression. Although the windows were all tightly shuttered, she couldn't hear any barking and the place was ghostly quiet. Silently cursing, she used her torch beam to guide her to the back of the building, where wild brambles and rotten lemon trees barred the path. Carefully she hoisted herself up onto a low wall and tiptoed through the briars to the rear garden. There were two small windows up above and she stood assessing whether she could safely mount the slippery rocks without putting herself in danger. Having decided not to take the risk, she returned to the front of the house and banged on the door. Surely if a dog was lurking inside, it would react to the noise?

As silence ensued, Isabel gave a growl and marched off to a campfire area some way off where a corrugated roof had been rigged. She could see the black remnants of carbonated wood, so presumed that barbecues and cooking took place here. Taking the plan of the property from her rucksack, she studied it closely. Llorenç had been able to give her a copy of the layout that was kept in the architectural records at the *ajuntament*. She looked up and scrutinised a path to her left. According to the plan, it led to a small outbuilding that was barely five metres in length. That wouldn't be large enough to accommodate a bunch of dogs. Still, she felt it worth exploring since the only nearby habitable building was an old stable that she had already explored.

The path meandered through heavy woodland and finally climbed up a small hill where to her astonishment she discovered a rectangular one-storey, purpose-built unit screened by bushy cypress trees. It was windowless and fabricated from concrete with a metal roll-up door.

'Well, well,' she muttered. Catching her breath, she consulted the plan again and realised that the erstwhile old building had evidently been demolished to make way for this larger, more secure lock-up. It had no doubt been built illegally, as so many rural outbuildings often were, as it failed to show on the records held by the town hall. She rattled the metal door and heard the sound of muffled whining from within. In frustration, she bent down and examined the secure lock. It wasn't going to be easy to penetrate the building and there were no other entry points visible. Taking out her phone, she saw that Pep had messaged her some minutes earlier. She read the text hurriedly and sent back an urgent reply. If the dogs were hidden inside, she would need the might of the Guardia to gain entry.

Slipping the phone back into her pocket, she crept around to the rear of the unit, and was disappointed to find neither door nor window. A piece of wasteland yawned before her, fringed by heavy shrubs. She was about to retrace her steps when her torch flashed an image that forced her to stop in her tracks. Someone had recently dug a deep trench beyond the building and in Isabel's mind, it could serve only one purpose. Bending down to examine her find, she felt a rage well up inside her. What kind of monster would kill the beloved dogs of people he knew, especially those who had already paid a ransom? As she stood up, a sudden rustle caught her attention. As quickly as she could, she killed her torchlight and, crouching, made her way stealthily towards a sodden woodpile that afforded some cover. Heavy footsteps clumped up to the front of the building before she heard the rattling of keys. She texted Pep again, and in some relief read that he had managed to open the gate and located Llorenç, and that both were on their way. Llorenç had also alerted the Guardia Civil. Weighing up whether to wait or act, she made her decision when she heard the hollow, booming sound of the metal door being opened.

Feeling her way in the darkness as rain blinded her, she peeped out from the side of the unit to see bright light flooding from the building. Carefully she crept up to the open doorway, and with no one in sight, entered. She was greeted by a blank and empty space, but a glass door to the right led onto a narrow corridor. Isabel controlled her breathing and slowly turned the handle. Once inside, she crept along, her mind whirring. A short distance ahead, she heard baleful barking and yapping, and the sound of a man talking soothingly but firmly. She could hear what sounded like chains being loosened and heavy panting and whining. The noise grew louder and suddenly Isabel arrived at the entrance to another stark room, where she discovered Teo Darder sitting on his knees with his back to her, surrounded by dogs she knew so well. At his side he had a rifle, and yet all of the animals were wagging their tails good-naturedly, relieved to have been released from chains within their individual pens.

Tears pricked her eyes, when she saw Perro limping towards his captor, a bewildered and sorrowful expression on his face. He seemed weak and broken and his body shivered uncontrollably. Without a second thought, she leapt forward and grabbed the rifle, pointing it directly at the builder. He spun round and for a moment stared at her in confusion until a sudden clarity hit him. While she stood with the gun directed at his head, he adjusted his position to face her. Perro gave a soft bark when he saw her and his tail wagged slowly like an old metronome. Sinking down on all fours, he panted, his eyes trained on her face.

Teo Darder fondled the dog's ears. 'Well done, Bel. You weren't fooled, after all.'

Isabel felt her hand shaking as she aimed the gun. 'So you were just going to shoot them all? Even one of your own beloved spaniels? I found the trench you prepared outside.'

Teo crossed his arms and smiled. 'I love dogs. To be honest, the thought of it broke my heart, but I had no choice. I couldn't afford to be found out. Besides, it would have been a swift death. I didn't reckon you'd catch on so fast.'

'You did all this for what? To take revenge on a few people who crossed you and to make a quick buck? The ransoms would never have cleared your debts.'

He shrugged. 'True, but at least I'd have had the satisfaction of breaking my enemies and causing them as much grief as possible.'

She stared at him in disbelief. 'How could you be so cruel? What has made you so callous and devoid of humanity?'

He laughed bitterly. 'Life, that's what. I had a thriving business and the whole thing fell apart through no fault of my own. Bad debtors, the tax system, complaining clients that lost me business, destroying everything I'd worked for here.'

Isabel remained mute, keeping the gun trained on him.

'So when did you know I was your famous Pied Piper?'

Isabel jerked the gun. 'Actually I had my suspicions the day you joined the vigilante group. Your fervour for the task didn't ring true. At first I sympathised when your spaniel had supposedly gone missing, but of course that acted as an excellent cover for your nefarious activities.'

'True.'

Isabel continued. 'The three white vans that we traced in the village at the time of the animal disappearances gave you away too. All were leased by your company to various local tradesmen who were given free parking facilities at your depot in Soller. When they returned from jobs, you had a spare set of keys and would use them to steal the pets. It created confusion and implicated them.'

'That was the aim,' he sneered.

'But you made so many mistakes. Sorry to be pedantic, but I discovered that at one time, you'd done repair work at every home where pets were stolen. That meant you were aware of where the animals were kept and how best to access them. You probably knew the owners' work shifts and habits.'

He nodded.

'The night I met you near Bernat's home convinced me that I was right about you. I deliberately gave you the evidence left at the scene as I knew you'd destroy it – you would have worried about traceable DNA. You dutifully took it to the town hall on Sunday as I requested but when Josep was doing his rounds, you slipped back into the building and took it. It's all on footage from a video camera that I had hidden in the entrance hall.'

The man offered her an insolent stare. 'Well, aren't you the clever one?'

'And that same night we walked back to the *plaça* together, you told me that you'd come on foot and I saw you heading off towards the *torrente*. In reality you were picking up the ransom money left in the old well by Pau. I walked about the village after you'd gone and discovered one of your white vans parked in a side street. No doubt once you'd picked up the money, you returned to it and drove home.'

'Spot on.'

'Of course, your final mistake was using letters cut out from *Ultima Hora*. It's a newspaper you read in Jordi's café every day. It was the final piece in the jigsaw.'

Teo let his arms swing by his sides. 'So what now?'

'I arrest you.'

'I don't think so, Bel,' he replied and in a fast move turned and grabbed Perro by the scruff of the neck. In a thrice, he'd pulled a small knife from his pocket and now held it to the dog's throat.

Isabel recoiled. 'If you so much as graze that dog, I will shoot you dead.'

He smiled. 'You won't shoot me, Bel. It's not in your nature. I'm going to take him with me and will tie him up once I'm safe and providing you don't follow. Otherwise, consider him gone.'

Isabel played for time. 'And where will you go? You tried to run me down in your van, you've stolen pets and money and held locals to ransom. The Guardia will hunt you down. There's no escape.'

'Trust me, I prepared for a quick getaway when and if the time came.'

'And what about your wife?'

'She'll be happier without me.'

Isabel heard the distinct sound of a creak in the corridor behind her and chose the moment to launch herself on the man. He was taken by surprise and fell backwards while Isabel squeezed his throat with both hands. While Teo Darder fought back, grabbing at Isabel's hair, Perro growled and tore at the man's shirt. The room suddenly erupted in chaos as Pep, Llorenç, Capitán Gómez and several Guardia officers poured into the room and the newly released dogs barked and ran about. Pep bent down and gently pulled Isabel free, forcing her to release her vice-like grip around Darder's neck. Her hair was askew and a thread of blood trickled down the side of her face. With irritation, she wiped it away with her fingers.

'It's over,' whispered Pep. After a struggle, Teo Darder was handcuffed and led away by two officers. Llorenç gasped. Sitting on a chair, he patted Llamp, Pau's Alsatian, as he tried to calm his breathing.

'Oh Bel, I'm getting too old for all this. Thank heavens you're alright and the dogs are all alive. This is a happy day for the residents of Sant Martí, though I feel sorrow at such betrayal from one of our citizens. To think a local could do this. If only it had been a foreign gang or…'

'But it wasn't,' replied Isabel firmly.

Capitán Gómez stood awkwardly in the doorway, one gloved hand resting on his cheek. 'I have to say, Isabel, that when Llorenç rang me from his hideout and told me of your bullish and defiant plan of action, I was highly displeased. I had categorically informed Llorenç earlier today that without proof, we could not risk a sting operation of any kind.'

Isabel stood with arms folded, eyeing him coolly. 'We had proof, but it just wasn't good enough for you, Capitán. If we hadn't acted, all of the dogs might have perished.'

'I concede that it has been an exceptionally busy time for our force of late. We've had far more pressing matters to deal with than a few village pets going missing.'

Llorenç coloured. 'You also seem to forget the ransom demands my citizens received and that Bel was nearly run over by Teo Darder.'

'Well, we have our criminal, and thankfully this highly unorthodox and ill-advised mission has ended happily. It appears that yet again, Isabel, Lady Luck was on your side.'

'She didn't get lucky, Capitán,' retorted Llorenç hotly. 'She used good policing methods and intuition to catch our Pied Piper.'

'That's as may be, but without our intervention tonight, the situation could have turned ugly.'

Pep frowned. 'But we'd asked you to help and you refused! That's why we had to act. Besides, we had the situation under control without you.'

'Young man, be careful or I might have to arrest you too for insubordination,' he growled. 'Don't let your gung-ho boss lead you astray.'

'It's okay, Capitán,' rejoined Isabel. 'I know how hard it is for you to be proven wrong. I'm just happy to have solved the case for you.'

She gathered up Perro in her arms. 'I trust you will care for these other poor mutts overnight and return them to their owners tomorrow?'

He offered a terse nod. 'I will, of course, need you urgently to file a report on the entire matter. First I will get a formal statement from the culprit.'

'I'll pop by early morning,' she replied.

Llorenç and Pep followed Isabel from the building as officers began rounding up the pets. Out in the crisp night air, Isabel yawned loudly and released Perro to amble at her side. 'At least it's stopped raining.'

'One small mercy,' said Llorenç. 'That man is such an ass. Come on, let me take you home. The car is just by the *casita*. It might be more comfortable for you both than Pep's damp *moto*!'

As they trudged off along the path, Capitán Gómez suddenly appeared on the steps of the building, and called out to Isabel.

She hesitated at the sound of her name and turned. 'You called?'

'Good job,' he blurted. 'A very good job indeed.'

TWENTY-FIVE

As Rafael pottered onto the terrace, he frowned when he saw the jumble of empty plates, cups and saucers. It seemed to him that the raucous crew that had taken over the best part of his café were all speaking at once.

'Any more orders, you lot?' he shouted.

Isabel turned to face him with a big smile. 'Maybe another *cortado*, my old friend, and two saucers of water for Furó and Perro.'

Idò, seated at her side with his beloved mutt on his lap, requested another black coffee and an *ensaïmada* pastry while Florentina, Marga and Pep ordered homemade lemonade. The mayor sat at the head of the table with a furrowed brow. 'It might only be eleven in the morning but it's been a tough week, so a bottle of San Miguel for me.'

'That's the spirit, Llorenç,' grinned Pep. 'How about some almonds and olives, too?'

Mumbling to himself, Rafael turned and almost collided with a tall blonde woman wearing a straw hat and shades.

'Oh!' she exclaimed, viewing the assembled throng in some distaste. 'There are live animals out here. That doesn't seem very hygienic.'

Rafael threw out his hands and said in his best English, 'I don't make the rules, lady!'

As the woman turned tail, laughter broke out at the table.

'So he *can* speak English,' said Pep to his sister.

'Only phrases he's learnt from the movies,' Marga replied.

Isabel gave her ferret a soothing pat. 'Don't listen, Furó, or you, Perro. We all love you.'

Florentina gave a sigh and sat forward in her chair. 'So how was Capitán Gómez

when you popped by earlier?'

All eyes turned to her.

Isabel sniggered. 'His usual cheery self. I gave him my report and the footage from the Vidcam I'd hidden at the entrance to the townhall early morning last Sunday. It clearly showed Teo sneeking off with the evidence he'd left earlier. Helpfully he had written a full statement admitting to his culpability anyway.'

Llorenç sat forward in his chair with a big grin on his lips. 'Placing that Vidcam there was so clever of you, Bel! You truly outfoxed Darder.'

'What I don't understand,' said Marga. 'was his reason for stealing those dogs. Why was he so angry with Idò and the others?'

Idò shrugged. 'I may have diddled him out of some loose change at a card game or two.'

'Is that all?' she replied with a grin.

He shook his head. 'I also complained about his work repairing my patio a year ago and refused to pay. We had a bit of a barney and he stormed off.'

Isabel nodded. 'He had an axe to grind with everyone: Gabriel for not extending his loan, Xavi for suing him on behalf of a client for shoddy work, Pau for having issued him parking fines and Alberto for denouncing him for a non-payment.'

He paused. 'Oh and he accused Bernat of fleecing him for car repair work.'

'What about poor old Magdalena Salas? asked Florentina.

'She complained about a supporting wall he'd built and told all her neighbours that he'd done a bad job. He claimed to have lost local business and she'd also insisted on a big discount.'

'Good for her,' chimed Pep. 'Sounds like he'd completely lost the plot.'

Florentina shook her head sadly. 'He has such a nice wife too. She's in my sewing bee and helps make the costumes for the *Moros y Cristianos fiesta* each May. No doubt she won't carry on.'

Llorenç banged the table. 'She has every right to continue. We must rally round and continue to make her feel part of the community. The poor woman will need all the friends she can get.'

'Will he go to prison for a long time?' asked Pep.

'Of course!' yelled Llorenç. 'He committed very serious crimes. How the mighty fall.'

'Gómez reckons he'll get at least eight years,' said Isabel.

'Serves him right,' replied Marga. 'He nearly ran over my best friend.'

Isabel leant over and squeezed her arm. 'I think he only meant to scare me, but it was a close shave.'

'Indeed it was,' grumbled Llorenç. 'He certainly took me for a fool all these years. He always had the fanciest cars and newest equipment. Even at his barbecues, he offered the classiest wines and most expensive steaks.'

'Appearances can be deceptive,' said Isabel. 'The peacock might puff up his feathers but he's just a skinny bird in the rain, like all the others.'

Her mother laughed. 'Wise words. So, will you take the rest of the day off to relax?'

Isabel shook her head. 'I'm afraid I can't. Tolo, Gaspar and I are having a meeting in Palma about our serial killer.'

'Are you getting any closer?' asked Marga.

Isabel nodded. 'Yes, I hope we will be making an arrest later today.'

There was a unified gasp.

'Today?' hissed Pep. 'But you said you'd need more time.'

Isabel turned to face him. 'I had a call from Ana Blanes, the former recruitment consultant, this morning. She remembered a piece of vital information that has confirmed my suspicions.'

'Why tonight?' he asked.

'Because our killer is becoming ever more reckless and another life is potentially at risk.'

'I want to help,' exclaimed Pep.

'Good,' Isabel replied. 'Tolo has requested a search warrant. Once we've got that, we'll map out our strategy.'

Florentina grimaced. 'Please don't take risks, Bel.'

'Furó needs you,' winked Idò.

Rafael bustled onto the terrace with a groaning tray and in some bemusement observed Isabel. 'I don't know about Furó but we all need you, so do as your mother says, catch the killer and come home to Sant Martí safe and sound.'

Llorenç grabbed his glass of lager. 'To Sant Martí, its residents, and to the one and only Bel!'

As everyone cheered, there came a cacophony of sound from the *plaça* below as a Guardia van rolled up and an officer released six happy, excitable dogs into the arms of their owners who were waiting patiently by the fountain. Everyone rose from their seats to view the happy scene and joined in with the whistling and clapping that rang out around the square. Pau was sitting on his haunches receiving huge licks from Llamp while Magdalena wept openly as she cuddled her poodle. Alberto was cupping his boxer's head in his hands while Xavi and Gabriel fussed around their respective hounds, a lively grey fox terrier and a black pug. Teo Darder's anxious wife stood apart from the others but threw her arms tearfully around the spaniel that ran towards her. Isabel smiled to see Alberto amble over to the woman to offer her a conciliatory hug.

'I do love a happy ending,' said Marga, between gulps of emotion.

'So do I,' replied Isabel as she hugged her old friend. 'So do I.'

*

Isabel had just parked her car at the Palma precinct when her phone buzzed. With a groan she surveyed the screen and propped herself up against the bonnet of the car.

'Josep! How are you doing?'

'All the better for hearing your voice, Bel. I just wanted to touch base about the animal thief in Sant Martí. I believe that an arrest was made last night?'

'Best to speak with the Guardia if you're in any doubt.'

Josep Casanovas took on a confidential air. 'I have spoken with Capitán Gómez actually. He explained how he'd set up a trap to flush out the felon and had already got a written confession.'

Isabel raised an eyebrow. 'The man's a genius.'

'Steady on, Bel. I wouldn't go that far, much as I admire him. He mentioned that you had played a small part in the affair.'

'Did he? How thoughtful.'

'So,' he simpered. 'Before I write up the story, I'd love to know how you were involved in the operation. Credit where it's due.'

'To be honest, Josep, I really played no part at all, so I'd be grateful if you could leave my name out of it.'

A pocket of silence made her question whether the obsequious editor was still on the line.

'The thing is, Bel, I don't believe you. I'm guessing that you masterminded the whole operation.'

'I'm touched, but that would be way beyond the remit of a rentals agent.'

'You see, when I asked the good captain for more details, he was somewhat foggy and flustered. It felt as if he'd played just a bit part.'

'He's very modest, and of course it would be inappropriate and a security breach for him to spell out the workings of the Guardia.'

'Have it your own way, but I hate only having one part of a jigsaw.'

'That makes two of us. Now, Josep, I really must be going.'

The editor stayed doggedly on the line. 'I believe that Gómez has been recommended for a promotion to *Comandante* and the apprehending of Teo Darder will no doubt go in his favour.'

'The wonders of a meritocracy, Josep,' she said playfully.

A sigh flooded the line. 'Unfortunately, should that happen, he'll inevitably be assigned to other duties and will no longer be in charge of the local force.'

'That would indeed be a tragedy for us all,' she replied with a ghost of a smile.

Isabel placed the phone back in her pocket and strode towards the precinct. *Comandante* had a good ring about it, and although some might question whether such an advancement was warranted, at least it meant that the exasperating captain would no longer be crowding her space. Every cloud had a silver lining.

As the lift door opened on the first floor, Isabel found herself face to face with Corc.

'Ah, Señorita Flores, I mean Bel, how opportune is this? The boss just asked me to fetch some coffees in anticipation of your visit. A *cortado* for you?'

'Perfect, Corc,' she replied. 'Is Gaspar here?'

'Yes indeed. They have been sitting in the office for hours. They both look very serious.'

'Crime is a serious matter, Corc.'

Tolo's highly-strung assistant stared at her in wonderment as he entered the lift, and continued to do so even when the doors closed tightly between them.

Gaspar stood up to greet her as she entered the office while Tolo smiled and waved her to a chair by his desk.

'Perfect timing. We've spent the morning trawling through the cold cases, forensic evidence and your detailed notes and reasoning. You make for a compelling case, but it's almost too preposterous and grotesque for words.'

'Horrific, Bel,' added Gaspar, shaking his head.

Isabel sat down. 'I wish I was wrong, but this morning I received a call from Ana Blanes which cemented the matter for me. I had left her a message about Lucy Vila, the maid who went missing eight years ago in Bunyola. She checked her files and discovered that she'd secured her a position at the Ses Fonts estate. She had been previously employed at Los Abetos.'

'How does that help exactly?' asked Gaspar.

'I'll explain in a minute. First, I want to know whether Nacho picked up anything of interest at my house.'

Gaspar nodded. 'He found a single hair, which is currently being analysed. If there's any follicular matter or blood detected, he'll run a DNA test on it.'

'Let's hope we get something from it. In the meantime, what about securing the search warrant?'

'The judge and commissioner were white at the gills reading your report, and issued it without a word,' replied Gaspar. 'I doubt any of us have come across a case like this before.'

Tolo gave her a penetrating stare. 'What we don't want to do is put lives in danger, particularly yours. As we agreed at lunch yesterday, you'll have a mic and transmitter and carry a piece.' He unlocked a desk drawer and placed a box in front of her. She slowly pulled out the semi-automatic pistol and examined it carefully.

'Heckler & Koch, a good, reliable German brand. We used Berettas in Madrid. Italian chic. Personally, I'd rather not carry a gun. A pepper spray would suffice.'

Tolo was curt. 'You don't have a choice. Take the gun or step down.'

Isabel replaced it in its home and shut the lid. 'That would rather jeopardise the operation, don't you think?'

Gaspar paced the room. 'Tolo's right. We're dealing with a deranged mind. We have no idea what might happen tonight, so you must carry a weapon. We'll be watching your back, but best to cover all fronts.'

Tolo fixed his gaze on her. 'The commissioner and judge are both adamant that we get a verbal confession via a bug so that no slick legal outfit can wriggle its way out of our net. The circumstantial evidence is overwhelming and yet there are still huge manholes to trip us up.'

Isabel sat in glum silence. 'I agree. This case could go two ways. Worst is not having any physical corpses.'

'Exactly,' Tolo replied. 'So much is historical, and without any hope of exhuming a body, we're on thin ice. Key witnesses are dead and we're dealing with powerful people.'

Gaspar came and sat down next to Isabel. 'We'll do a rehearsal with the technical team shortly to check the wire and then we'll discuss timing. Much as we'd all like this to run like clockwork, as you well know, operations can be unpredictable, especially with so many factors at play.'

'That's part of the thrill of it, though,' replied Isabel. 'Just knowing that I'll have you as back-up close by is good enough for me.'

Gaspar grinned. 'We'll be on your tail the whole time, so be warned.'

'You can count on us one hundred per cent,' said Tolo sombrely. 'We'll have the whole *cava*lry on standby.'

'I want Pep along too. He's become a real asset.'

Tolo seemed reluctant. 'As long as he doesn't get in our way and just stays safely beyond the perimeter as an observer.'

Isabel smiled as Corc entered, bearing a tray of coffees and sugared *churros*.

'Now that is a sight to brighten the greyest of days,' she said.

As they all helped themselves to the sticky doughnuts, Gaspar raised his coffee cup. 'Here's to a successful operation.'

Tolo nodded thoughtfully. 'Hopefully by this time tomorrow, everyone on the island will be able to sleep a little more easily in their beds.'

TWENTY-SIX

As Isabel followed the dark, winding mountain road towards Escorca, she marvelled at the silence. She had passed only one other car, its bright headlights jarring with her own until both drivers had dimmed them at exactly the same time. The vehicle was travelling at some speed, confidently navigating every curve in the road as it romped downhill. Isabel pondered whether the driver was on the way home after a long working day, or perhaps visiting friends and family for supper. Ridiculously, she felt envious of the stranger whose car would soon be entering her beloved valley, which was as welcoming and as cosy as a cashmere blanket.

Queasily, she contemplated having dinner with Nicolas, not an occasion she would relish. Whether they would actually get to complete the meal depended on how things unravelled in the household. She had spent much of the afternoon rehearsing with the armed response team of the National Police, and had in the breast pocket of her black blazer a non-descript pen fitted with a powerful microphone and transmitter. Pep would be joining the team in one of the surveillance vehicles which would be positioned on the edge of the estate. Tolo had ensured that his elite team would have the latest technology at their disposal, including handheld night-vision devices and telescopic cameras. They were well-prepared, and when she'd been able to extract a confession from the suspect, her role would expire as the *cava*lry stormed in.

All the same, what if something went wrong? This wasn't a straightforward scenario and she would need her wits about her. She shifted in her seat, feeling the unnatural heaviness of the semi-automatic pistol strapped onto her belt. For many years while in the police force, Isabel had grown accustomed to wearing a hip holster on undercover operations. Each day, when she got dressed, she would strap on her pistol without a thought, but now it felt unnatural and burdensome on her waist. She had chosen her outfit carefully for maximum comfort and flexibility. The stretchy fabric of her black trousers had a luxurious sheen but was robust enough to support a gun on the belt without sagging. Equally, the length of her jacket easily allowed for the concealment of her weapon and the plastic wrist restraints she'd brought could be stowed in the pockets. Having passed the placid Cuber and Gorg Blau reservoirs, both bathed in golden light cast from a full moon, Isabel followed the empty road, trying to dispel her anxious thoughts. As the sharp left turning to the estate's rural track came into view, she flicked Pequeñito's amber indicator, and took a deep breath as she rumbled along.

'In a few hours, it'll all be over,' she reassured her panting car. 'We'll be heading home to bed, without a care in the world.'

Pequeñito issued a loud gasp and shuddered as the track narrowed and rose ever higher.

'*Venga, amigo mío*. We must be brave in the face of adversity, enough of this spineless shaking!'

As smooth tarmac replaced rocks and silt, Pequeñito ceased his juddering and received an approving pat on the dashboard from Isabel. Using her headlights to follow the curves in the road and surprise hairpin bends, Isabel became aware of the tall sombre gates of Ses Fonts. To her disappointment, she noted that they were firmly closed, which might prove an added obstacle. Still, scaling the stone walls would require little effort for her fit police colleagues and would attract far less attention than using a vehicle to storm the grounds.

Under the cover of darkness, she could see nothing but bundles of sooty-hued trees and wild scrubland on either side of the track, but somewhere, concealed in the undergrowth, a team would already be in place and Tolo, Gaspar and Pep would no doubt arrive shortly. As she drove slowly up to the gates, she spoke quietly into her microphone, confirming her position. The team had pre-agreed that *calambre* would be her trigger word should she need immediate back-up, although the audio equipment in the police van would hopefully pick up on any signs of conflict well before that might be necessary.

A friendly male voice which she didn't immediately recognise greeted her via the intercom and the gates pulled open. Without a watch, she estimated that it must be just before 8 p.m., so she and Nicolas would surely be sitting down for dinner soon. She knew that her host was accustomed to retiring to bed early, so punctuality was probably expected.

As she coursed up the drive and parked in front of the house, Andel came over to greet her and opened her door.

'It's lovely to have you back with us,' he smiled. 'Nicolas is on the back terrace, so I'll show you through.'

Isabel stepped out of the car, this time determinedly taking her ignition key with her. In the brightly lit hallway, a young man bowed politely.

'This is our agency chef,' replied Andel. 'With Lourdes leaving at such short notice, the estate has been thrown into some turmoil. We all relied on her a great deal.'

'It must have been a shock for you all. How is Ismael?'

'Very upset,' he remarked. 'He knew nothing of her plans but we are all supporting him and he continues to work with us on the estate.'

Isabel shook her head in puzzlement. 'Has he no idea where she might have gone?'

He shrugged. 'Apparently not, but we are carrying out our own investigations. She could be in some kind of trouble.'

Nicolas was sitting peacefully in his wheelchair on the terrace, a woollen rug wrapped tightly about his knees. He was wearing a thick, stylish sweater in heather tones.

'I'm enjoying a glass of champagne,' he said by way of greeting. 'I do hope you'll join me.'

Isabel had anticipated this and gracefully accepted the glass proffered by the new chef. She raised it in his direction and took a tiny sip.

'Thank you for inviting me to dinner. During the week when I'm working, I usually feast on dishes left for me in the fridge by my mother.'

'Well, I'm glad you've made this an exception.' He turned to Andel. 'Could you lead us through into the dining room. It's growing chilly outside.'

Andel nodded and gently closed the French doors as Nicolas directed his wheelchair through the doorway. Isabel found herself sitting at one end of a polished mahogany table dominated by a grand silver candelabra. The linen place settings had been perfectly starched and the phalanx of gilt cutlery twinkled alluringly in the candlelight. An elaborate array of crystal glasses huddled expectantly by a bone-china bread plate while a silver water bowl stood to attention close by. As Nicolas faced her at the other end of the table, the chef and Andel fussed around, pouring mineral water and white wine, and serving bread and an array of appetising dips. Isabel, a self-confessed *gourmande*, for once felt not remotely hungry, and fiddled with the olive bread on her plate. Nicolas held up his glass of white wine.

'May I congratulate you on identifying the animal thief, Isabel. I know that my Misha was not among the captives but I am happy that others had their beloved pets returned.'

Isabel raised her glass but failed to sip the wine. She wanted to keep a clear head. 'It was a combined operation with the Guardia so I can't take all the credit,' she replied. 'Still, it was a success and the animals were returned safe and sound to their owners. That's what matters most.'

'Indeed it does,' he smiled. 'And do you know how the National Police are proceeding with Paloma's disappearance? When I met Llorenç by chance in Soller recently, he mentioned that you were assisting the force with the case. You are so multi-talented, Isabel.'

She glimpsed at the delicate pieces of fresh lobster and dill sauce placed in front of her and wished she had a doggie bag with her. Instead she took a small mouthful and attempted to appear relaxed.

'I am just in the wings should the force need my help. In confidence, the chief of police and his team appear to be closing in on the main suspect.'

Nicolas nodded slowly as he took a hefty forkful of food. He dabbed at his mouth with a napkin. 'So do you anticipate an imminent arrest?'

'Most definitely,' she replied. 'It's been quite a complicated case to unravel. And of course, the police have needed to re-examine cold cases that might have related to Paloma's abduction and that of Gunter Weber, the German, abducted in Artà. You may have read about it in the press?'

'A shocking series of events, but I just don't see how the two could be related – then again, I'm no detective.'

'Both were itinerant workers and took on freelance assignments and held positions on various estates such as Paloma did here at Ses Fonts.'

Nicolas held her gaze. 'Of course we were recommended Paloma thanks to the team at Los Abetos in Bunyola.'

'I remember. Apparently, Gunter Weber had also worked there at one time.'

Nicolas gasped. 'Is that so? I must confess that I feel some odd things have been going on over there recently.'

'Really?'

'Call it gut instinct, but I visited recently for lunch at the behest of Vincente Diaz, the butler I've known for many years, and I found him unsettled, as if hiding something. Marc, the chef, seemed unnaturally surly and after serving lunch zoomed off on his motorbike without waiting to serve coffee.'

'Strange behaviour indeed. You are very perceptive. I shouldn't say this but the police are also concerned about the goings-on over there.'

Nicolas sighed heavily. 'I'm not surprised. Since Paloma's abduction, I have had my suspicions about Vincente. We have always had a lot in common, especially as we hail from South America, but these days he seems furtive and stressed. I'd hate to think that he had any involvement in Paloma's disappearance or is covering up for someone.'

'And who might that be?'

He placed a hand to his forehead. 'I'm not one to speculate but Marc is someone I'd keep under the radar. Paloma mentioned being afraid of a creepy guy, and frankly, he was by all accounts obsessed with the poor girl.'

'That's concerning,' replied Isabel.

'Let's just hope that the police are on the ball.'

Isabel managed to consume small amounts of her starter and was relieved to see the plate whisked away by Andel. As he removed her fork and knife, she noticed a cut on his left wrist.

She flinched. 'That looks painful.'

He eyed her steadily. 'I was cutting through a tube in the garage and the saw slipped. My own fault for not concentrating.'

'What bad luck,' she replied.

The main course and dessert came and went, consumed alongside exhaustive discussions about the garden and local wildlife. Nicolas expressed concern about Isabel's tiny appetite.

'It's been quite a long day and if I'm honest I was eating churros with some friends late afternoon. It was an unexpected indulgence.'

He laughed. 'Well, in that case I shan't worry about you wasting away.'

'No chance of that.' Isabel placed her napkin decisively on the table. 'The meal was delicious, so bravo to your temporary chef.'

'Yes, he came with excellent references. Of course we're all devastated by the disappearance of Lourdes. We are actively trying to find her to bring her home.'

Isabel stiffened. 'Has she family on the island?'

'No. It's anybody's guess where she might be. Her husband, Ismael, did admit that she'd seemed downbeat and anxious of late.'

'It's odd that she should just take off like that when she's been so happy here. There must surely have been a very good reason.'

'People let you down when least expected, Isabel. It's a sad fact of life,' he replied.

Isabel placed her hands on her lap and felt the holster of her gun brush her arm. 'It's disappointing when that happens but it's how one reacts that matters,' she retorted.

He frowned. 'In what way?'

'Some might accept the situation and forgive and forget while others might consider retribution.'

'What a terrible thought,' he said. 'I am disappointed with Lourdes but I feel nothing but love for her.'

'I believe that,' replied Isabel with a sad smile.

Nicolas looked up brightly. 'As the night is still young, I wonder whether I might lure you for a stroll through the sculpture park. It is beautifully under-lit.'

Isabel hesitated and then smiled. 'Actually that would be perfect.'

Nicolas pressed a button on the arm of his wheelchair, and Andel arrived, carrying Isabel's Puffa jacket and scarf, and two warm blankets which he wrapped around his boss's waist and legs.

'Will you join us, Andel?' asked Nicolas with a sideways glance.

'Of course.'

The valet smiled warmly and opened the French doors that led onto the stone pathway. The moon shone like a smooth white pebble in the peppery sky, and outdoor lanterns flooded the lawns and rocky walls with ivory light. With some pathos, Isabel walked at Nicolas's side as he powered himself along, thinking about how magical it all appeared. When they reached the sculpture park, Andel held open the gate and ushered them through. The garden had taken on new meaning for Isabel. Now as she stood and admired Artemis and her sparrows, her eyes filled with sudden tears. Nicolas wheeled himself ahead and stopped at a bronze cat on a plinth. Isabel knew it was the sculpture made from the maquette of Misha. Somehow the sculptor had masterfully managed to create a mane of shaggy hair and a wonderfully expressive face.

'This is Misha, isn't it? She must have been a beautiful cat.'

Nicolas nodded. 'Yes, there'll never be another, but now she is here with us forever.'

At the side of a bare and scrawny apple tree, Isabel's eyes rested on the bronze of an elderly woman tucked away in the long grasses. She was wearing an apron and smiled wistfully into the distance. Isabel lowered her head and unable to control her emotions, turned to face Nicolas.

'Let's dispense with the charade. I'm guessing this is Luz Pujals?'

He was silent for a few moments and then threw a meaningful look at his valet.

'I told you she was clever.'

Isabel pointed towards the gate. 'And beautiful Artemis with the sparrows is Lucy Vila from Bunyola who disappeared eight years ago. When I saw her photo in the cold case file I knew I'd seen her before somewhere. You captured the essence of her perfectly.'

'Thank you. She was very special to me and she adored sparrows. I transformed a humble maid into a goddess.'

'No, you and your demented valet murdered a beautiful girl with everything to live for simply because she wanted to take up a new position in another estate.'

'She had abandoned our family. It was hurtful.'

Isabel felt her heartbeat quickening. 'So, where is Manolo Suarez, the shoe shiner?'

Andel suddenly lost his composure. 'She knows everything!'

'Calm yourself, Andel. I'm sure Isabel will understand the importance of our mission when it's been explained to her. Manolo was a champion swimmer. Did you know that?'

Isabel could barely form words. 'Yes, I did.'

'Come, here he is.' Nicolas's chair glided along a narrow path close to the studio. High above a stone wall rose the statue of a sinewy man clad in trunks, a towel slung over his shoulder. His hair was short but wavy, and heavy lines marked his face.

'Now he is immortalised. No longer a humble shoe shiner but a veritable Titon.'

Isabel rounded on him angrily. 'Who gave you the right to play God or comment on the worthiness of his profession? I imagine Manolo was more than happy with his existence.'

'I brought him back into the heart of his family.'

'You are delusional. He had his own beloved son and family. And where are Paloma Crespí and Gunter Weber?'

'Still works in progress, but I'd like you to see them,' he replied.

'That won't be necessary,' she rejoined.

'Oh but it is.' Nicolas's voice took on a steely note. 'I'd value your opinion.'

'You're a monster, and you and your misguided protégé are beyond redemption.'

'I'm disappointed by your reaction, Isabel. I had high hopes but evidently you don't have the depth of emotion to understand what I have been trying to achieve all these years. These people were lost and directionless. I had done my utmost to bring them into the heart of our family, but they betrayed and left me. Through forgiveness, I had to guide them back home, like a loving shepherd with his wayward flock, and guarantee them eternal life. Thanks to me, their memory will live on forever. Why don't you see?'

'You are a narcissist and a deranged magpie who selfishly stole bright and beautiful souls as if they were trinkets to feather your own nest. You were too selfish and self-absorbed to accept that people had the right to lead their own lives.'

'I lost the love of my life many years ago and swore that I would never relinquish those I loved ever again.'

'All you offered them was cloying patronage. It was a trap. It wasn't motivated by love but control.'

Andel came up close behind Isabel and pushed her forward. Something hard and metallic dug into her back. Was it a gun? He was terse. 'Keep walking. We are going to the foundry.'

She stopped and rubbed her leg, crying out, '*Calambre*!'

'Cramp? A good try. Keep moving,' Andel sneered.

Isabel was tempted to pounce but knew that by the time she'd reached for the holster, Andel would be close enough to overpower her. She breathed more easily knowing that at this very moment, police officers would be entering the grounds. Focusing on her hidden listening device, she decided to extract as much information as she could from them both.

'I was on to you from the outset, Nicolas. Early on, I knew you were trying to frame Vincente Diaz and his chef, Marc, at Los Abetos. For example, the Alfa Romeo used on the Bunyola estate sported Continental brand tyres. When I examined the cars in the garage at Ses Fonts, I discovered a Renault with brand new tyres. I'm guessing they were originally Continental brand but you had them changed after Paloma's abduction, to deflect blame to those at Los Abetos estate.'

'True,' replied Nicolas.

'I'm also sure that Andel has a motorbike with a faulty chain drive. Where does he keep it? Somewhere hidden on your land, I'm certain.'

'It's not important.'

'We will find it, be sure of that. You mentioned earlier that Marc had ridden off on a motorbike after your lunch at Los Abetos, again to put me off the scent and to try to implicate him.'

'It's all ephemeral now,' he replied impatiently.

'And of course you and Andel were each other's alibi the night of Paloma's abduction. In reality, your valet followed poor Paloma home that wet night and lay in wait for her near her uncle's land. She was a lamb to the slaughter.'

'Andel struck too soon. He was impulsive and acted without my instruction. He was angry that Paloma had rejected him. I would never have condoned such immediate action.'

'No, sadistically, you used to bide your time for a few years to ensure enough time had elapsed before you struck. That way no one would suspect your involvement.' She turned to Andel. 'If you hadn't been so reckless, you could both have carried on, perhaps for years, making people disappear. Key was that your victims were itinerant and that there was little trace of their varied work history.'

He glared at her. 'Hurry up!'

Nicolas led them all into the studio and Andel carefully locked the door behind them. To Isabel's dismay, he pressed a handheld device and a steel barrier began to descend, blanking out the windows and door.

Isabel gave a wry chuckle. 'Your wound wasn't caused by cutting a tube but by my brave ferret who gave you a good bite when you broke into my home hoping to steal cold case files. I knew you would come. '

'I hope I killed the beast,' he growled.

'Well you failed and you left valuable DNA behind.'

When she hesitated at the sloping passageway leading down to the foundry, he pushed her and shouted, 'Move!'

Isabel found herself taking reluctant steps behind Nicolas's wheelchair. Her thoughts were racing around her head but she maintained a sense of calm, focusing on the gun wedged into her belt and the pepper spray in her pocket.

Once in the foundry, Andel double-locked the door behind them and switched on the lights. Isabel blinked at the sudden brightness. Angrily she turned to Nicolas.

'You made a mistake at dinner mentioning the creepy guy Paloma had alluded to. You couldn't have known that unless you'd got Andel to bug my car. Last Sunday, I deliberately lay a trap for you by mentioning it to Tolo, the head of homicide, when he called while I was driving. Paloma had been referring to Andel but you tried to point the finger at Marc at Los Abetos.'

'And why not?'

'You did the same with Vincente. I deliberately showed you the wooden heart, which I presume you crafted and that Andel placed at each crime scene. You insinuated that the laurel wood used by the Mapuche people was prevalent in Argentina, where Vincente came from. I discovered from a Colombian police contact that this wood is most popular with the Mapuche community in Chile, your provenance. I'm assuming you have a good source there.'

'I do.'

'The Mapuche have long used laurel to make their large chemamüll statues, which signal the grave of a corpse. Maybe you found it ironic to create your own chemamüll in the shape of a heart whenever Andel abducted one of your victims.'

'It was a mark of respect and love. Their physical forms ceased to be but I gave them immortality here on the estate. All of these people betrayed me, Isabel.'

'They wanted independence.'

He shrugged. 'The same thing in my book. Everyone who works here is part of a big family. Family sticks together.'

Andel shifted uncomfortably behind her. 'I am putting her in the cage. She can't leave us now. She knows far too much.'

He thrust his gun with venom into the small of her back as he nudged her into the secure locked zone that guarded commissioned sculptures.

Seemingly oblivious, Nicolas smiled at Isabel. 'If you turn to your right, you will see the unfinished works of both Paloma and Gunter. Are they not beautiful?'

Horrified, she jolted back against the wall and eyed two sombre, unpolished life-sized statues. One was holding a posy of flowers, the other leaning against the trunk of a tree with a spade. She stared at them wordlessly as Andel secured her inside, locking fast the metal grille. He stood back with revolver extended while Nicolas appeared lost in his own thoughts.

Hoping to buy some time, Isabel called to Andel. 'So why did Lourdes leave so suddenly? Did you frighten her away too with unwanted advances? I do know that you placed my car keys in the pocket of her apron when I last visited. Why was that? To implicate her or confuse me?'

He shrugged. 'To send you on as many wild goose chases as possible. As for Lourdes, she wasn't worried by me. I had no problem with her.'

Isabel nodded. 'I believe you, because I came to realise that she was in love with Nicolas. Whenever I visited the estate she became increasingly distant and cold towards me.' She turned to Nicolas. 'I must admit to having distrusted her, but she was simply jealous of any other woman that had an audience with you.'

'She was infatuated with me, poor girl. I would hardly be interested in pursuing a member of my staff,' he replied tersely.

'I imagine she felt that she was living a lie with her husband, Ismael, when she was smitten with you. That is why she left.'

Isabel looked across at Andel. 'I feel pity for you. You haven't had much of a life.'

'You know nothing about me,' he spat.

'I know enough from INTERPOL, which I made contact with. Your name means "God's messenger" in your mother tongue and unsurprisingly, your family was deeply religious. Your father was abusive and controlling and was accused of embezzling funds from his last company in Prague, so he fled Czechoslovakia for Mallorca with your mother when you were a young boy. The police in Prague told me that he remains a person of interest. You had a disciplined upbringing and you worked hard at the local school here, but while your mother smothered you with unwanted affection, your father was a brute and beat you. Life was all about order, and to survive, you were an obedient son. When you'd just turned eighteen, your parents were killed in a freak car accident on the road to Lluc and Nicolas took you in. You were liberated but in shock and alone in the world. He became your father figure and convinced you that in carrying out his deranged killings, you were doing a noble deed. In effect he groomed you to become his messenger of evil.'

He stared at her with zealous eyes. 'God abandoned me as a child but relieved me of my hateful father and weak mother when I turned eighteen. I was reborn thanks to Nicolas, my new father. He saved me, and also many other miserable souls that had lost their way. I helped them to leave this world peacefully so that they would live on eternally through Nicolas's creations.'

'How did you kill them?' she whispered.

He was matter-of-fact. 'Chloroform. They just drifted to sleep. It was all very painless.'

Isabel shook her head, unable to fully comprehend what she was hearing.

'Heartlessly you killed Paloma. You had placed a bug in her boyfriend, Pere's, car the day he came to collect her from the estate. You knew she was walking home alone in the rain and you knew she was terrified of you. She had told a friend that you were obsessed with her. Presumably when she spurned your advances, you decided to murder her.'

'I gave her immortality,' he shouted.

'But Nicolas wasn't happy with you. You acted on impulse and broke the careful pattern that your master had crafted, undetected by the police, for years. He would wait patiently before instructing you to abduct another victim. This time you disobeyed him.'

'He was a silly, impetuous boy,' replied Nicolas, as he charged the steel furnace. Isabel heard a roar from the machine and wondered about his intention. 'He became obsessed with the girl and her disappearance set off a chain of unfortunate events.'

'By that I imagine you mean the killing of Gunter Weber and his friend, Archie Brookes? Your apprentice decided to play with fire. He took decisions without consulting you. When he heard that Gunter was back on the island, he decided to strike again, and when he discovered I was hot on the trail, killed Archie Brookes by default.'

'It was a nuisance, I agree. Very reckless and I told Andel so. That is why we tried to point you and the police in the direction of the staff at Los Abetos.'

'When we first met, you told me that Andel adored dogs and that he always walked your Labrador, Harry.'

'What an excellent memory you have,' Nicolas replied.

'That's what raised my suspicions at the crime scenes of Archie Brookes and Gunter Weber. The two dogs had bizarrely been spared and given food and water. Andel immediately entered my thoughts.'

Nicolas rounded on his valet. 'Very careless, Andel. What were you thinking? You should have disposed of them.'

Andel was now pacing the room in a turbulent state of mind. 'We must dispose of *her*!' he yelled.

'Calm down. We need to think.'

Isabel laughed. 'You're both a pair of amateurs.' She looked at Nicolas. 'When you told Llorenç that Misha had possibly been taken by the animal thief in Sant Martí, it made no sense at all. Your estate is miles from our village. I began wondering why you would have invented such a story. Gradually it dawned on me. Llorenç served a useful purpose as he introduced me to you. Through your close friendship with the commissioner at the National Police, you had discovered that I was being seconded to help in the disappearance of Paloma. That's why you got Andel to put a device in my car to track my movements.'

'I can't argue with that.'

'And at dinner you feigned that you'd met Llorenç in Soller recently and that he'd told you that I was working on the Paloma case. As if my mayor would divulge such details. You've known all the time.'

'He has a big mouth, you must admit.'

Isabel ignored him. 'What was insidious was that you offered a reward and funded a vigilante group in our village to keep us all close. I presume Misha ended up in the furnace too?"

'She was elderly and had died in her sleep, and naturally I wanted to immortalise her, too. Her magic lives on.'

'When it became clear that the animal thief had nothing to do with her disappearance, you invented a fictitious car apparently seen by your valet in the middle of the night. And then you told me about a theft in your studio. Why? To imply that you were vulnerable and that dark forces were at play, external to the estate?'

Nicolas sat quietly in his chair and ignored the angry demeanour of his valet, whose gun remained trained on Isabel's head.

She gave a bitter laugh. 'Another bizarre coincidence occurred. A friend showed me a book about the archaeology of death and burial. In the Bronze Age the corpses of the dead were often burnt in furnaces to a very high temperature along with molten metal in order to gain immortality. The human particles merged with the liquid bronze, which was fashioned into swords or everyday objects. In effect, the deceased were smelted into something new and eternal. Flesh acted as the fuel that married technology and cosmology.'

'Beautifully put, Isabel.'

She ignored him. 'I visited Ses Paisses recently, the Talayotic site near Artà, and saw where a furnace had once existed. The Talayotic people believed that the particles that remained following cremation contained the pure essence of a person. It allowed those left behind to control the identity of the parting soul and to transform them into something new and everlasting, be it coins, vessels or weapons. Local archaeologists found fragments of bone in the same furnaces used to smelt bronze.'

Nicolas sighed heavily. 'I must say, I'm impressed. You certainly did your homework. It was a fascinating practice by a highly evolved ancient culture.'

'I thought so too, but your version is so much more grotesque. You killed the living for the purpose instead of using those already deceased.'

'I did it out of pure love,' he replied.

'Love? To incinerate in cold blood those who showed you nothing but loyalty and transform them into lifeless and mute statues on the estate – for what?'

'No, Isabel. I *gave* them life.'

The heat from the furnace was now fierce and Nicolas sat in front of it, mesmerised by the sound of the motor and the roar of the flames. 'Would you like to see how bronze is melted, Isabel?' he asked pleasantly, his eyes strangely opaque in the half-light. 'We could melt an ingot or two, couldn't we, Andel?'

Isabel's ears detected a dull sound from somewhere above the room. Andel twitched and stared at her. 'You didn't come alone, did you?'

She spoke quietly. 'It's too late, Andel. The police are here. This is the end of the line for you both.'

In fury, he pointed the gun at her. 'But first you will die. You will not be immortalised like the beautiful souls here on the estate but will rot in the soil or burn in a municipal crematorium. Gone in a whisper.'

As Isabel used the moment to pull out her pepper spray, Nicolas wheeled himself towards Andel and pulled at his sleeve. 'Stop! My beautiful boy, my son, it's over. You have gone too far.'

Furiously, Andel ripped his arm away from his mentor just as Isabel aimed the spray at his face. While he recoiled and screamed, she removed her pistol and blasted the lock, ducking down as it exploded. Pushing the door open in the acrid and putrid air, she coughed on her sleeve and directed the gun at Andel, but in a second two shots rang out just as the room burst into life. Police officers in protective equipment and with guns raised raced inside and soon Isabel found herself being led firmly out of the chaos by Tolo, his face as pale as the ash of the furnace.

TWENTY-SEVEN

It was nine o'clock and the village clock began pounding just as Llorenç attempted to bring order to the meeting. He looked at his watch, and with a sigh, drummed his fingers on the desk, waiting until the last reverberating chime had ceased.

He had convened the Sant Martí event committee in the hope of allocating key tasks to the various incumbents before the festive season got underway. Traditionally, the town hall held an annual event on Christmas Eve after the church service at which a young girl from the village was given the honour of singing the famed *El Cant de la Sibil.la, the Song of the Sibyl*. This spine-tingling and sombre rendition of a medieval poem about the final judgement was performed from the pulpit and the chosen singer, dressed in a white robe, had to keep a sword erect throughout. This was no mean feat, nor was having to sing with no accompaniment save an organ blast between stanzas. Following the service, piping hot chocolate and *ensaïmadas* were served to all the villagers either at Café Jordi or Bar Castell. The two bar owners were gracious in accepting that the event would be held at their respective premises on alternate years.

The festivities didn't end there. While private family celebrations took place on Christmas Day, there was a special gift-giving ceremony of turkeys and fruit baskets for local elderly citizens on New Year's Eve and in the evening, a party in the village square. Llorenç ensured that a famed valley oom-pah band was hired and that the *cava* flowed while packets of twelve celebratory grapes were freely available to all. When the village clock struck midnight, citizens would get ready to gulp down one grape with every chime of the clock. Woe betide anyone unable to guzzle down all the grapes in time as this signified potential bad luck.

Llorenç offered a tight smile as silence once again reigned. 'Ah, peace at last,' he sighed. 'Now, as time is not on our side and we all have work to do, is everyone clear about their respective roles at the Christmas Eve church service and also on New Year's Eve?'

There was a general mumbling and nodding of heads. Isabel was keen to break loose, and with a Chupa Chup in her mouth, began quietly placing her notebook and pen in her pannier. Llorenç smiled across at her.

'Padre Agustí tells me that you will be giving a reading at the service on Christmas Eve, Bel.'

Isabel withdrew her lollipop. 'Yes, apparently so,' she replied with a wink.

'And remember, everyone, that the presentation of the unusual Indonesian cockerel to our dear Señora Coll takes place at seven o'clock today in the *plaça*. It will be a complete surprise for her, although she knows to be there on time. We will be serving *cava* and *coca*.'

Pep stole a glance at Isabel and mouthed *coca* then rolled his eyes when Llorenç wasn't looking. She waggled a finger at him and grinned as everyone rose from their chairs, talking animatedly.

Alfonso signalled to the mayor with a frantic wave. 'Llorenç, you will ensure that I have enough responsible volunteers to run the *cava* stand this year? It was a bun fight last New Year's Eve! Remember how Pau's nephew got very drunk and crashed onto the table?'

'*Sí, sí*,' he said, putting a placatory arm around the shoulder of the fretful artist. 'Don't worry. I will personally select the young people to help you this time.'

At the door, Llorenç beckoned to Isabel when the others were chatting. 'I hear that you had quite a night over at Ses Fonts.'

'It certainly was action-packed,' she replied with a wry smile. 'How did you hear about it?'

'Our friend, Capitán Gómez, called me at the crack of dawn with a full-blown report.'

Isabel chuckled. 'He wasn't even there! It was a National Police operation.'

He shrugged. 'I know, but he hates to miss out. His life isn't so exciting. Who would have thought such a wonderful sculptor could have done such unthinkable things?'

Isabel nodded in agreement. 'It's a tragedy. He had lost his mind and turned Andel into his puppet and murder machine.'

'And ironically, Andel ended up killing his master.'

'True. It's hard to know whether he shot Nicolas deliberately or it was just an unfortunate accident as they struggled with the gun. He will be questioned at the station this morning, so I might hear more from Tolo later.'

'The important thing is that you didn't get hurt. It was risky.'

'Any undercover operation involves a degree of danger, but Tolo and the special operations team had my back.'

Isabel and Llorenç walked slowly down the main staircase of the town hall and stopped by the formidable wooden front door.

Isabel kissed him on both cheeks and was about to leave when her lips parted in a huge smile.

'The door handle is fixed!'

Llorenç laughed. 'It is indeed, Miss King Kong, so please don't touch it on your way out.'

*

As Isabel dawdled outside the town hall, Padre Agustí bustled over to her. He was smiling broadly and waving a sheet of paper in his hand.

'Bel, I wonder if you'd kindly read my speech for the Señora Coll presentation tonight. I wanted to strike a happy note, highlighting how God works in so many mysterious ways, bringing about peace and light.'

Isabel nodded. 'Of course, but in truth, I haven't seen much peace and light the last few days.'

He hung his head for a moment. 'Ah but you must have faith, Bel, and all will come good. Sometimes the darkness can be overwhelming, but we must persevere in order to reach the light.'

She took the piece of paper and read through the contents, smiling at the *padre*'s biblical reference to Peter the disciple denying Jesus three times before the cockerel crowed. The priest had also referred to how the Chinese regarded the the cockerel as a symbol of honesty.

She passed it back to him. 'A lot of nice irony in there too.'

Padre Agustí frowned. 'I don't think that was my intention.'

'Ah well, an added bonus, in that case. Well done, Padre.'

Isabel smiled and strode off in the direction of Ca'n Moix, keen not to be late for her mother and uncle, who had arranged to bring fresh *ensaïmadas* for breakfast. Before she reached the garden gate, she heard fast footsteps behind her and turned to see a panting Pep a few paces away. He stopped to catch his breath, taking big gulps of air.

'You could have waited for me. I got caught up with the event committee.'

'You're getting rather unfit, young man. Time to give up smoking, perhaps?' she baited.

He followed her into the house. 'I've already stopped. Angélica gave me hell for starting again. Besides, now all these pet thieves and murderers are no longer on the loose, I won't feel so stressed.'

'All the same, I was happy that you came to Ses Fonts last night. It was reassuring to see you at the gate.'

Pep shrugged. 'Tolo wouldn't let me join the officers breaking into the grounds. I had to stay in the police van watching them on the screen. A bit boring.'

'It was a job for trained firearms officers and I would not have been happy if your life had been put at such risk.'

'But it was okay for you?'

Isabel laughed as she stood at the bottom of the staircase, listening to her mother and uncle chatting animatedly from the room above.

She tapped Pep's arm. 'Yes it was, because that was my job for many years and I know the drill.'

In the office, Isabel found her mother and uncle sitting comfortably on the sofa, a big pot of coffee in front of them on the table and a pile of *ensaïmadas* still wrapped in white tissue paper.

Florentina jumped up and hugged her tightly. 'We heard on the news that Nicolas Garcia was killed last night on his estate and his valet, Andel Picó, taken in for questioning. Were you there?'

Idò chuckled. 'Of course she was there. Where else would she be?'

Her mother mumbled a short prayer. 'Thank heavens you're safe. I wish you'd give up all this police work. It's that Tolo Cabot, luring you back when you could be leading a peaceful and safe life here in Sant Martí.'

'And be bored stiff!' yelled Pep.

'I have to agree,' replied Idò. 'Besides, she and lover boy make a great team on all fronts.'

'Careful, Idò,' Isabel growled, giving him a hug. 'So is someone pouring us coffee?'

'We were waiting for you!' exclaimed Florentina as she fussed over plates and cups. 'So tell us what happened last night.'

Isabel shot a wary look at Pep. 'In a nutshell, Nicolas Garcia and Andel Picó were both responsible for the deaths of Paloma Crespí, Gunter Weber and Archie Brookes. Andel carried out the abductions and killings but it was on the instructions of Nicolas.'

'It is too shocking to imagine,' gasped Florentina.

'We also know that they abducted and killed at least three others: Luz Pujals and Manolo Suarez, who were both pensioners, and a young maid named Lucy Vila. I fear there were more that we may never know about, although the other statues dotted around the grounds may lead us to fresh investigations.'

'But why did they do it?' asked Idò. 'It makes no sense at all.'

'It did to them. Nicolas genuinely believed in his deluded mind that he was bringing members of his flock home. He regarded all his staff as his possessions, a warped idea of family. If anyone left his employ, sooner or later, they would be abducted and brought back to the estate to be fashioned into a statue. All of his staff were on freelance contracts and paid in cash. They also had peripatetic work assignments. All of this meant that it was difficult to trace them back to the estate when they went missing.'

'And also he waited a few years after they left the estate before he pounced,' said Pep.

'That was true until Andel got cocky and started acting alone and impetuously abducted and killed Paloma.'

'Why did he change?' asked Idò.

'He was angry that Paloma had rejected his advances before she left. He wanted to punish her and wasn't prepared to bide his time before meting out retribution,' Isabel replied.

'So they cremated all the bodies and turned them into statues?' asked Idò.

Isabel grimaced. 'It's not a pleasant subject, but yes, the bodies were burnt for several hours at a temperature of about one thousand centigrade in the foundry. The sand-like particles were then mixed with the melted copper and tin and formed into bronze statues. Human matter is easily broken down in extreme heat.'

'What about bone and teeth?' asked Idò.

'A good point. Teeth can burn completely if the temperature is high enough, but I imagine that our killers would have needed to sift out small fragments of bone and teeth from the furnace. Of course, if victims had had metal hip replacements or porcelain teeth, they'd have needed to be removed.'

'It's impossible to think that anyone could dream up such a grotesque idea,' said Florentina.

'That's the interesting part. A few weeks ago I met with Aina in Morells and she showed me a book about the archaeology of death and burial. It turns out that six thousand years ago during Neolithic times, pottery kilns could withstand temperatures of nine hundred centigrade, and so human cremation would have been totally feasible. By the time of the Bronze Age, copper and tin were being smelted and human remains were often melded with liquid copper to create weapons and keepsakes so that the deceased lived on in a new guise with the living.'

'It's so macabre,' Pep said while chomping on his *ensaïmada*. 'Ingenious, though, because the victims' DNA would cease to exist.'

'More deranged than ingenious,' sniffed Idò. 'I doubt Neolithic man would have worried about DNA though. So what will happen to all the statues on the estate, Bel?'

She took a sip of coffee. 'I don't know. Tolo is coming over for the cockerel presentation and later we'll be dining at Can Busquets, so hopefully he'll have more news.'

Florentina gave Idò a knowing wink. 'That's lovely. We all like Tolo very much, don't we?'

Pep laughed. 'Come on, Florentina. Let's leave them to it. I'm sure they'll get it together when the time is right.'

'Thanks, partner,' replied Isabel. 'We're happy as we are, so no more on the matter, please, Mama.'

Idò thumped the table. 'I'm with Pep. It's none of our business, dear sister. More to the point, what's going on with you and the good doctor?'

'Yes, tell us about that,' heckled Isabel.

Florentina blushed pink. 'What, Miguel and I? Don't be ridiculous. We're just old friends having a little fun together.'

Pep smirked and started humming Wagner's bridal chorus, much to Isabel's amusement.

She prodded her mother affectionately. 'Now you know what it feels like!'

'*Touché*,' she replied. 'I'll stop pestering you. I just want to think you'll be happily settled down one day.'

'Maybe I will, but it will be on my own terms,' Isabel replied.

Idò got to his feet. 'Well, I've work to get done. Come on, Florentina, you and the village ladies are baking for the event tonight. Better get cracking.'

'More *coca*,' grumbled Pep.

'Actually, young man, we will also have sausages on sticks and tuna pasties.'

'*Madre de dios!*' he shouted. 'Let's celebrate.'

'No need to blaspheme, young man,' growled Idò, as he threw open the office door. 'We'll see you lot later tonight.'

When they'd scuttled off down the stairs, Isabel and Pep grinned at one another.

'So, back to work,' Pep yawned.

'Indeed. I must call Julian Mosquera.'

'To thank him for his help?'

'Yes. He discovered from his Chilean police contacts that laurel wood was popular with the Mapuche indigenous community and that it had great significance when crafted into chemamüll statues. That got me thinking early on about the meaning of the laurel hearts at the crime scenes.'

'So in Nicolas's twisted way, they signified love?'

'Indeed, and also served as a marker, just like the huge chemamüll statues for the deceased.'

'So he wanted the police to know that the person was deceased?'

'I'm not sure. Whatever the weather, the heart was his calling card, and those that commit serial killings or crimes often leave a tantalising and symbolic artefact.'

'What will happen to Andel Picó?'

'I don't know, but I think he'll be going to prison for a very long time.'

Pep gave a sigh. 'Now it's all over, life's going to be a bit dull.'

'Of course it won't be. It's nearly Christmas and then we'll have all the *fiestas* and lots of holiday bookings in the lead up to Easter. Then of course, there's Colombia to think about.'

'What do you mean?'

'Julian Mosquera is now liaising with Emilio Navarro, my private investigator, to locate Uncle Hugo. Julian and Emilio both believe that he is still alive and being kept in captivity. I am keen to visit to pick up the trail.'

Pep remonstrated. 'But it's too dangerous to go alone.'

'Who said I'd be going alone?'

'Well, who'd be going with you?'

'Tolo, of course,' she replied with a smile.

*

It was early evening and the pale lilac sky was threaded with wispy cream clouds. Isabel and Tolo sat in the garden basking in the last rays of sunshine while sipping on cool beers.

Tolo smacked his lips together. 'This is the life.'

'It seems hard to imagine that only last night I was staring down the barrel of a gun,' she replied.

'As always you kept your cool under pressure, but that metal grille covering the studio door foxed us. We were shadowing you all night but hadn't anticipated you heading off to the foundry.'

'Me neither, but in a way it had to be. I needed to get a full confession and to understand what had really happened down there. It makes me shiver.'

Tolo nodded. 'A veritable tomb. By the way, my team did a major search of the estate today and discovered Andel's faulty motorbike hidden near the gardener's cottage. The old man and his wife were totally unaware of all that had gone on.'

'Now that Nicolas is dead, will his and Andel's verbal confession be enough for a conviction?'

'Yes, the recording is perfect but Nacho has also provided solid proof. After Andel broke into your house, you'll recall that Nacho discovered a single hair in your *entrada*. The DNA present in the follicular material exhibited class characteristics such as race.'

'It showed that the perpetrator was Czech?'

'Spot on. Thanks to your little ferret having a tousle with him that night, a fatal error was made.'

Isabel called to Furó under the table. 'Did you hear that?'

Fast asleep on an old rug, the ferret continued to slumber, his breathing slow and rhythmic. 'I won't awaken him but he'll have a special treat for breakfast tomorrow.'

Tolo drained his glass. 'On a brighter note, we heard from Nicolas's lawyer. He left his entire estate to his staff, so they'll all be quids in.'

'What about Lourdes? Have you found her yet?'

Tolo smiled. 'She contacted us this morning when she saw the news about Nicolas. Apparently she had been staying with an old school friend in Campos until she'd decided what to do with her life.'

'And what is that?'

'She told us that she was infatuated with Nicolas but that after speaking with Ismael she would give the marriage another try.'

'Maybe the thought of such a huge inheritance helped soothe her pain at Nicolas's death,' Isabel replied with a grin.

'Maybe they'll all stay on the estate, although that seems unlikely. I imagine they'll split the funds once the government and lawyers have had their slice.'

'But what about the fate of the statues?' she asked.

Tolo shrugged. 'That's for discussion. They may even be offered to the families of the victims. After all, they contain the ashes of the deceased.'

'I feel so much for the relatives,' Isabel sighed.

Tolo nodded. 'At least they'll have some sort of closure. We must be grateful for that.'

She turned to him. 'Do you think Andel meant to kill Nicolas?'

He clicked his teeth. 'It's hard to know and somehow I don't think we'll ever have the answer. So far Andel has remained doggedly taciturn under questioning.'

Isabel took a sip of her lager and brightened up. 'Capitán Gómez will be joining us all this evening. I hope he's not too sore about last night.'

Tolo laughed. 'He'll no doubt try to take credit for the operation, even though he was tucked up in his bed. Hopefully if he gets his promotion, he'll move on and give us all some peace.'

'Don't bet on it,' she grinned. 'So, dinner at Can Busquets tonight?'

'You bet. Besides, I need to pick up my wine order.'

'Me too. We can have a nightcap back here later.'

He grinned. 'That was my hope.'

The magic of the moment was rudely interrupted when Idò erupted from the kitchen door. 'Come on. The event's going to start soon. We need everyone at their stations.'

Isabel gave a groan. 'It's not even seven o'clock yet.'

'That's as may be, but Señora Coll is already waiting in the square in her Sunday best and the villagers have started on the wine and tuna pasties.'

'Where's my mother?' she asked.

'Serving sausages and *coca* in the square with Miguel, Marga and Pep and her lady friends.'

She laughed. 'Come on, then! I can't wait to see the Ayam Katawa in action. We'd better leave Furó to his slumbers.'

Isabel accepted Tolo's hand as he pulled her up from the comfortable wicker chair and gallantly passed her the shawl draped on the back of it.

With Idò excitedly leading the way, they set off along Calle Pastor and arrived in the *plaça* just as Llorenç and Padre Agustí took their places up by the fountain. The old church clock still had ten minutes to catch its breath before it was required to emit seven loud chimes. Isabel snatched a glimpse of Doctor Ramis and her mother cheerily handing around plates of *coca* to the appreciative hordes while Pep seemed to be steadily scoffing more sausages than he was serving. As people milled around, various neighbours and friends came over to greet Isabel and Tolo, allowing Idò the opportunity to fetch them all glasses of *cava*. While they chatted, and caught up on local news, Isabel suddenly spotted a flash of dark green fabric, and there before her was Capitán Gómez. He was attired in full uniform and stood offering her an intense stare.

'It is a shame that I missed out on the operation last night, but I am told it was a success,' he opined.

Tolo took a sharp intake of breath. 'We missed your input.'

'I'm sure,' he replied acidly. 'So what next, Isabel? Will you return to police work full-time after yet another triumph?'

Isabel offered him a broad smile. 'To be honest, I prefer a quiet life, so for now I'll stick to holiday rentals. If I get bored, I'm sure Tolo can provide me with some action.'

He smirked. 'That's probably true. I can't imagine that his department will cope without you.'

Tolo shook his head and laughed. 'So, tell us, Álvaro, when does your new promotion come into force?'

The captain stood stock still for a few seconds and then folded his arms tightly. 'My promotion was turned down. I have been told to reapply next year.'

'That's disappointing. I'm really sorry,' Isabel replied gently.

Zealously, he gripped her arm. 'But Isabel, this means that you, Tolo and I will continue to occupy the same orbit. Surely that is something to celebrate?'

'It certainly is,' said Tolo stiffly.

'I'm happy that you won't be heading off to greener pastures just yet,' said Isabel with as much cheer as she could muster. 'Here's to us,' she said, raising her glass. 'The three musketeers!'

'Always, such a developed sense of humour, Isabel.' He replied dismissively. 'I'd love to chat but duty calls. My team needs to ensure that certain protocols are observed during this village affair. There are always parking infringements, and of course the possibility of locals driving while under the influence of alcohol. The residents of Sant Martí are notoriously lax.'

He doffed his cap in Isabel's direction, and with a nod to Tolo, marched off into the crowd.

'He's always such a bundle of joy,' Tolo muttered.

'Actually, I feel for him. He really thought he'd get that promotion.'

'Hubris,' he replied and gave a groan when he saw a vintage yellow *moto* draw up by the pavement. 'Look who's here?'

Isabel peered through the crowds and spied the head of Josep Casanovas as he removed his helmet. His sleek, blond, highlighted hair fell in soft waves about his face.

'He looks more like a woman every day,' scoffed Tolo.

She giggled. 'He thinks he's a god. Don't disillusion him. His ego is fragile. Remember how helpful he was to us during the investigation.'

He shrugged. 'I suppose it's better to keep the creep onside.'

Isabel smiled politely as Josep bounded towards them.

'Beautiful Bel, and you too, Cabot! What a catch. I'm here to cover the presentation, but I hope you'll give me the full scoop on last night's events. Maybe dinner later?'

'We're otherwise engaged but I'll call you in the morning, Josep. We'd be happy to cooperate,' she said.

'No doubt you'll be toasting the success of your operation? I heard on the grapevine that you were involved, Bel?'

'Then you must hire better informants,' she said.

Tolo managed a thin smile. 'Never forget, Casanovas. It's always about mutual cooperation.'

He slapped his arm. 'Sure thing, my friend.'

As Tolo winced, Josep set off towards Señora Coll, who, dressed in a dark woollen dress with pink shawl, stood by the fountain in a state of wonderment. It was evident from her facial expression that she had little idea why she was being made the centre of attention. Josep produced his camera and busied himself taking snaps and whipping up the locals with promises of coverage in his esteemed organ. Meanwhile, making his way through the merry throng came Señora Coll's neighbour, Gori Bauza. Laboriously, he carried a large wooden box, aided by his shy teenage son. Having mounted the marble steps to the fountain, he somewhat sheepishly delivered a peck on Señora Coll's cheek.

'What's in that box?' she whispered to him.

'You'll find out soon enough!' he said mysteriously.

With a nervous smile, she waited patiently at his side as Llorenç cleared his throat and hushed the crowd.

'I am delighted to bring happy tidings to you all. As you will recall, not long ago, the life of Carlos, the beloved cockerel of our dear postmistress, was cruelly cut short by an unknown felon.'

Llorenç paused for a second, shooting a knowing glance in Gori Bauza's direction. 'But luckily, Señora Coll's neighbour, Gori, was so saddened by the incident that out of the goodness of his heart he decided to find a fitting replacement. What he has bought at his own expense is a marvel to behold. Gori, please unveil the Ayam Ketawa!'

As he pulled back the door of the wooden box, a splendid cockerel emerged, and flaunting its glossy, russet plumage, began hollering at the top of its voice.

At the sound of the cry, the crowds whooped in amazement and began laughing. This was no ordinary crowing but a Grace Poole cackle that grew and grew so that it might more easily have felt at home drifting along the white corridors of a mental asylum.

'It's laughing!' cried Señora Coll, clapping her hands together in glee. 'It's got a real human laugh! Thank you, dear Gori. It is spectacular.'

And with that, the normally hypochondriac and frail postmistress flung her arms around his neck and sobbed in happiness. Her neighbour, still pricked with guilt, felt tears spring to his own eyes. He hated the damned noisy cockerel with a vengeance and in truth it was one hundred times worse than the previous horror that he'd silenced, but in that moment, he felt lighter and happier than he'd done in years. He had unexpectedly made someone happy and that person was evidently desperately lonely. How had he not realised this before?

He had lived next door to Señora Coll for four years but had never seen eye to eye. After all, she was such an old busybody and always complaining about this and that. Widowed and living alone with her cats and cockerel, it now dawned on him that perhaps they gave her comfort. Yes, he could see that now. He had been thoughtless and cruel but now he would make amends.

He would do his best to be a kinder and better neighbour. With a cheer, he raised the cockerel in the air and smiled as the crowds clapped and roared in appreciation.

Padre Agustí, his white, wispy hair rising in the breeze, wandered over to the microphone and calmed the crowds. 'Today,' he began, 'I met Isabel Flores Montserrat in the *plaça* and we spoke briefly of the terrible events that have recently taken place in our midst. We had a pet thief and worse still, a tortured soul who robbed innocent people of their lives.'

He paused and regarded the crowds. 'And yet in darkness comes light, and in despair comes hope. We must always chase the light, come what may. Sometimes, we feel anger, confusion and fear, but if we stick together as a community and support one another, we will always find our way back. Now as Jesus said on the day that his apostle, Peter.....'

Isabel turned to Tolo but his eyes were already smiling at her. He scrunched her hand as the *padre* addressed the crowds, making them giggle with his view that Ayam Ketawa cockerels symbolised good luck in Southeast Asia.

'Pity the poor mugs living in a one-mile radius of that demented creature,' muttered one wag to another. 'Not quite so lucky when it begins cackling at dawn!'

As Padre Agustí ended his speech, applause broke out, and the hapless cockerel was placed back in his box, ready for a new life in the postmistress's backyard.

Tolo and Isabel strolled off in the direction of Can Busquets. As they reached the door, he turned to her with a puzzled expression.

'So Gori Bauza killed the postmistress's cockerel because it was noisy and instead bought one that was even noisier. How does that make sense?'

'It wasn't necessarily his choice.'

He narrowed his eyes. 'Do I sense that this was a cunning scheme cooked up by you and Llorenç?'

'Possibly.'

'Rough justice in a small village,' he replied dryly.

'Better than going to prison or being exposed as a villain to the community at large, surely?'

'Perhaps you're right, but has he really paid for his crime?'

Fabian, the jolly owner, welcomed them into the warm and cosy interior and showed them both to a snug table in the corner of the room, close to the roaring fire. Isabel smiled at Tolo.

'In answer to your question, I think so. Gori is aware that a small group of us know exactly what he did and he will have to live with his conscience. But the most fitting penance is surely that Señora Coll has decided to christen her new pet Gori?'

He shook his head. 'That's definitely punishment enough.'

As Isabel nibbled on tart green olives and fresh bread smeared with *alioli*, Fabian reappeared with a carafe of red wine and the menu. Isabel gave it a cursory glance and started chuckling. She passed it to Tolo. 'We simply must have the special of the day!'

In some bemusement, he followed her gaze and roared with laughter when he saw the words: *Coq au vin*.

'What's so funny?' asked Fabian in some alarm.

'Nothing, dear Fabian,' said Isabel, between bursts of hysterical giggles. 'Absolutely nothing at all.'

Acknowledgements

Heartfelt thanks, as ever, to my friend and partner in crime, illustrator, Christopher Corr, as well as to my talented design team, Chris Jones and Ben Ottridge and editor, Clem Moulaert. A special mention to my agent, Francine Fletcher of Fletcher Associates, for her excellent media guidance and expertise.

It goes without saying that big hugs are due to my hugely supportive husband, Alan, son Ollie, sister, Cecilia and nephew, Alex, for their constant cheerleading and encouragement.

Finally, immeasurable thanks to you, my readers, for having supported me thus far on my publishing journey. Without you, it simply wouldn't have been possible.

ANNA NICHOLAS

AN ISABEL FLORES MALLORCAN MYSTERY

THE DEVIL'S HORN

THE DEVIL'S HORN

An Isabel Flores Mallorcan Mystery

Anna Nicholas

Paperback: 978-1-9996618-4-7
Ebook: 978-1-9996618-5-4

When 33-year-old Isabel Flores Montserrat quits her promising career with the Spanish police to run her mother's holiday rentals agency in rural Mallorca, her crime-fighting days seem far behind.

Basking in the Mediterranean sunshine with pet ferret Furó, she indulges her passion for local cuisine, swimming in the sea and raising her pampered hens.

However, in just a few days, the disappearance of a young British girl, violent murder of an elderly neighbour, and discovery of a Colombian drug cartel threaten to tear apart Isabel's idyllic life.

Together with local chief inspector Tolo Cabot, an old admirer of her unorthodox methods, Isabel must race against the clock to untangle a sinister web of crime and restore peace to the island once more.

burrobooks

www.burrobooks.co.uk